BECOMING brianna

tip tip tip

TERRI LIBENSON

BALZER + BRAY
An Imprint of HarperCollins*Publishers*

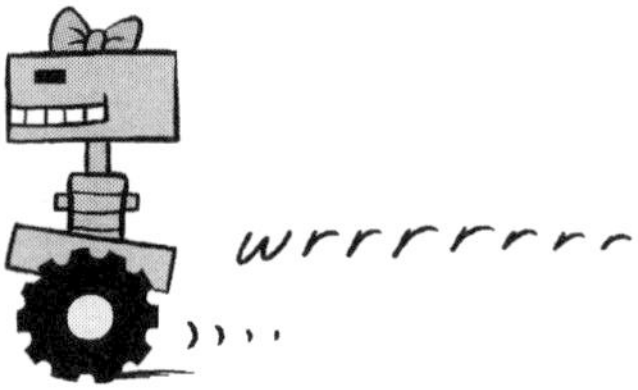
wrrrrrrr

Balzer + Bray is an imprint of HarperCollins Publishers.

Becoming Brianna

 For information address HarperCollins Children's Books, a division of HarperCollins Publishers, 195 Broadway, New York, NY 10007.
www.harpercollinschildrens.com

Library of Congress Control Number: 2019956234
ISBN 978-0-06-289454-0 (trade bdg.)
ISBN 978-0-06-289453-3 (pbk.)
ISBN 978-0-06-301814-3 (special edition)
ISBN 978-0-06-302664-3 (special edition)
ISBN 978-0-06-302571-4 (special edition)
ISBN 978-0-06-302903-3 (special edition)
ISBN 978-0-06-303973-5 (special edition)

Typography by Terri Libenson and Laura Mock
20 21 22 23 24 PC/LSCC 10 9 8 7 6 5 4 3 2 1

First Edition

To the clergy and educators at Fairmount Temple, who helped shape my kids and gave them a home away from home

Author at age 13

wasn't as blurry in real life

hair looked uncombed (but wasn't, I swear)

dressed for big event (by mom)

nervous, excited, itchy (the days of lace)

PROLOGUE

Well, here I am again. How, how, how did I get myself into this TWICE?

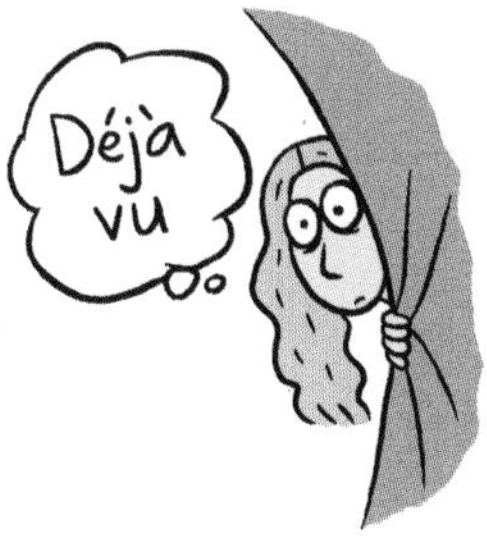
Déjà vu

Maybe I'm a glutton for punishment. Or just a sucker. That last one probably nails it. Why else would I put myself in the spotlight again?

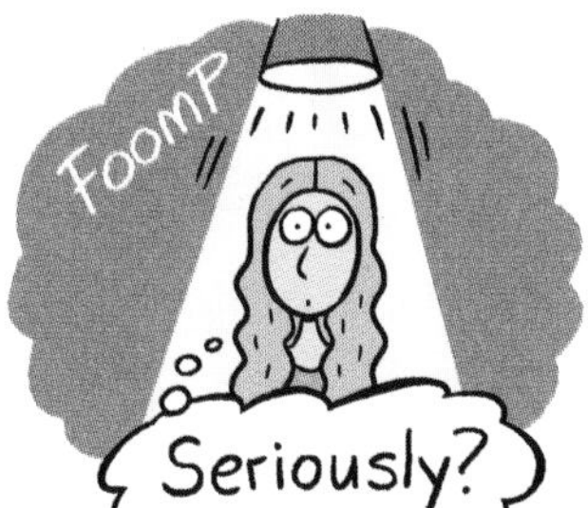
FoomP
Seriously?

Peeking through the curtains, I see my parents and lots of friends. At least I have support.

Or witnesses for this train wreck.

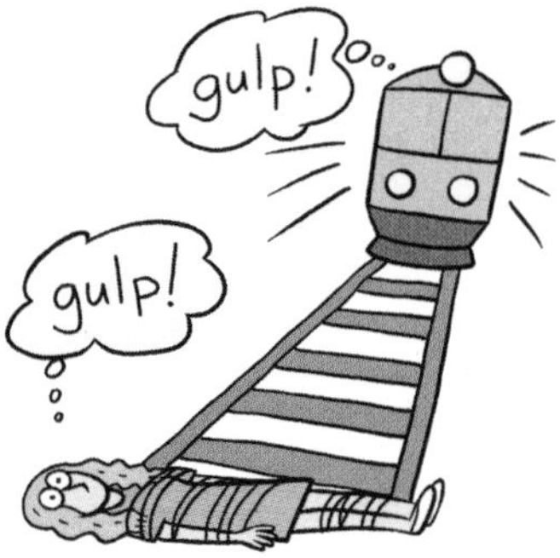
gulp!
gulp!

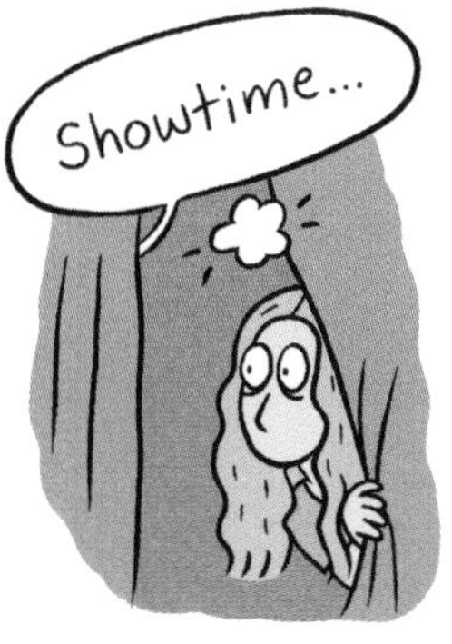
Showtime...

Okay, here I go. I hope I know my part well. I hope I don't screw up. I hope I don't trip on my face. I hope, I hope, I hope . . .

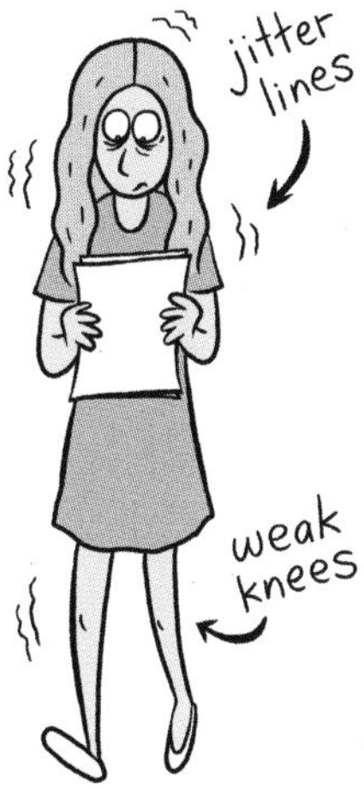
jitter lines
weak knees

I hope I get this over with FAST.

EIGHT MONTHS AGO

Mom and I are sitting at the kitchen table, shoving pizza in our faces. It's homemade pizza. Mom started making it from scratch when she realized it was just about the only thing I ever ate without complaining. Also, she figured it would be healthier.

regular pizza

semi-sweet sauce

crispy crust

drippy and gooey (yum)

healthy pizza

semi-sweet sauce

not as drippy and gooey

slightly burnt crust* (but still good)

* sometimes made with cauliflower (ick!)

It's not bad. I like Ramone's Pizza the best, but I've gotta hand it to Mom. She badgered the owner for the sauce recipe a thousand times until he finally gave in. Ramone made her swear she wouldn't give it away and would burn the photocopy of his handwritten recipe.

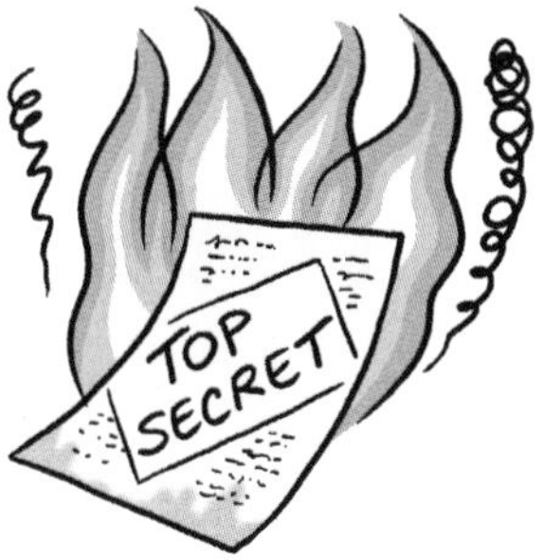
TOP SECRET

I'm at Mom's condo this week. My parents are divorced and share custody. They trade off weeks. It can be a pain going back and forth, but I'm pretty used to it.

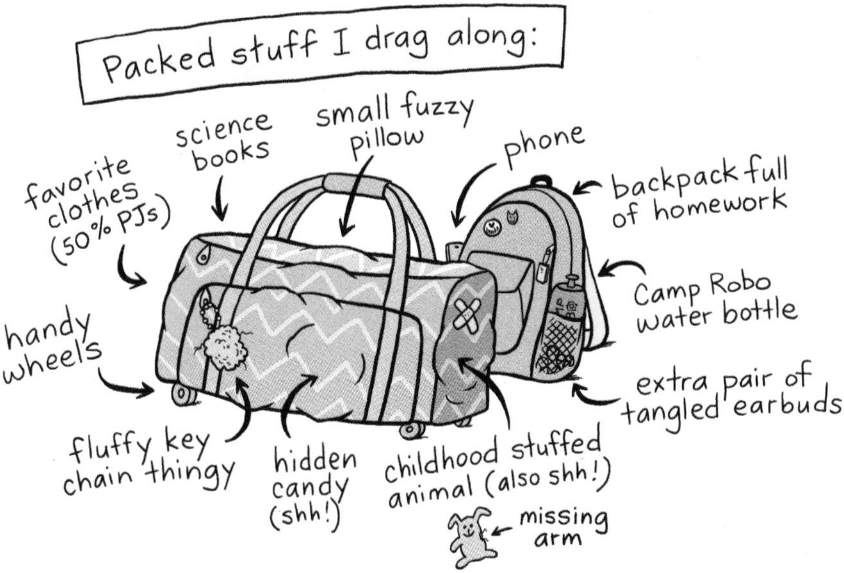
Packed stuff I drag along:
science books
small fuzzy pillow
phone
favorite clothes (50% PJs)
backpack full of homework
Camp Robo water bottle
handy wheels
extra pair of tangled earbuds
fluffy key chain thingy
hidden candy (shh!)
childhood stuffed animal (also shh!)
missing arm

Anyway, here I sit, stuffing myself with pizza. At least, I try.

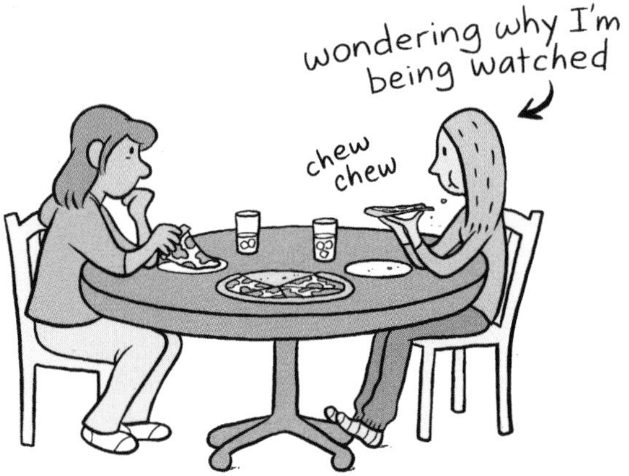
wondering why I'm being watched
chew chew

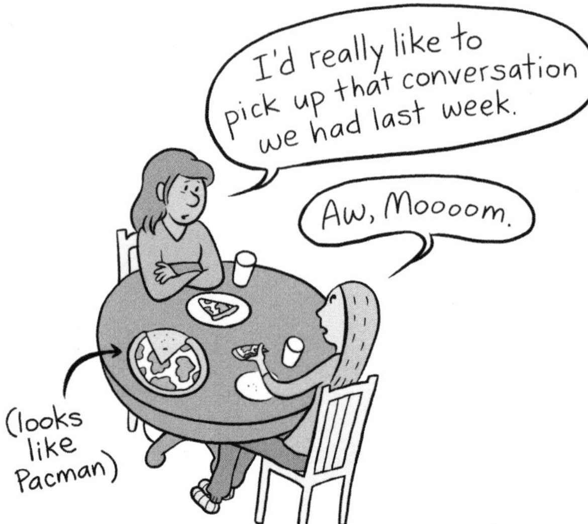
I'd really like to pick up that conversation we had last week.
Aw, Moooom.
(looks like Pacman)

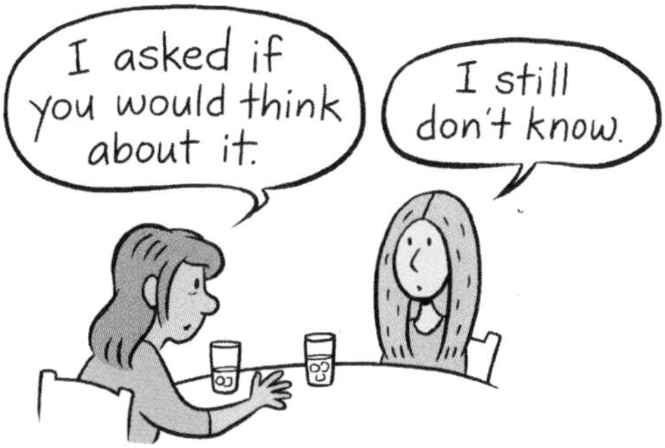
I asked if you would think about it.
I still don't know.

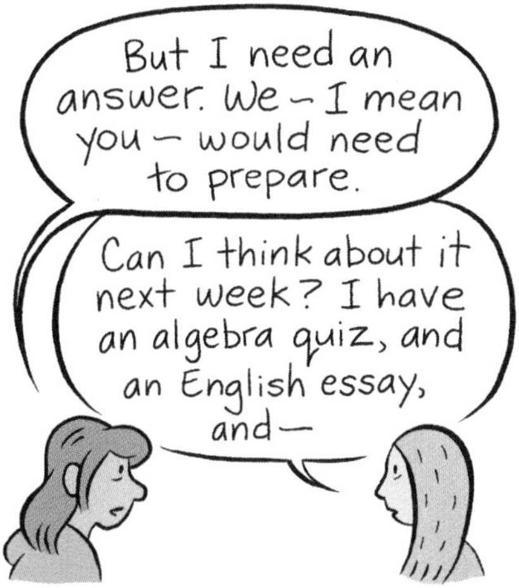
But I need an answer. We – I mean you – would need to prepare.
Can I think about it next week? I have an algebra quiz, and an English essay, and–

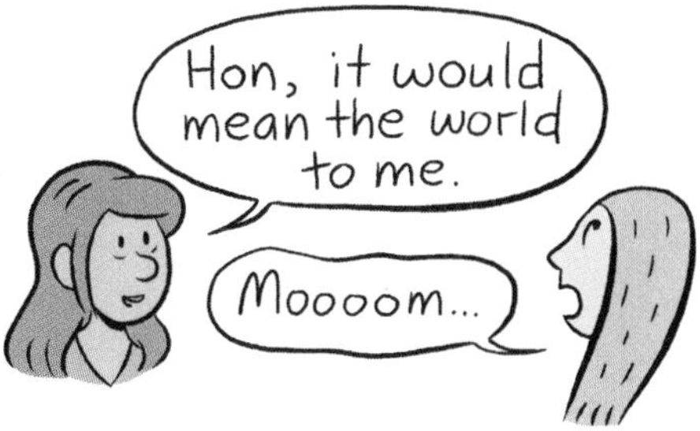
Hon, it would mean the world to me.
Mooooom...

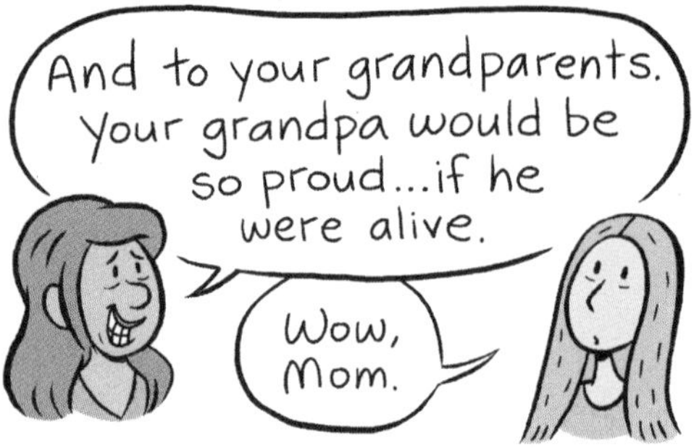
And to your grandparents. Your grandpa would be so proud...if he were alive.
Wow, Mom.

Did I mention she is the Queen of Guilt?

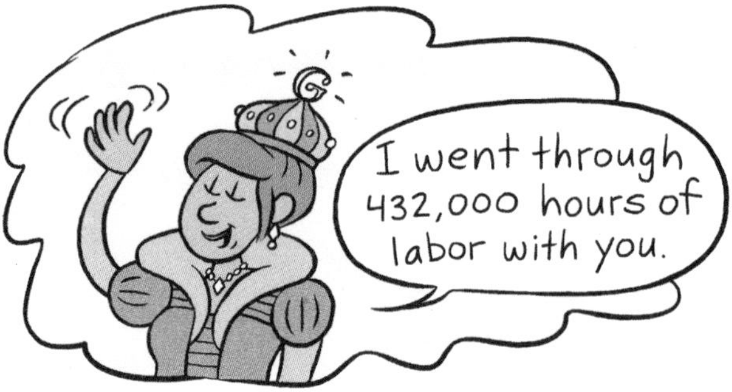
G
I went through 432,000 hours of labor with you.

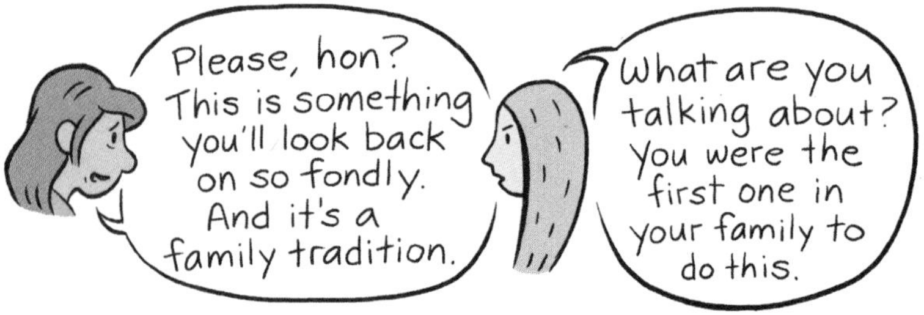
Please, hon? This is something you'll look back on so fondly. And it's a family tradition.
What are you talking about? You were the first one in your family to do this.

The first female. And that's another thing. It's so important that women should be honored this way.

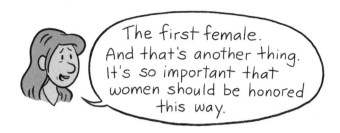

That is the **ultimate** guilt. Mom knows I've been a feminist since I was, like, five. She just touched a nerve.

Fiiiiiiiiine.

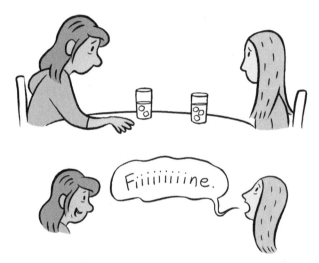

So fast, I almost don't see her get up, Mom races over and engulfs me in a powerful hug.

I'm so glad, hon! You are ***NOT*** going to regret this.
oof!

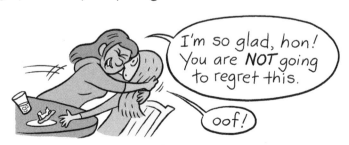

What Mom doesn't know is that any time she says that . . .

. . . I usually do.

NOW

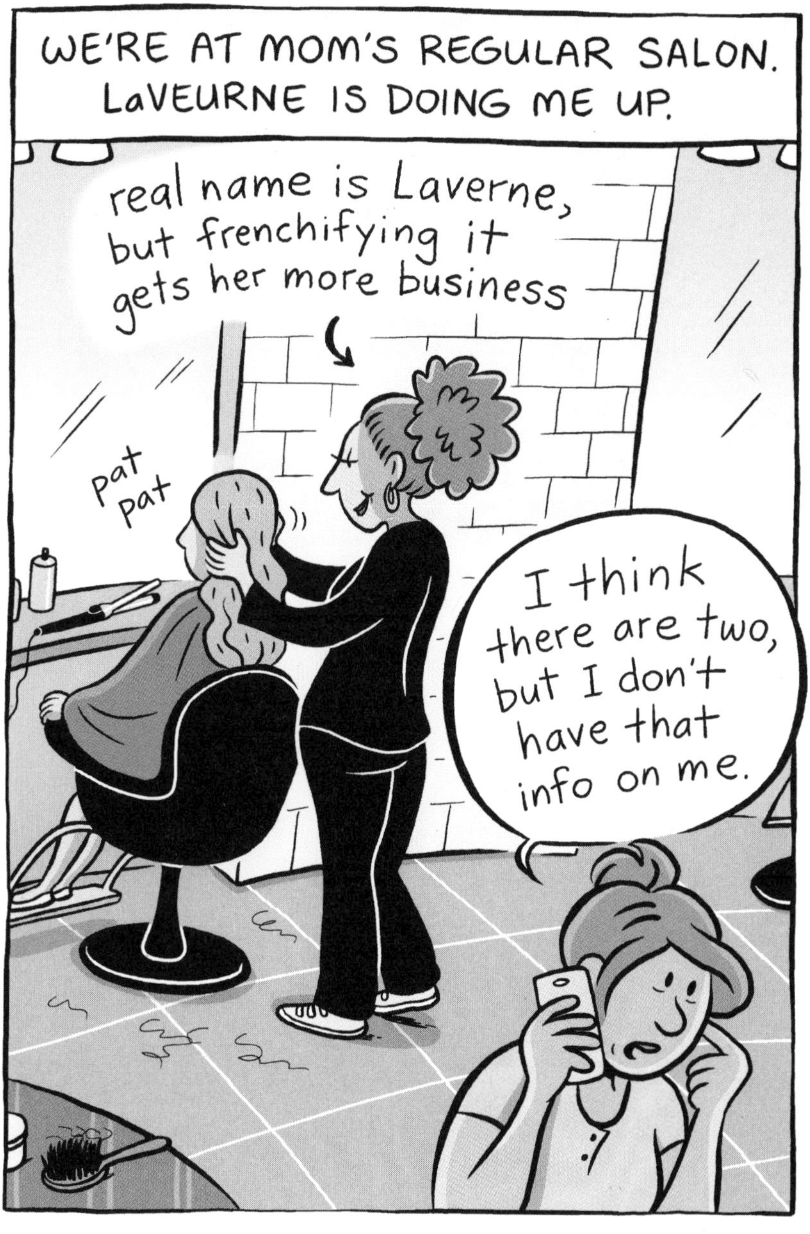
WE'RE AT MOM'S REGULAR SALON. LaVEURNE IS DOING ME UP.
real name is Laverne, but frenchifying it gets her more business
pat pat
I think there are two, but I don't have that info on me.

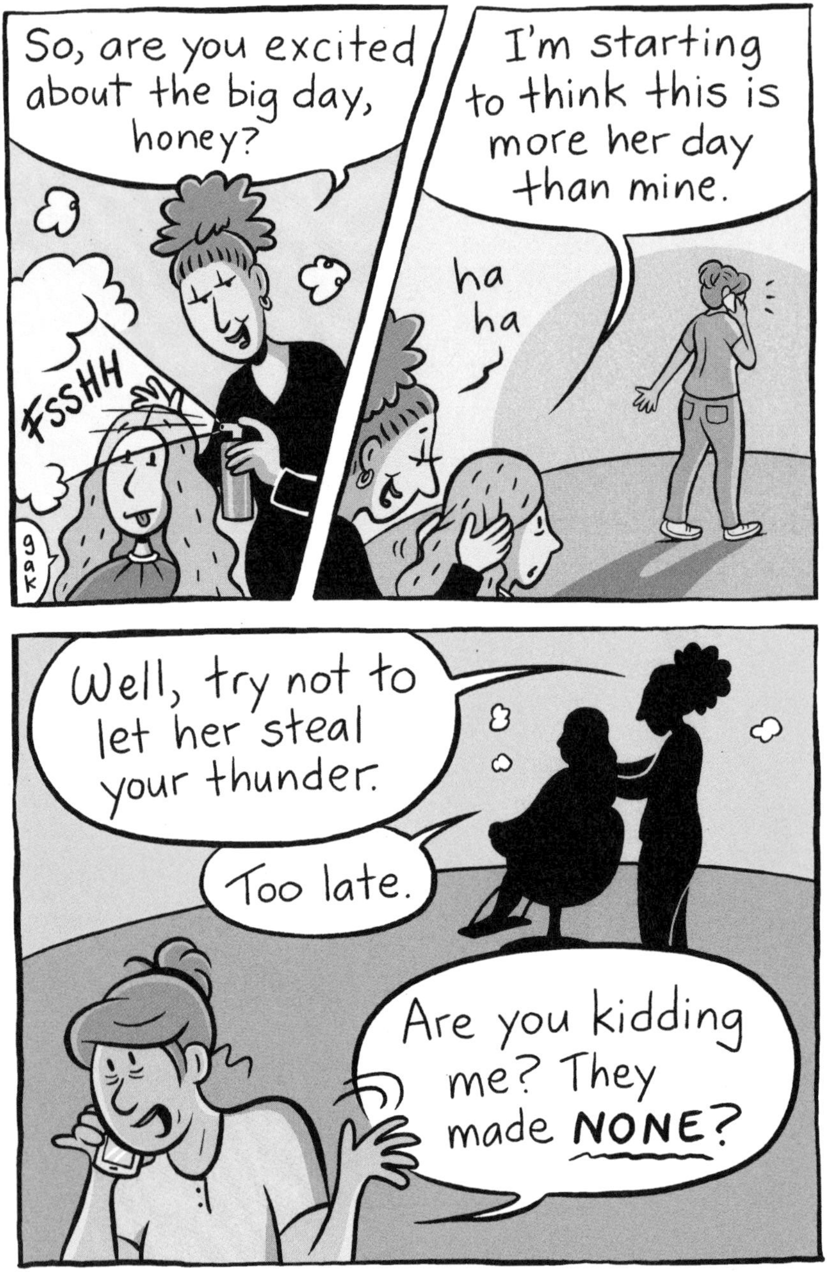
So, are you excited about the big day, honey?
FSSHH
gak
I'm starting to think this is more her day than mine.
ha ha
Well, try not to let her steal your thunder.
Too late.
Are you kidding me? They made **NONE**?

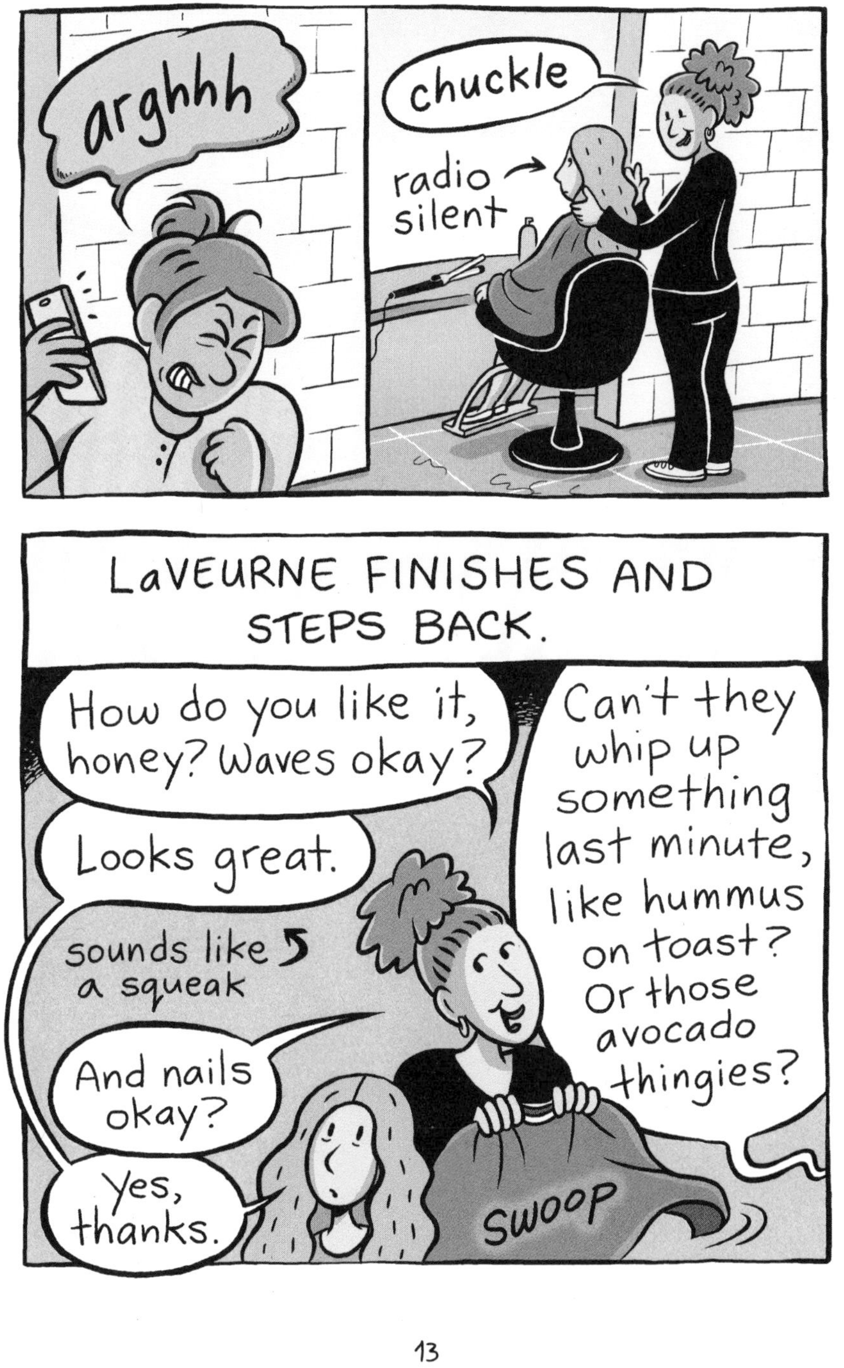
arghhh
chuckle
radio silent
LaVEURNE FINISHES AND STEPS BACK.
How do you like it, honey? Waves okay?
Looks great.
sounds like a squeak
And nails okay?
Yes, thanks.
Can't they whip up something last minute, like hummus on toast? Or those avocado thingies?
SWOOP

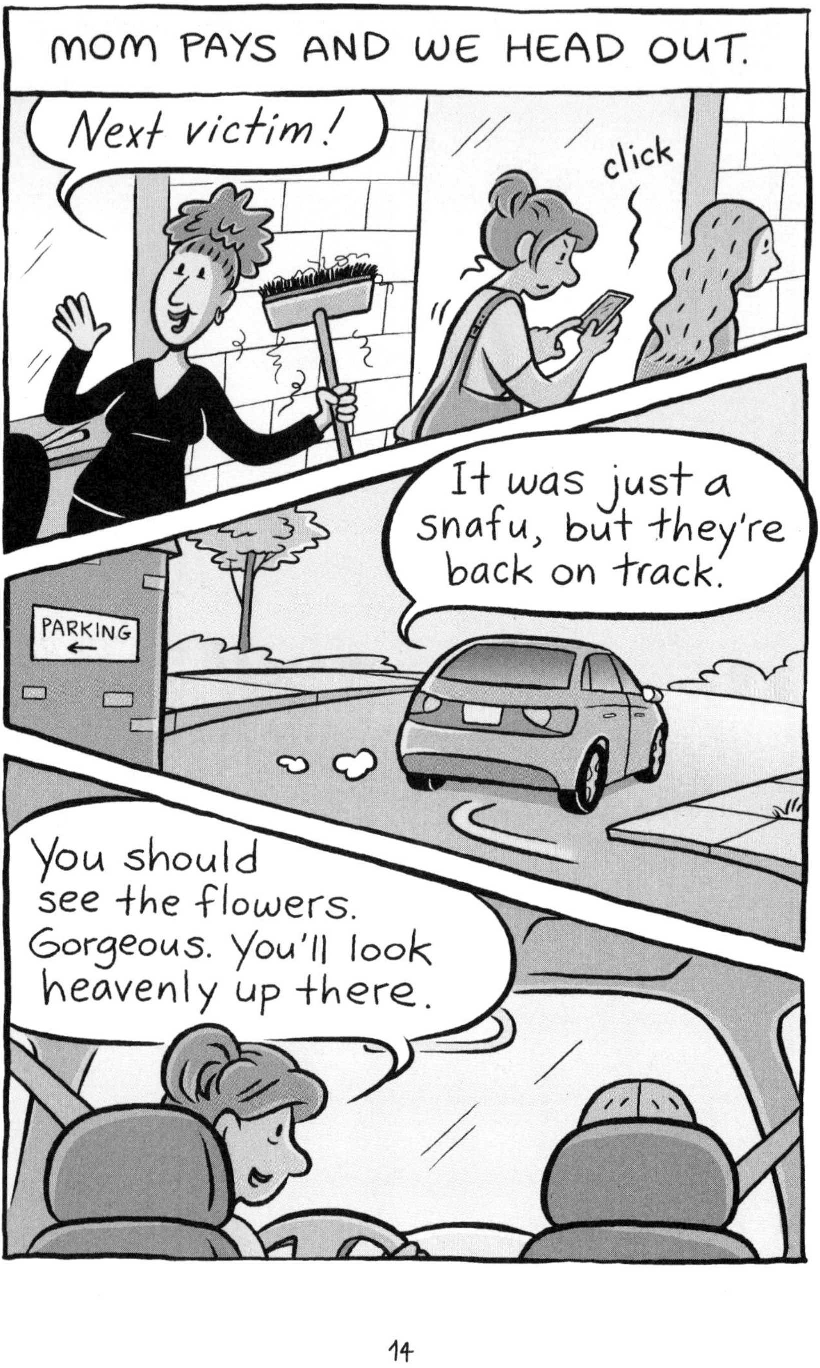
MOM PAYS AND WE HEAD OUT.
Next victim!
click
It was just a snafu, but they're back on track.
PARKING
You should see the flowers. Gorgeous. You'll look heavenly up there.

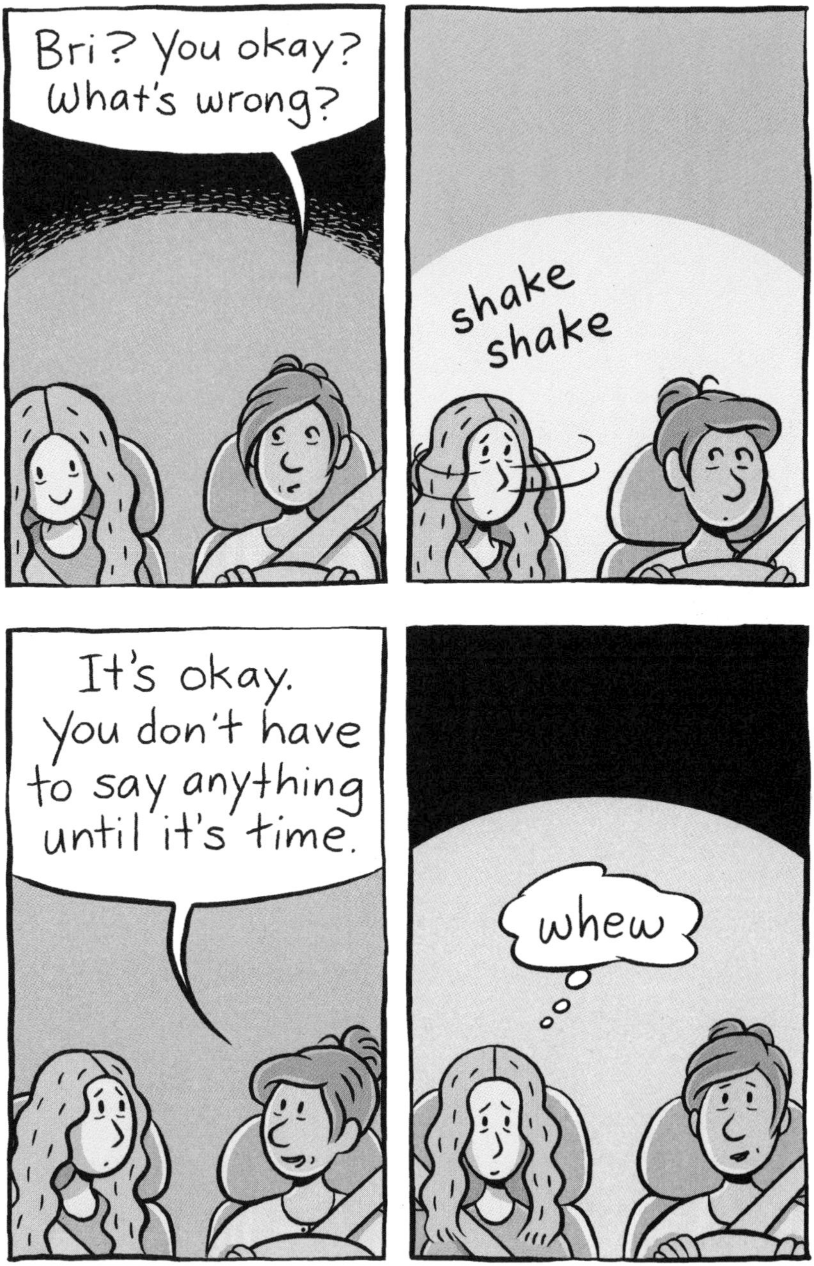
Bri? You okay? What's wrong?
shake shake
It's okay. You don't have to say anything until it's time.
whew

EIGHT MONTHS AGO

So, by now you might be wondering what exactly I just agreed to. If you're twelve or thirteen years old and Jewish, you've probably guessed.

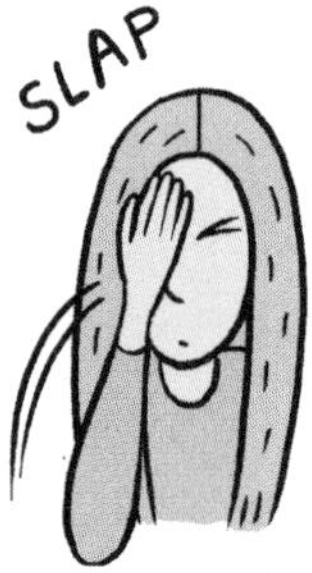
SLAP

Yep, I just agreed to have a bat mitzvah.

Kids have bar or bat mitzvahs ("bar" for boys, "bat" for girls) around age thirteen (sometimes younger for girls 'cause, you know, we're mature and stuff). It marks a "coming of age" in Jewish tradition. The boy or girl leads the service—in Hebrew!—usually at a synagogue in front of family, friends, and even strangers (aka relatives you've never met).

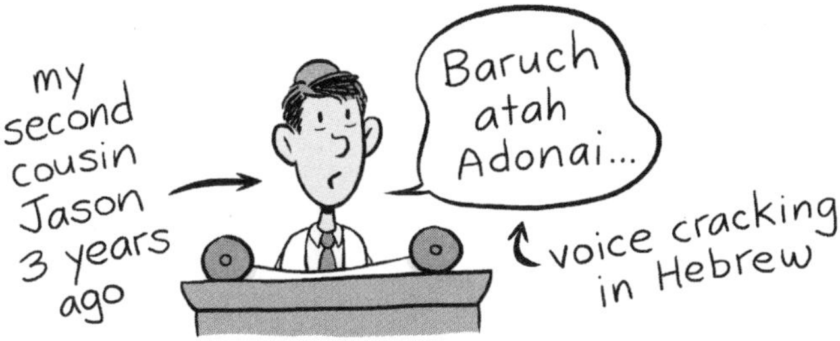
my second cousin Jason 3 years ago
Baruch atah Adonai...
voice cracking in Hebrew

This is no little thing, believe me. You have to start preparing about six months ahead. Or longer, if you don't know Hebrew too well. Which I don't.

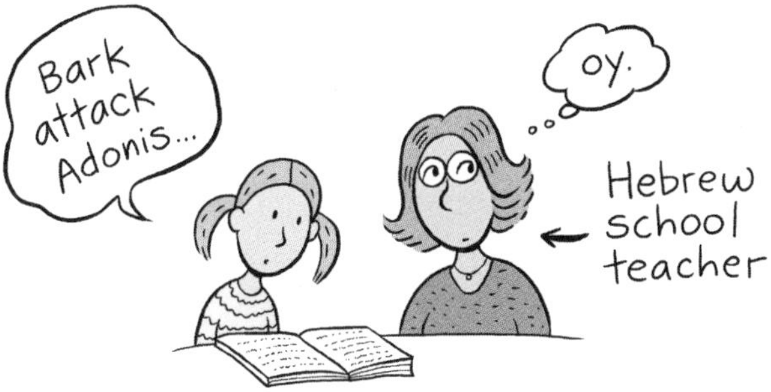
Bark attack Adonis...
oy.
Hebrew school teacher

Here's the story. My mom is Jewish; my dad isn't. Traditionally, this means I'm considered Jewish. If it were reversed, I wouldn't be. Weird, considering the usual religious patriarchy* thing.

*(men in charge, big surprise)

Traditional view

Jewish | not Jewish | not Jewish

not Jewish | Jewish | Jewish

Nontraditional view*
*(our temple, in a nutshell)

Jewish | not Jewish | Jewish

not Jewish | Jewish | Jewish

not Jewish | Jewish | Jewish

When I was growing up, Mom **encouraged** me to go to religious school (aka made me). That meant a couple weeknights and Sunday mornings. Because my studies came first, I didn't always have time to go.

And **maybe** I used that as an excuse once too often.

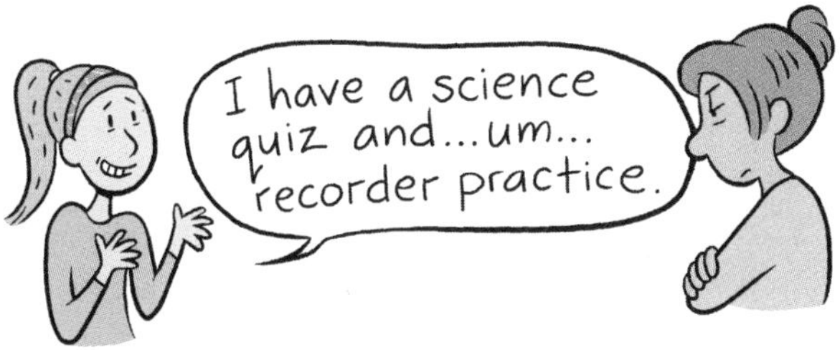
I have a science quiz and...um... recorder practice.

It's not that it was horrible. The teachers were nice, and they tried to make the lessons interesting, like with games and stuff. But most of the kids went to the local Jewish day camp during summers and were used to hanging out together. I didn't go to that camp, so I always felt a little left out.

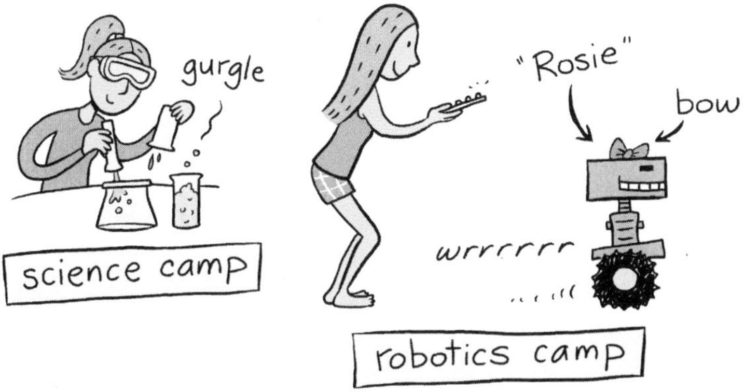
gurgle
science camp
"Rosie"
bow
wrrrrrr
robotics camp

Also, I was pretty bad at Hebrew.

I know what you're thinking: me, bad at a class? But languages aren't my thing. I'm not even that great at Spanish. I just study extra hard for it, and that's how I get As.

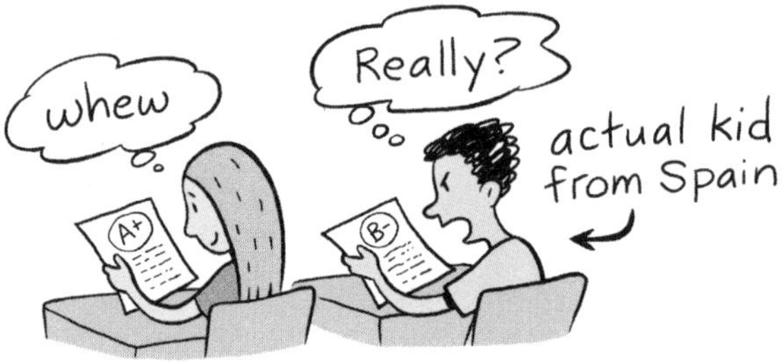
whew
A+
Really?
B-
actual kid from Spain

Anyway, I put my foot down and stopped going to religious school after fifth grade. I had way more important things to do, and I really wasn't that into it. Dad couldn't care less.

Mom agreed and seemed to stop pressing the issue.

But around September, she brought up the idea of a bat mitzvah.

At first, I was like:

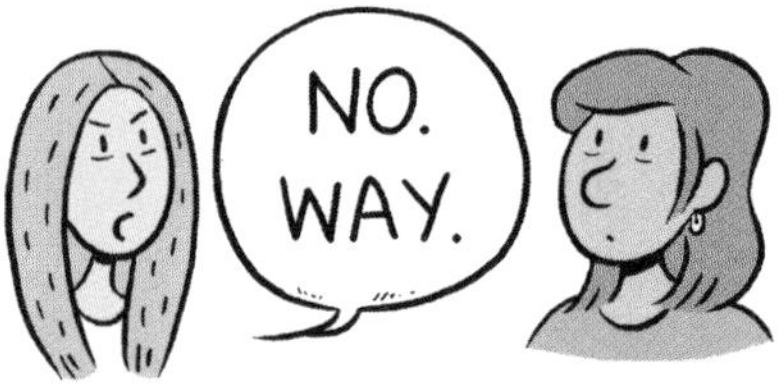
NO. WAY.

But she kept insisting. And insisting. And . . .

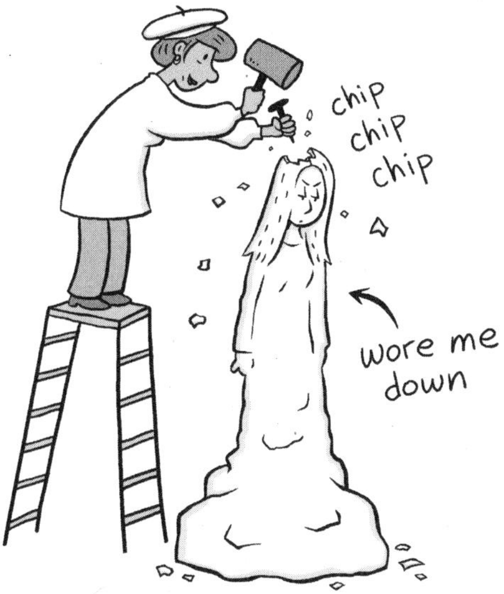
chip
chip
chip
wore me down

So here I am wondering—not for the first time—what I just got myself into.

It's true. Mom was the first girl in her family to have a bat mitzvah. Her temple didn't allow 'em for girls until then. Even her older sister, my aunt Dani, didn't have one. (Her younger sister, my aunt Ashley, was just plain against it, for some reason.)

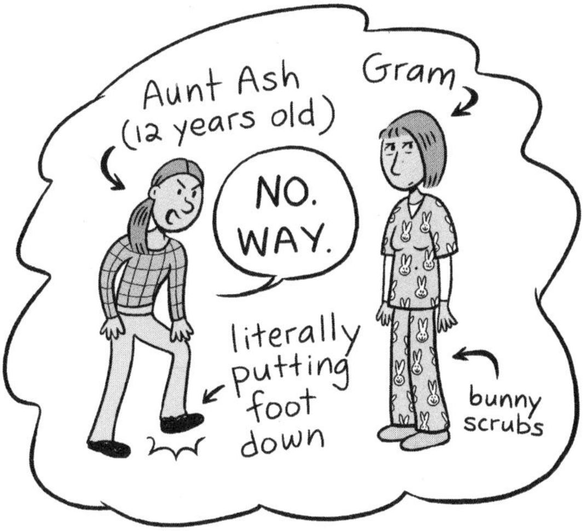
Aunt Ash (12 years old)
Gram
NO. WAY.
literally putting foot down
bunny scrubs

I know Mom just wants me to carry on the tradition she started. I can't really blame her. I'm her only child, so this is her one big chance.

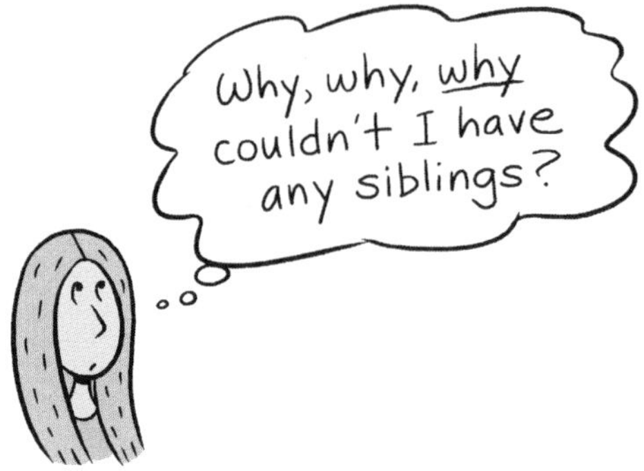
Why, why, why couldn't I have any siblings?

I also know I'm doing this more for her than me.

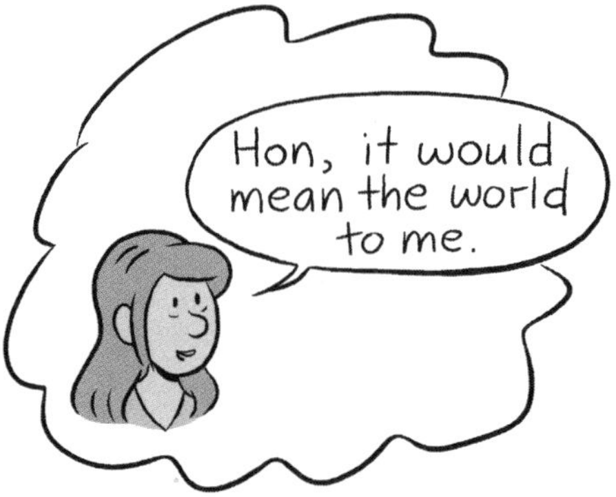
Hon, it would mean the world to me.

But . . .

. . . I'm still trying to figure out **why**.

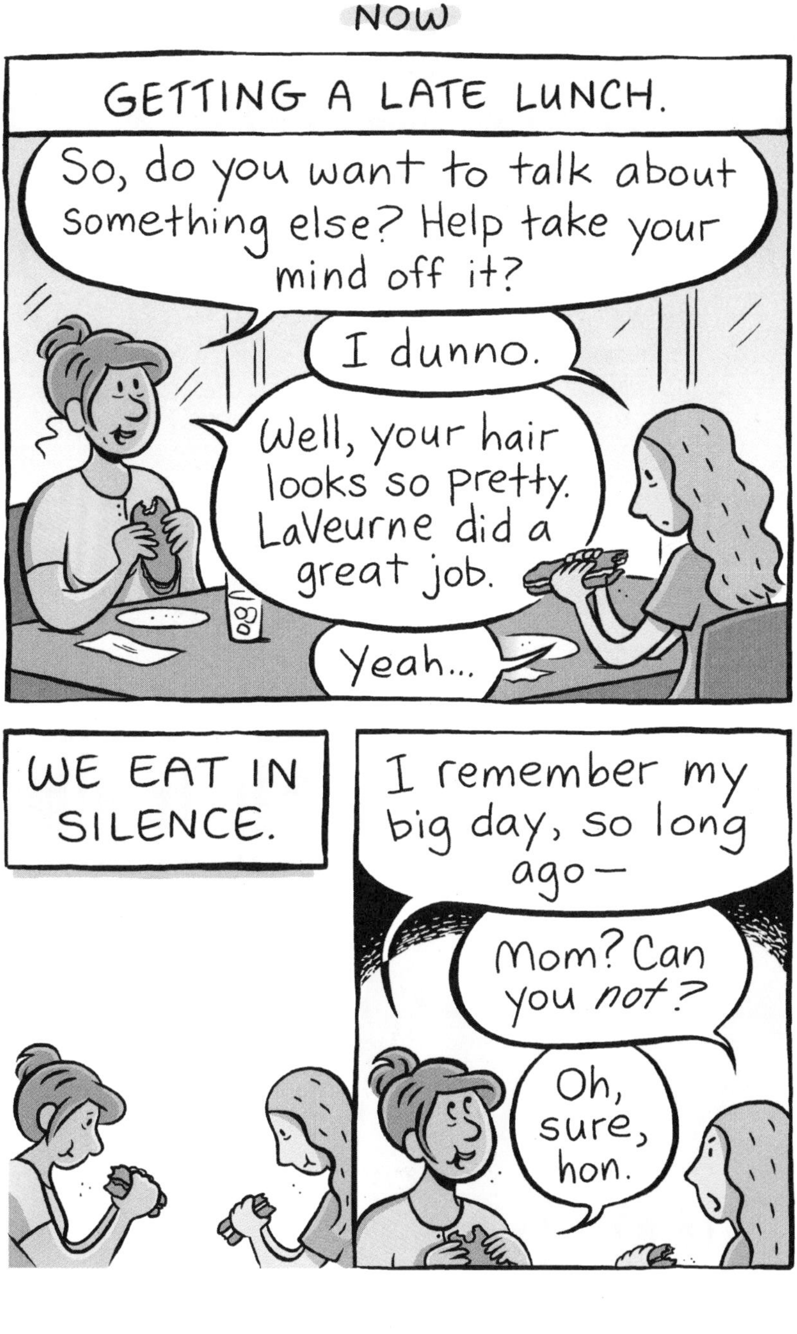
NOW
GETTING A LATE LUNCH.
So, do you want to talk about something else? Help take your mind off it?
I dunno.
Well, your hair looks so pretty. LaVeurne did a great job.
Yeah...
WE EAT IN SILENCE.
I remember my big day, so long ago—
Mom? Can you *not*?
Oh, sure, hon.

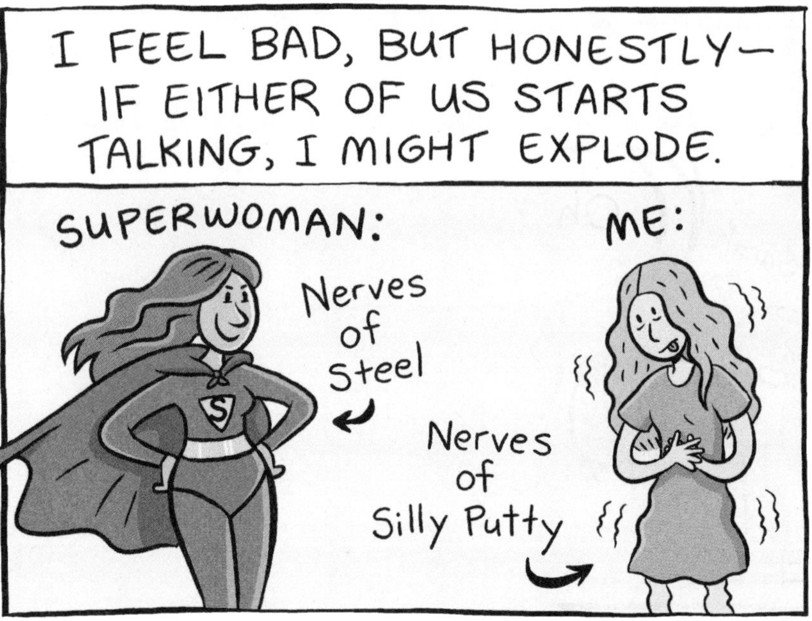
I FEEL BAD, BUT HONESTLY—IF EITHER OF US STARTS TALKING, I MIGHT EXPLODE.
SUPERWOMAN:
ME:
Nerves of Steel
Nerves of Silly Putty

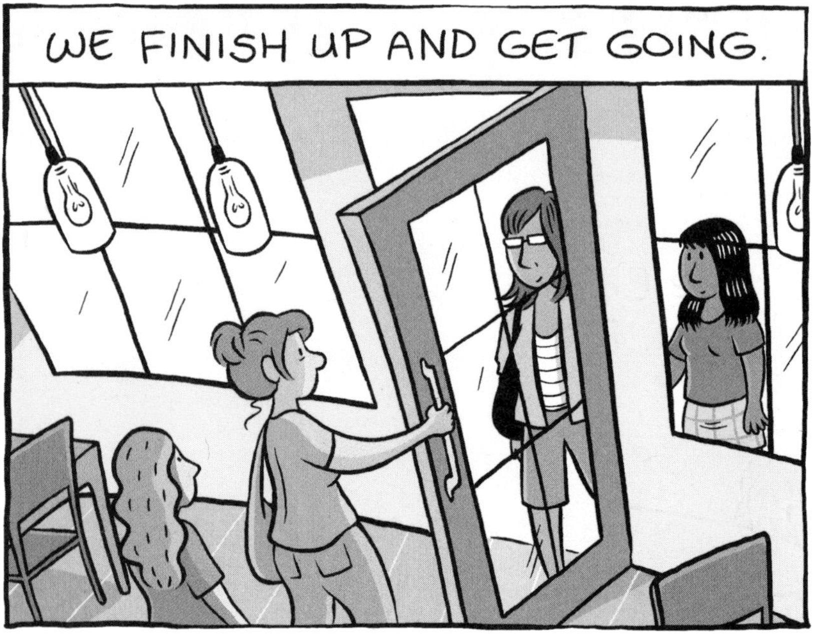
WE FINISH UP AND GET GOING.

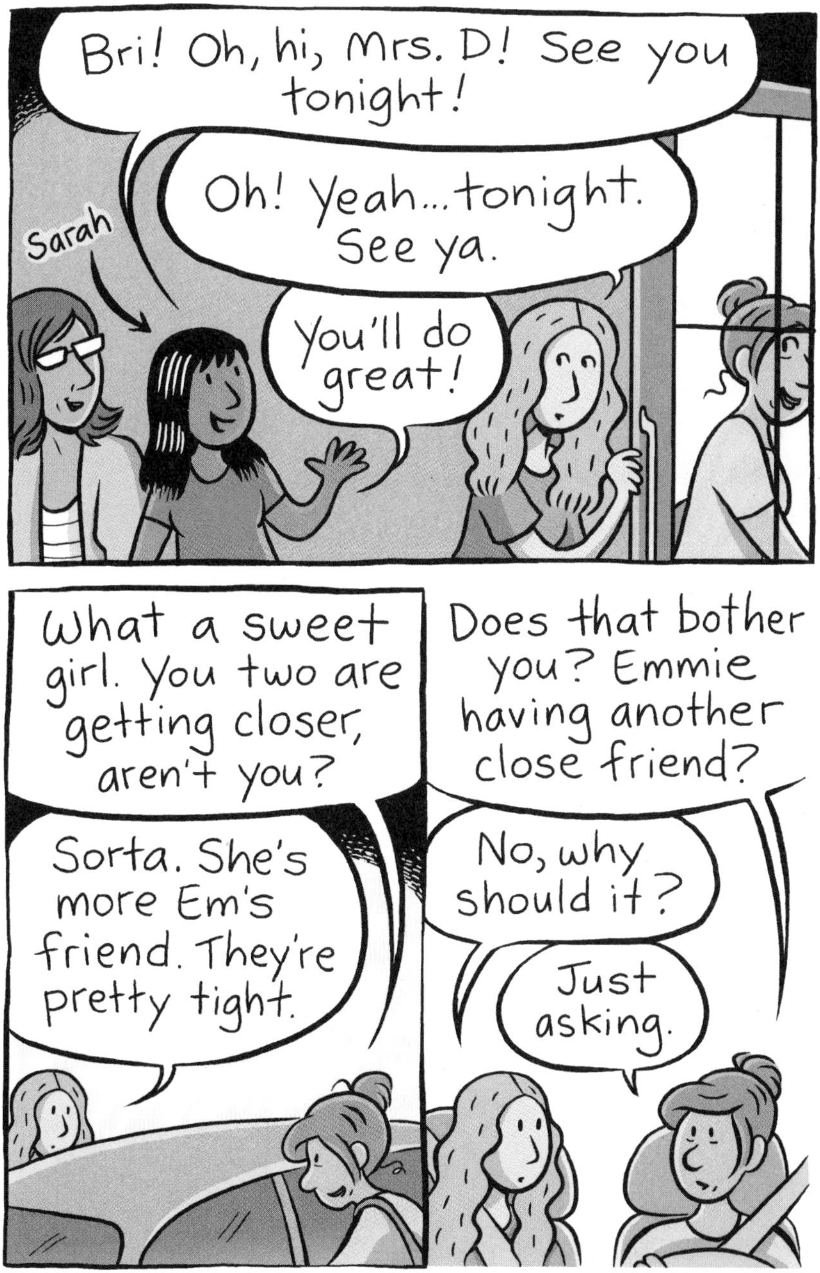
Bri! Oh, hi, Mrs. D! See you tonight!
Oh! Yeah...tonight. See ya.
Sarah
You'll do great!
What a sweet girl. You two are getting closer, aren't you?
Sorta. She's more Em's friend. They're pretty tight.
Does that bother you? Emmie having another close friend?
No, why should it?
Just asking.

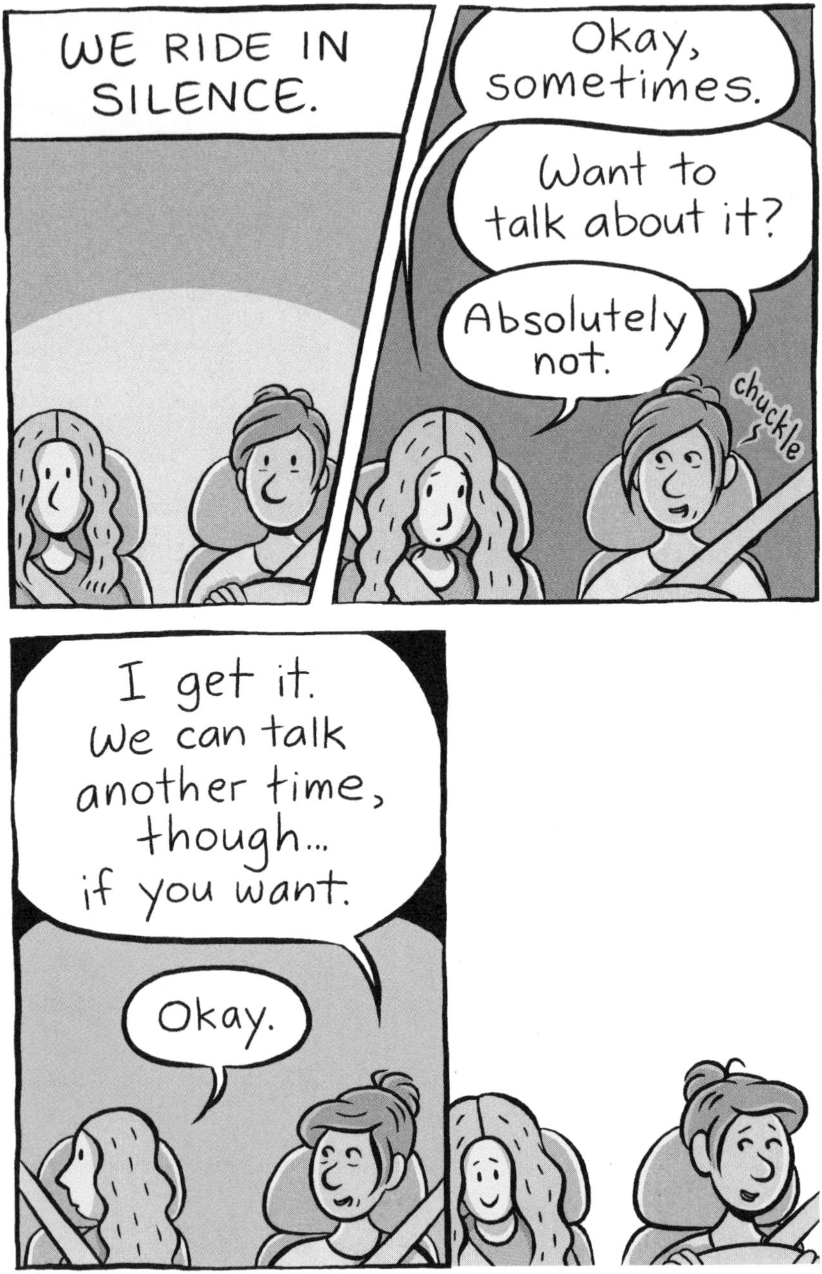
WE RIDE IN SILENCE.
Okay, sometimes.
Want to talk about it?
Absolutely not.
chuckle
I get it. We can talk another time, though... if you want.
Okay.

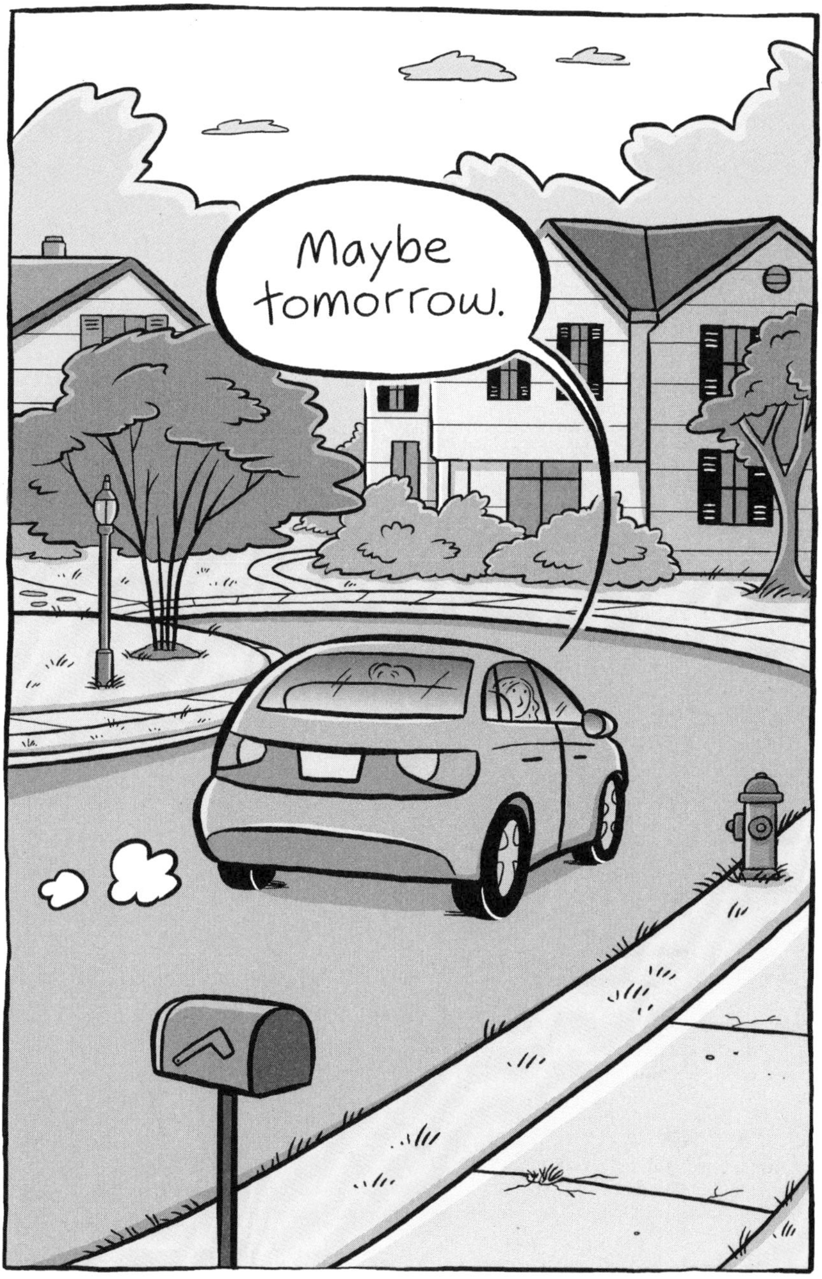
Maybe tomorrow.

SEVEN MONTHS AGO

Em and I are at lunch. It's pretty loud today. Everyone's excited because Thanksgiving break starts tomorrow. The enthusiasm is echoed by the force of the ice cream freezer lid slamming.

art club kids

Emo girl

SLAMMO

table earthquake

I make a face at Emmie's lunch.

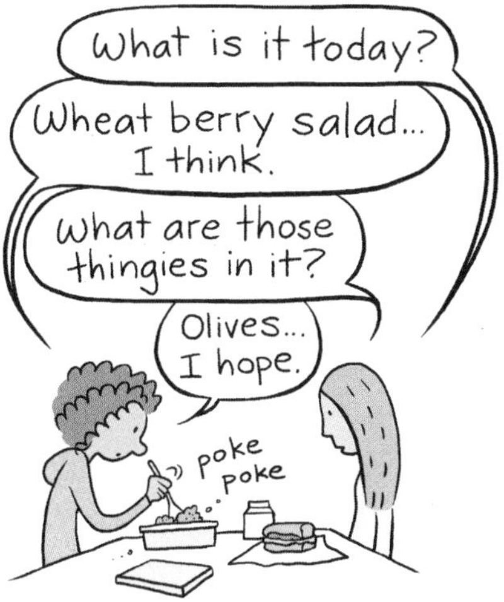
What is it today?
Wheat berry salad... I think.
What are those thingies in it?
Olives... I hope.
poke poke

She pokes one with her spork.

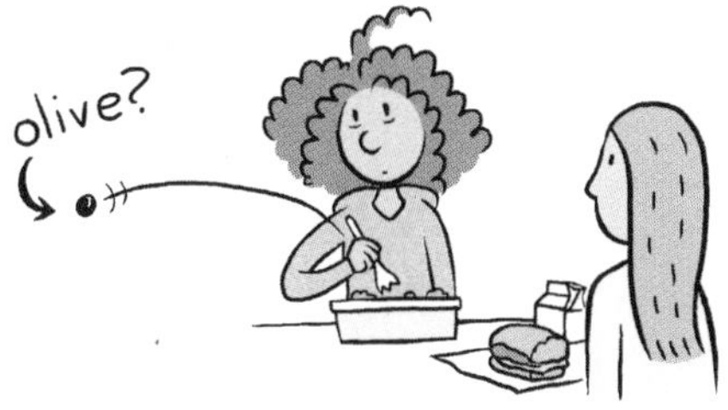
olive?

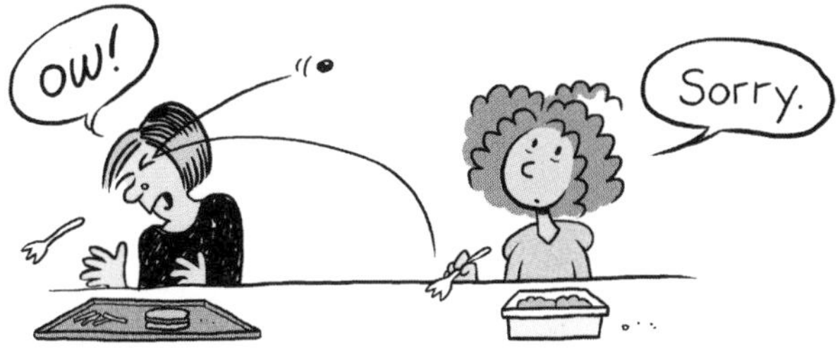
OW!
Sorry.

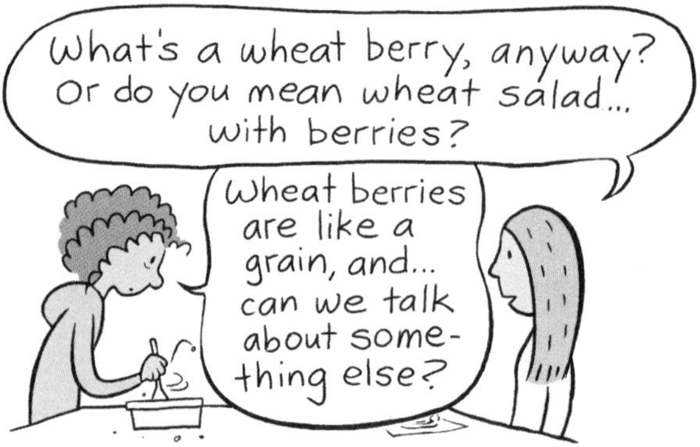
What's a wheat berry, anyway? Or do you mean wheat salad... with berries?
Wheat berries are like a grain, and... can we talk about some-thing else?

It's hard not to make fun of Emmie's lunches, which are usually leftovers from home. Her mom's kind of a health nut. "Nut" being the key word.

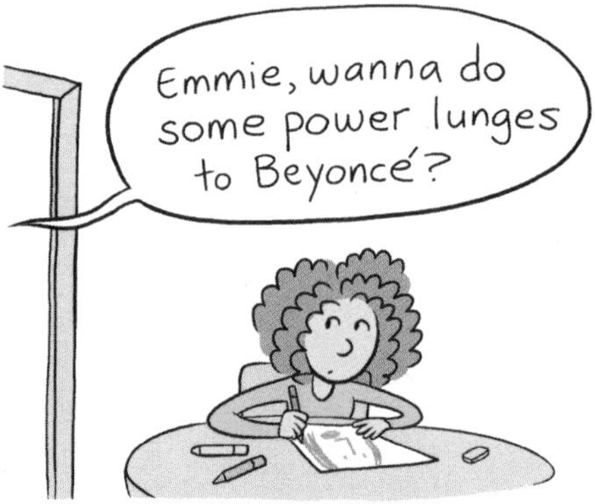
Emmie, wanna do some power lunges to Beyoncé?

But I know Em's so over it, so I try not to push it.

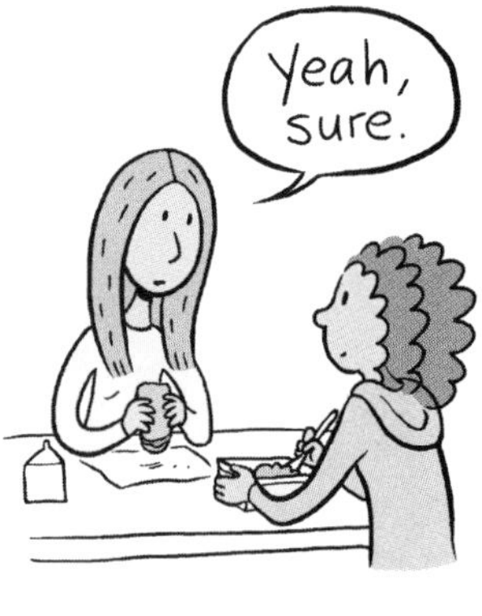
Yeah, sure.

I bite into my sandwich. I'm attempting to branch out from pizza. Dad packed me his leftover sub from a faculty meeting yesterday. Turkey with gravy, of course.

I immediately spit it out.

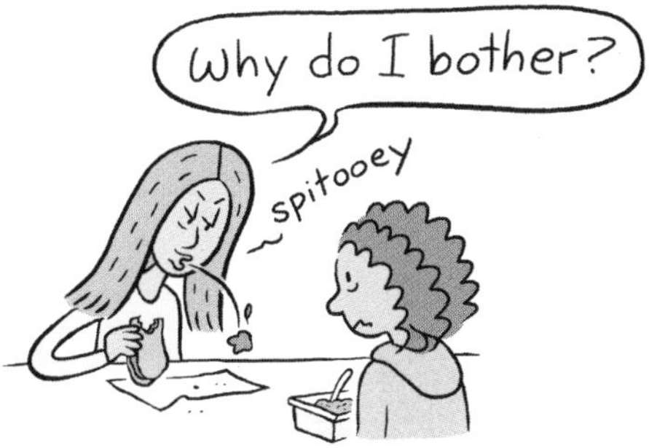
Why do I bother?
spitooey

I sip my milk.

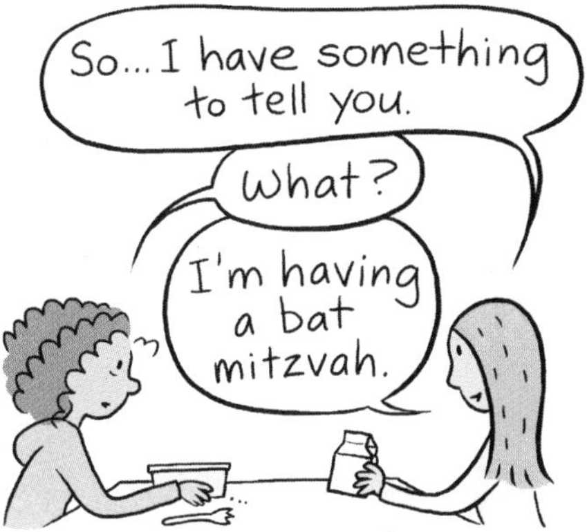
So... I have something to tell you.
What?
I'm having a bat mitzvah.

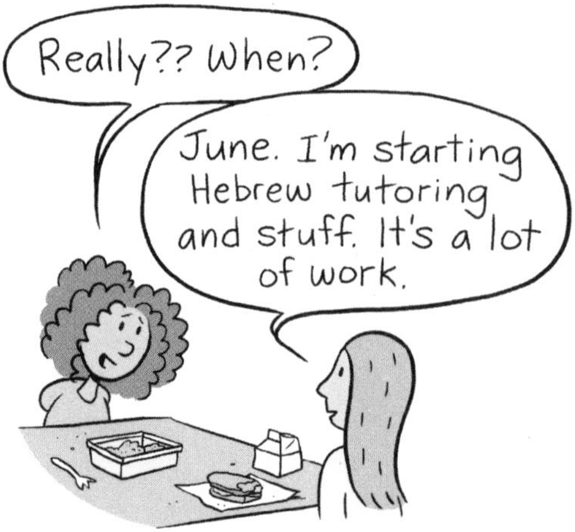
Really?? When?
June. I'm starting Hebrew tutoring and stuff. It's a lot of work.

Joe Lungo grabs three ice cream sandwiches and slams the freezer lid so hard, my turkey and gravy separate.

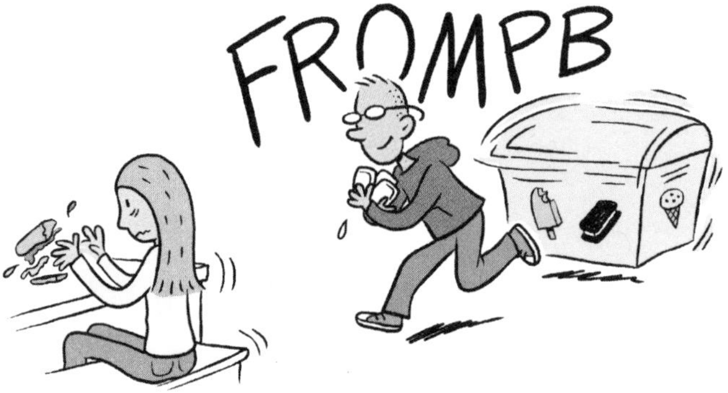
FROMPB

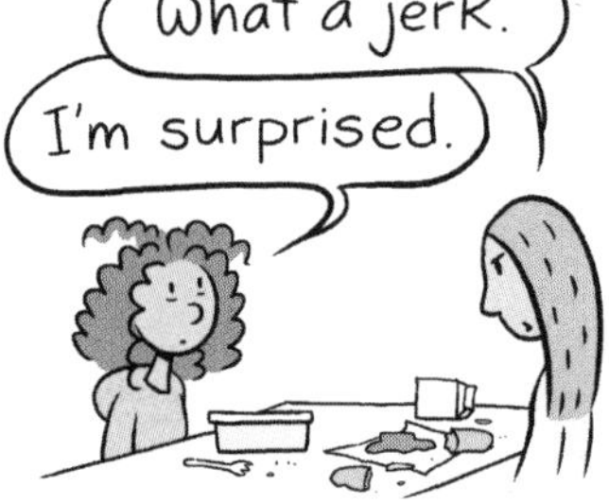
What a jerk.
I'm surprised.

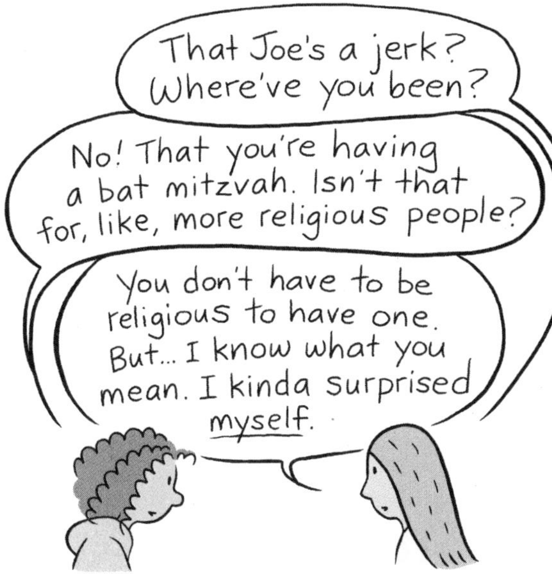
That Joe's a jerk? Where've you been?
No! That you're having a bat mitzvah. Isn't that for, like, more religious people?
You don't have to be religious to have one. But... I know what you mean. I kinda surprised myself.

The chatty art club kids get up and leave.

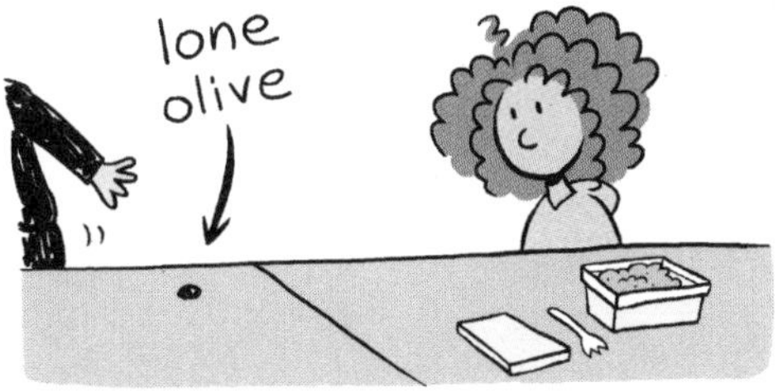
lone olive

Tyler Ross suddenly runs by our table and tries to catch a flying Styrofoam plate. It misses and lands in front of us.

gray, lumpy,
and slimy
(probably gravy)

Hey, sorry!
I'll get that.

He grabs the greasy plate and flings it at Anthony Randall. They're playing some kind of Frisbee game with Joe L. They're each in a corner of the cafeteria in triangle formation. Except they're trying to eat ice cream sandwiches and play at once. Not very effective.

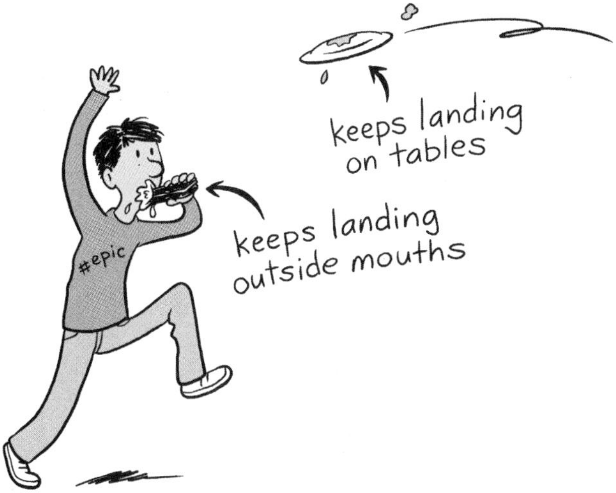
#epic
keeps landing on tables
keeps landing outside mouths

The lunch monitor must be on break. I turn toward Emmie, whose face is bright violet.

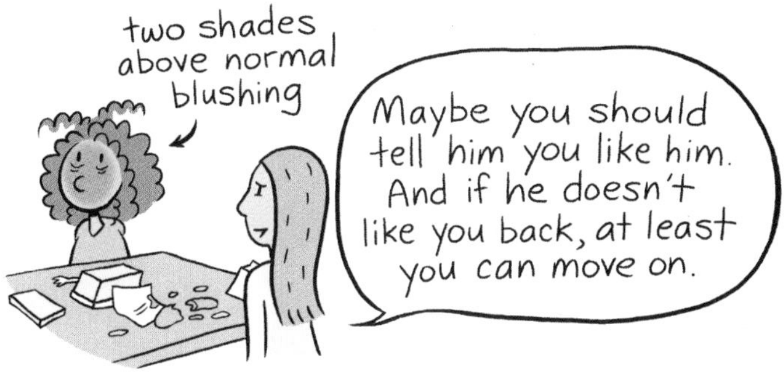
two shades above normal blushing
Maybe you should tell him you like him. And if he doesn't like you back, at least you can move on.

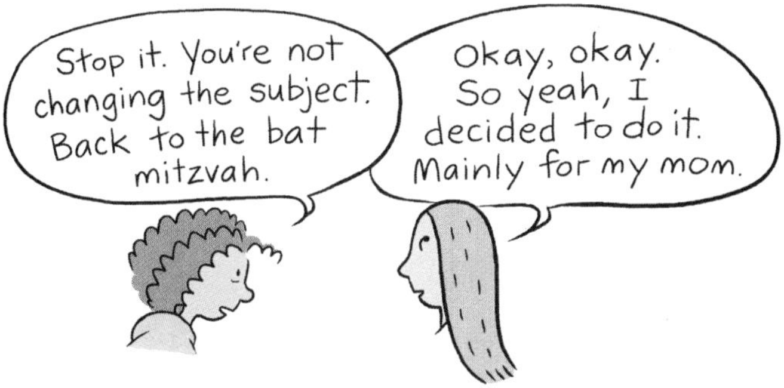
Stop it. You're not changing the subject. Back to the bat mitzvah.
Okay, okay. So yeah, I decided to do it. Mainly for my mom.

Oh, Briii.

Like you should talk. How many half marathons has your mom dragged you to?

To watch, not to <u>do</u>.

Okay, fine. I guess I can take it back and not have one. But a small part of me wants to, I think. I don't know why.

Maybe underneath, you have a spiritual side.

SNORT

Yeah, that's it.

Maybe you'll figure it out as you go along.

Maybe.

The plate lands in front of us again, this time knocking over my milk. I jump up. Luckily there's not much in the carton. It dribbles down the side of the table and just misses my shoes.

This time Anthony rushes over and grabs the plate, half an ice cream sandwich sticking out of his mouth.

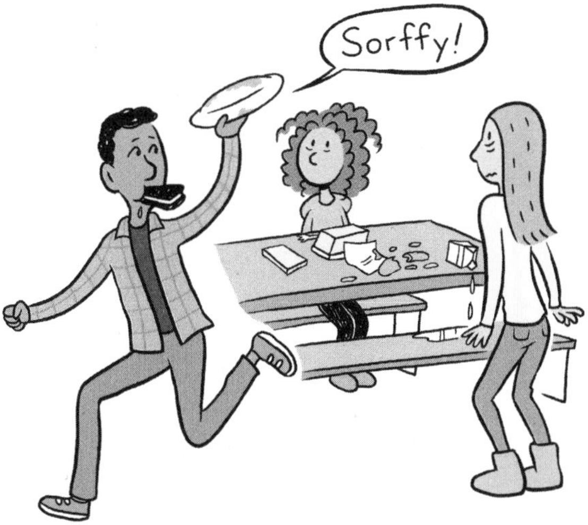
Sorffy!

Now it's my turn to blush.

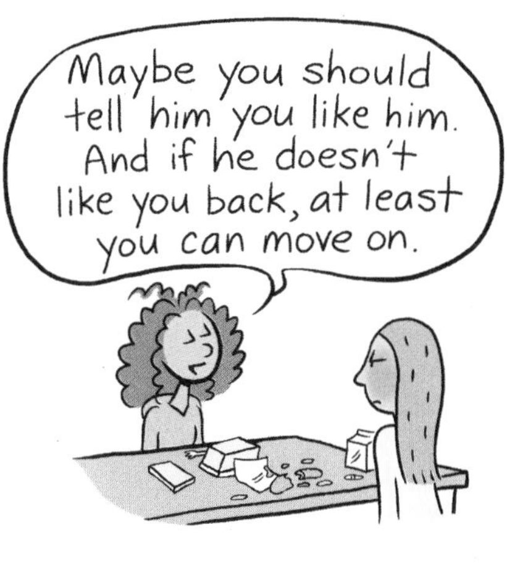
Maybe you should tell him you like him. And if he doesn't like you back, at least you can move on.

I feel myself turning the same shade of violet. Yeah, okay, I deserved that. Still, I won't admit it.

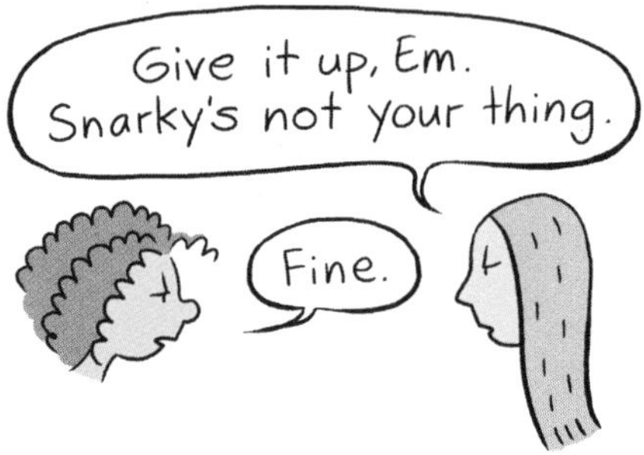
Give it up, Em.
Snarky's not your thing.
Fine.

We look at each other and burst out laughing. At the same time, some lone girl passes us, balancing an overflowing lunch tray. (How'd she score **three** tacos? I mean, yuck, but still . . .)

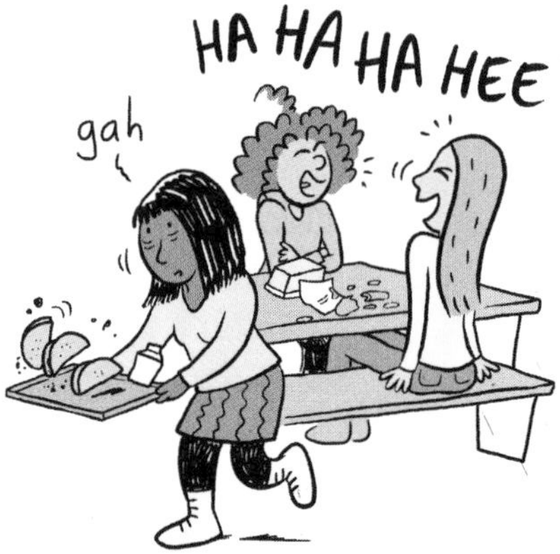
HA HA HA HEE
gah

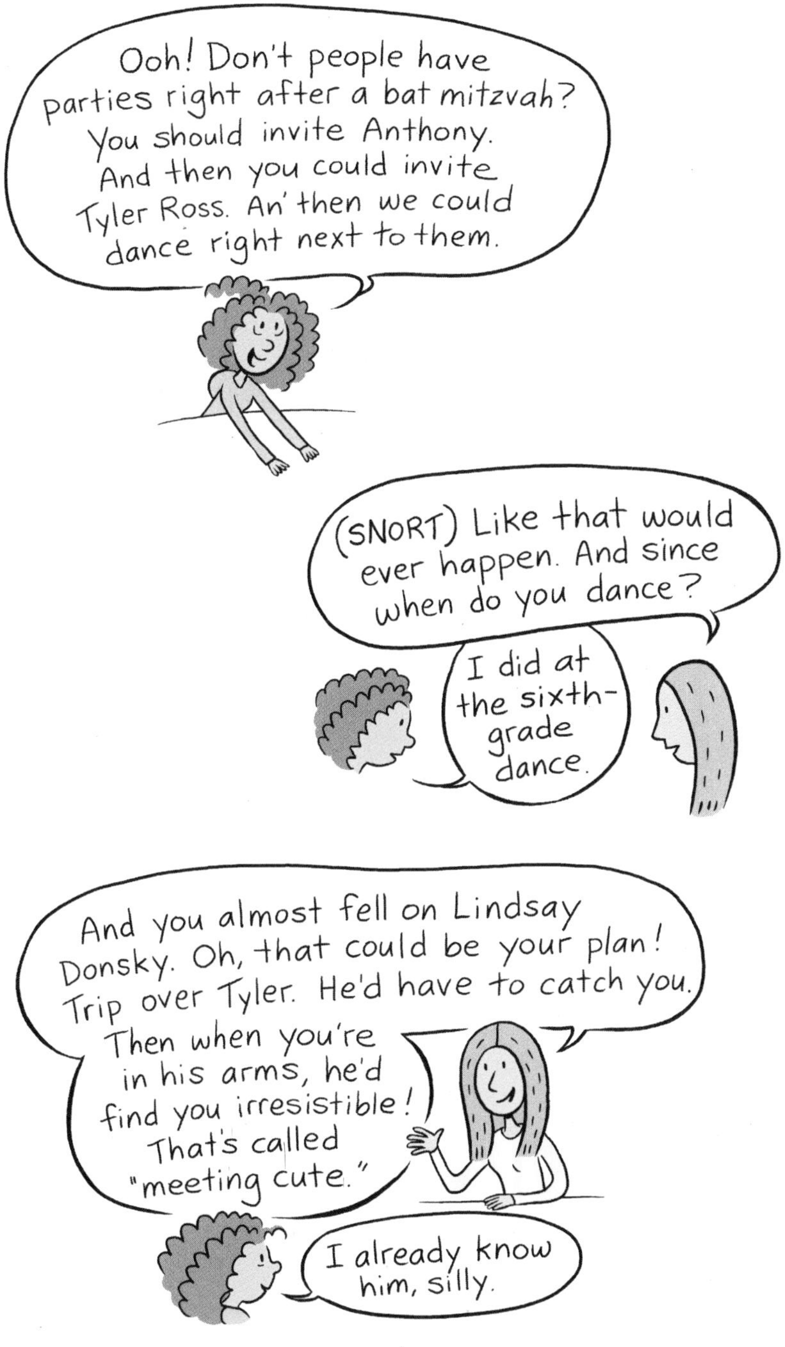
Ooh! Don't people have parties right after a bat mitzvah? You should invite Anthony. And then you could invite Tyler Ross. An' then we could dance right next to them.
(SNORT) Like that would ever happen. And since when do you dance?
I did at the sixth-grade dance.
And you almost fell on Lindsay Donsky. Oh, that could be your plan! Trip over Tyler. He'd have to catch you.
Then when you're in his arms, he'd find you irresistible! That's called "meeting cute."
I already know him, silly.

But you don't <u>know</u> <u>him</u>-know him. Falling in love is like getting to know someone all over again.

And how would <u>you</u> know?

I look across the room at Anthony. He just sat down and is avoiding the lunchroom monitor, who finally showed up. He spits into his napkin. I still don't know why that doesn't gross me out. I guess love really is blind.

I read a lot... remember?

NOW

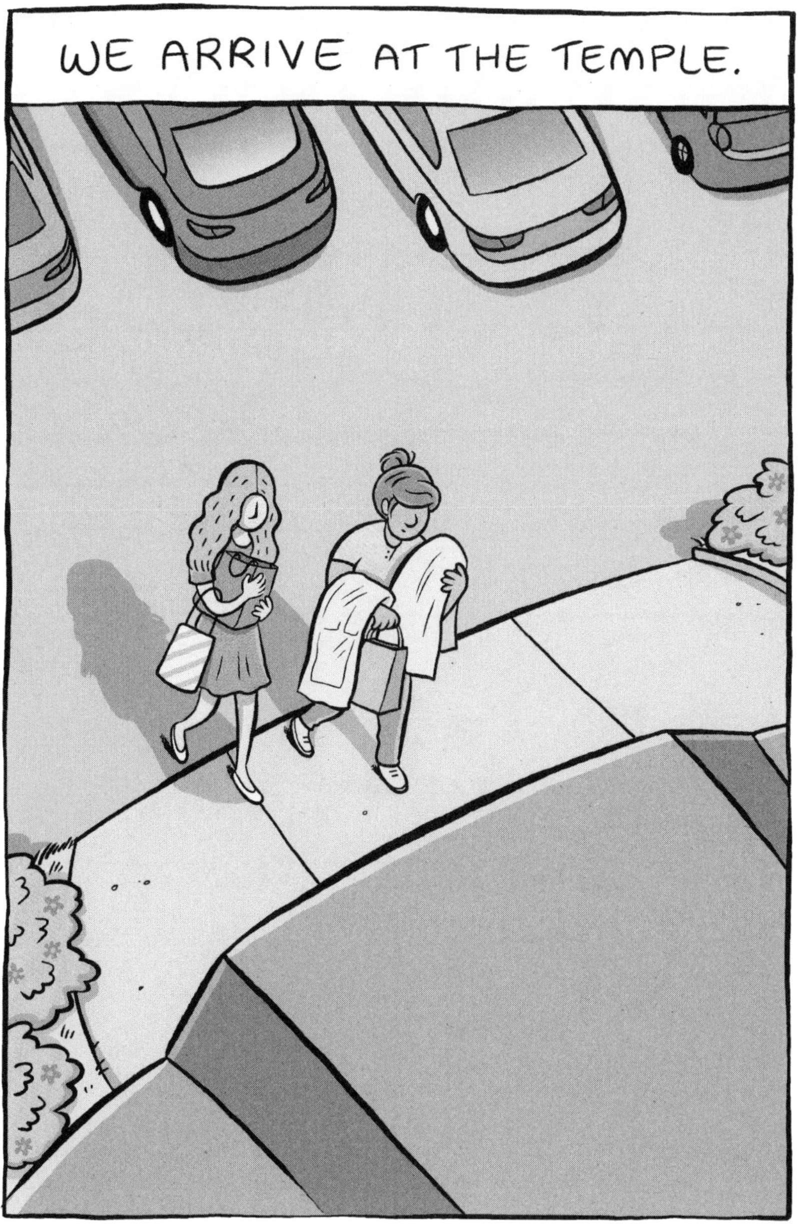
WE ARRIVE AT THE TEMPLE.

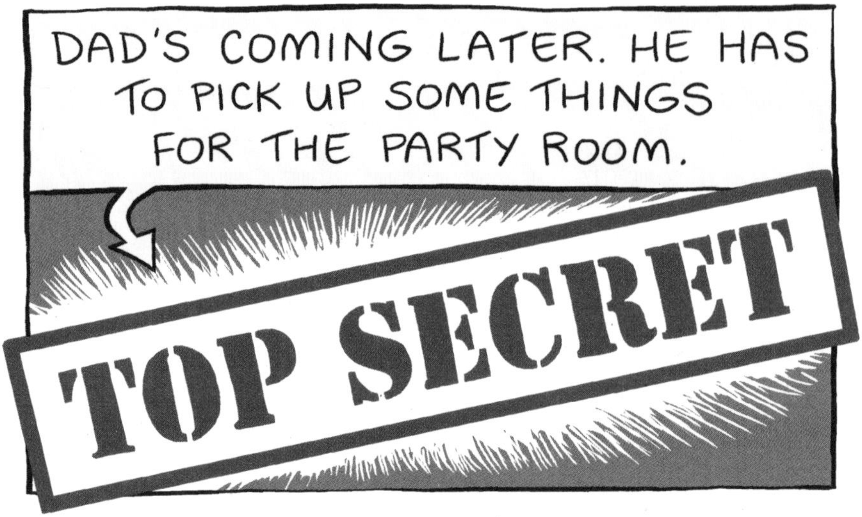
DAD'S COMING LATER. HE HAS TO PICK UP SOME THINGS FOR THE PARTY ROOM.
TOP SECRET

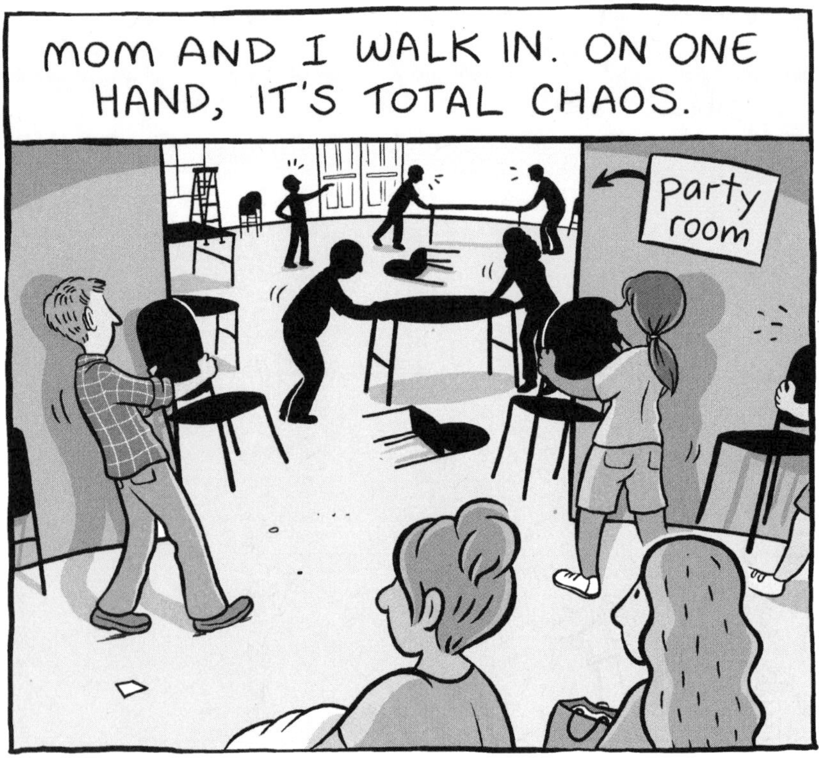
MOM AND I WALK IN. ON ONE HAND, IT'S TOTAL CHAOS.
party room

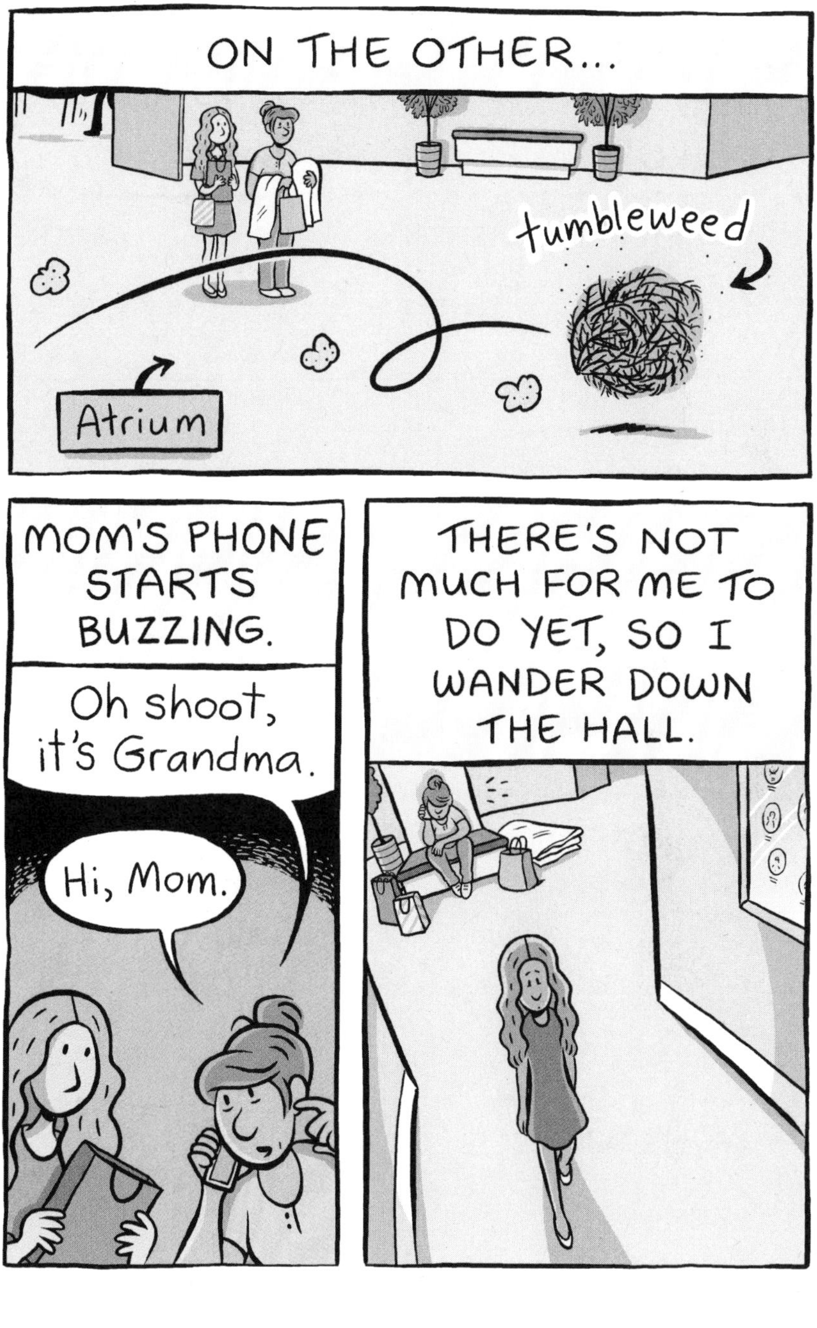
ON THE OTHER...
tumbleweed
Atrium
MOM'S PHONE STARTS BUZZING.
Oh shoot, it's Grandma.
Hi, Mom.
THERE'S NOT MUCH FOR ME TO DO YET, SO I WANDER DOWN THE HALL.

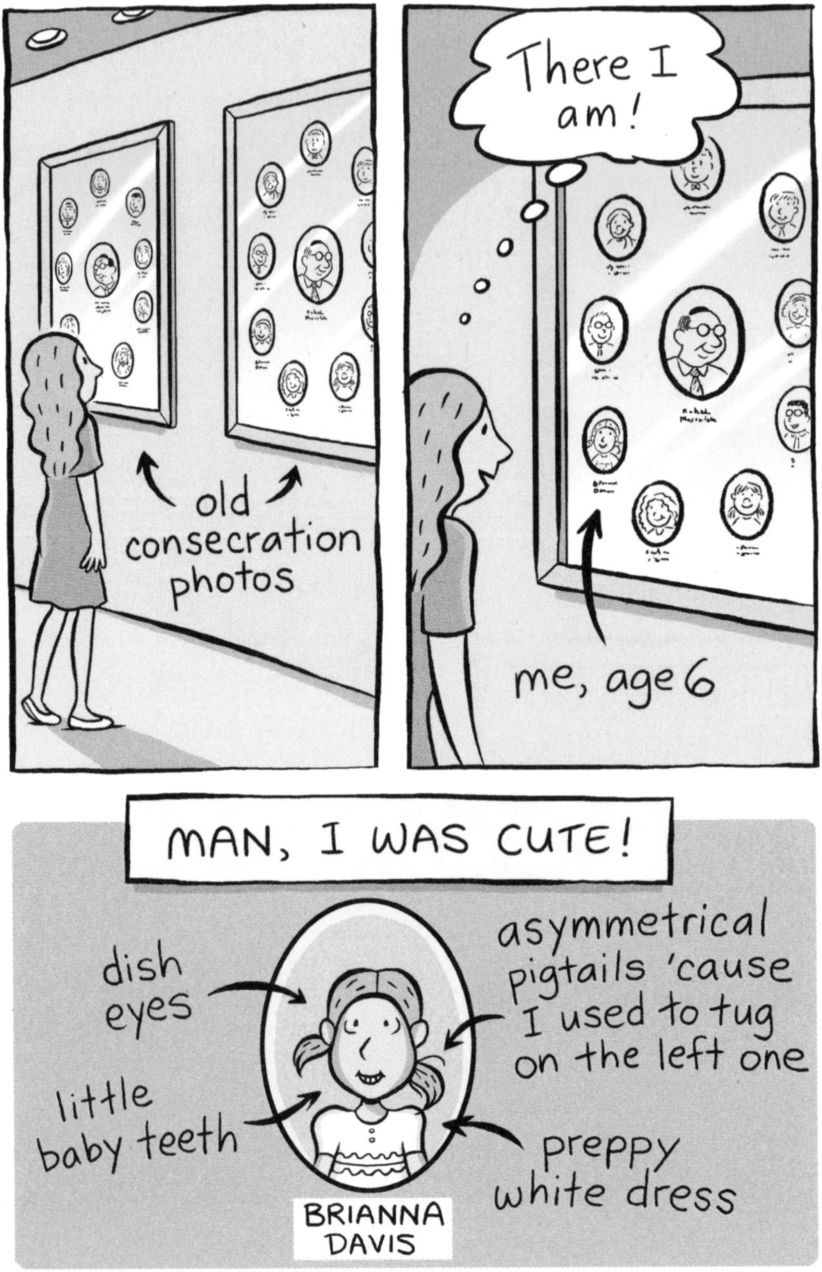
old consecration photos
There I am!
me, age 6
MAN, I WAS CUTE!
dish eyes
asymmetrical pigtails 'cause I used to tug on the left one
little baby teeth
preppy white dress
BRIANNA DAVIS

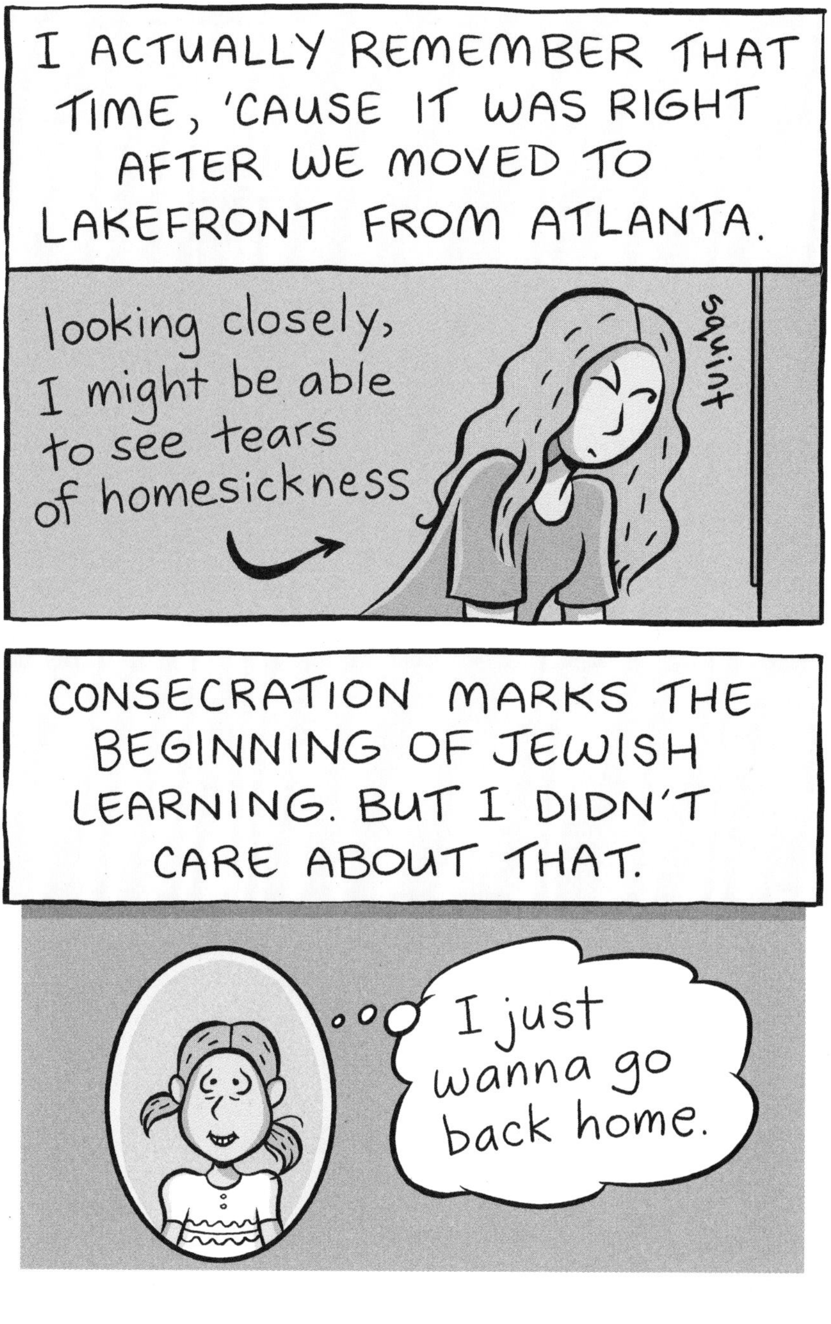
I ACTUALLY REMEMBER THAT TIME, 'CAUSE IT WAS RIGHT AFTER WE MOVED TO LAKEFRONT FROM ATLANTA.
looking closely, I might be able to see tears of homesickness
squint
CONSECRATION MARKS THE BEGINNING OF JEWISH LEARNING. BUT I DIDN'T CARE ABOUT THAT.
I just wanna go back home.

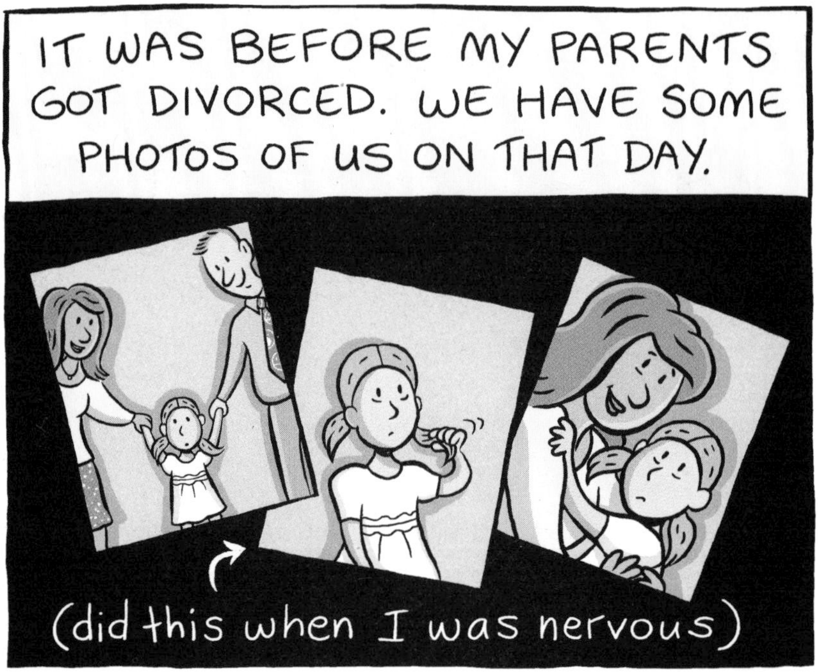
IT WAS BEFORE MY PARENTS GOT DIVORCED. WE HAVE SOME PHOTOS OF US ON THAT DAY.
(did this when I was nervous)

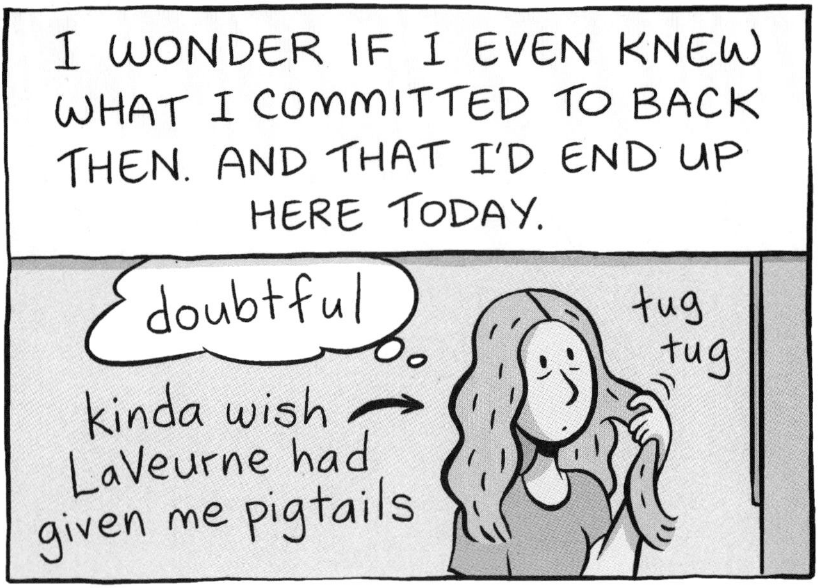
I WONDER IF I EVEN KNEW WHAT I COMMITTED TO BACK THEN. AND THAT I'D END UP HERE TODAY.
doubtful
tug tug
kinda wish LaVeurne had given me pigtails

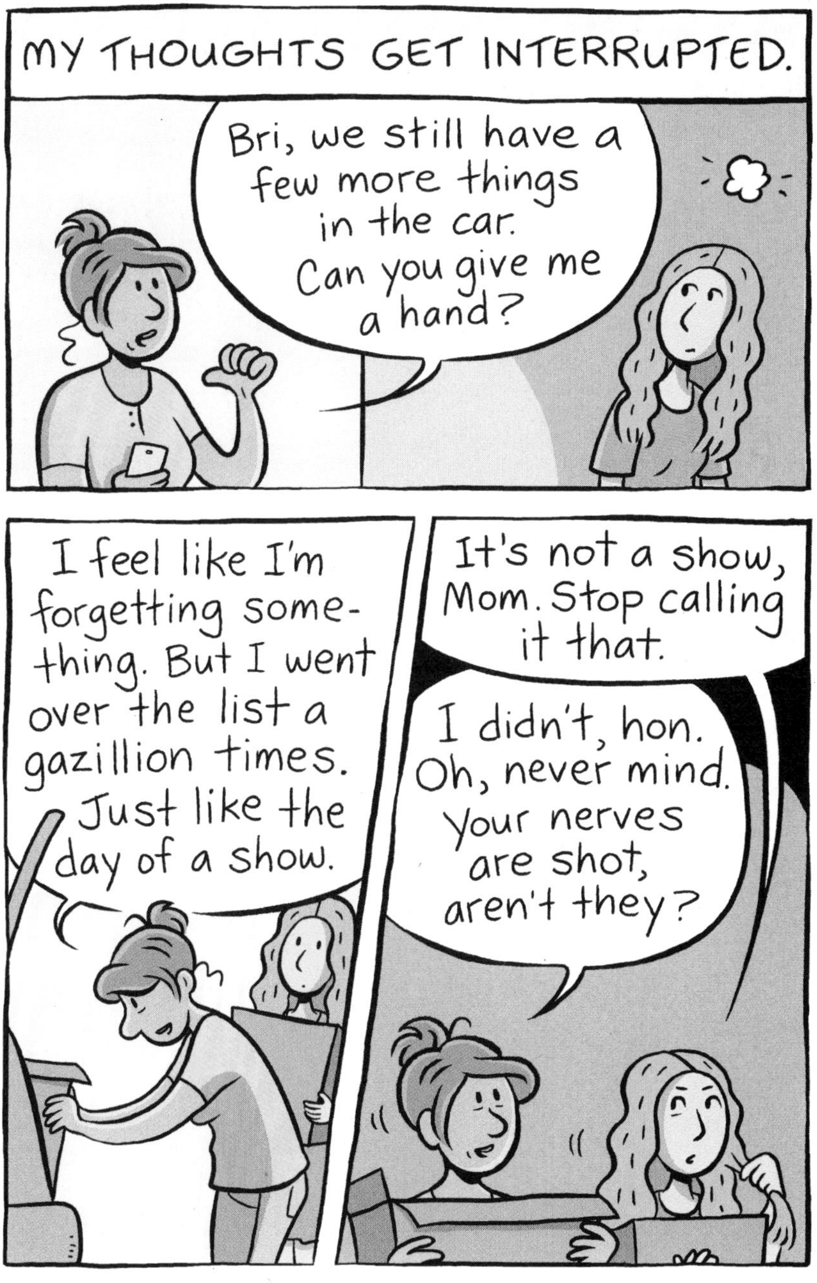
MY THOUGHTS GET INTERRUPTED.
Bri, we still have a few more things in the car. Can you give me a hand?
I feel like I'm forgetting some-thing. But I went over the list a gazillion times. Just like the day of a show.
It's not a show, Mom. Stop calling it that.
I didn't, hon. Oh, never mind. Your nerves are shot, aren't they?

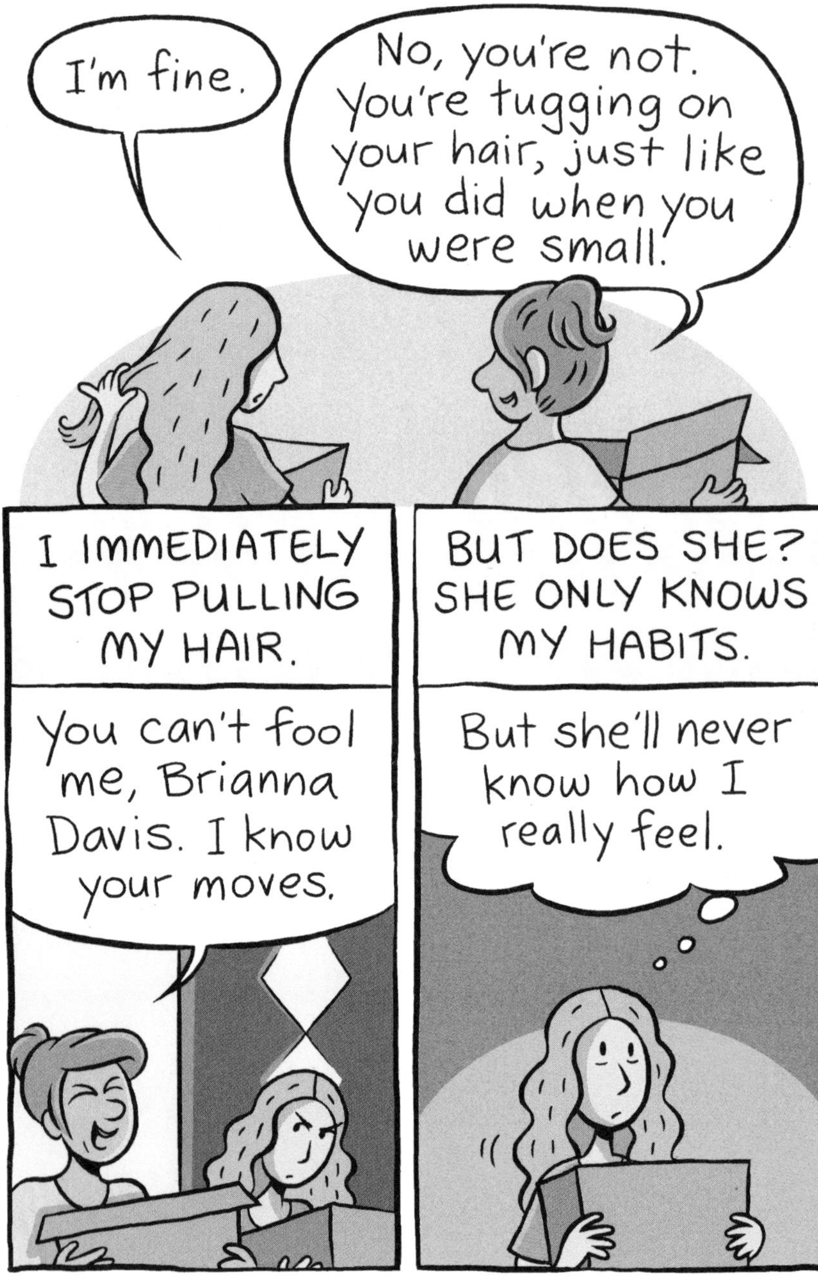

I'm fine.
No, you're not. You're tugging on your hair, just like you did when you were small.
I IMMEDIATELY STOP PULLING MY HAIR.
You can't fool me, Brianna Davis. I know your moves.
BUT DOES SHE? SHE ONLY KNOWS MY HABITS.
But she'll never know how I really feel.

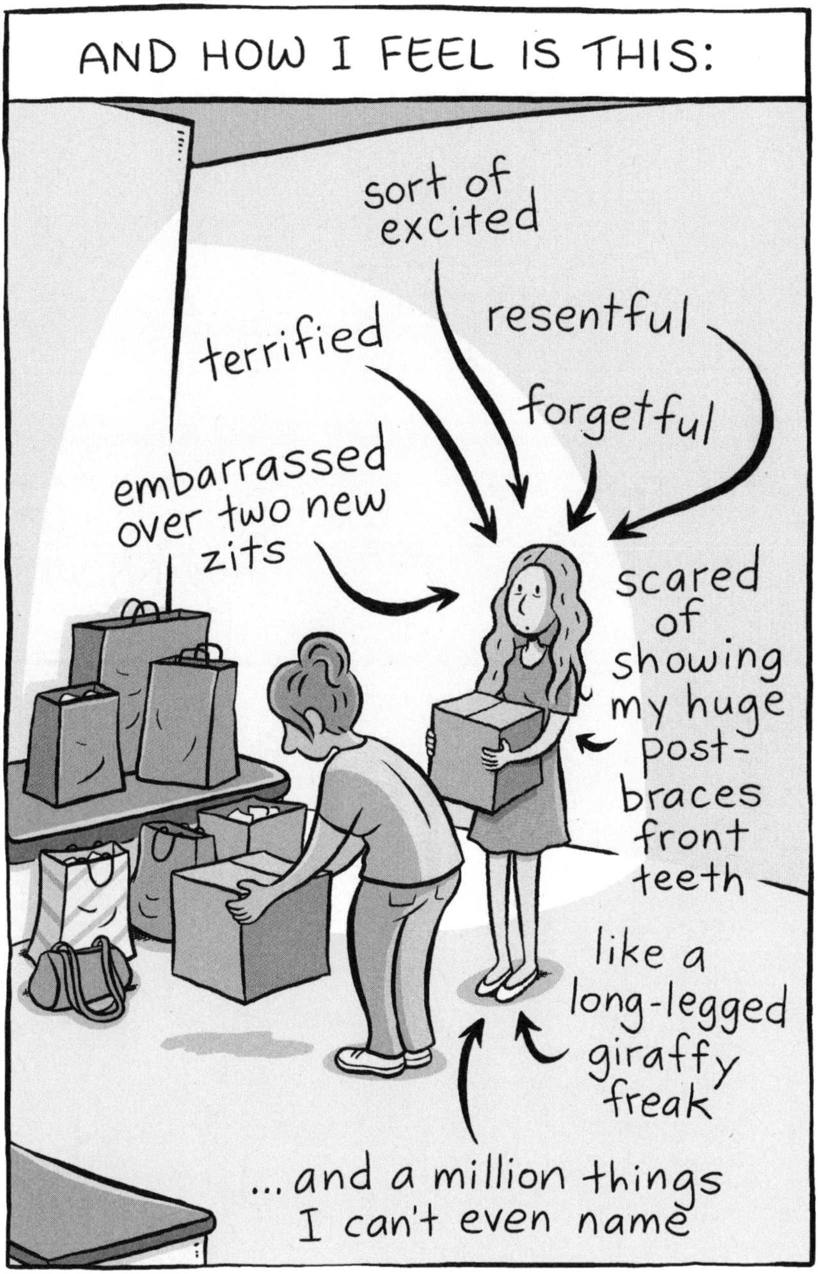
AND HOW I FEEL IS THIS:
sort of excited
terrified
resentful
forgetful
embarrassed over two new zits
scared of showing my huge post-braces front teeth
like a long-legged giraffy freak
...and a million things I can't even name

SIX MONTHS AGO

I'm hanging out by Emmie's locker. It's right before homeroom, and the hallway's crowded.

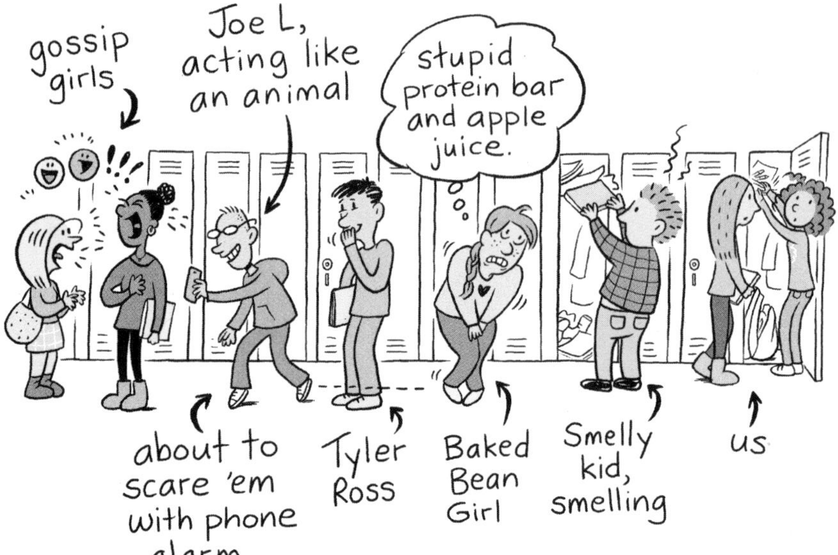
gossip girls
Joe L, acting like an animal
stupid protein bar and apple juice.
about to scare 'em with phone alarm
Tyler Ross
Baked Bean Girl
Smelly kid, smelling
us

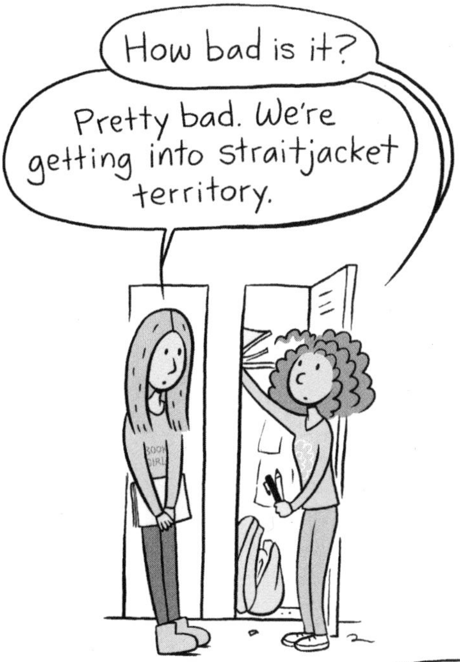
How bad is it?
Pretty bad. We're getting into straitjacket territory.

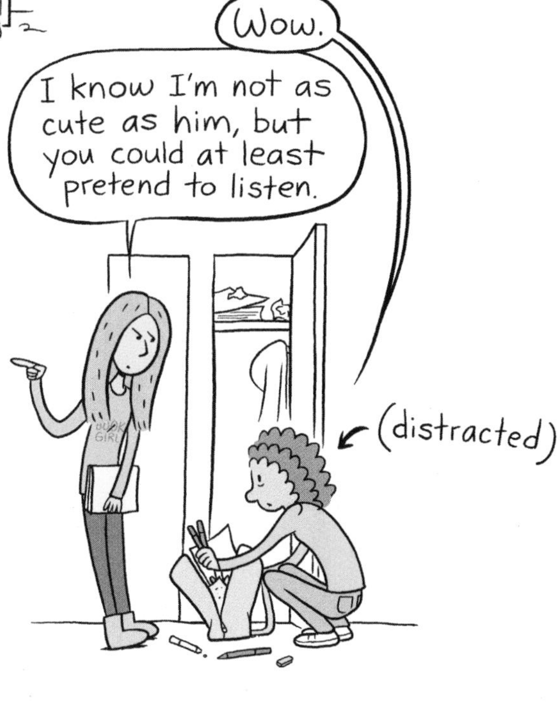
Wow.
I know I'm not as cute as him, but you could at least pretend to listen.
(distracted)

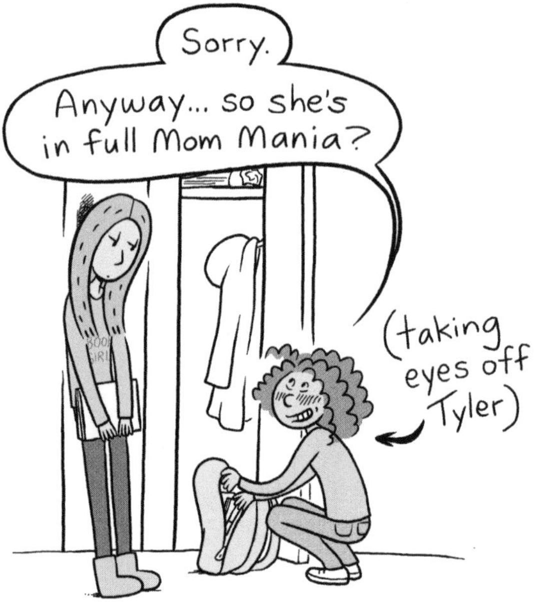
Sorry.
Anyway... so she's in full Mom Mania?
(taking eyes off Tyler)
BOOK GIRL

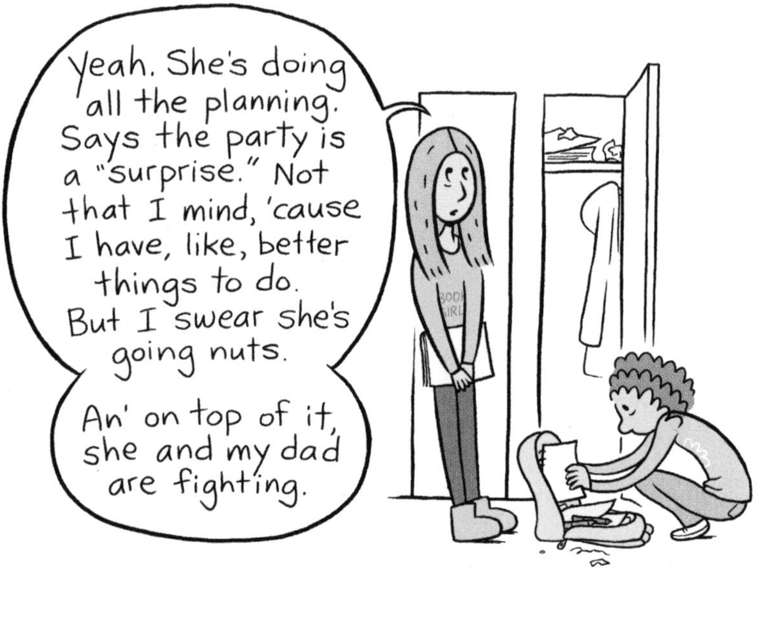
Yeah. She's doing all the planning. Says the party is a "surprise." Not that I mind, 'cause I have, like, better things to do. But I swear she's going nuts.
An' on top of it, she and my dad are fighting.
BOOK GIRL

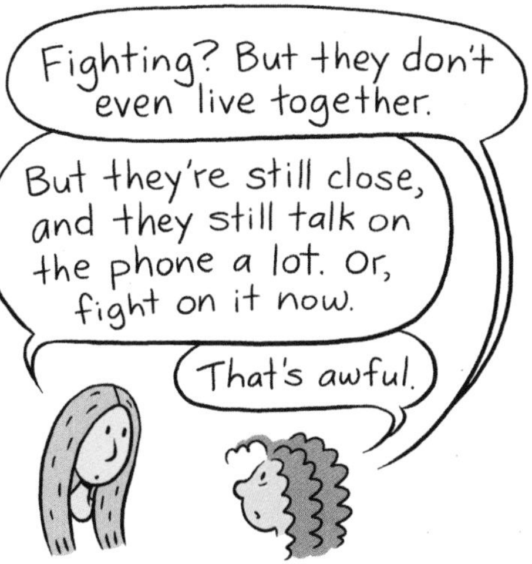
Fighting? But they don't even live together.
But they're still close, and they still talk on the phone a lot. Or, fight on it now.
That's awful.

Em finishes shoving art supplies in her backpack and grabs her book. She closes her locker door, and we walk by Joe Lungo and Tyler. Actually, I have to step over Joe Lungo because he's rolling on the floor and howling like a dog.

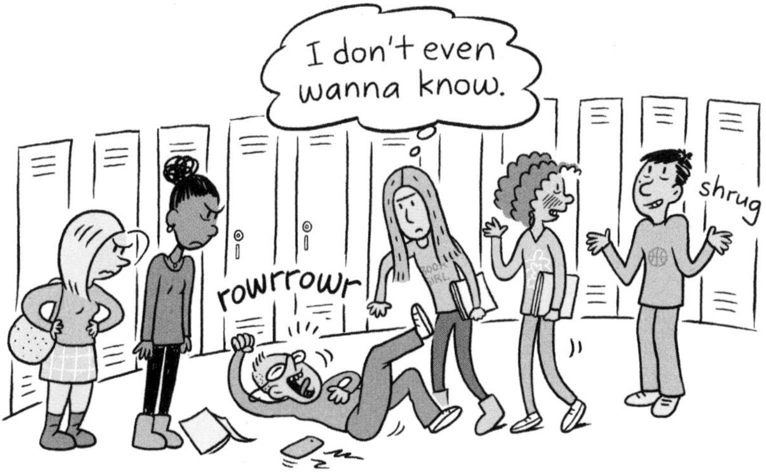
I don't even wanna know.
rowrrowr
shrug

We stop around the corner from homeroom.

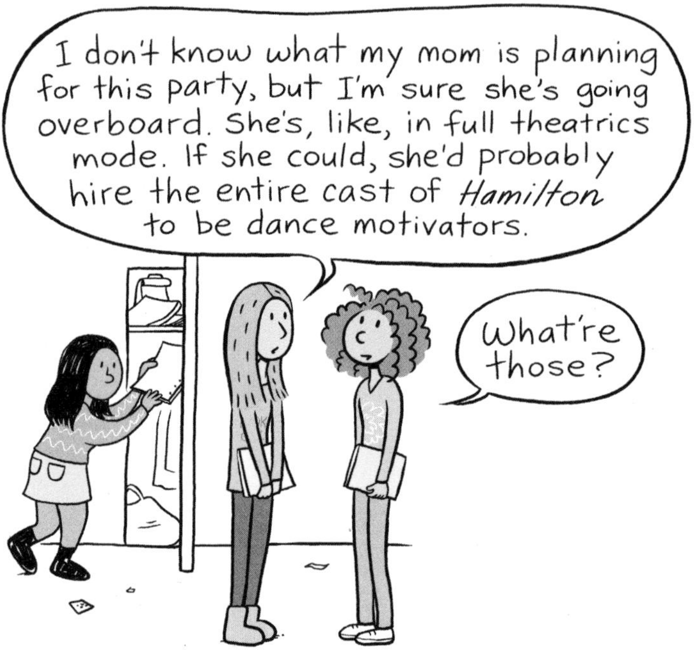
I don't know what my mom is planning for this party, but I'm sure she's going overboard. She's, like, in full theatrics mode. If she could, she'd probably hire the entire cast of *Hamilton* to be dance motivators.
What're those?

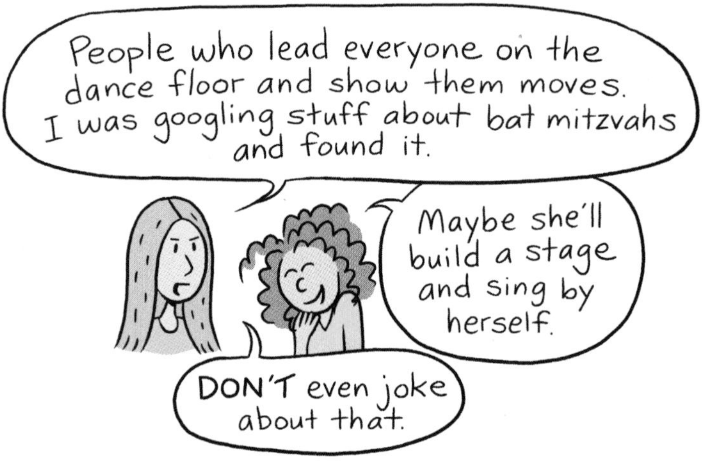
People who lead everyone on the dance floor and show them moves. I was googling stuff about bat mitzvahs and found it.
Maybe she'll build a stage and sing by herself.
DON'T even joke about that.

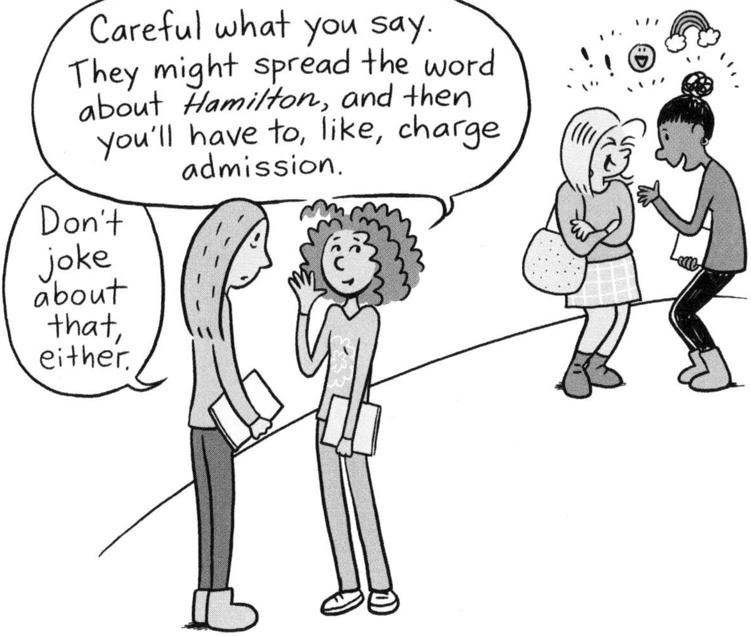
Careful what you say. They might spread the word about *Hamilton*, and then you'll have to, like, charge admission.
Don't joke about that, either.
! !

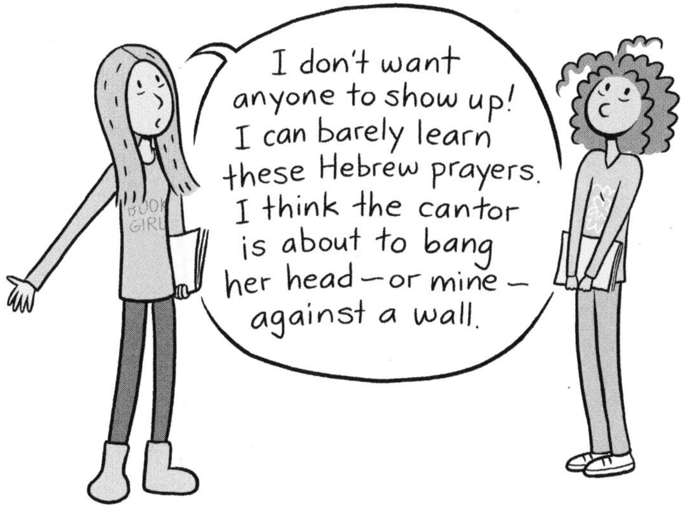
I don't want anyone to show up! I can barely learn these Hebrew prayers. I think the cantor is about to bang her head—or mine—against a wall.
BOOK GIRL

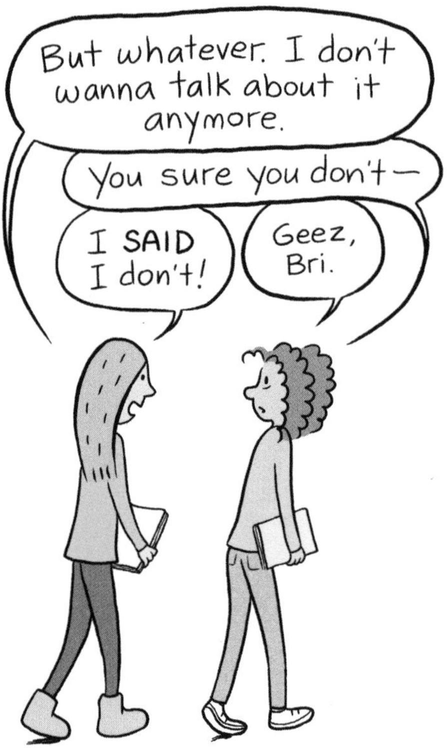
But whatever. I don't wanna talk about it anymore.
You sure you don't—
I **SAID** I don't!
Geez, Bri.

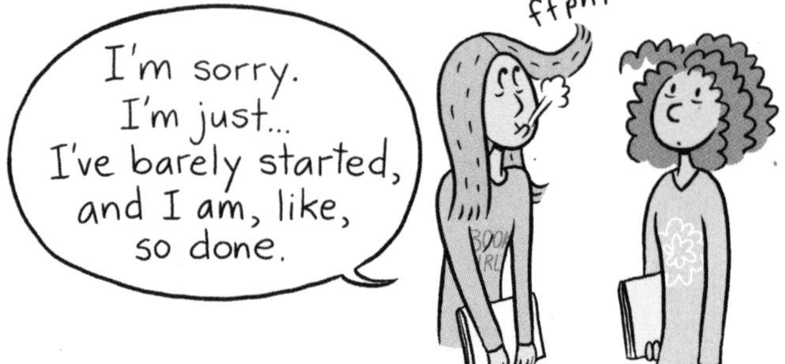
ffpht
I'm sorry. I'm just... I've barely started, and I am, like, so done.

Across the hall, we see Em's new friend from art class, Sarah. She waves and comes over. I feel a little pang inside, like a hand just squeezed my guts.

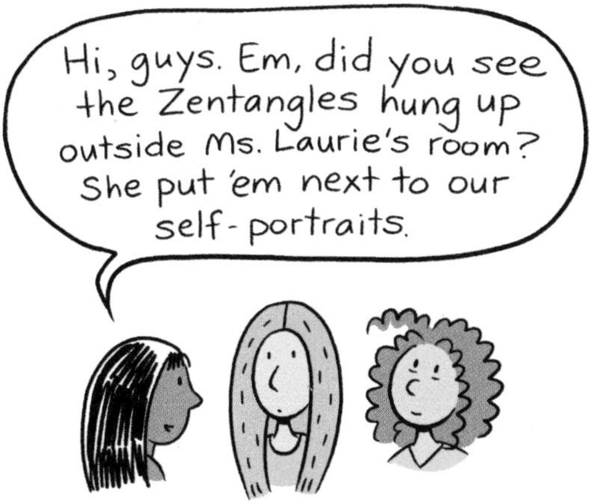
Hi, guys. Em, did you see the Zentangles hung up outside Ms. Laurie's room? She put 'em next to our self-portraits.

Em. Now they're on shortened-name terms. That's when you know people are getting to be good friends.

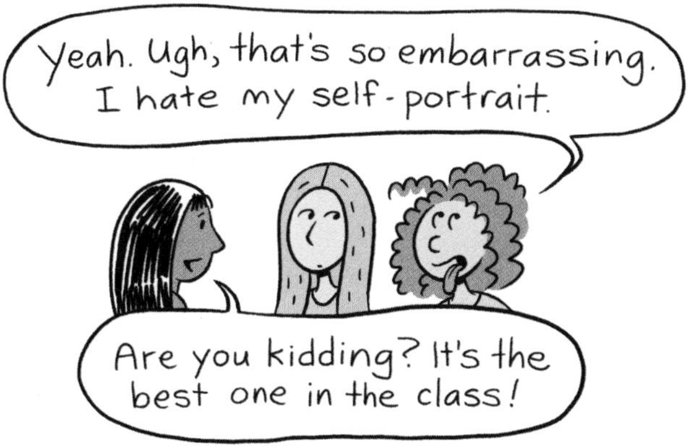
Yeah. Ugh, that's so embarrassing. I hate my self-portrait.
Are you kidding? It's the best one in the class!

I want to gag. But I hold it in because the bell's about to ring, and I realize we're gonna be late for homeroom. That's a good excuse to nudge Em away from Sarah.

I tug on her sweater sleeve.

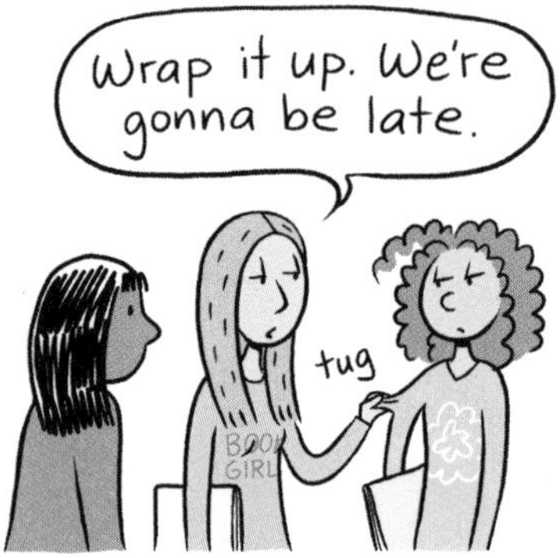
Wrap it up. We're gonna be late.
tug
BOOK GIRL

She throws me an annoyed look. I keep forgetting myself.

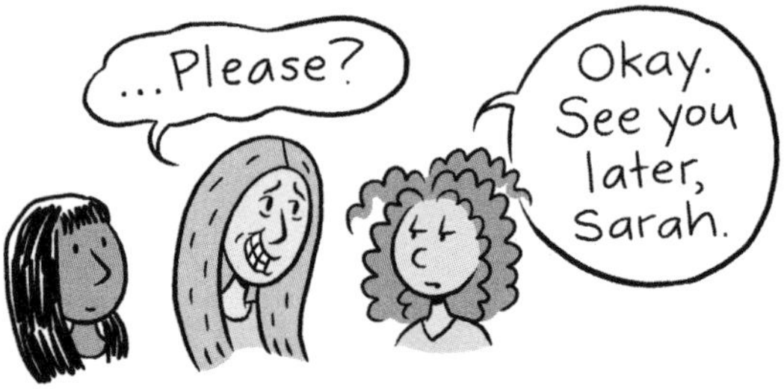
...Please?
Okay. See you later, Sarah.

We walk toward homeroom, and I try to put all this bat mitzvah and Sarah stuff behind me. For now.

Someone taps me on the shoulder.

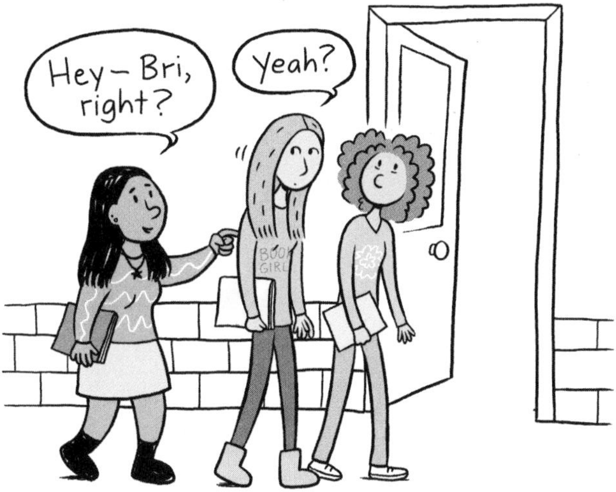
Hey – Bri, right?
Yeah?
BOOK GIRL

Emmie and I do a double take. Zoe Torres is one of the coolest kids in our grade. Popular but not too popular. She's pretty friendly, which is one of the reasons why people like her. But it's the first time she's ever spoken to me.

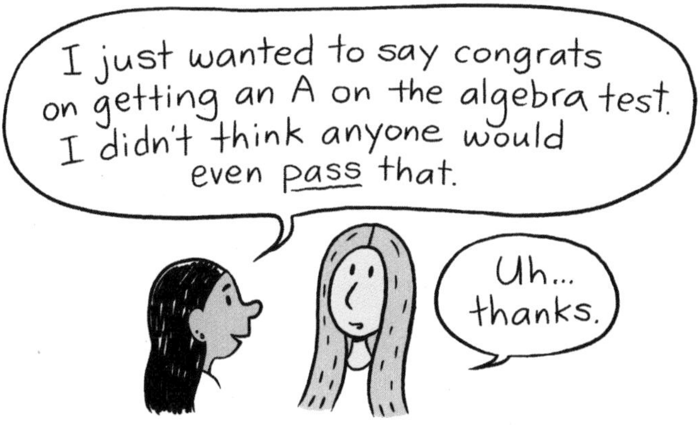
I just wanted to say congrats on getting an A on the algebra test. I didn't think anyone would even pass that.
Uh... thanks.

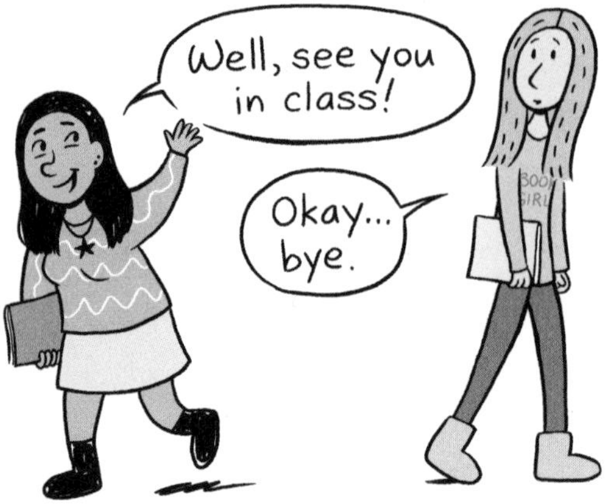
Well, see you in class!
Okay... bye.

That was nice . . . but weird. No one's ever congratulated me on getting an A before. Usually I get a reaction like:

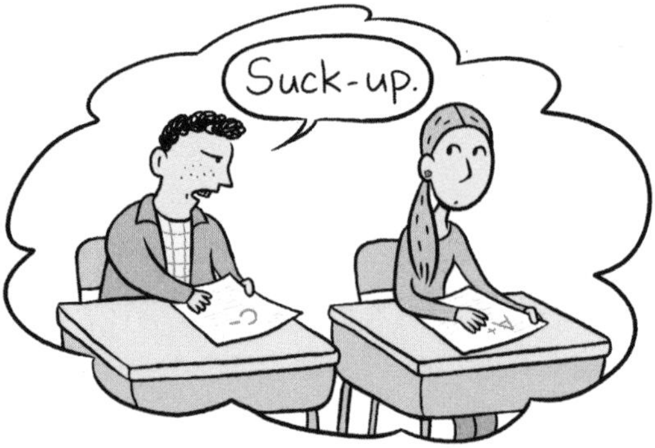
Suck-up.

Emmie and I shrug at the same time and walk into homeroom.

WE'RE BACK IN THE ATRIUM.
I GET THE SUDDEN FEELING
I FORGOT SOMETHING.

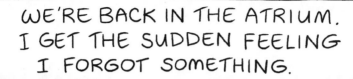

Mom. No, Mom,
we don't need extra
sweaters for the
sanctuary. It's
like a hundred
degrees. Mom.

?

THERE'S MORE COMMOTION
COMING FROM THE PARTY ROOM,
BUT THE DOORS ARE CLOSED.

Fine. Just
bring them.
*I DON'T CARE
WHAT SIZE!*

feel like
a volcano
of nerves
about to
erupt

cantor

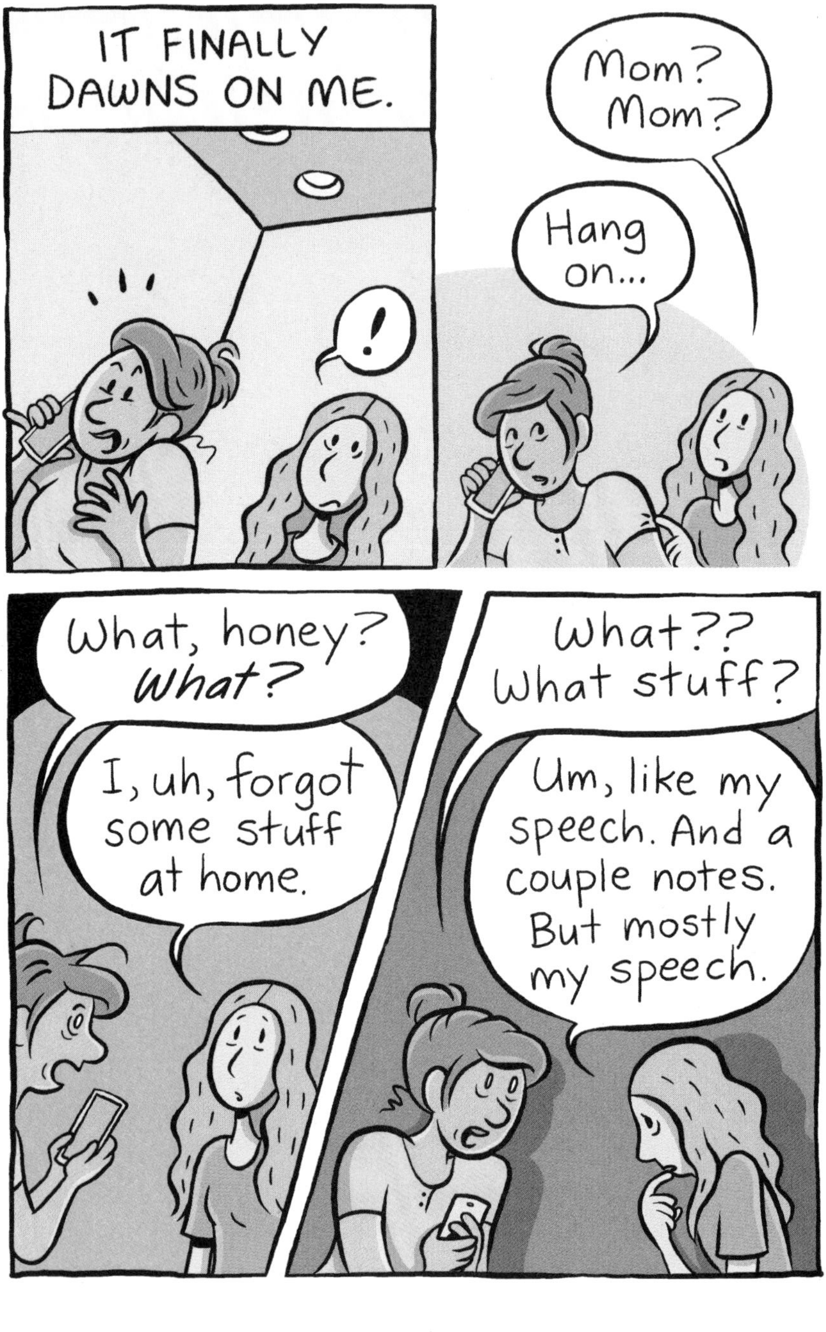
IT FINALLY DAWNS ON ME.
!
Mom? Mom?
Hang on...
What, honey? *What?*
I, uh, forgot some stuff at home.
What?? What stuff?
Um, like my speech. And a couple notes. But mostly my speech.

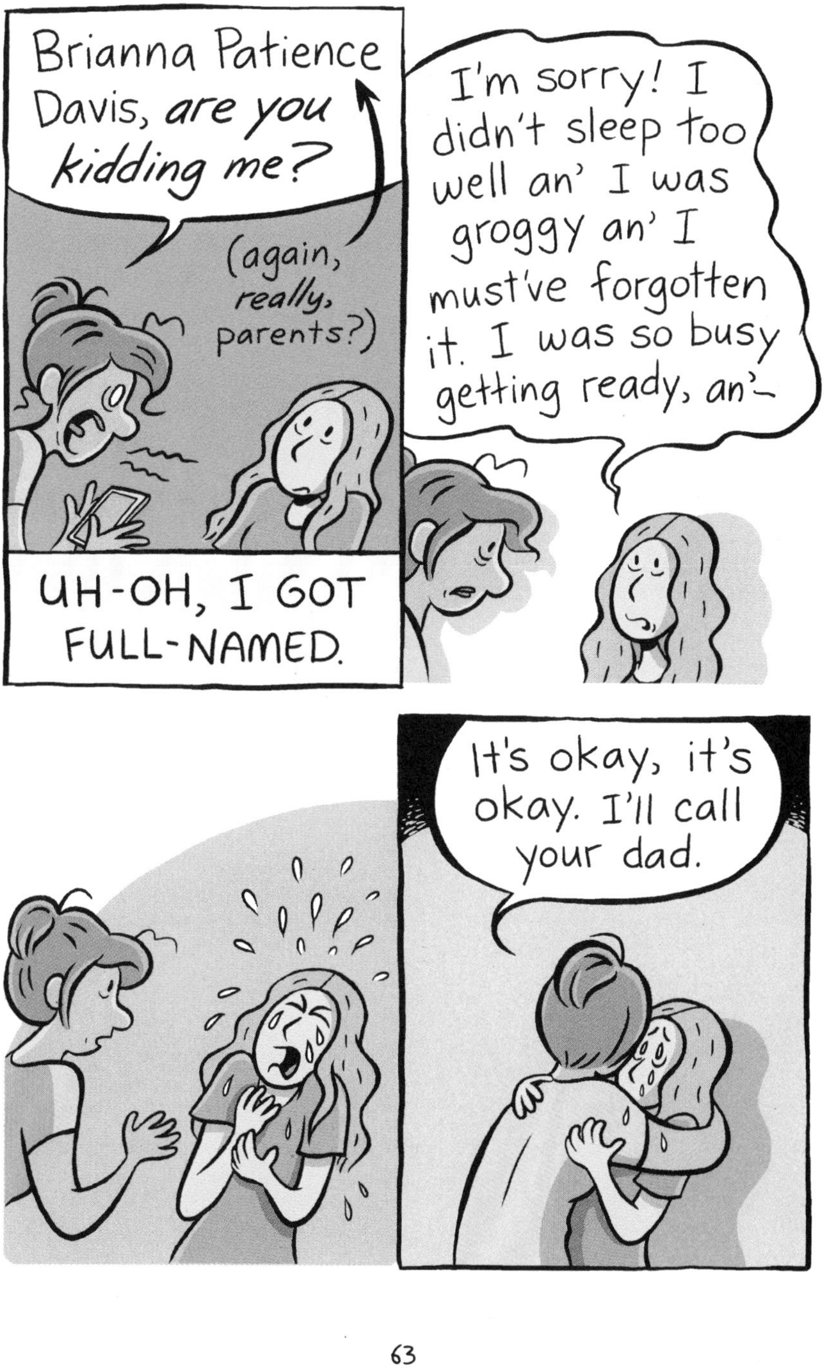
Brianna Patience Davis, *are you kidding me?*
(again, *really,* parents?)
UH-OH, I GOT FULL-NAMED.
I'm sorry! I didn't sleep too well an' I was groggy an' I must've forgotten it. I was so busy getting ready, an'—
It's okay, it's okay. I'll call your dad.

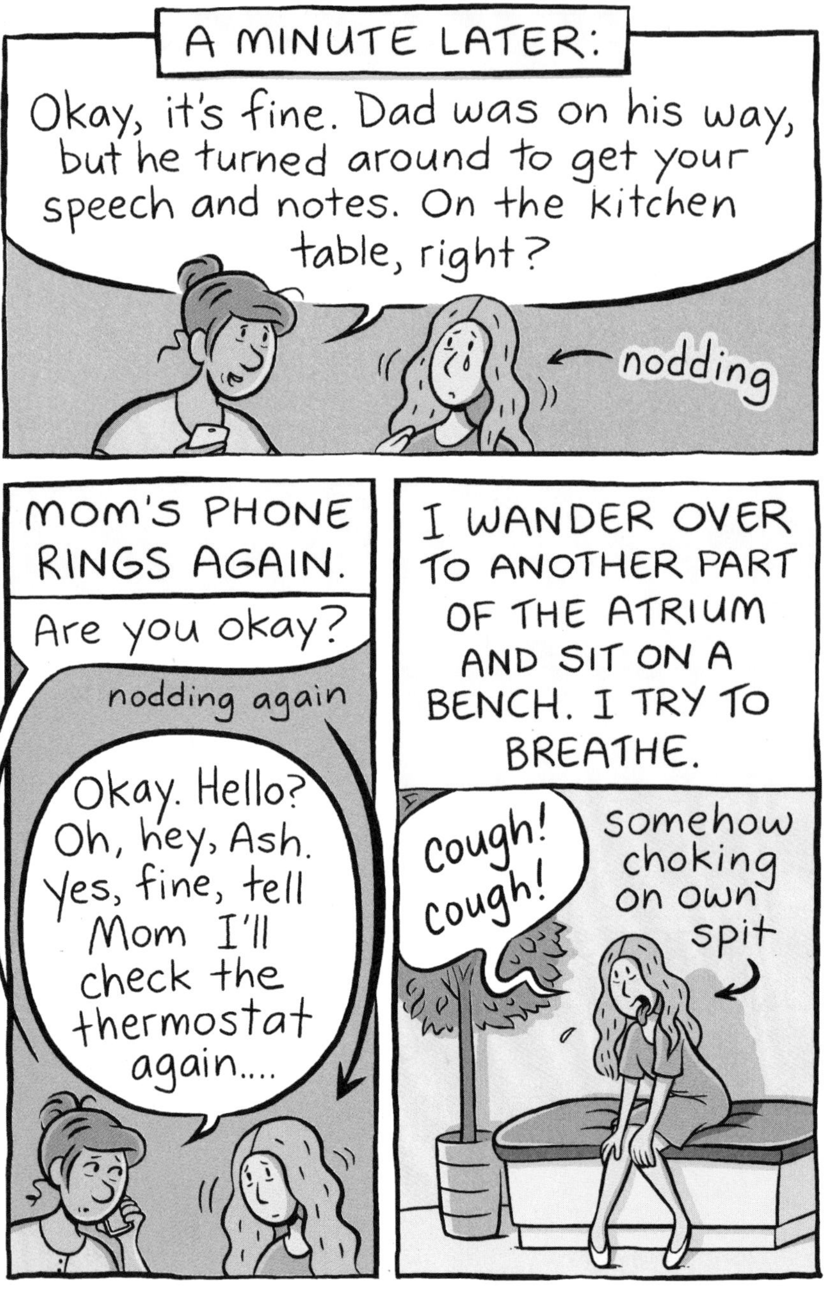
A MINUTE LATER:
Okay, it's fine. Dad was on his way, but he turned around to get your speech and notes. On the kitchen table, right?
nodding
MOM'S PHONE RINGS AGAIN.
Are you okay?
nodding again
Okay. Hello? Oh, hey, Ash. Yes, fine, tell Mom I'll check the thermostat again....
I WANDER OVER TO ANOTHER PART OF THE ATRIUM AND SIT ON A BENCH. I TRY TO BREATHE.
Cough! Cough!
somehow choking on own spit

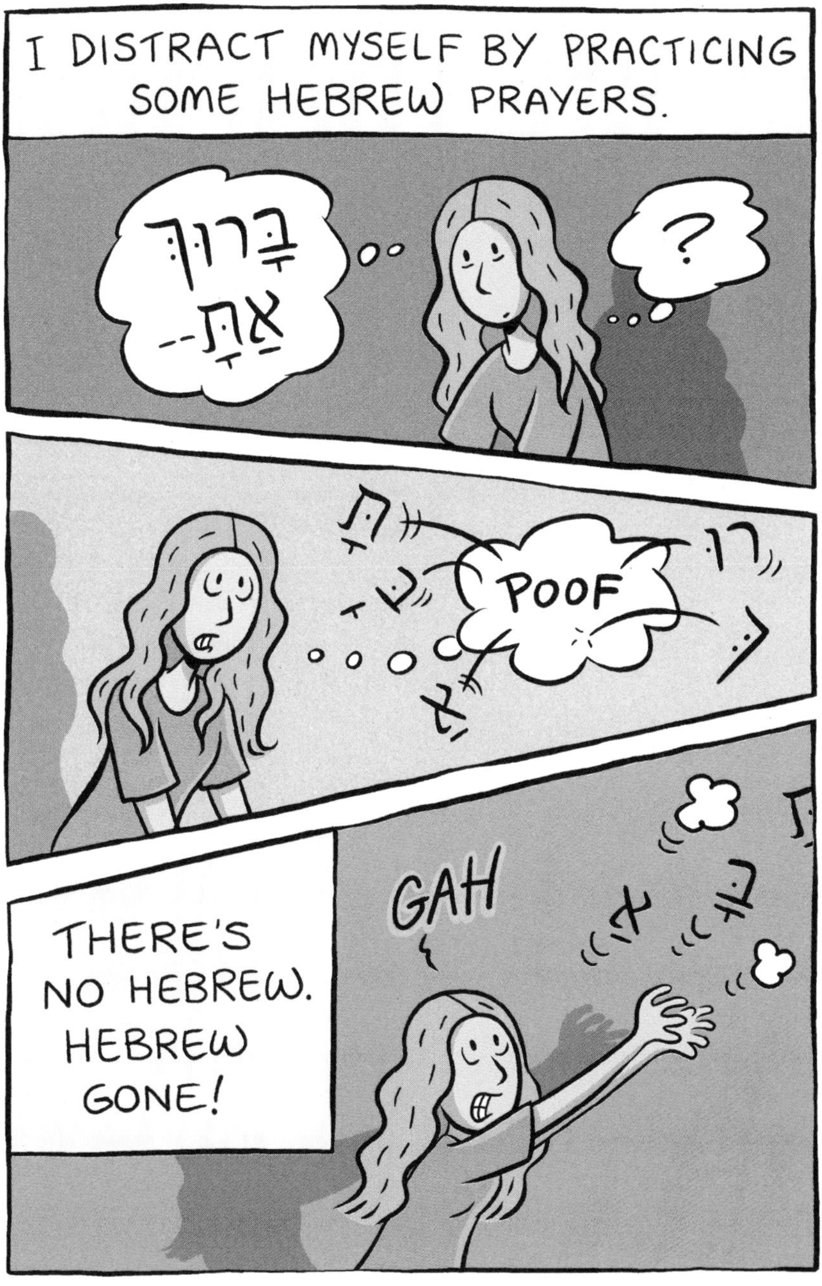
I DISTRACT MYSELF BY PRACTICING SOME HEBREW PRAYERS.
בָּרוּךְ אַתָּ--
?
POOF
GAH
THERE'S NO HEBREW. HEBREW GONE!

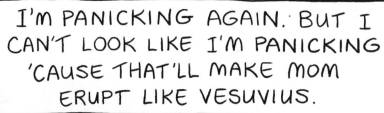

I'M PANICKING AGAIN. BUT I CAN'T LOOK LIKE I'M PANICKING 'CAUSE THAT'LL MAKE MOM ERUPT LIKE VESUVIUS.

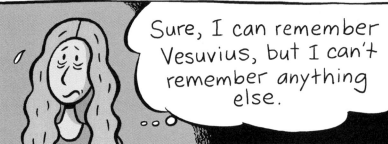

Sure, I can remember Vesuvius, but I can't remember anything else.

OKAY, MOM'S BUSY. DAD'S STILL GONE. I NEED SOMEBODY.

Somebody else.

text
text
text
text

FIVE MONTHS AGO

I'm at the temple, sitting in Cantor Jordana Caruso-Sager's office (fun to say ten times fast). I just (barely) got through practicing the first of many Hebrew blessings. On the plus side, I think I'm now reading at a second-grade level.

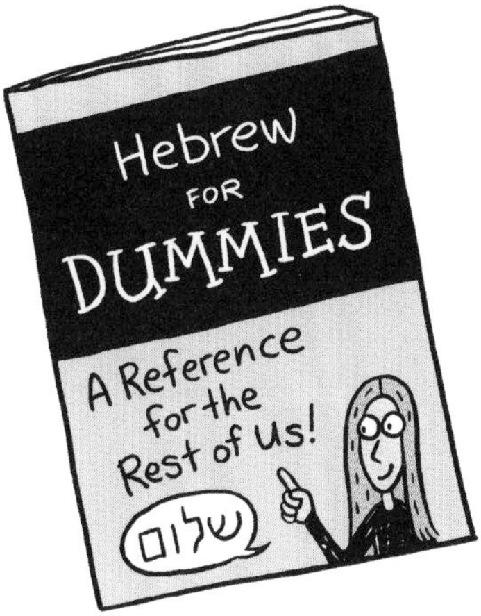
Hebrew FOR DUMMIES
A Reference for the Rest of Us!
שלום

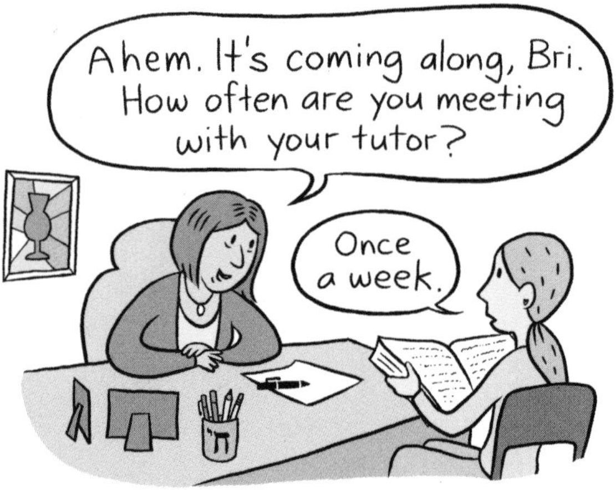
Ahem. It's coming along, Bri. How often are you meeting with your tutor?
Once a week.

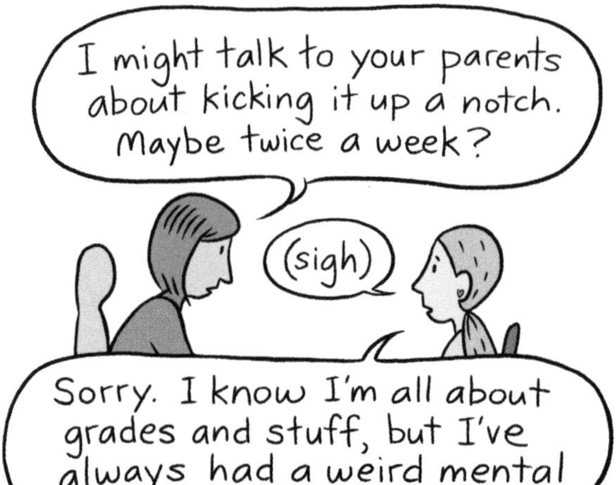
I might talk to your parents about kicking it up a notch. Maybe twice a week?
(sigh)
Sorry. I know I'm all about grades and stuff, but I've always had a weird mental block with Hebrew.

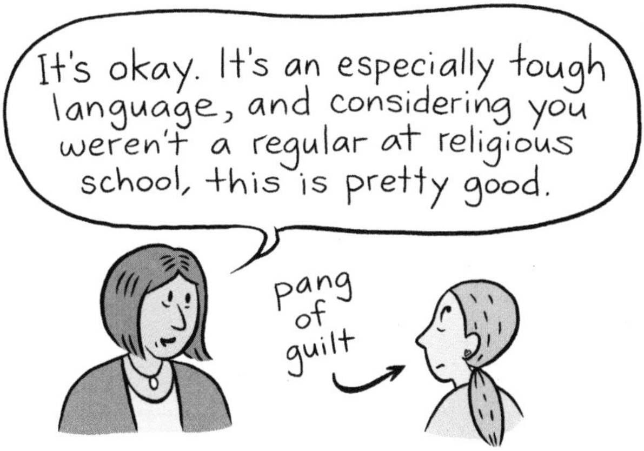
It's okay. It's an especially tough language, and considering you weren't a regular at religious school, this is pretty good.
pang of guilt

I'm supposed to meet with the cantor about three or four times before the bat mitzvah so she can see how I'm coming along with the prayers. This is our first meeting, and I'm not exactly shining.

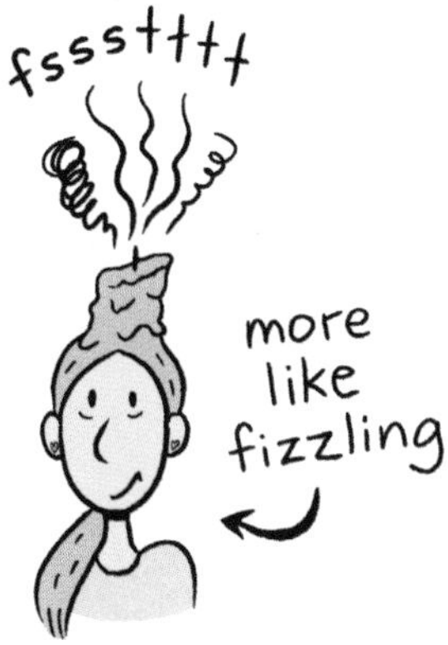
fssstttt
more like fizzling

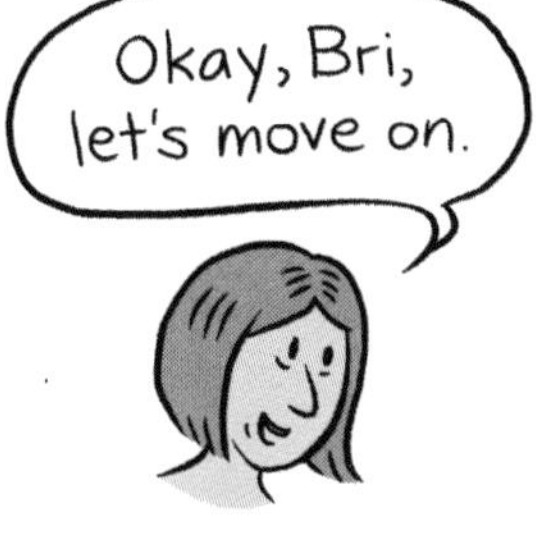
Okay, Bri, let's move on.

She hands me a prayer book earmarked with little fluorescent sticky notes.

This is the Torah portion, or parashah, for your bat mitzvah. I'd like you to read over the English translation and find three paragraphs that have meaning for you.

That's the section you'll read in Hebrew on The Big Day.

It's a good one, Bri! It's a celebration, all about the holiday of Shavuot. It talks about the giving of the Torah to our ancestors.

It's basically an agreement between our people and God.

Inwardly I groan. Because, honestly, I don't even know if I believe in any of this. So does this mean my bat mitzvah will just be one big sham?

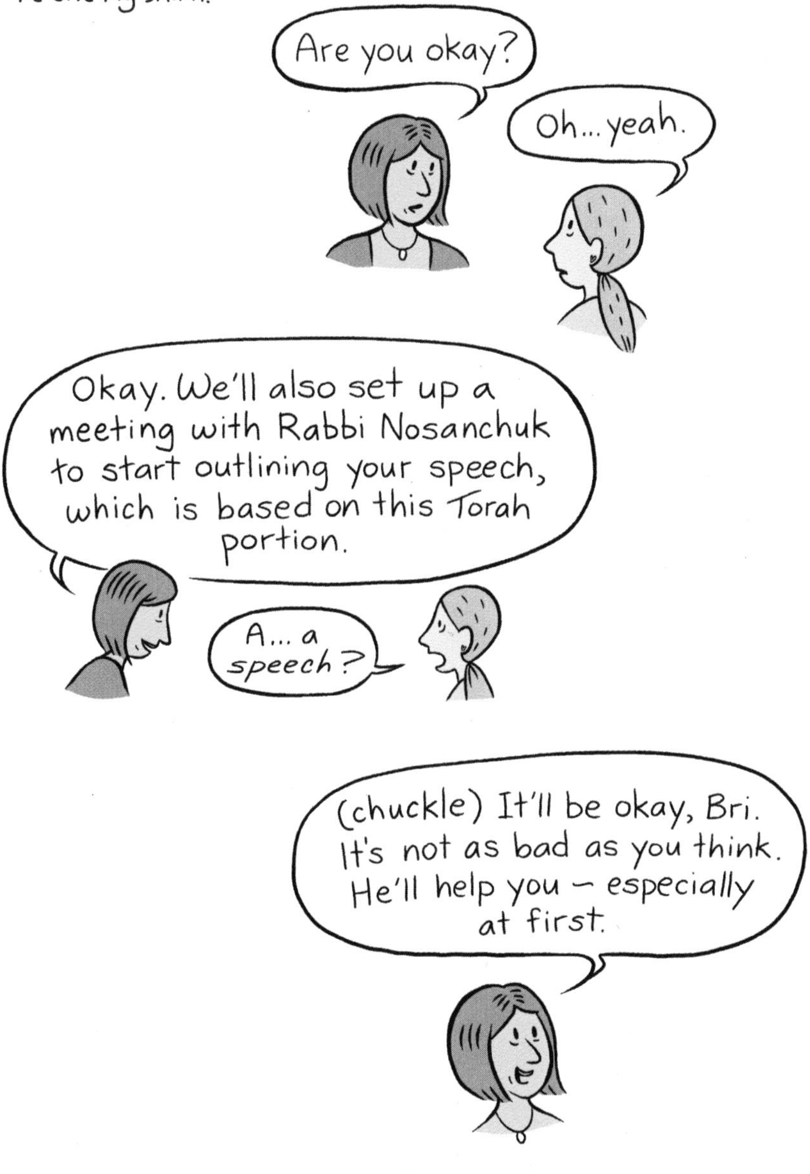
Are you okay?
Oh... yeah.
Okay. We'll also set up a meeting with Rabbi Nosanchuk to start outlining your speech, which is based on this Torah portion.
A... a speech?
(chuckle) It'll be okay, Bri. It's not as bad as you think. He'll help you – especially at first.

Inwardly I groan again. A speech? It's bad enough I have to get up in front of everyone and chant Hebrew. Making a speech just adds to the . . . the . . .

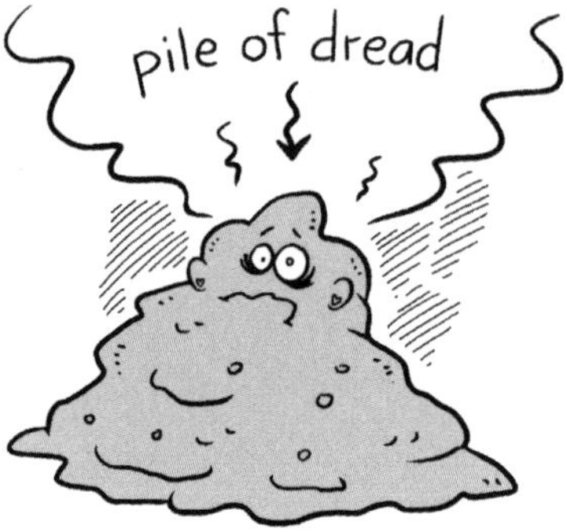
pile of dread

I must look exactly how I feel because Cantor Caruso-Sager chuckles louder.

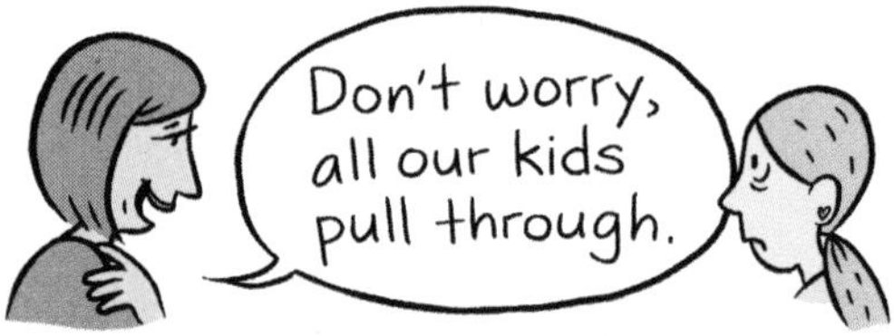
Don't worry, all our kids pull through.

Easy for her to say. Besides, there's always a first.

She gives me one final little pep talk, and then we say goodbye.

Dad's waiting for me in the hall. I'm relieved he's here instead of Mom. She's been in hyper-planning mode and won't stop talking about seating charts. You'd think I was getting married.

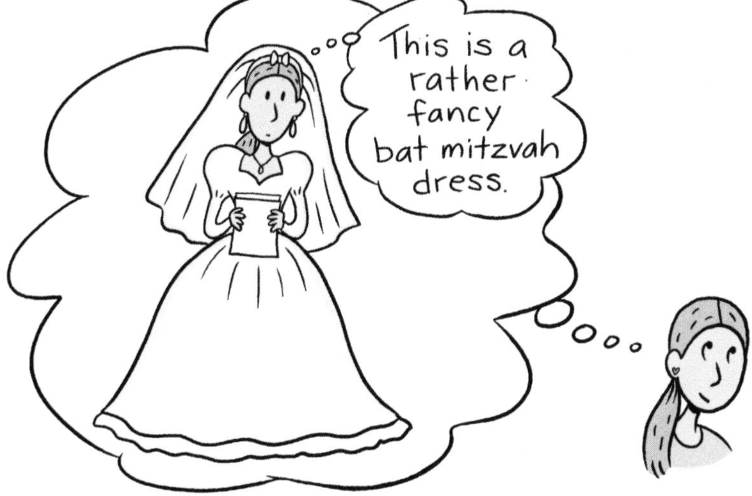
This is a rather fancy bat mitzvah dress.

We walk to his car.

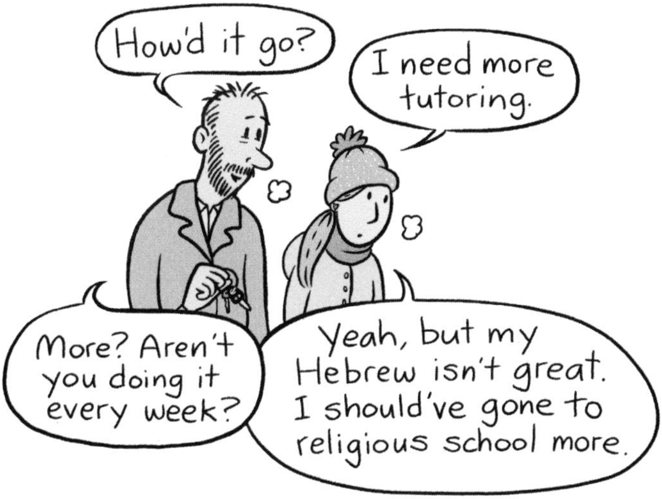
How'd it go?
I need more tutoring.
More? Aren't you doing it every week?
Yeah, but my Hebrew isn't great. I should've gone to religious school more.

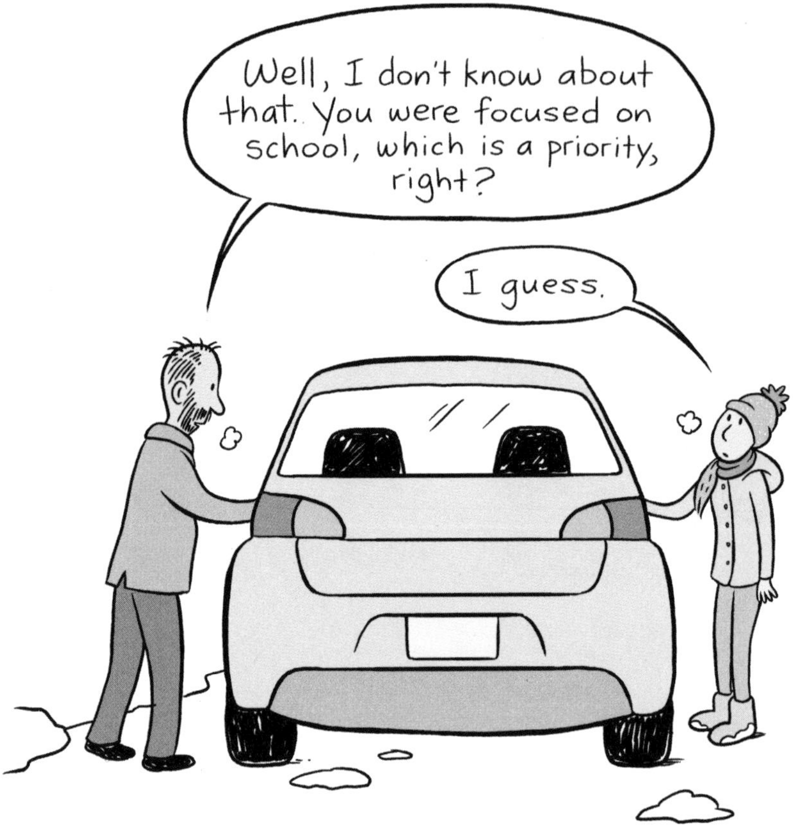
Well, I don't know about that. You were focused on school, which is a priority, right?
I guess.

He's trying to make me feel better, but at the same time, part of me wonders why he never encouraged me to come here more often.

Oh geez, now I sound like Mom.

Anyway, how could he have known I was gonna do this?

We get in the car and start driving.

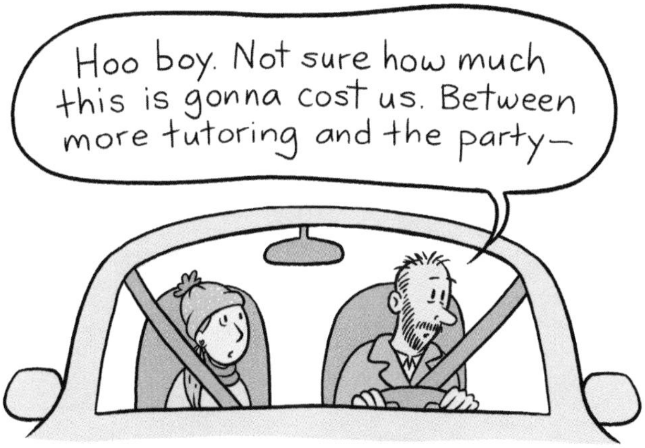
Hoo boy. Not sure how much this is gonna cost us. Between more tutoring and the party—

I must have a horrified look on my face because he stops himself.

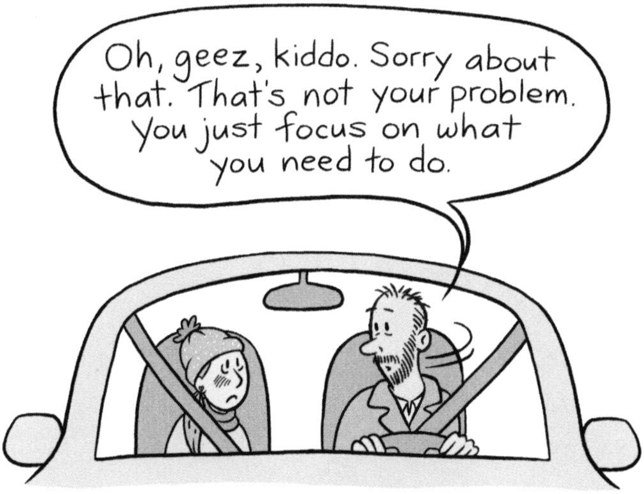
Oh, geez, kiddo. Sorry about that. That's not your problem. You just focus on what you need to do.

I squeeze my eyes shut. Both my parents are teachers, which means they don't earn the highest salaries. Proven by all the stuff they make by hand.

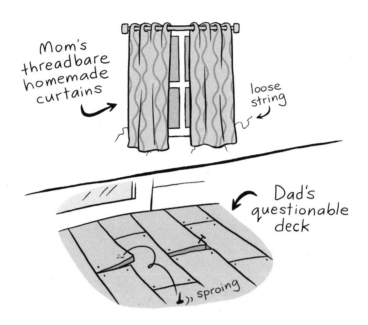

Mom's threadbare homemade curtains

loose string

Dad's questionable deck

sproing

Great. Now I add "feel guilty" to the top of my to-do list. I ask myself for the fourteen hundredth time this month:

Why am I having a bat mitzvah?

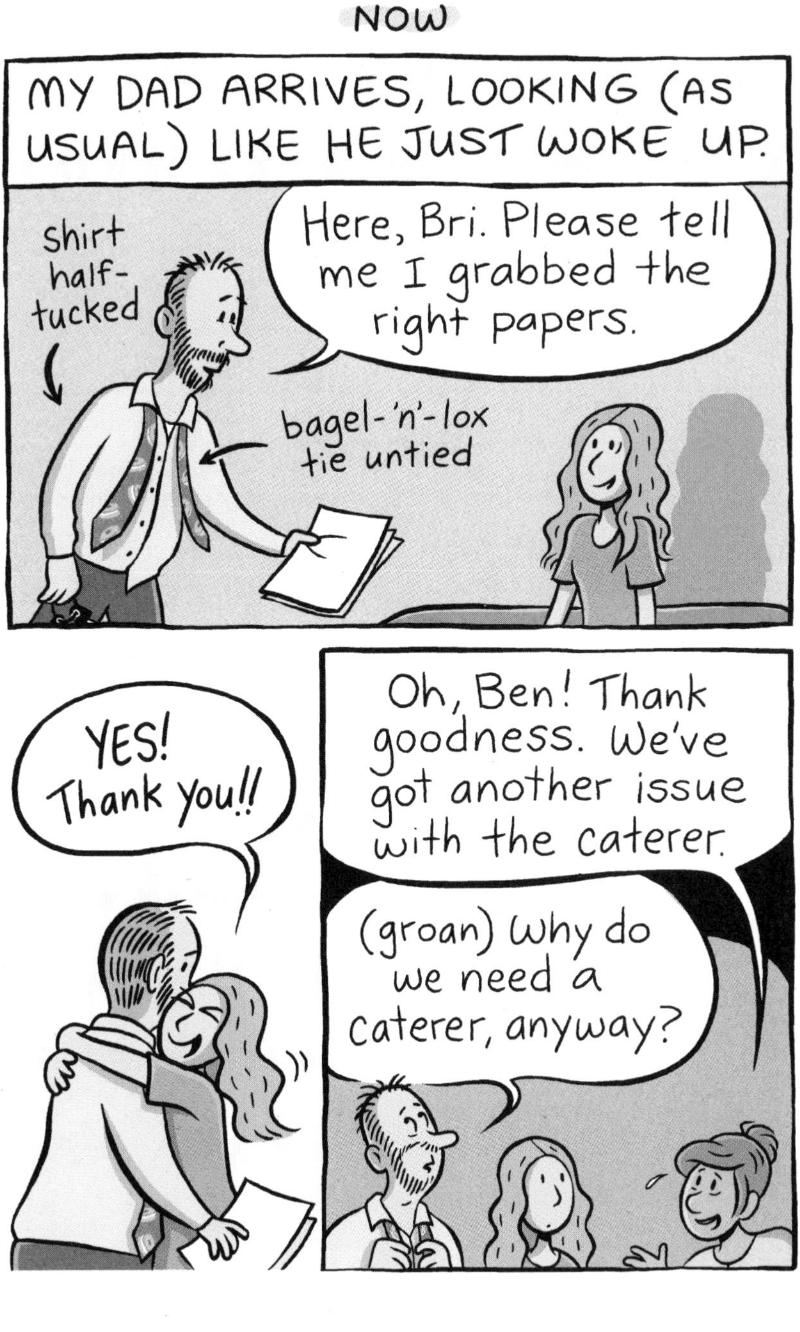
NOW
MY DAD ARRIVES, LOOKING (AS USUAL) LIKE HE JUST WOKE UP.
Here, Bri. Please tell me I grabbed the right papers.
shirt half-tucked
bagel-'n'-lox tie untied
YES! Thank you!!
Oh, Ben! Thank goodness. We've got another issue with the caterer.
(groan) Why do we need a caterer, anyway?

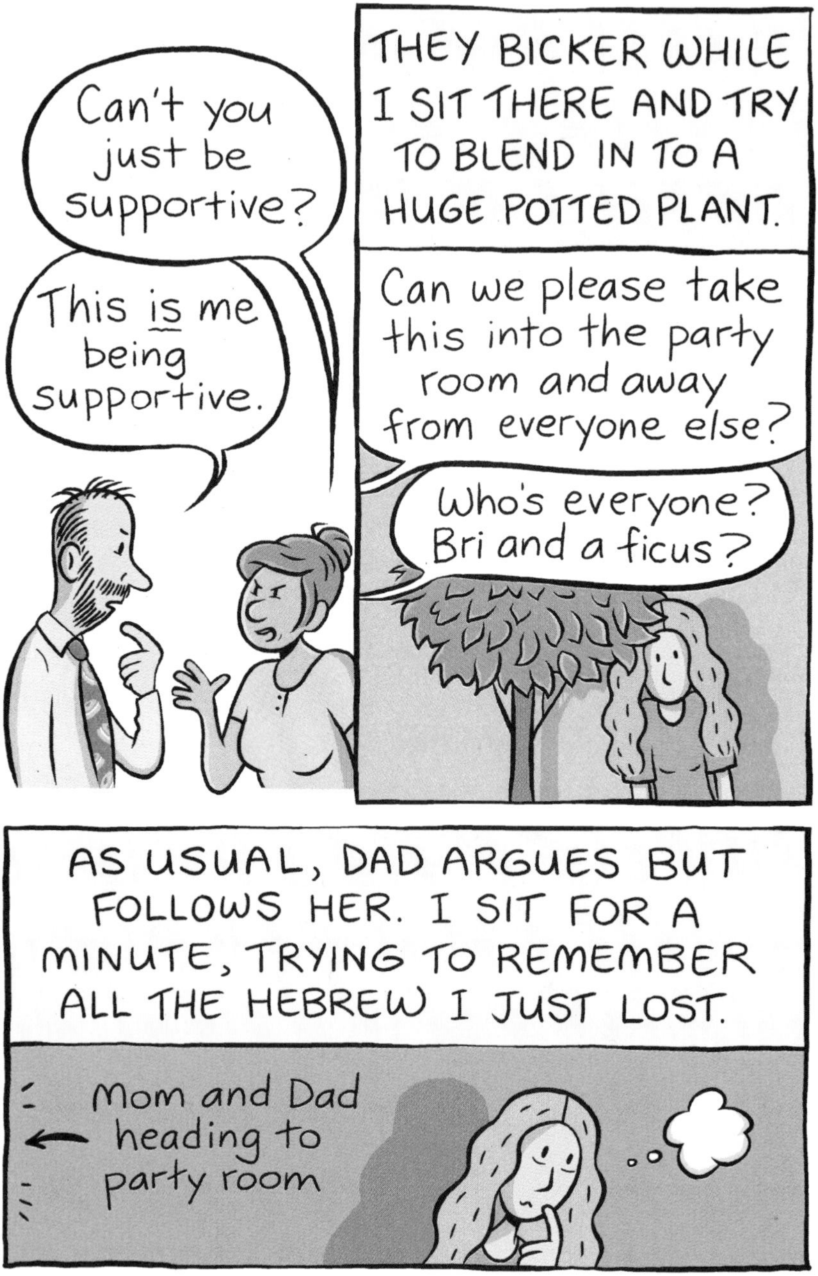
Can't you just be supportive?
This is me being supportive.
THEY BICKER WHILE I SIT THERE AND TRY TO BLEND IN TO A HUGE POTTED PLANT.
Can we please take this into the party room and away from everyone else?
Who's everyone? Bri and a ficus?
AS USUAL, DAD ARGUES BUT FOLLOWS HER. I SIT FOR A MINUTE, TRYING TO REMEMBER ALL THE HEBREW I JUST LOST.
Mom and Dad heading to party room

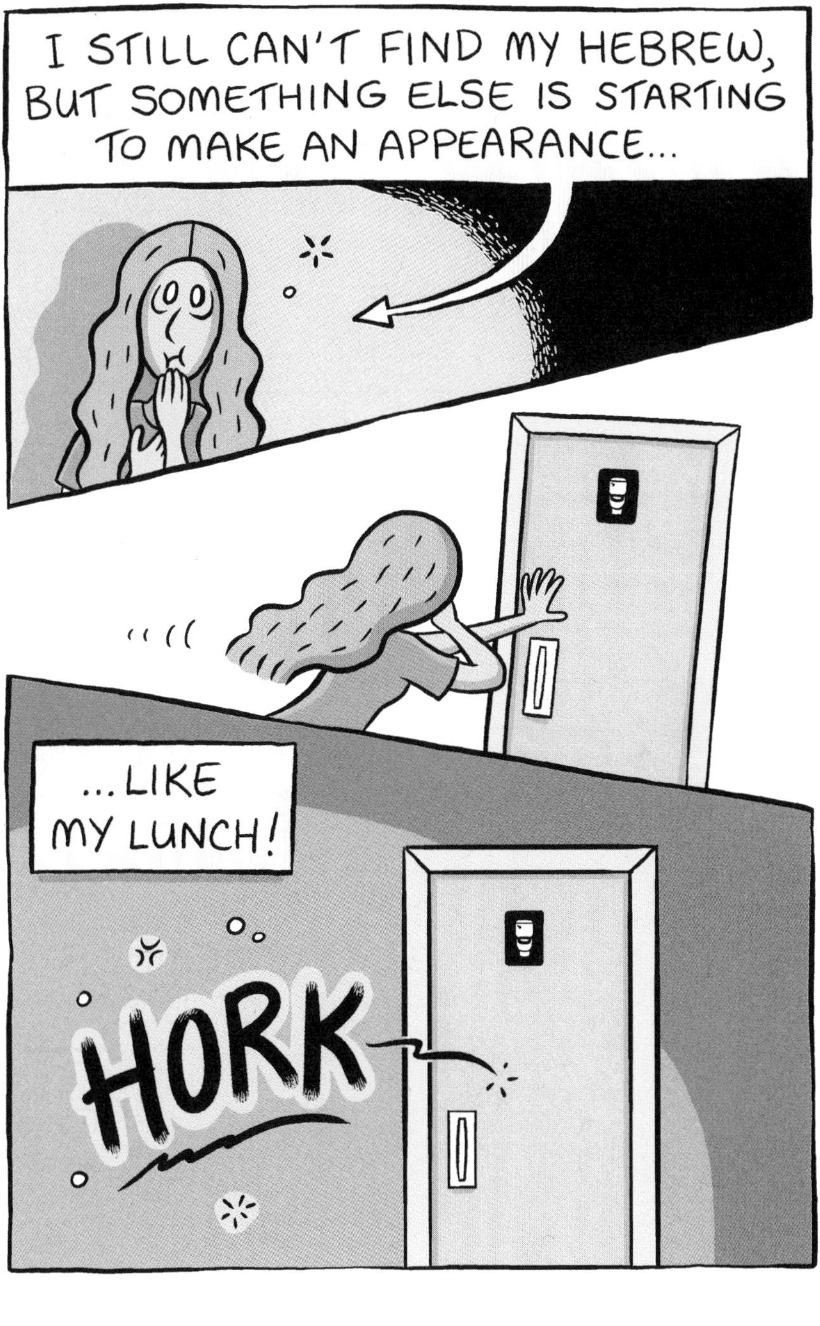
I STILL CAN'T FIND MY HEBREW, BUT SOMETHING ELSE IS STARTING TO MAKE AN APPEARANCE...
...LIKE MY LUNCH!
HORK

FOUR MONTHS AGO

Emmie's over. We're hanging in my room.

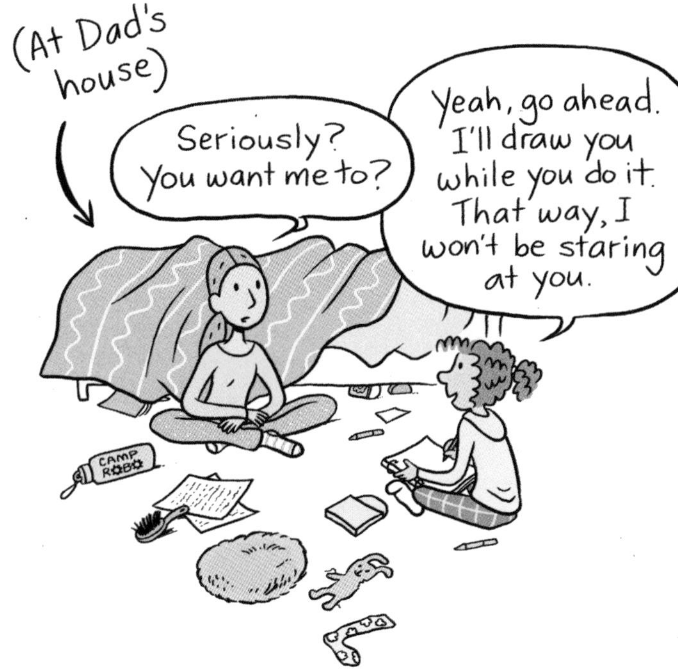
(At Dad's house)
Seriously? You want me to?
Yeah, go ahead. I'll draw you while you do it. That way, I won't be staring at you.
CAMP ROBO

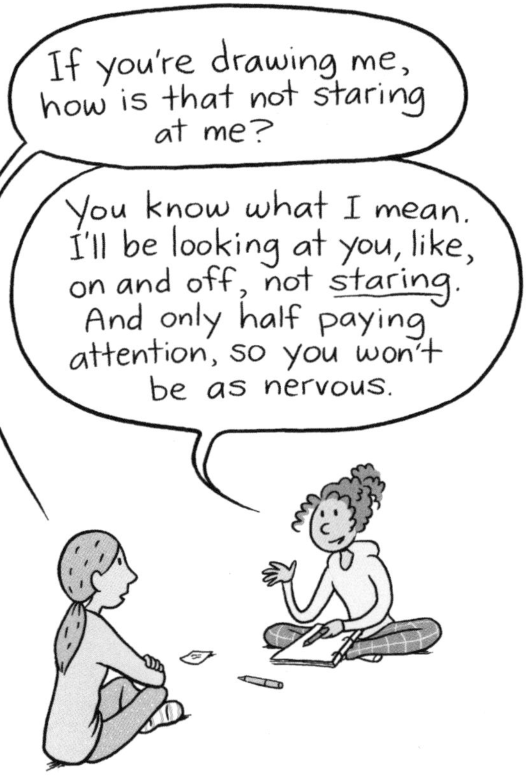
If you're drawing me, how is that not staring at me?
You know what I mean. I'll be looking at you, like, on and off, not staring. And only half paying attention, so you won't be as nervous.

I get it. I'm used to Em sketching me, anyway. It probably **would** make me less jittery.

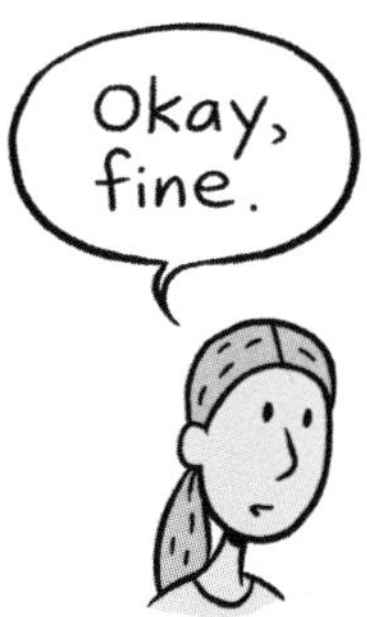
Okay, fine.

I start reading my Hebrew blessings. I stumble a lot, but I keep going. At the same time, Emmie draws me in her sketchbook. That thing is full of **mes**. I don't mind; she only does it to practice her faces, and she sure wouldn't dare draw anyone else except her family.

Although . . . I once snuck a peek at her book while she was in the bathroom and saw a few sketches from memory of Tyler. They weren't half bad. I was surprised she hadn't put little hearts in his eyes and floating around his head. That girl is a **goner**.

But I should talk. If I could draw Anthony, I totally would. I don't even have the nerve to sneak selfies with him in the background, like a lot of girls with crushes do. (Which, by the way, is **so** obvious!)

I finish the four blessings. Em looks up.

That was good.

Nah, it wasn't.

Well, I couldn't tell, except, for, like, five times. Anyway, most of your friends aren't Jewish and wouldn't care.

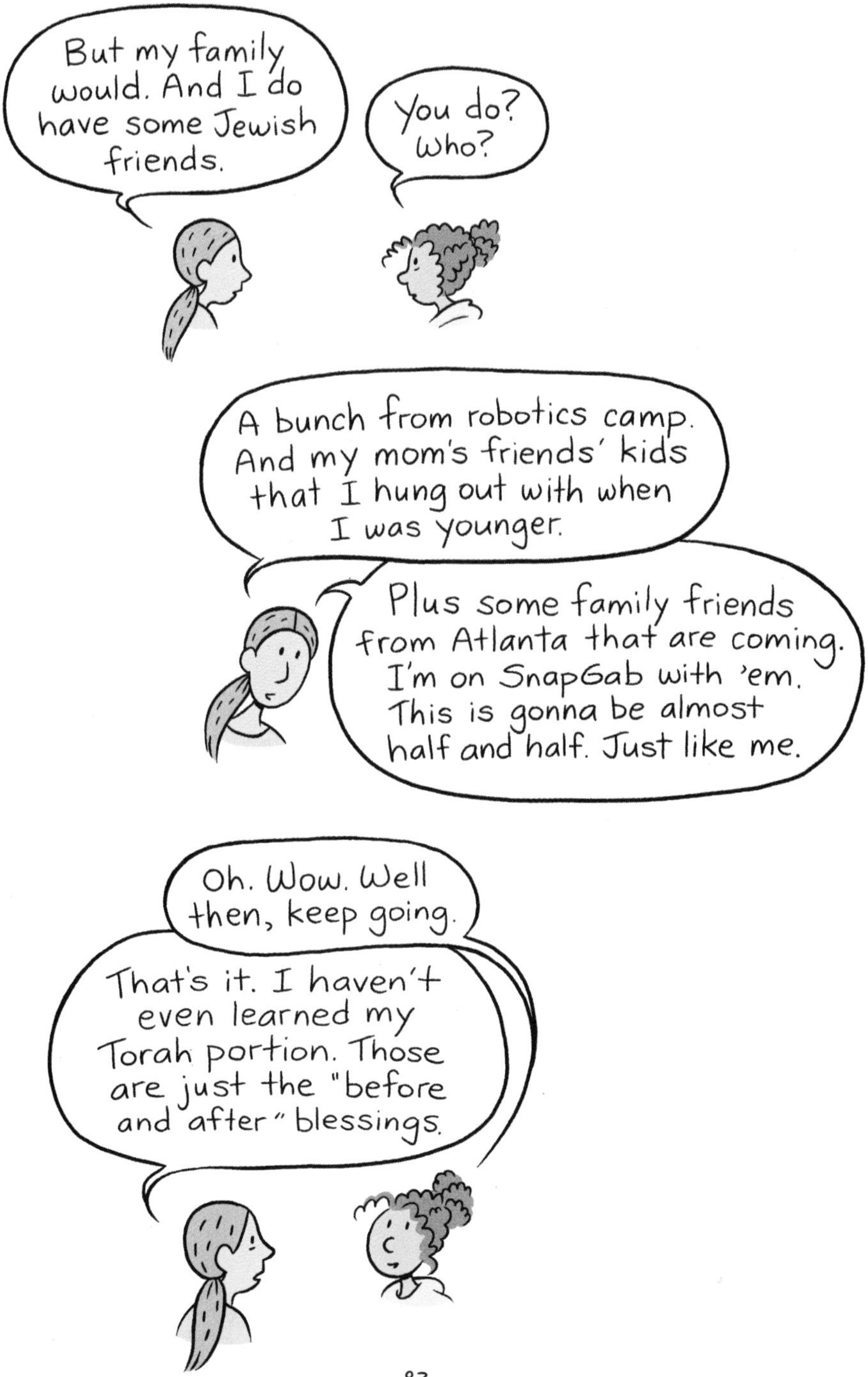
But my family would. And I do have some Jewish friends.
You do? Who?
A bunch from robotics camp. And my mom's friends' kids that I hung out with when I was younger.
Plus some family friends from Atlanta that are coming. I'm on SnapGab with 'em. This is gonna be almost half and half. Just like me.
Oh. Wow. Well then, keep going.
That's it. I haven't even learned my Torah portion. Those are just the "before and after" blessings.

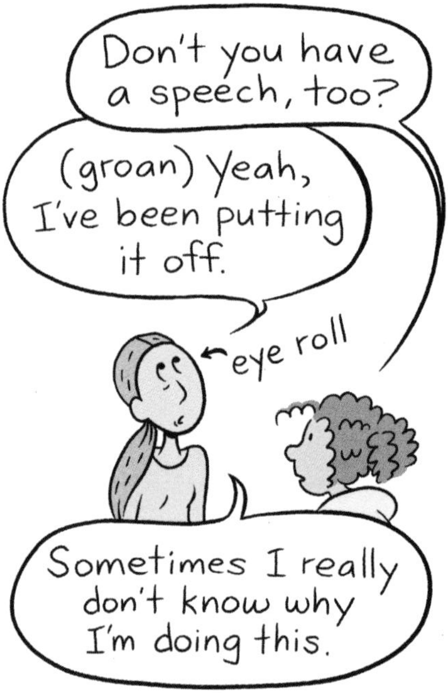
Don't you have a speech, too?
(groan) Yeah, I've been putting it off.
eye roll
Sometimes I really don't know why I'm doing this.

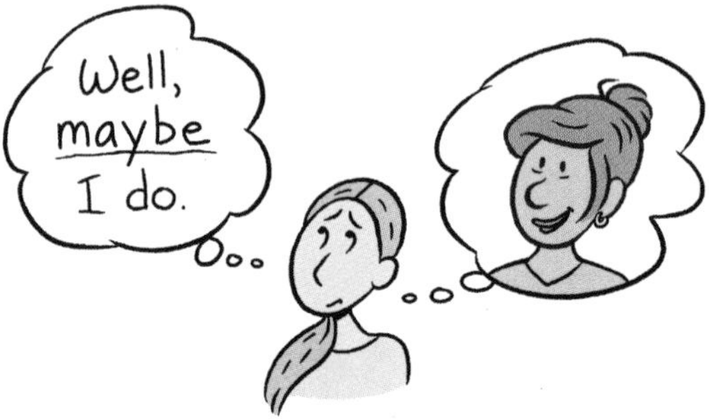
Well, maybe I do.

My dad knocks on the door.

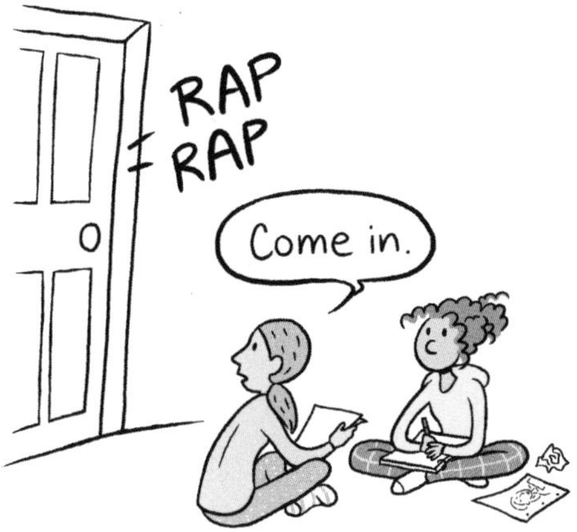
RAP
RAP
Come in.

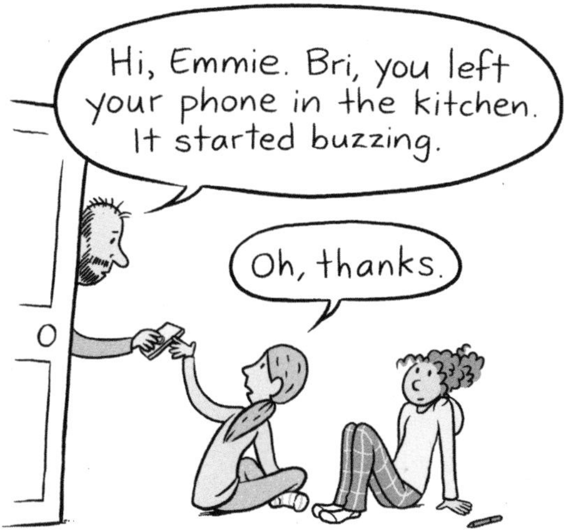
Hi, Emmie. Bri, you left your phone in the kitchen. It started buzzing.
Oh, thanks.

He raises an eyebrow at all the books and old clothes scattered like mulch across the floor but doesn't say anything, which I'm grateful for. I know I have to get rid of some of it already.

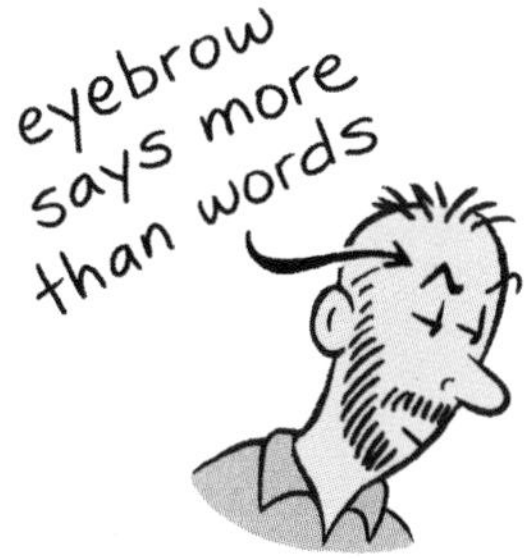
eyebrow says more than words

He raises a hand to signal goodbye and leaves.

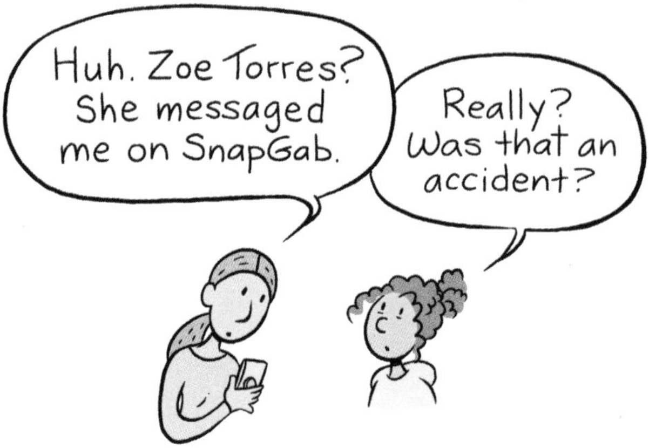
Huh. Zoe Torres? She messaged me on SnapGab.
Really? Was that an accident?

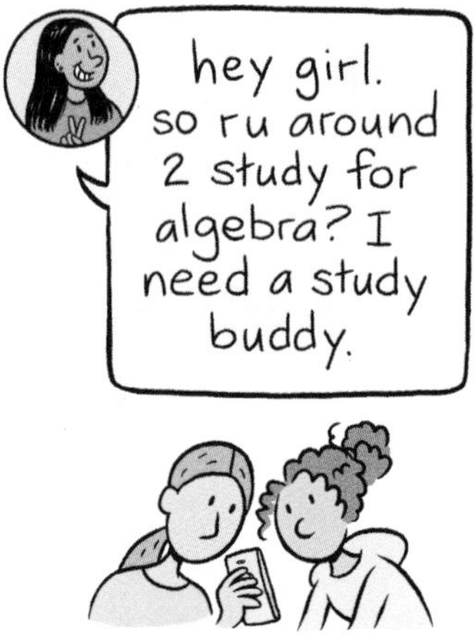
hey girl. so ru around 2 study for algebra? I need a study buddy.

That is the weirdest of weird. I mean, I know we have a test in a couple days, but this is the first time Zoe T. ever asked **me** for help. And I thought she was okay at math.

Still . . . wow. Kinda flattering.

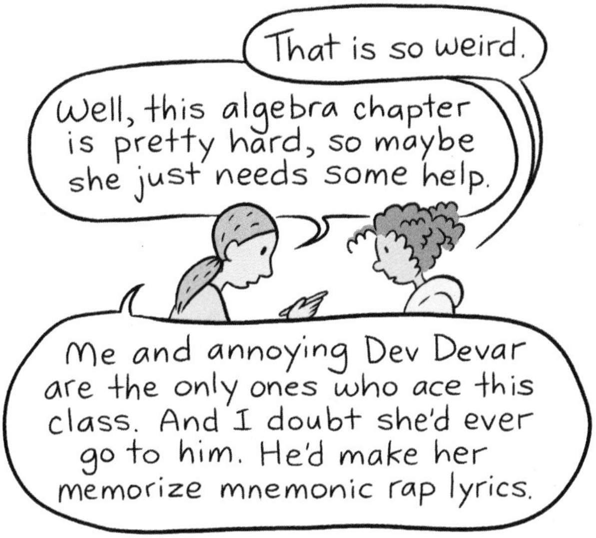
That is so weird.
Well, this algebra chapter is pretty hard, so maybe she just needs some help.
Me and annoying Dev Devar are the only ones who ace this class. And I doubt she'd ever go to him. He'd make her memorize mnemonic rap lyrics.

I text back.

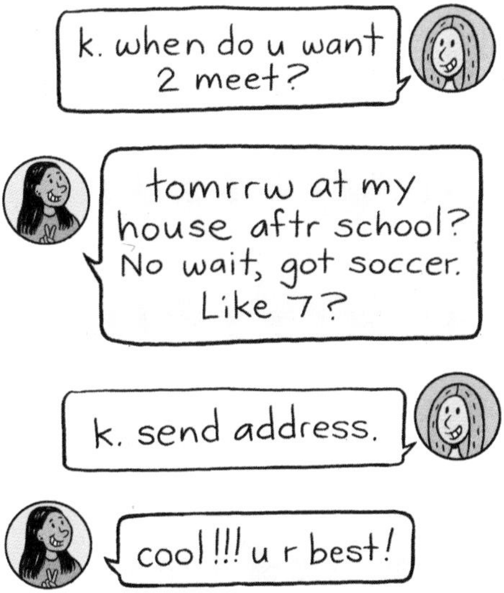
k. when do u want 2 meet?
tomrrw at my house aftr school? No wait, got soccer. Like 7?
k. send address.
cool!!! u r best!

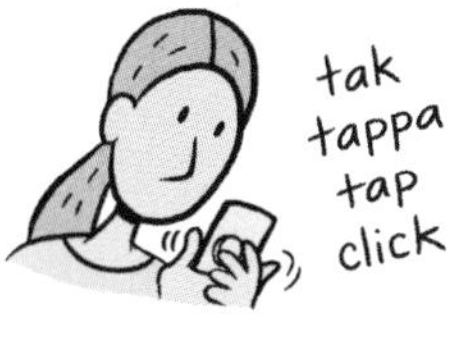
tak
tappa
tap
click

I stare at my phone for a sec, then toss it casually on my bed. It slides off into a pile of dirty clothes.

So weird. But also kind of exciting. I'm not caught up in coolness or anything, but I have to admit: studying with Zoe gives me a little thrill-chill.

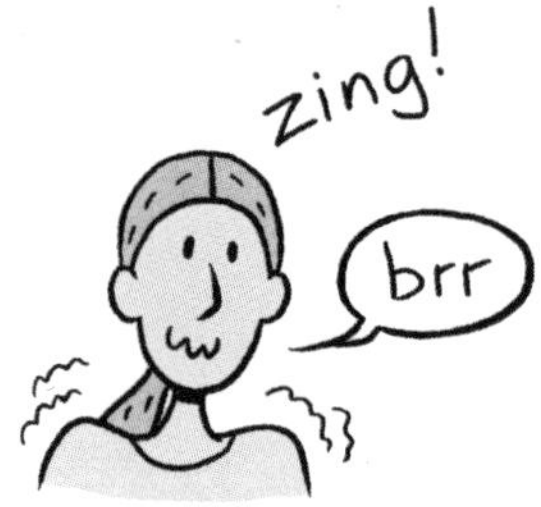
zing!
brr

I start to wonder what her house looks like.

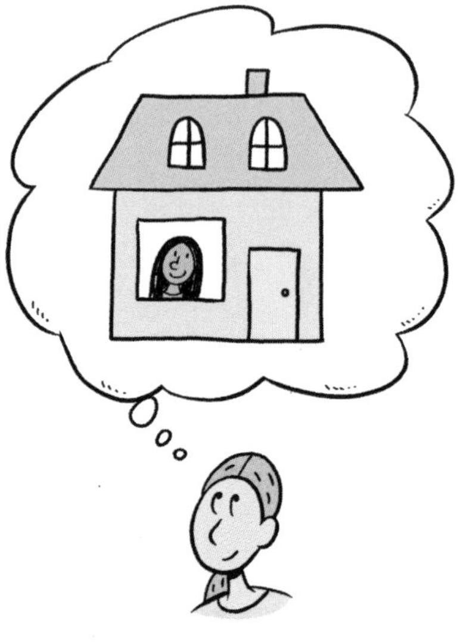

Then I start to wonder if we could become friends.

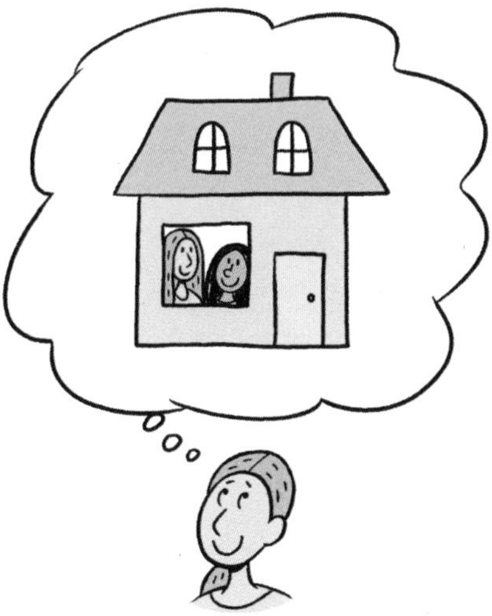

I look at Em, hunched over her sketchbook like an armadillo while she scratches away again. I think of her and Sarah in art class, bonding over landscapes.

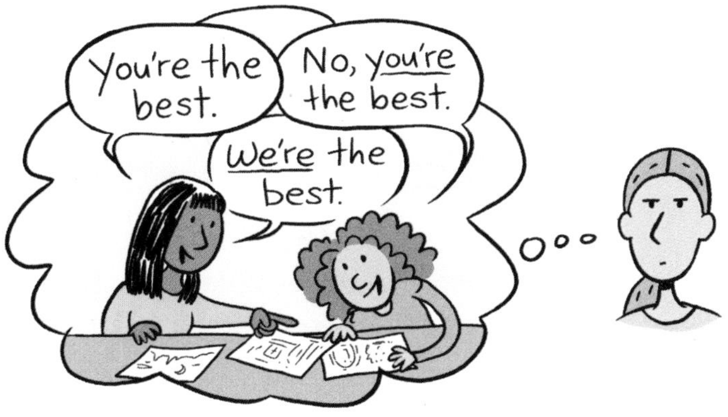
You're the best.
No, you're the best.
We're the best.

Maybe it wouldn't be the worst thing to try and branch out a little.

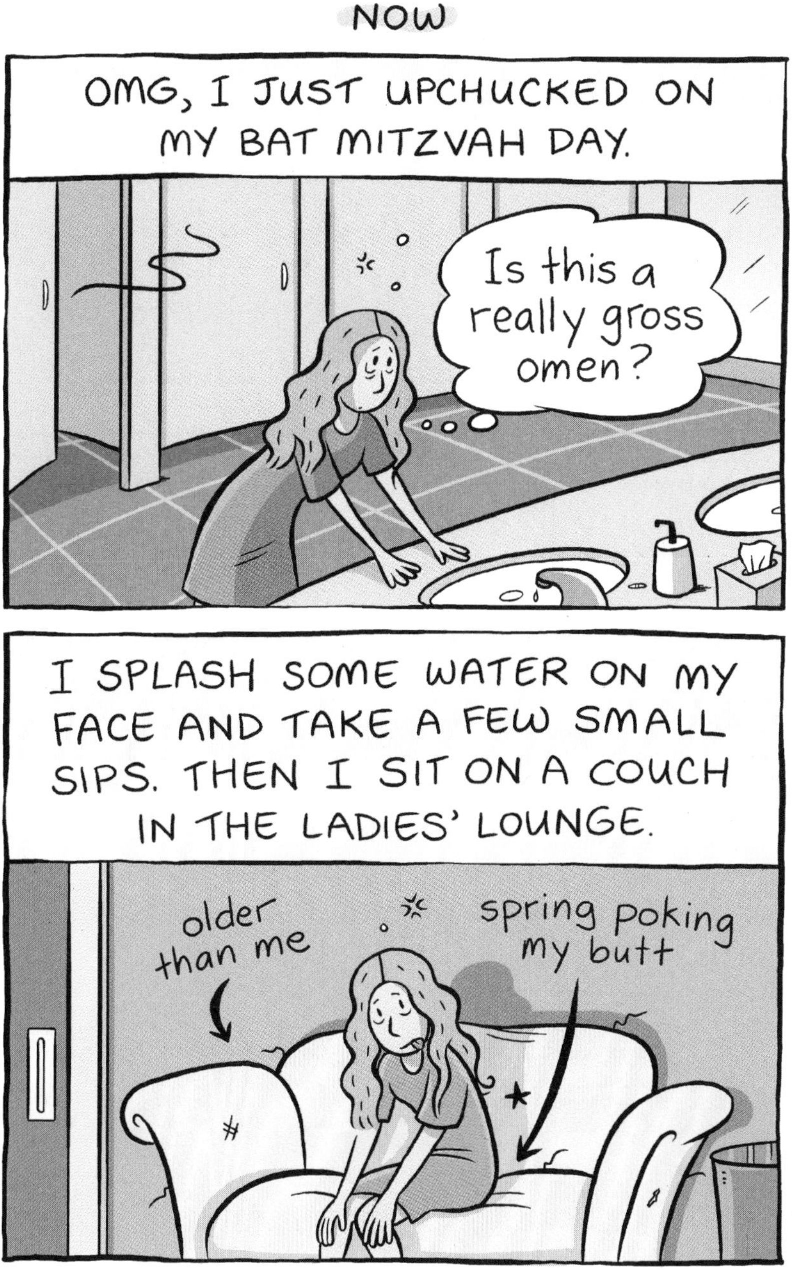
NOW
OMG, I JUST UPCHUCKED ON MY BAT MITZVAH DAY.
Is this a really gross omen?
I SPLASH SOME WATER ON MY FACE AND TAKE A FEW SMALL SIPS. THEN I SIT ON A COUCH IN THE LADIES' LOUNGE.
older than me
spring poking my butt

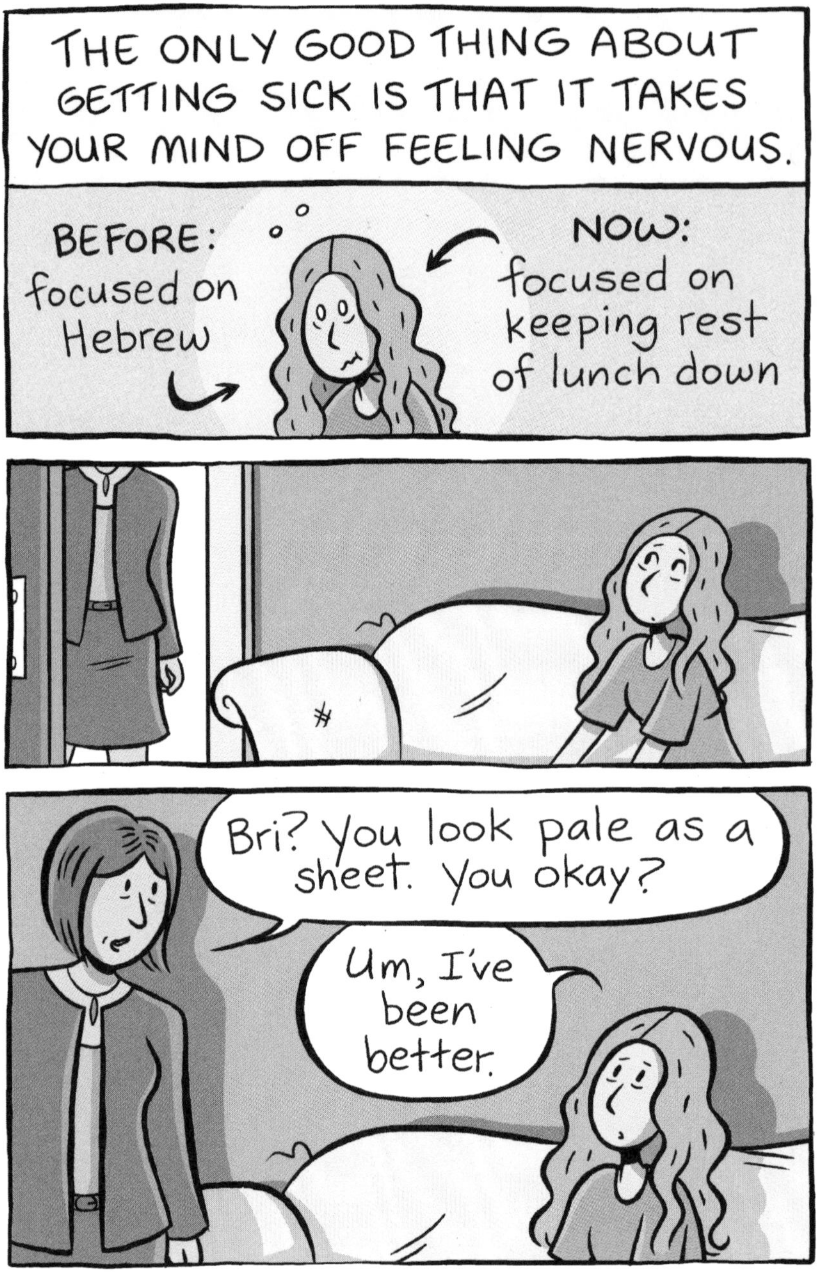
THE ONLY GOOD THING ABOUT GETTING SICK IS THAT IT TAKES YOUR MIND OFF FEELING NERVOUS.
BEFORE: focused on Hebrew
NOW: focused on keeping rest of lunch down
Bri? You look pale as a sheet. You okay?
Um, I've been better.

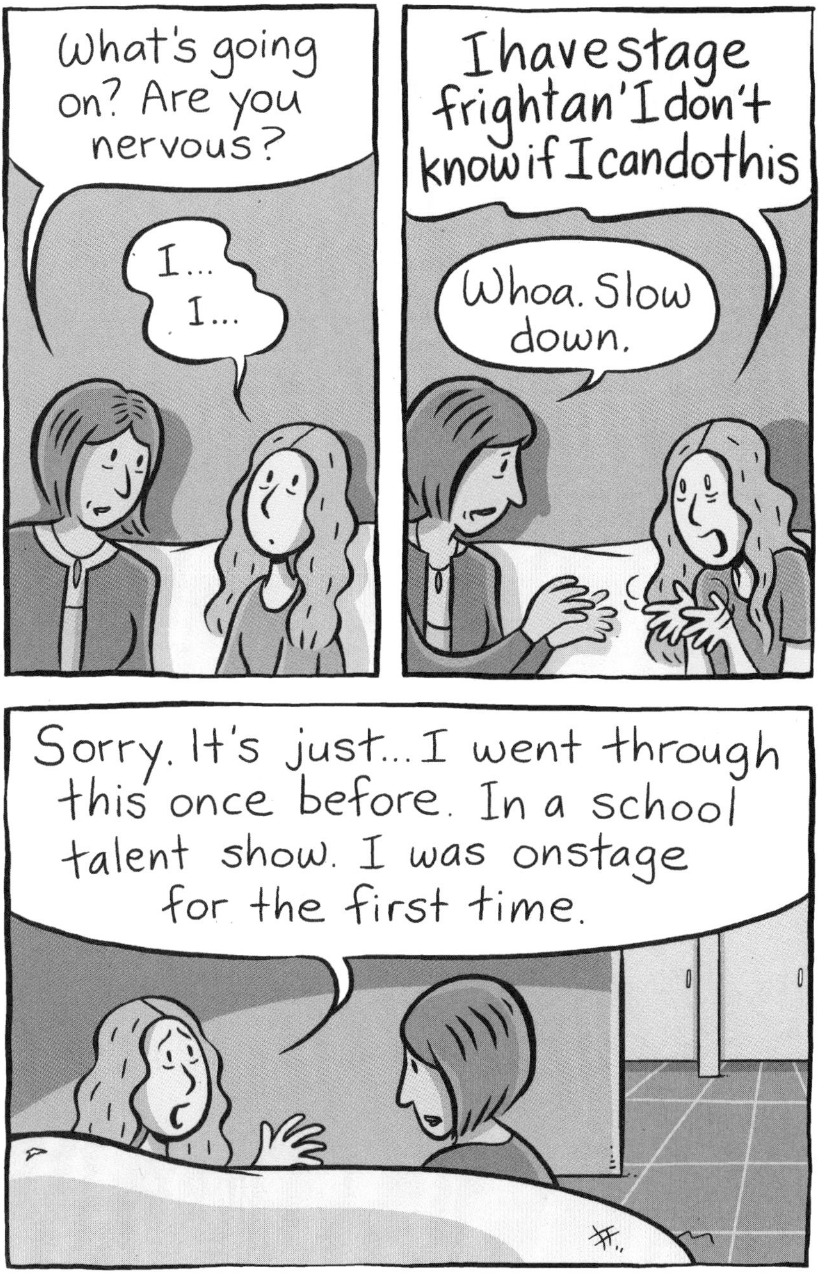
What's going on? Are you nervous?
I... I...
Ihavestage frightan'Idon't knowifIcandothis
Whoa. Slow down.
Sorry. It's just... I went through this once before. In a school talent show. I was onstage for the first time.

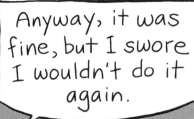

Anyway, it was fine, but I swore I wouldn't do it again.

An' now here I am...and I have to do everything in Hebrew. An' give a <u>speech</u>. And—

And I just threw up. Ick. Sorry.

First of all, don't apologize. It's natural to be nervous. Second, do you need anything? Crackers? Ginger Ale?

shaking head

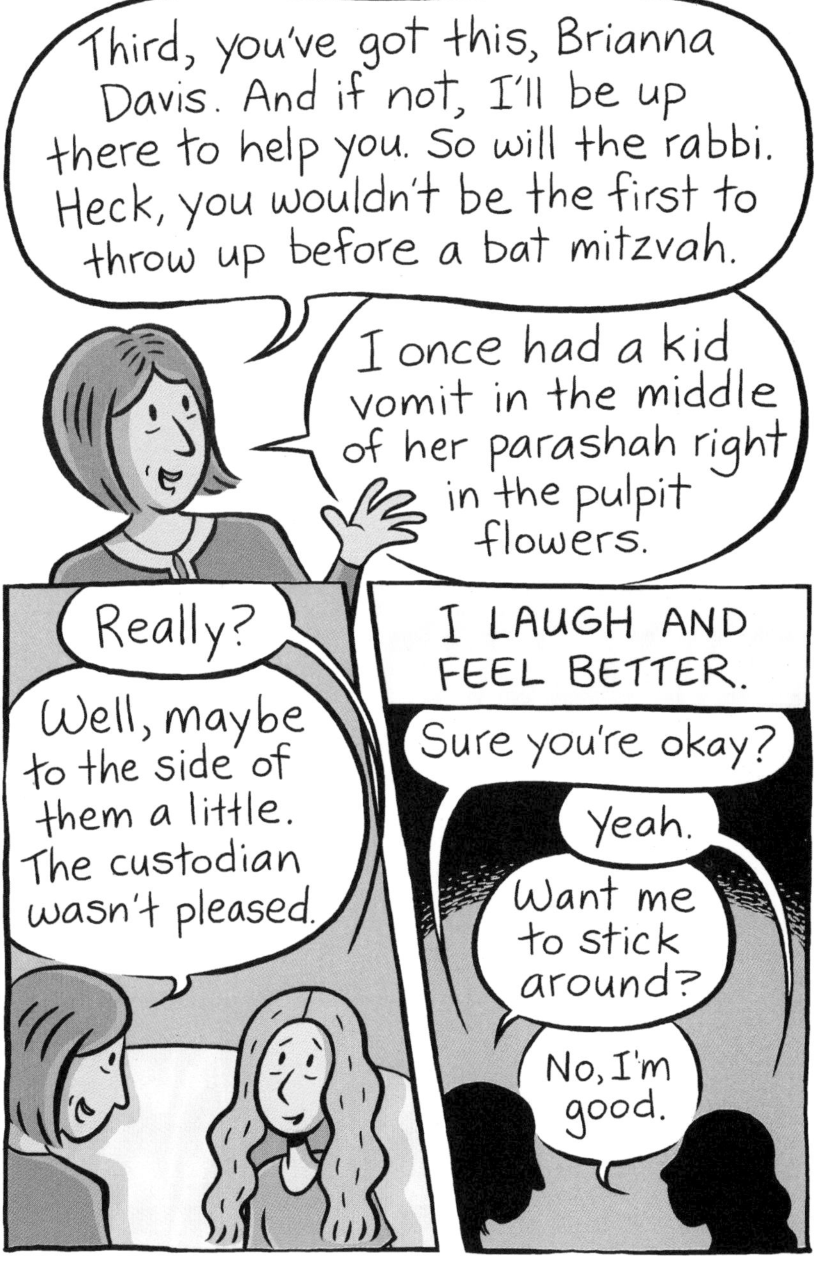
Third, you've got this, Brianna Davis. And if not, I'll be up there to help you. So will the rabbi. Heck, you wouldn't be the first to throw up before a bat mitzvah.
I once had a kid vomit in the middle of her parashah right in the pulpit flowers.
Really?
Well, maybe to the side of them a little. The custodian wasn't pleased.
I LAUGH AND FEEL BETTER.
Sure you're okay?
Yeah.
Want me to stick around?
No, I'm good.

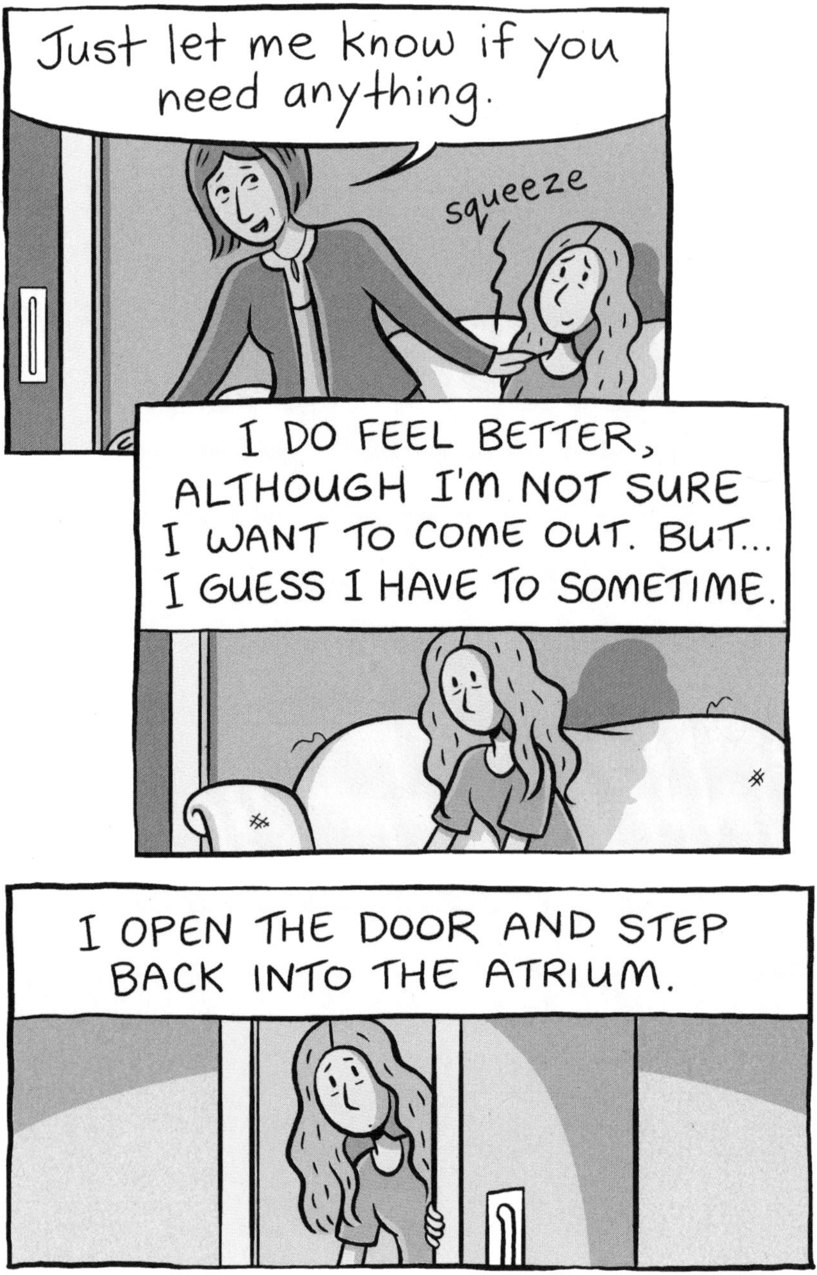
Just let me know if you need anything.
squeeze
I DO FEEL BETTER, ALTHOUGH I'M NOT SURE I WANT TO COME OUT. BUT... I GUESS I HAVE TO SOMETIME.
I OPEN THE DOOR AND STEP BACK INTO THE ATRIUM.

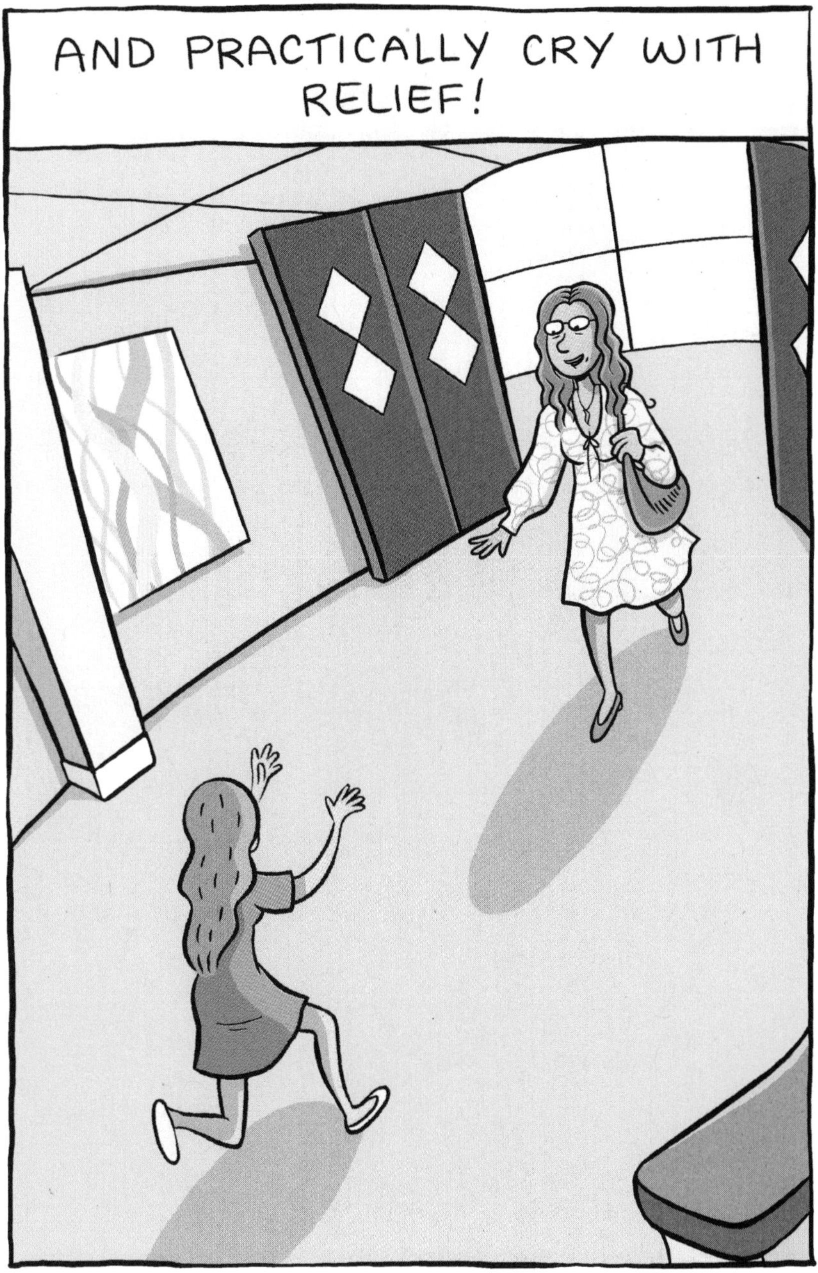
AND PRACTICALLY CRY WITH RELIEF!

THREE MONTHS AGO

I've stopped talking about the bat mitzvah at school. Trying to stop thinking about it, too. It's been getting in the way of everything. Hebrew tutoring and practice take up so much time. I need to . . . What's that word? Compartmentalize.

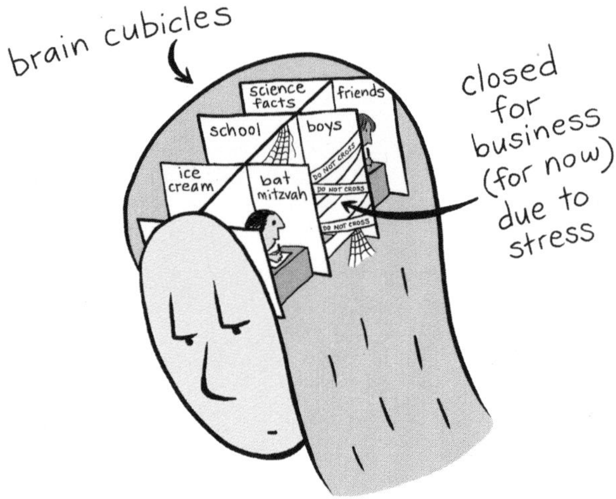
brain cubicles
science facts
friends
school
boys
ice cream
bat mitzvah
DO NOT CROSS
DO NOT CROSS
DO NOT CROSS
closed for business (for now) due to stress

I did take a break from it for a day when Mom roped me into doing the talent show.

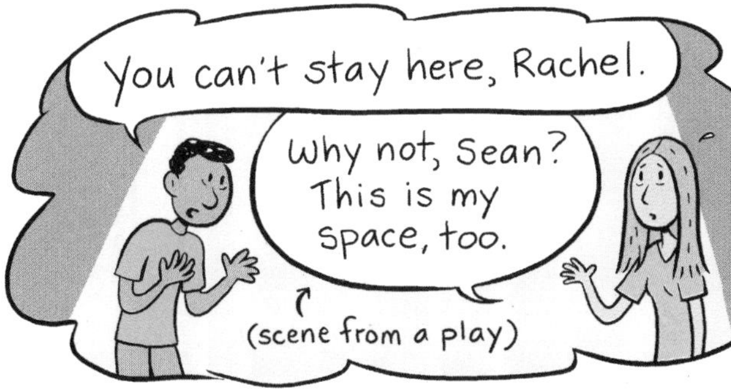
You can't stay here, Rachel.
Why not, Sean? This is my space, too.
(scene from a play)

I won't even go into **that**. Let's just say it did not help my bat mitzvah jitters. Okay, it was kinda fun, and I actually got a (surprising) friend out of it.

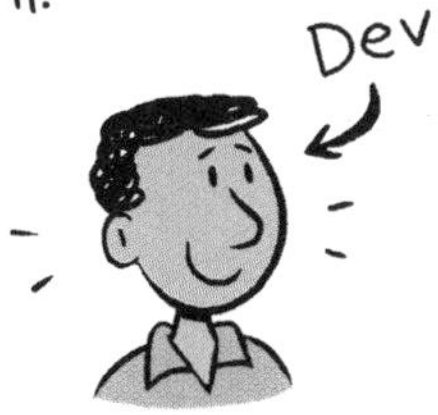
Dev

But it also reminded me that I **hate** being the center of attention. Besides, it's one thing to memorize a bunch of lines and act 'em out. . . . It's another to—

Oh, forget it. **Compartmentalizing.**

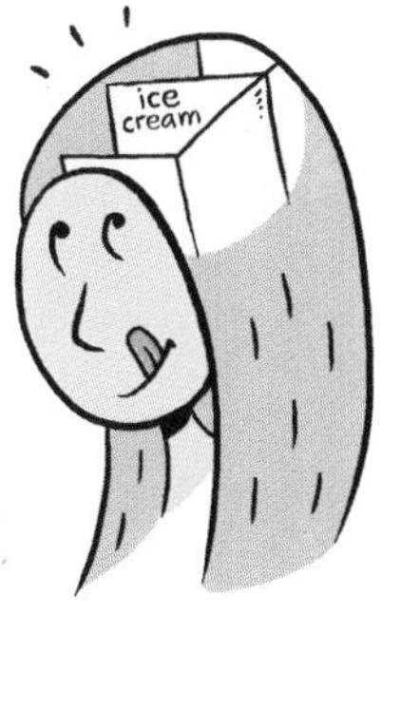
ice cream

It's the end of the day, and I'm grabbing everything from my locker.

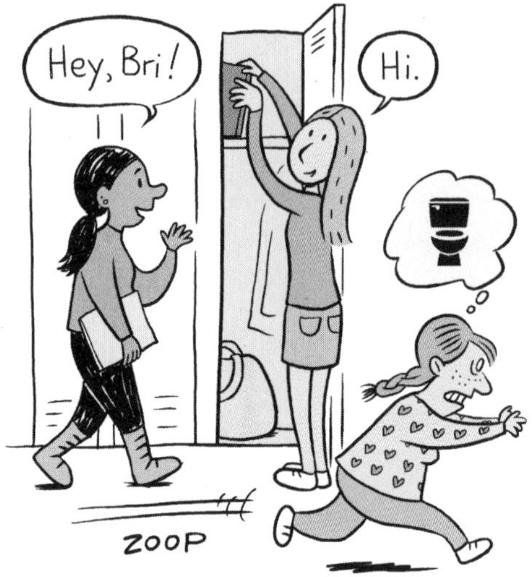

Hey, Bri!
Hi.
ZOOP

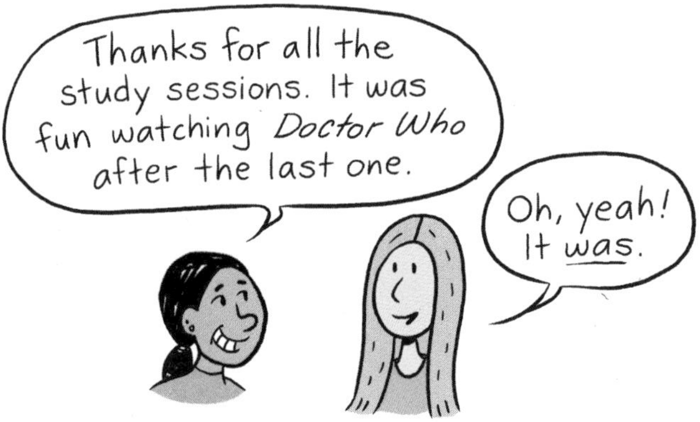

Thanks for all the study sessions. It was fun watching *Doctor Who* after the last one.
Oh, yeah! It was.

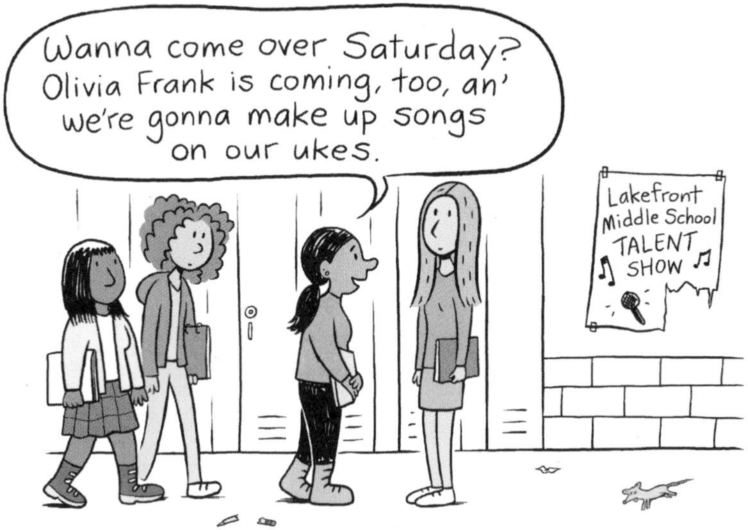
Wanna come over Saturday? Olivia Frank is coming, too, an' we're gonna make up songs on our ukes.
Lakefront Middle School TALENT SHOW

Everyone and their sister are buying ukuleles now. It's the latest nerd rage (after nerd glasses). I like to say I had one before it became trendy.

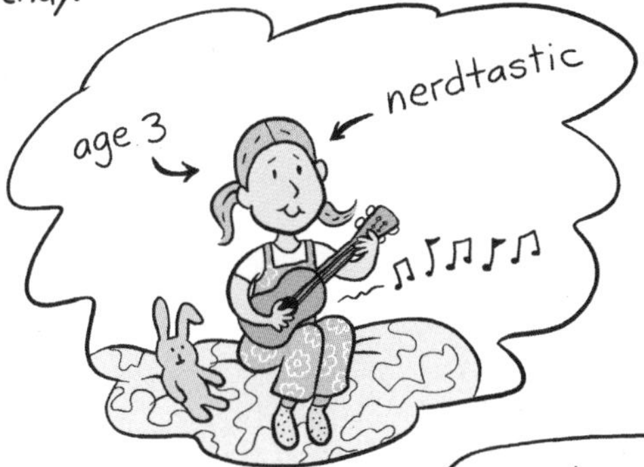
age 3
nerdtastic

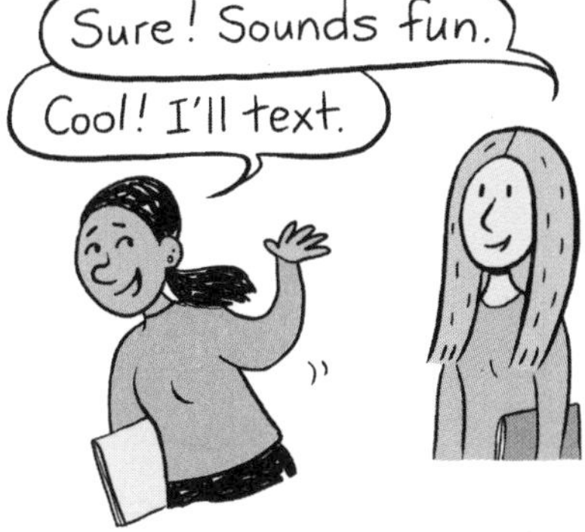
Sure! Sounds fun.
Cool! I'll text.

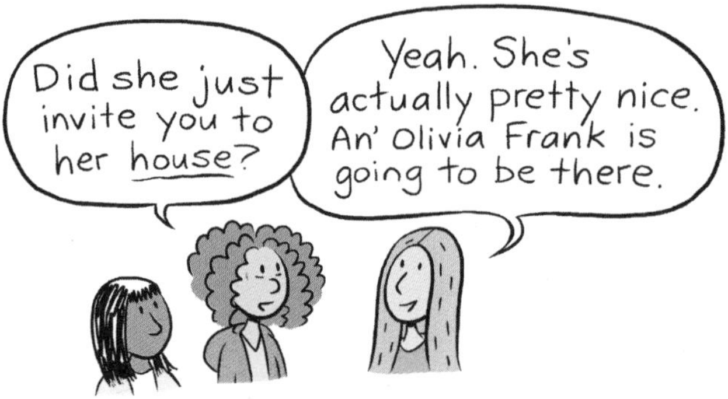
Did she just invite you to her house?
Yeah. She's actually pretty nice. An' Olivia Frank is going to be there.

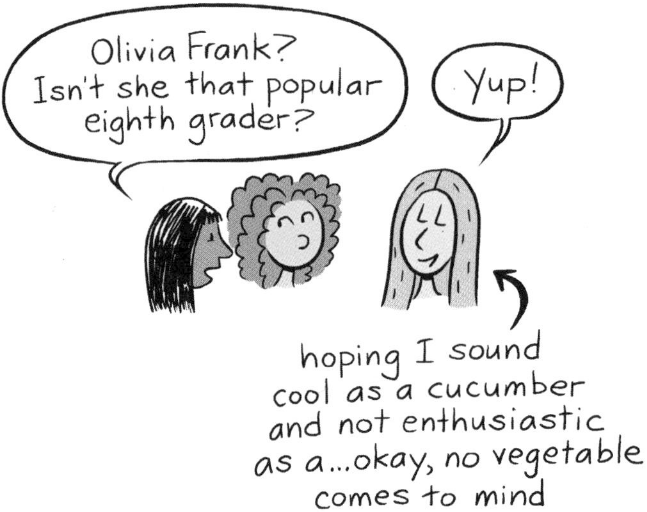
Olivia Frank? Isn't she that popular eighth grader?
Yup!
hoping I sound cool as a cucumber and not enthusiastic as a...okay, no vegetable comes to mind

The final bell rings, and we head to our buses. Sarah waves bye and gets on hers. Em and I get on ours. We sit in our usual seats.

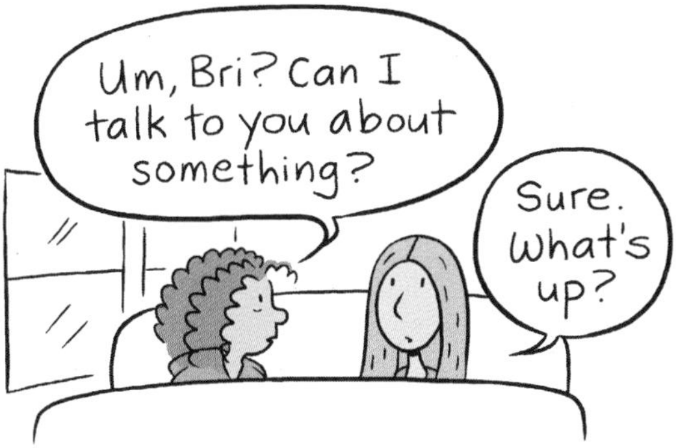
Um, Bri? Can I talk to you about something?
Sure. What's up?

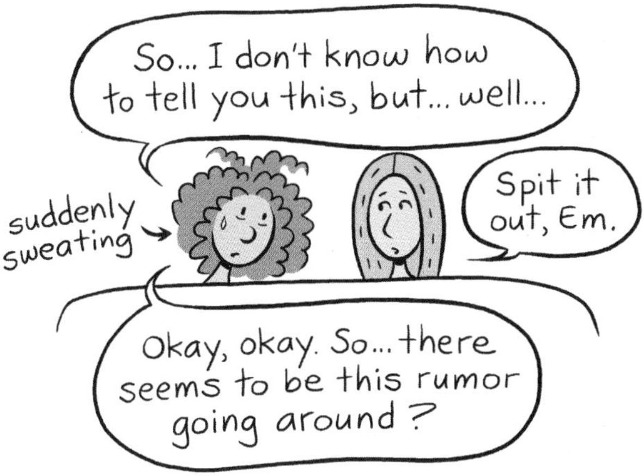
So... I don't know how to tell you this, but... well...
suddenly sweating
Spit it out, Em.
Okay, okay. So... there seems to be this rumor going around?

When Em gets nervous, everything she says sounds like a question.

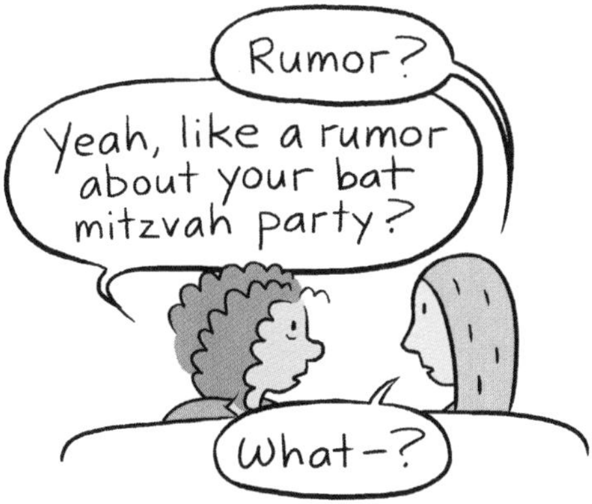
Rumor?
Yeah, like a rumor about your bat mitzvah party?
What-?

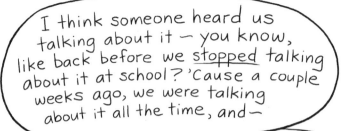

I think someone heard us talking about it — you know, like back before we _stopped_ talking about it at school? 'Cause a couple weeks ago, we were talking about it all the time, and—

Yeah, I get it. So what's the rumor?

People think it's gonna be this huge blowout.

WHAT?

You know how rumors travel through school — it's like a game of Telephone. I overheard the Gossip Girls talking.

People think it's gonna be *the* summer experience, and now some kids wanna score an invite. One kid called it "Briannapalooza."

There are rumors of Drake coming and a huge Dippin' Dots truck.

My jaw drops. Then I start laughing hysterically because it's so over-the-top.

That's pure craziness.

I know, but now everyone's googling bat mitzvah parties, and of course all they see are, like, the celebrity ones.

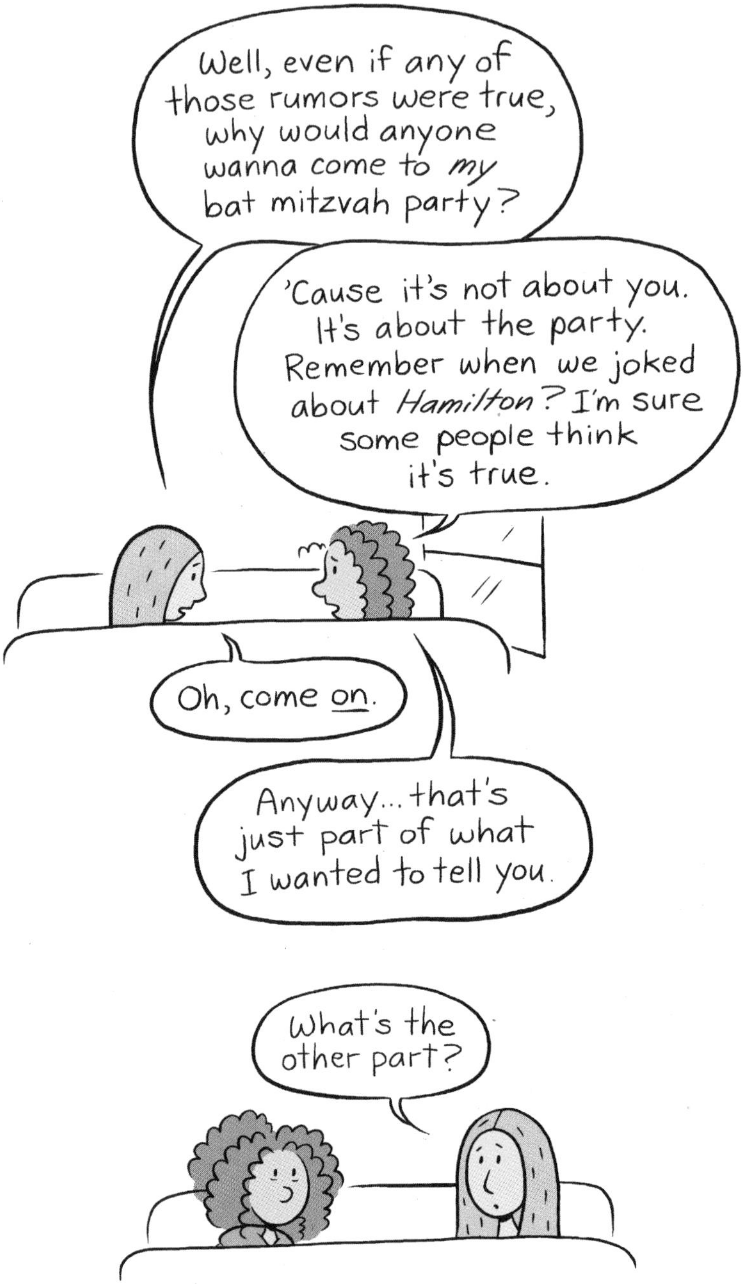
Well, even if any of those rumors were true, why would anyone wanna come to *my* bat mitzvah party?
'Cause it's not about you. It's about the party. Remember when we joked about *Hamilton*? I'm sure some people think it's true.
Oh, come on.
Anyway... that's just part of what I wanted to tell you.
What's the other part?

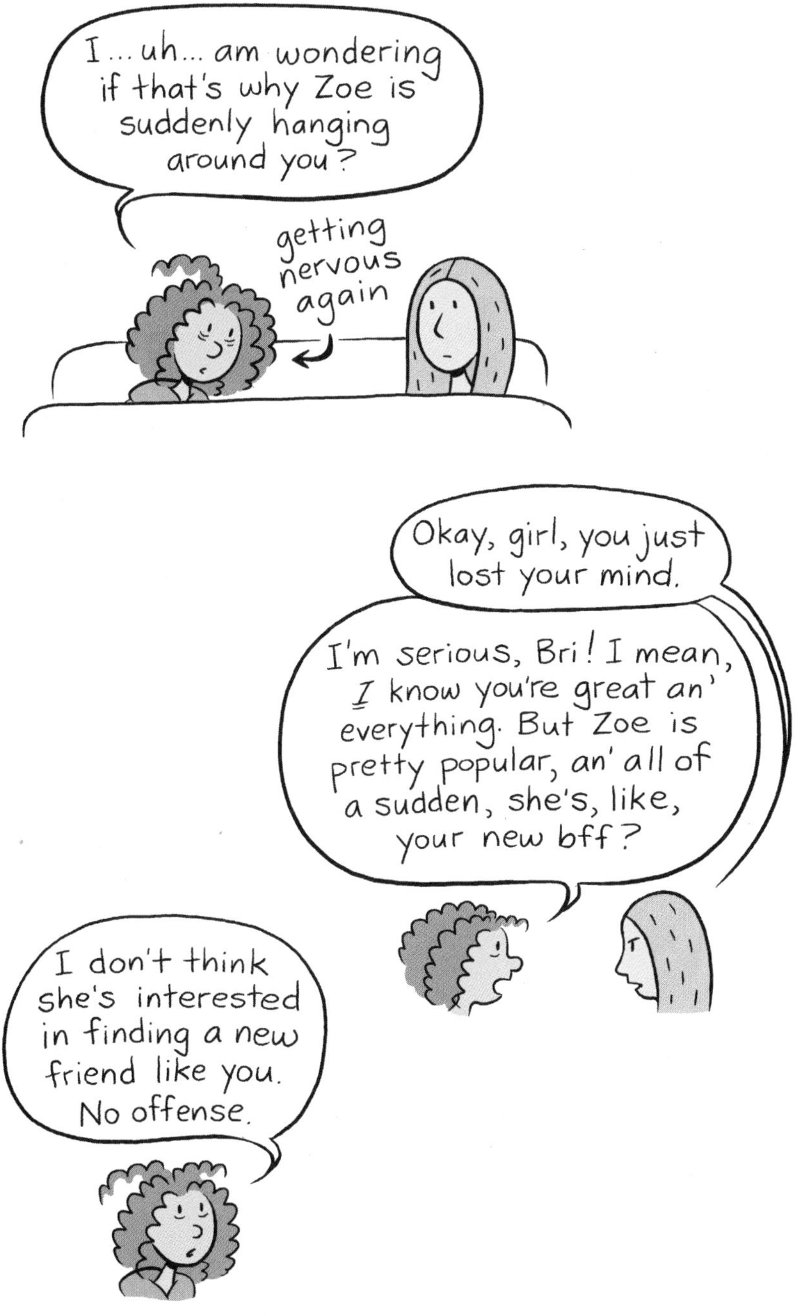
I... uh... am wondering if that's why Zoe is suddenly hanging around you?
getting nervous again
Okay, girl, you just lost your mind.
I'm serious, Bri! I mean, I know you're great an' everything. But Zoe is pretty popular, an' all of a sudden, she's, like, your new bff?
I don't think she's interested in finding a new friend like you. No offense.

No offense? You just said the only reason Zoe wants to hang out with me is 'cause of the bat mitzvah party.
Well, think about it. She's one of the cool kids, and you're... uh... not that you aren't cool, but...
I may not be as cool, but did you ever think she might still like me for my personality? Something you might not know much about?
slack-jawed
(icy)
I can't believe you just said that.

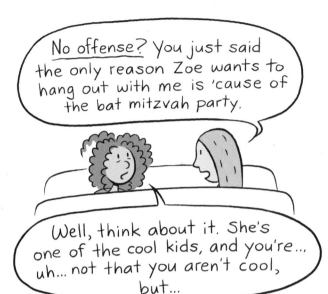

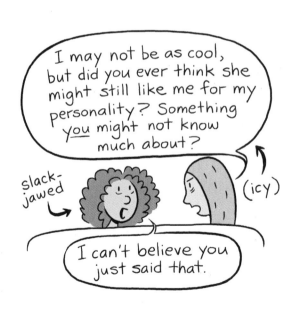

The bus stops and I get up.

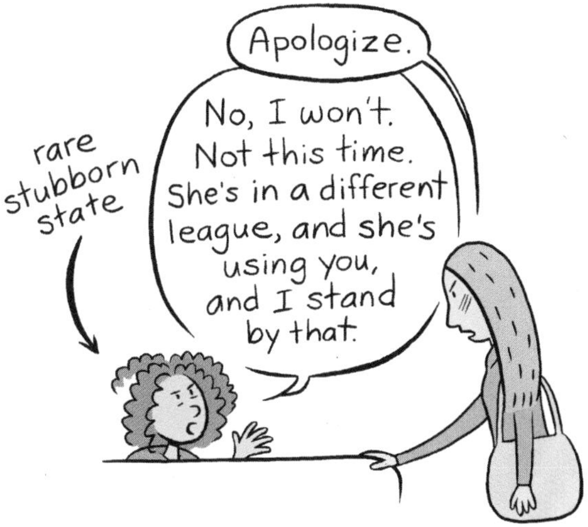
Apologize.
No, I won't. Not this time. She's in a different league, and she's using you, and I stand by that.
rare stubborn state

Even she seems surprised by her bluntness. Back in December, she stood up for herself in front of Joe Lungo. After that, she gained some confidence and two new friends, Sarah and Tyler. Ever since, Emmie's been trying to live her "truth." But that's her truth.

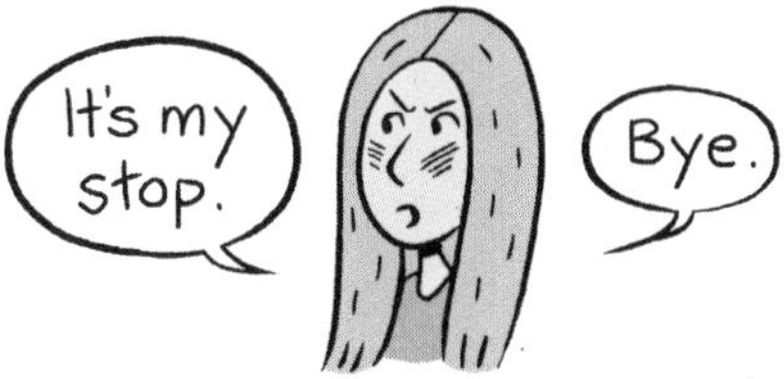
It's my stop.
Bye.

I get off and don't even turn around to look back at Em through the bus window.

can feel her gaze like a torch, though

The **nerve!** Yeah, okay, I may not be top tier. But I'm not a social pariah either! Maybe Emmie's just jealous that I'm starting to hang out with Zoe. But it's not like she hasn't branched out.

And anyway, I'm not "suddenly" friends with Zoe. We studied together a bunch of times, and it's been growing from there. We text. We watch **Doctor Who**. We're becoming friends. It's not magic; it's just natural.

Evolution of a friendship:

strangers

acquaintances

Hi   Hi

friends

uke pals!*

*regular evolution does not include ukuleles

My thoughts bounce between disbelieving those crazy party rumors and being mad at Emmie.

thoughtnado

I stomp home. I can't remember the last time I was so steamed. Even when she lost a love letter I wrote to Anthony at school in December. I mean, that was an accident. (An' I don't even think I like him anymore.) But this?

This is just . . .

. . . mean.

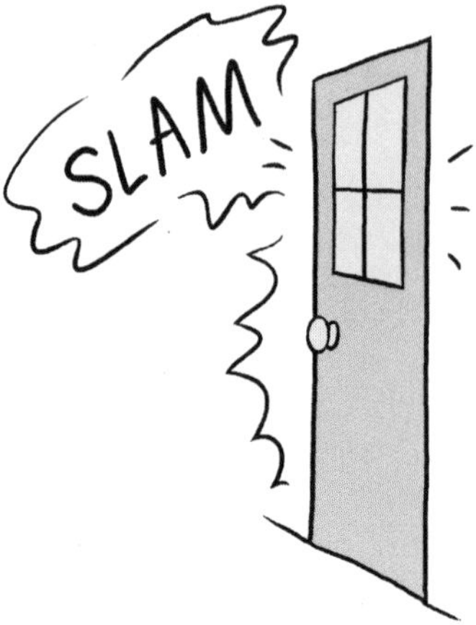
SLAM

Something I never knew Emmie had in her.

NOW

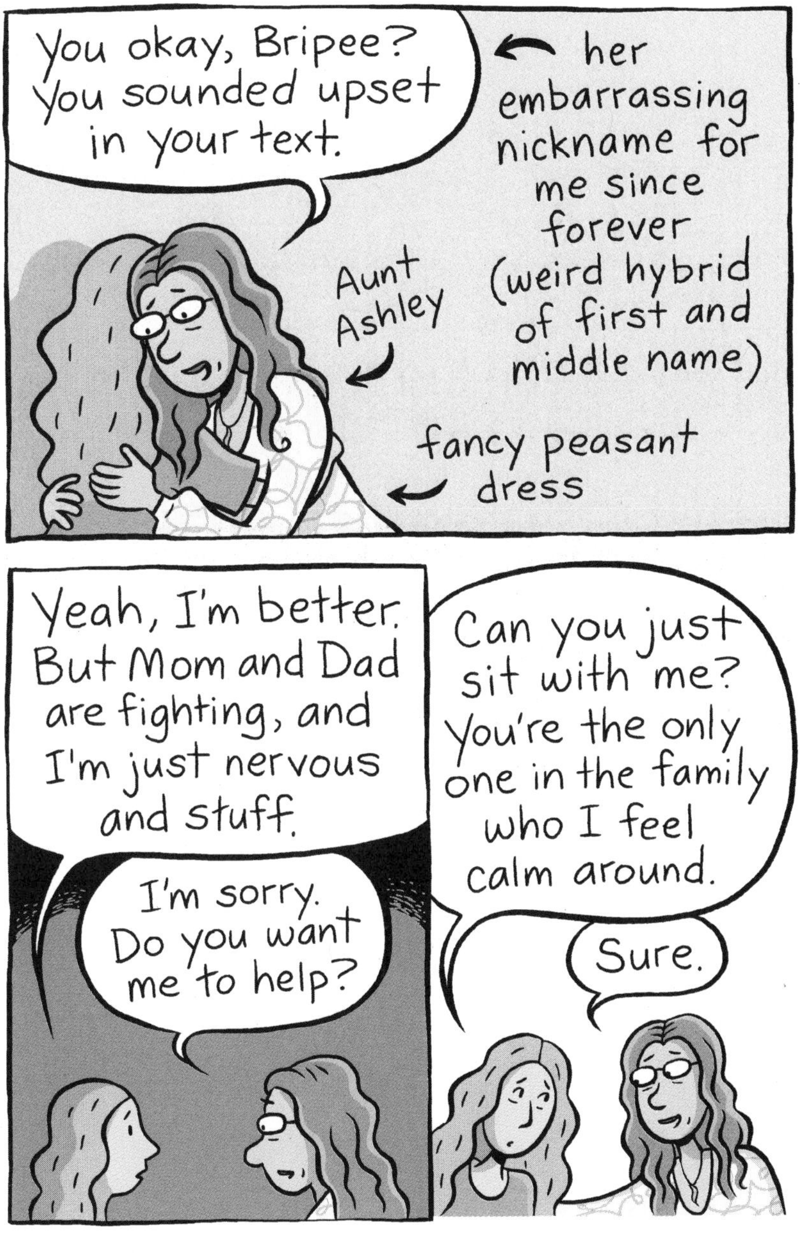
You okay, Bripee? You sounded upset in your text.
her embarrassing nickname for me since forever (weird hybrid of first and middle name)
Aunt Ashley
fancy peasant dress
Yeah, I'm better. But Mom and Dad are fighting, and I'm just nervous and stuff.
I'm sorry. Do you want me to help?
Can you just sit with me? You're the only one in the family who I feel calm around.
Sure.

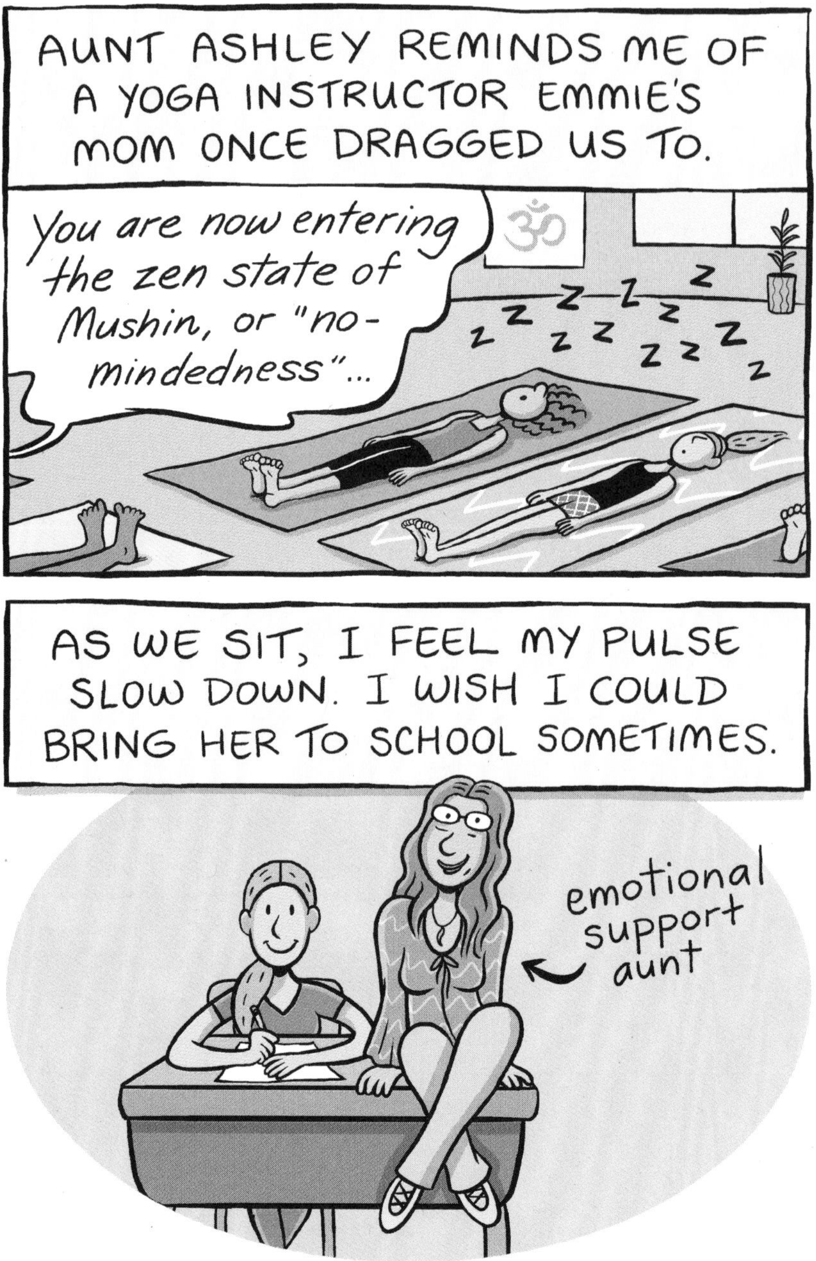
AUNT ASHLEY REMINDS ME OF A YOGA INSTRUCTOR EMMIE'S MOM ONCE DRAGGED US TO.
You are now entering the zen state of Mushin, or "no-mindedness"...
Z Z Z Z Z Z Z Z Z Z Z Z Z
AS WE SIT, I FEEL MY PULSE SLOW DOWN. I WISH I COULD BRING HER TO SCHOOL SOMETIMES.
emotional support aunt

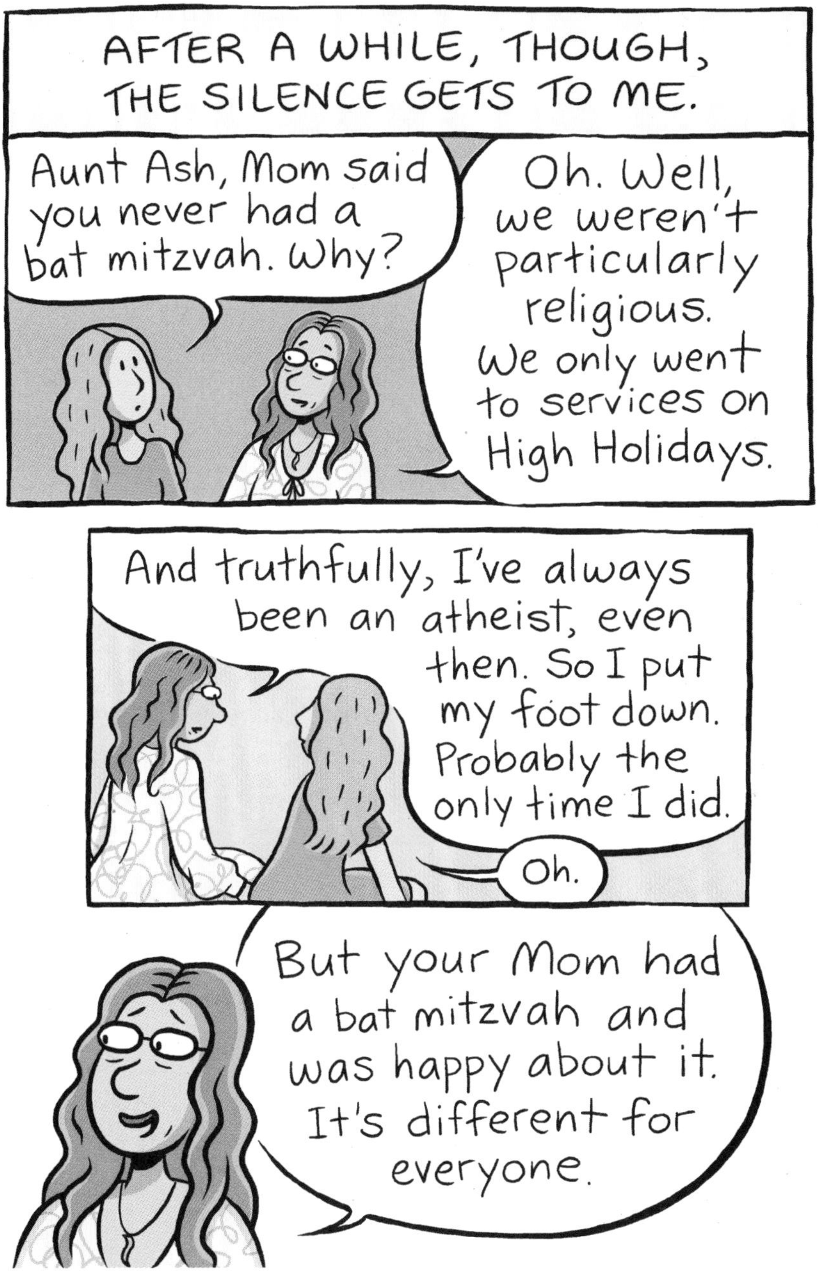
AFTER A WHILE, THOUGH, THE SILENCE GETS TO ME.
Aunt Ash, Mom said you never had a bat mitzvah. Why?
Oh. Well, we weren't particularly religious. We only went to services on High Holidays.
And truthfully, I've always been an atheist, even then. So I put my foot down. Probably the only time I did.
Oh.
But your Mom had a bat mitzvah and was happy about it. It's different for everyone.

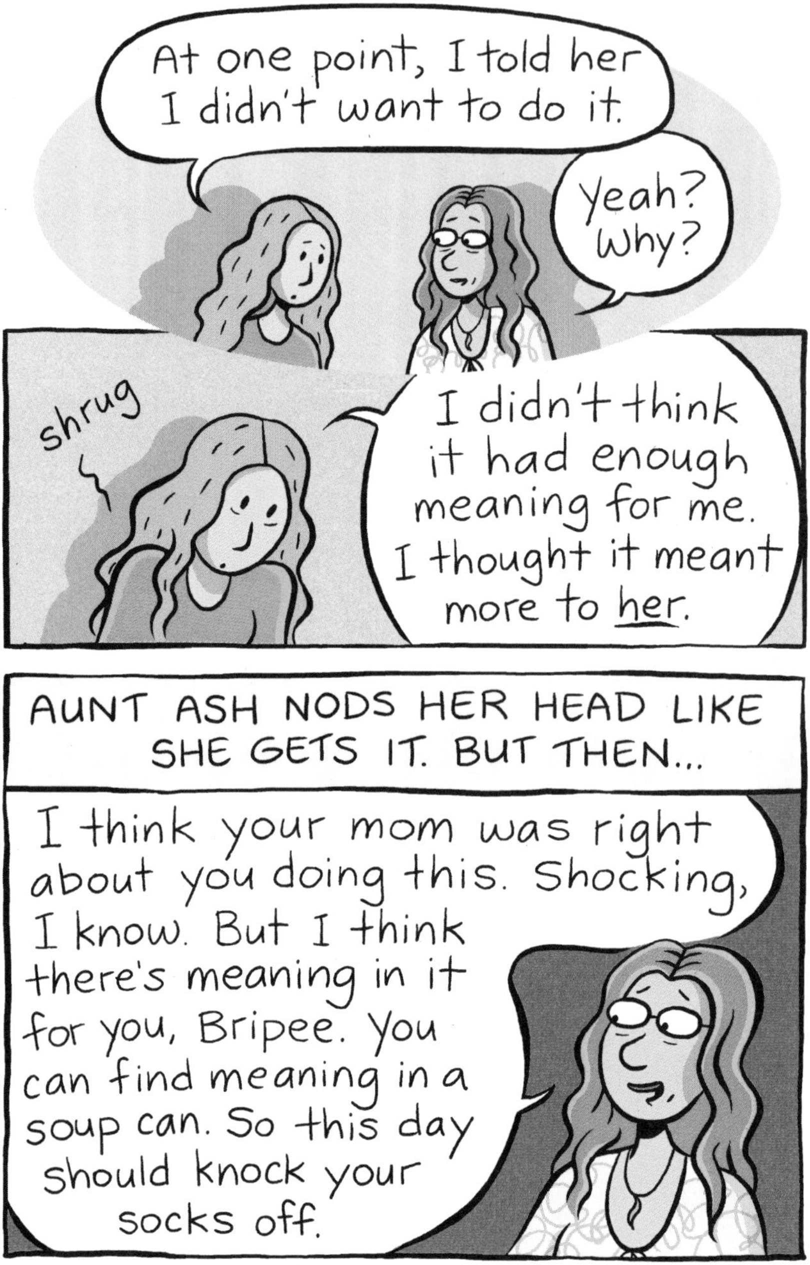
At one point, I told her I didn't want to do it.
Yeah? Why?
shrug
I didn't think it had enough meaning for me. I thought it meant more to her.
AUNT ASH NODS HER HEAD LIKE SHE GETS IT. BUT THEN...
I think your mom was right about you doing this. Shocking, I know. But I think there's meaning in it for you, Bripee. You can find meaning in a soup can. So this day should knock your socks off.

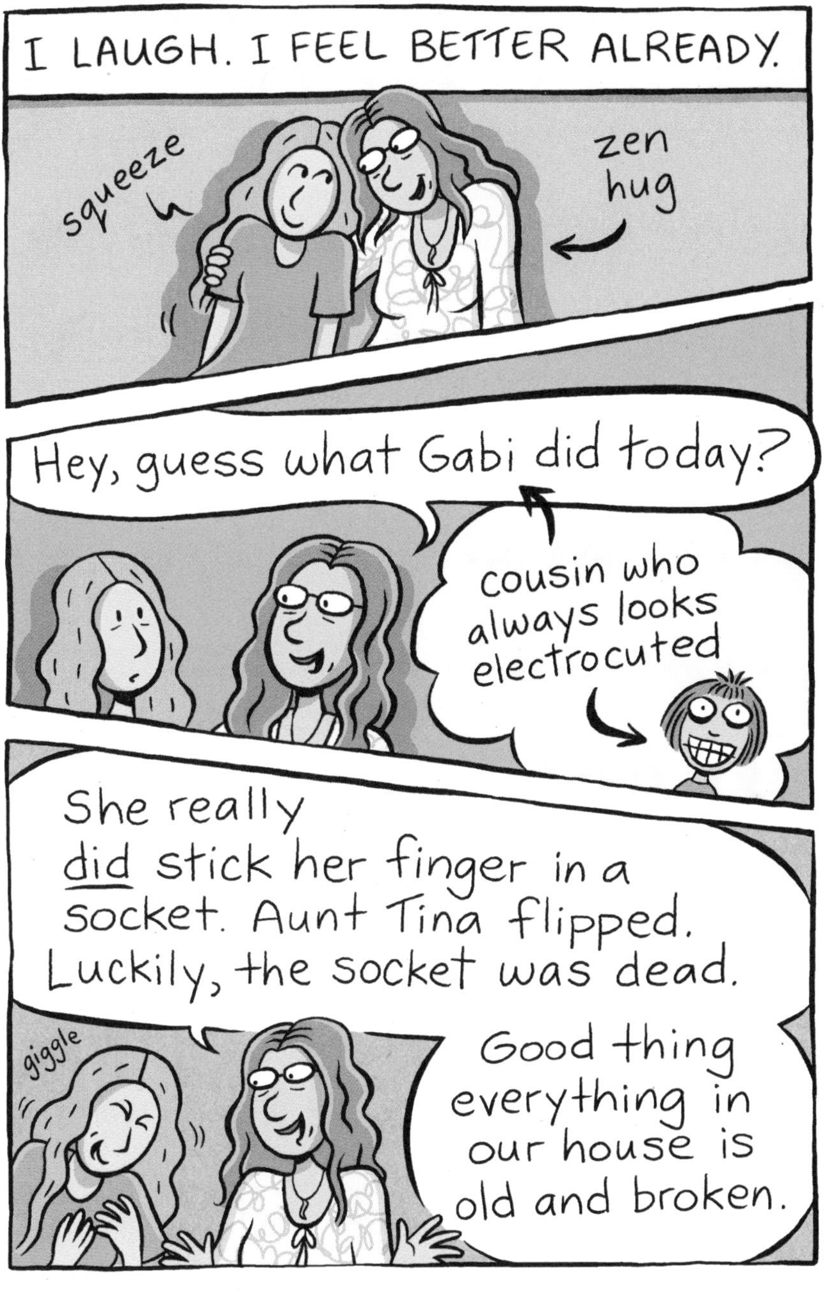

I LAUGH. I FEEL BETTER ALREADY.
squeeze
zen hug
Hey, guess what Gabi did today?
cousin who always looks electrocuted
She really did stick her finger in a socket. Aunt Tina flipped. Luckily, the socket was dead.
giggle
Good thing everything in our house is old and broken.

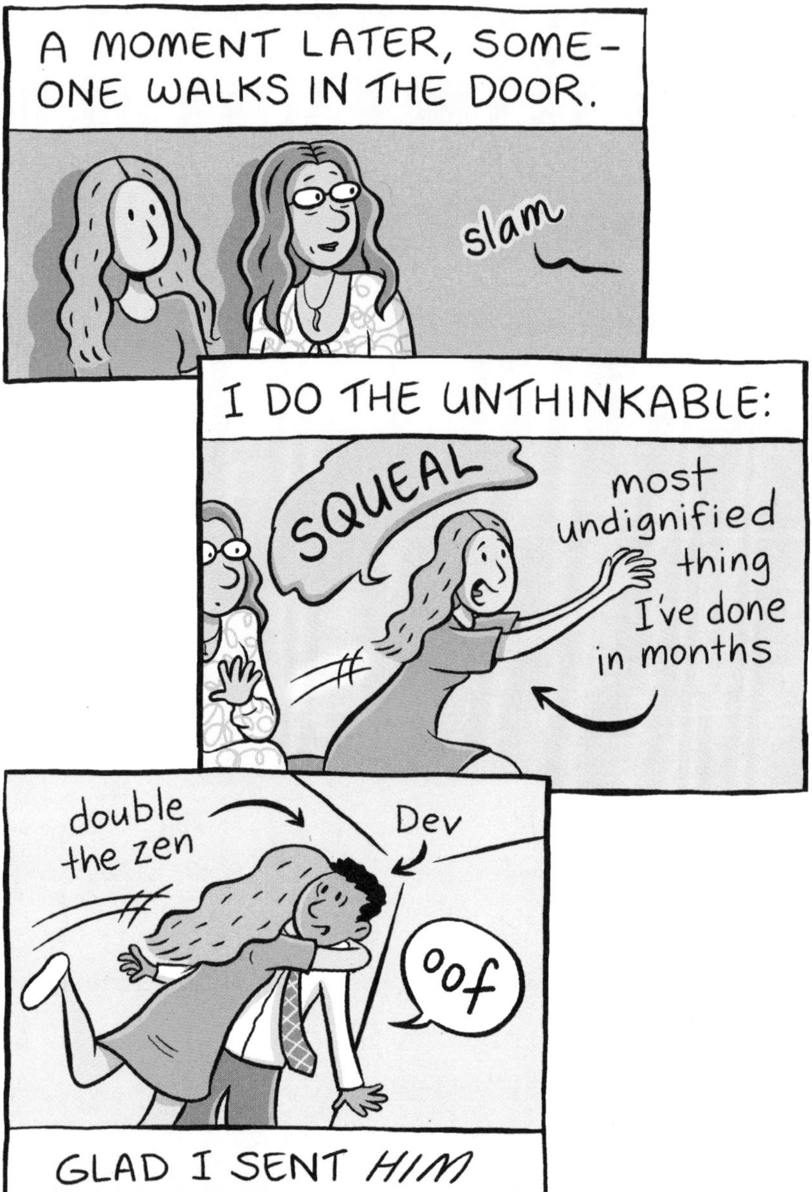
A MOMENT LATER, SOME-ONE WALKS IN THE DOOR.
slam
I DO THE UNTHINKABLE:
SQUEAL
most undignified thing I've done in months
double the zen
Dev
oof
GLAD I SENT *HIM* A TEXT, TOO!

TWO AND THREE-QUARTER MONTHS AGO

I'm sitting on the deck steps at my dad's. We finally got the patio all set for spring.

furniture hosed down

old lemonade can tossed

loose plank fixed

new weed

I'm rolling a disgusting tennis ball with my foot. It got into the yard by accident. Probably belongs to the neighbor's dog.

chew marks

slobber

cracked
on one side

This is usually where I come out to think. My bedroom is my thinking room all winter, but as soon as warm weather hits, I come out here. Even my brain needs some air.

think

Besides, my room is getting too distracting with all the homework, STEM stuff, and Hebrew notes spread everywhere. Not to mention the books and clothes that I still haven't done anything with.

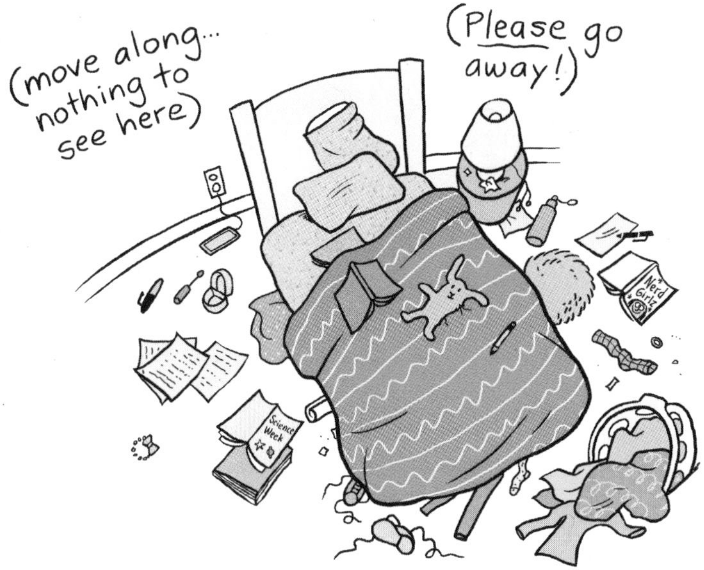
(move along... nothing to see here)
(Please go away!)
Science Week
Nerd Girlz

I feel really depressed. It's been a week since Emmie and I have spoken to each other. This is the longest we've ever been apart. I haven't been this lonely since, well . . .

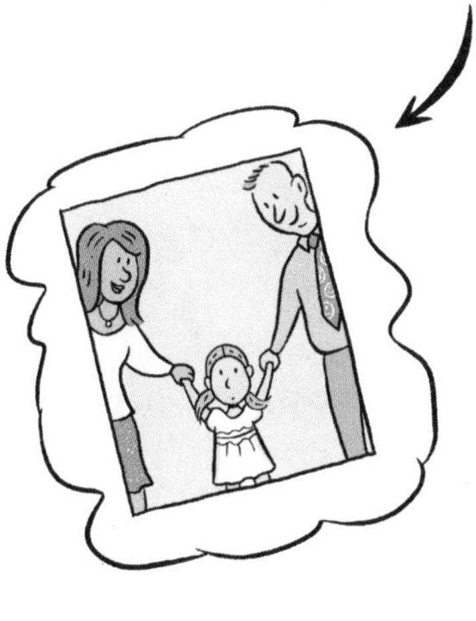

The ball slips away and rolls downhill into a hedge separating our yard from the neighbor's. A furry paw suddenly pokes out of the hedge and pulls in the ball. They both disappear.

The thing is, I may be lonely, but I'm also mad. Hopping mad! And for me, that always beats lonely. Because there's usually a valid reason behind "mad." You can't argue with data.

scientist

official-looking pointer

facts

SAD
MAD

I texted both Dev and Zoe the day after Em and I had our fight. I guess I needed some friends.

Zoe came over, which kinda surprised me. She usually likes to hang at her house. (I get it, it's pretty posh.)

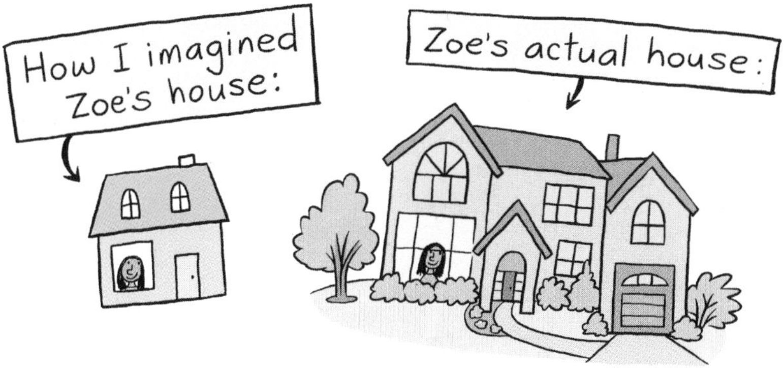
How I imagined Zoe's house:
Zoe's actual house:

Mostly we hung out and watched TV. She briefly tried to cheer me up.

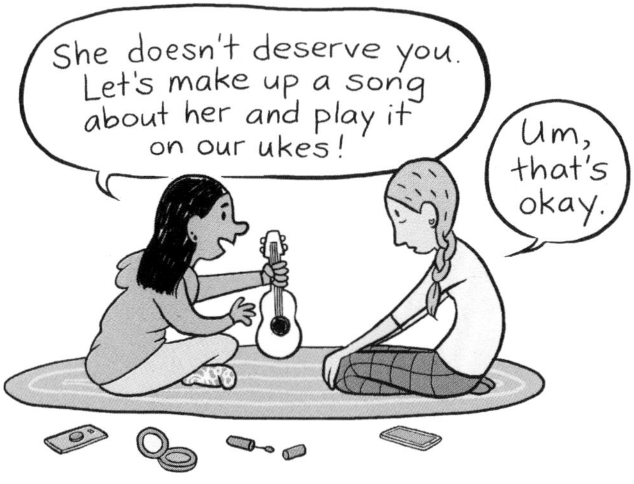
She doesn't deserve you. Let's make up a song about her and play it on our ukes!
Um, that's okay.

After that, we really didn't say much. But she tried.

Dev came over the next day. Funny how I used to think he was annoying. Things sure have changed.

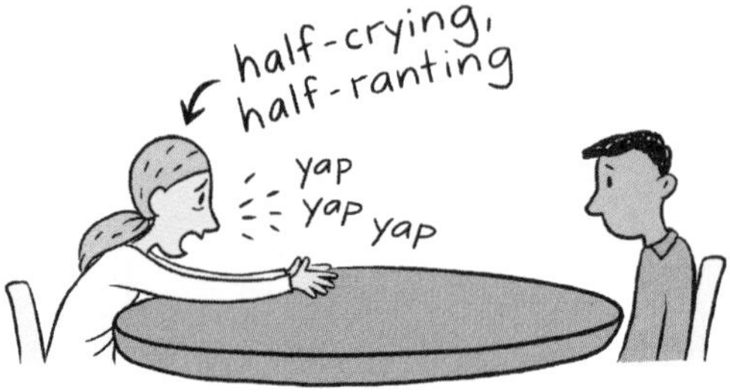
half-crying,
half-ranting
yap
yap
yap

He's a good listener. Especially over ice cream.

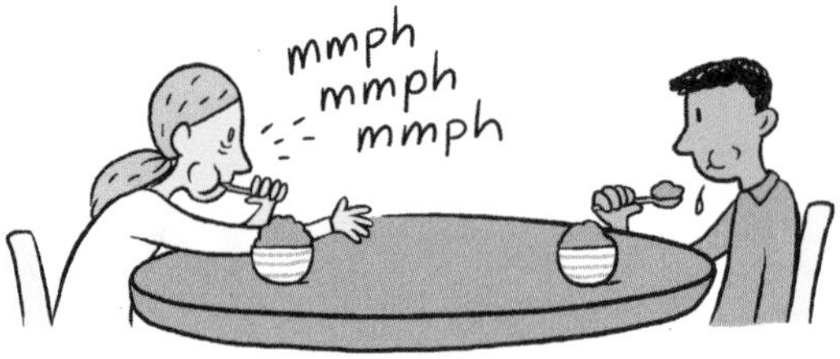
mmph
mmph
mmph

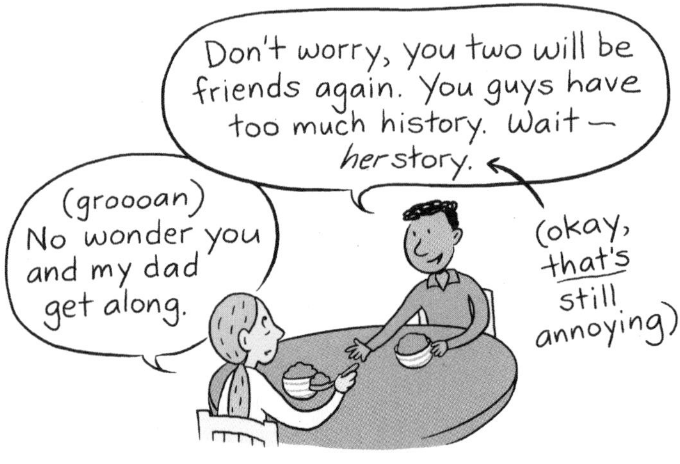
Don't worry, you two will be friends again. You guys have too much history. Wait — *her*story.
(okay, that's still annoying)
(grooooan) No wonder you and my dad get along.

What kills me, though, is that Emmie is spending more time with Sarah, and I know I'm quickly being replaced. Which actually makes me madder! And doesn't exactly help the situation.

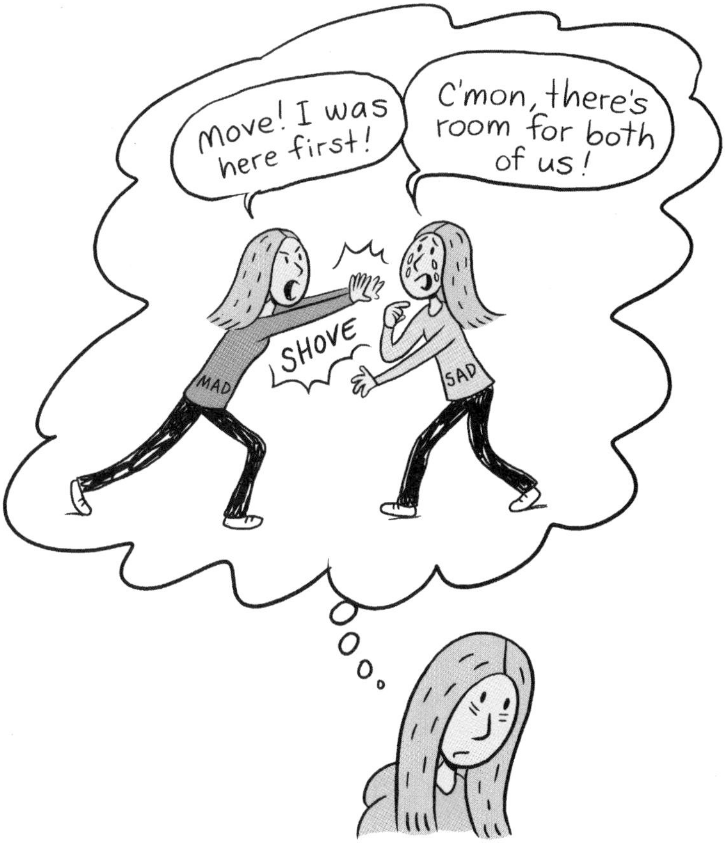
Move! I was here first!
C'mon, there's room for both of us!
SHOVE
MAD
SAD

The back door opens.

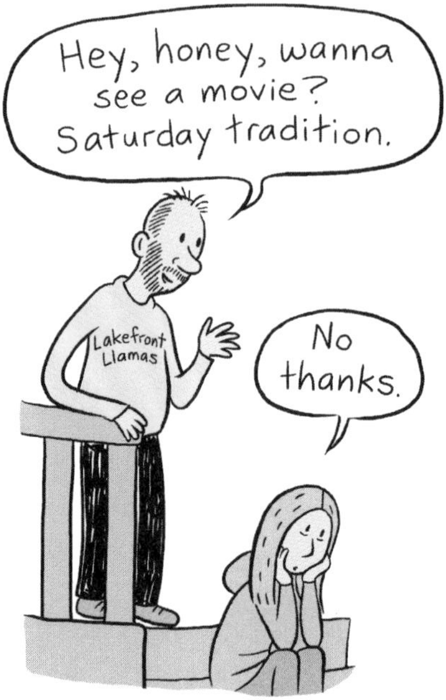
Hey, honey, wanna see a movie? Saturday tradition.
No thanks.
Lakefront Llamas

Dad comes over and sits next to me on the steps.

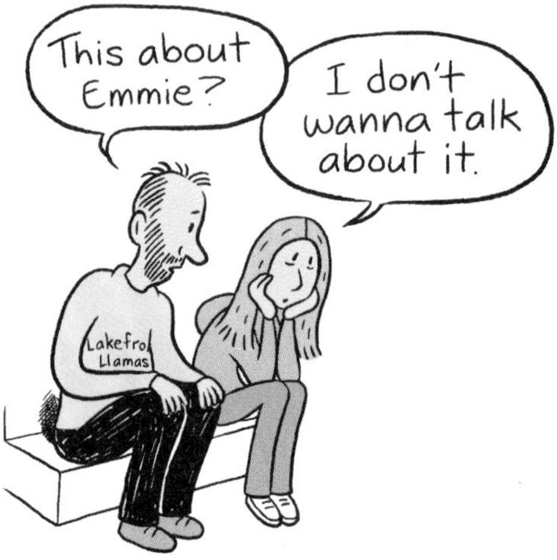
This about Emmie?
I don't wanna talk about it.

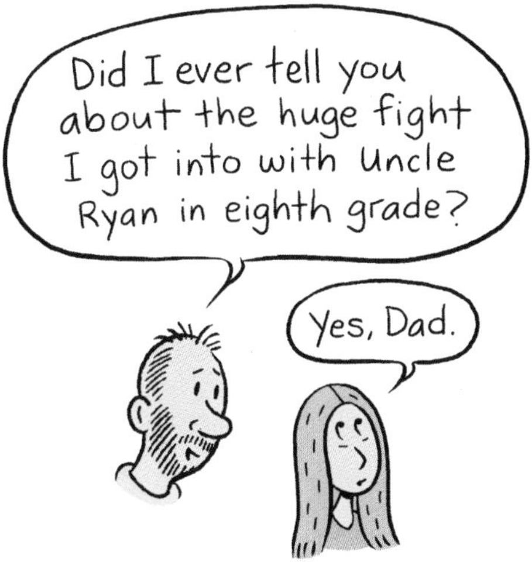
Did I ever tell you about the huge fight I got into with Uncle Ryan in eighth grade?
Yes, Dad.

Actually, he didn't. But the last thing I need is a "back in my day" story.

We sit quietly for a moment.

As usual, the silence gets to me.

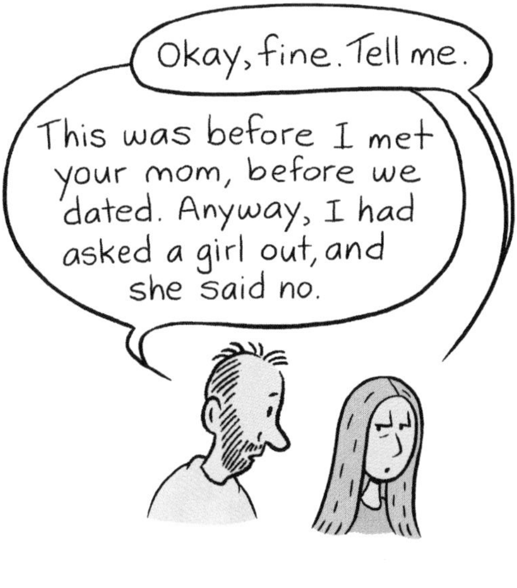
Okay, fine. Tell me.
This was before I met your mom, before we dated. Anyway, I had asked a girl out, and she said no.

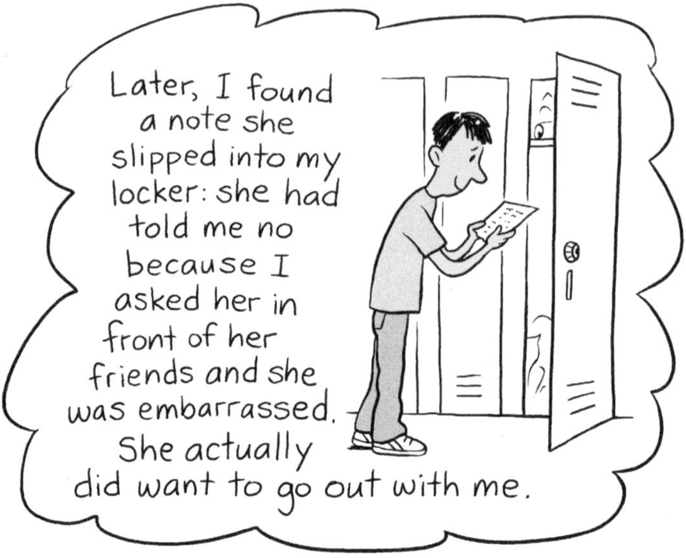
Later, I found a note she slipped into my locker: she had told me no because I asked her in front of her friends and she was embarrassed. She actually did want to go out with me.

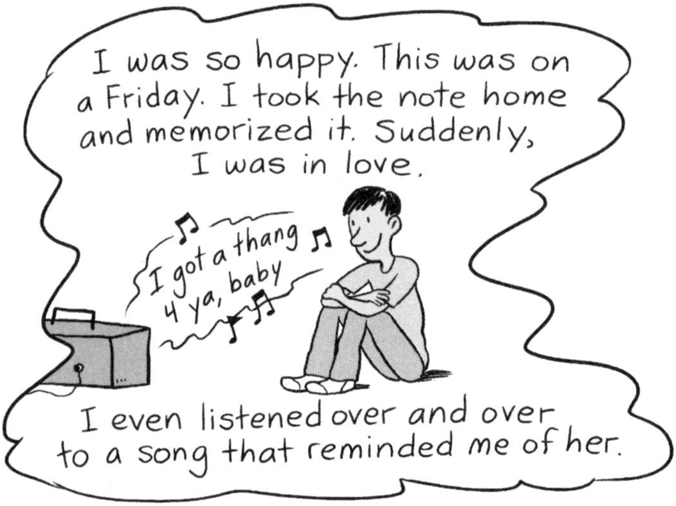
I was so happy. This was on a Friday. I took the note home and memorized it. Suddenly, I was in love.
I got a thang 4 ya, baby
I even listened over and over to a song that reminded me of her.

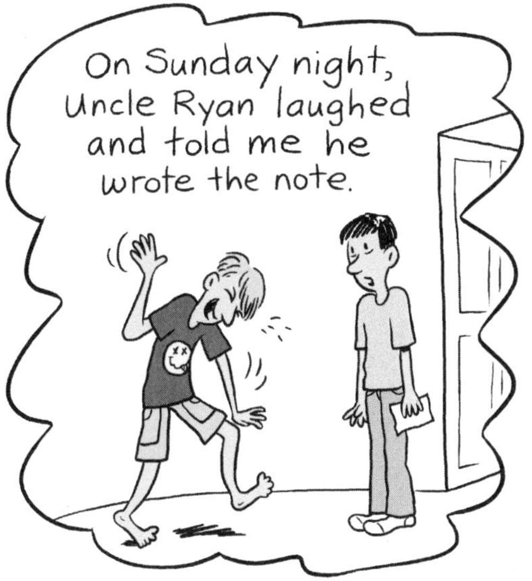
On Sunday night, Uncle Ryan laughed and told me he wrote the note.

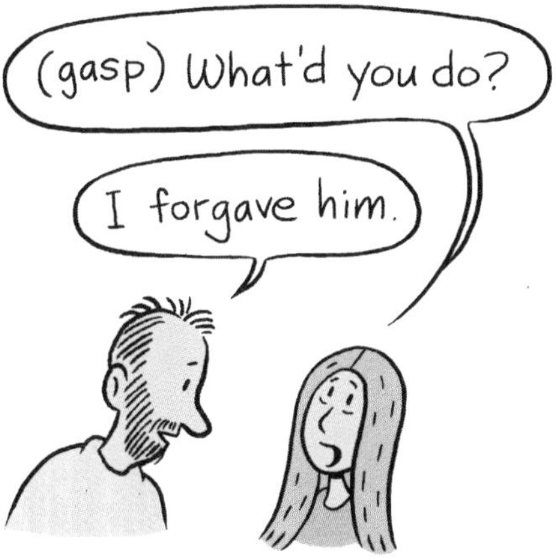
(gasp) What'd you do?
I forgave him.

What? You did?

Yeah. After about a week and one brutal prank of freezing a Mentos in an ice cube and sticking it in his soda.

AHHH!

soda bomb

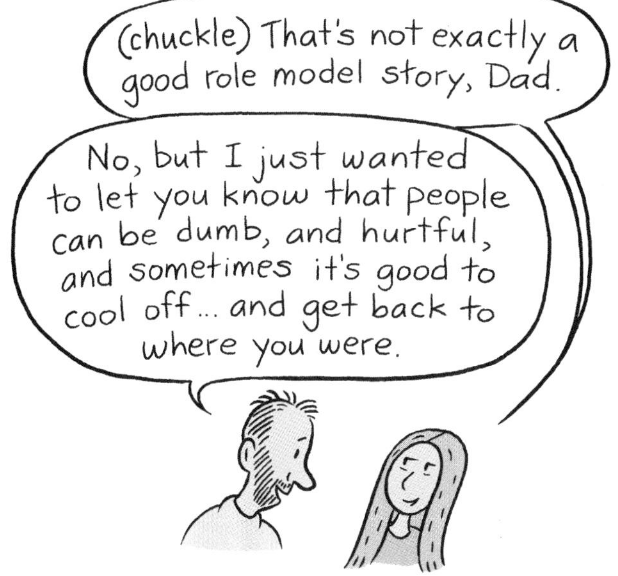
(chuckle) That's not exactly a good role model story, Dad.
No, but I just wanted to let you know that people can be dumb, and hurtful, and sometimes it's good to cool off... and get back to where you were.

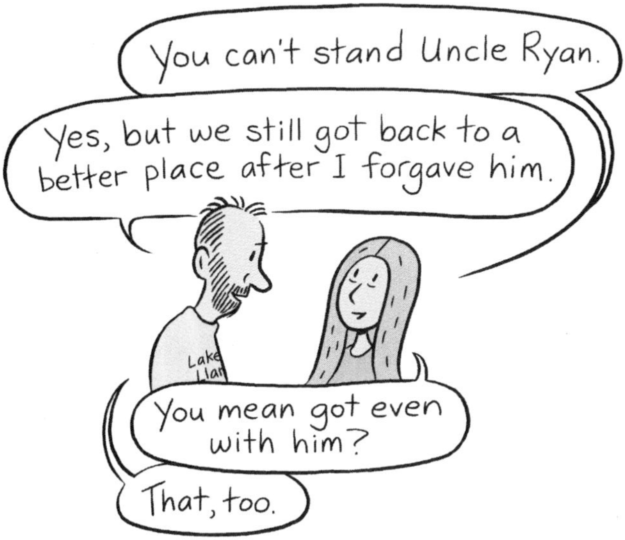
You can't stand Uncle Ryan.
Yes, but we still got back to a better place after I forgave him.
You mean got even with him?
That, too.

I smile, but I'm still not ready to forgive Emmie.

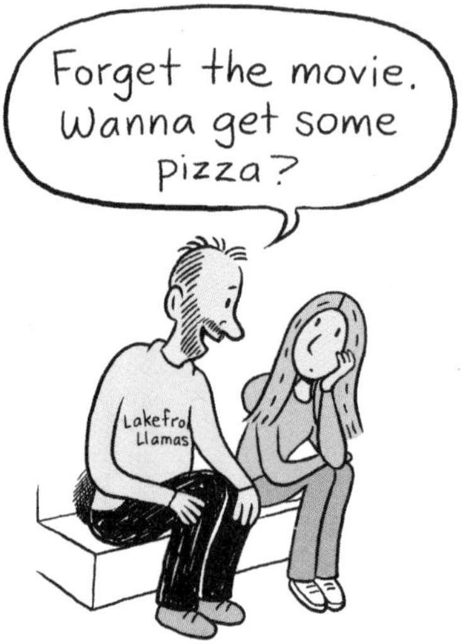
Forget the movie. Wanna get some pizza?
Lakefro
Llamas

I think about it, but only for a second.

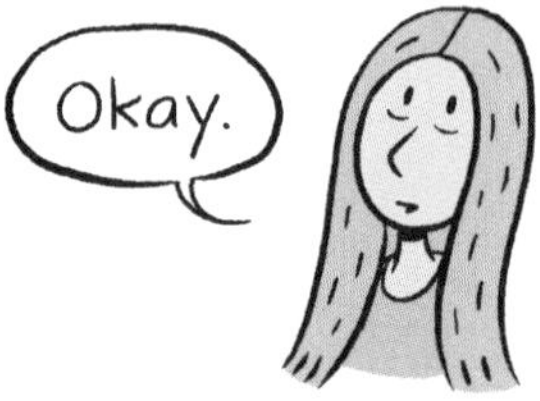
Okay.

We stand up and are about to head back inside when something shoots out of the hedges.

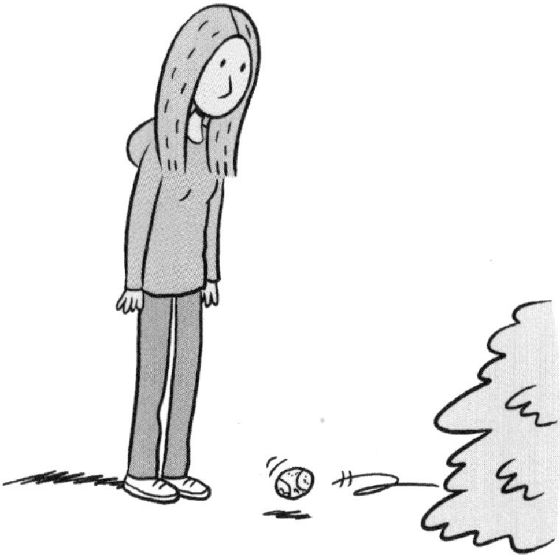

I don't believe in signs, but maybe that's one. Like, you get what you give, and maybe **that's** Emmie's anger rolling back to **me**.

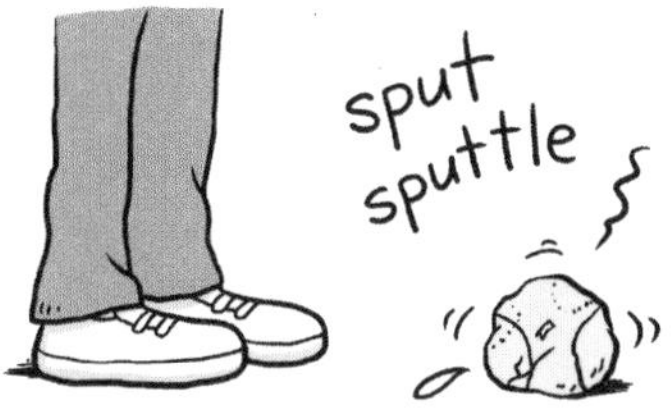
sput
sputtle

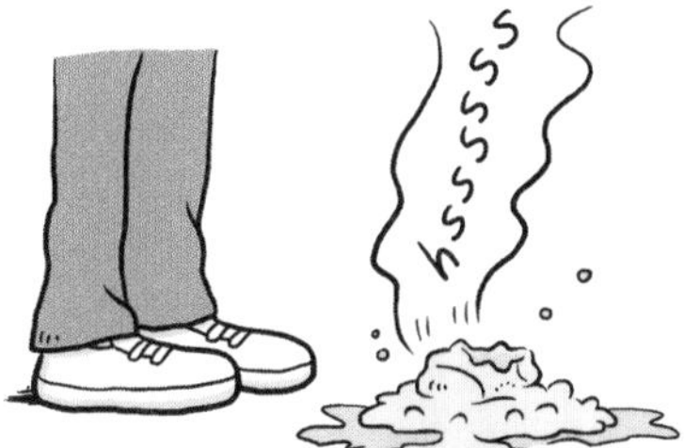
hssssss

Or maybe it's time for the neighbors to get their dog a new ball.

NOW

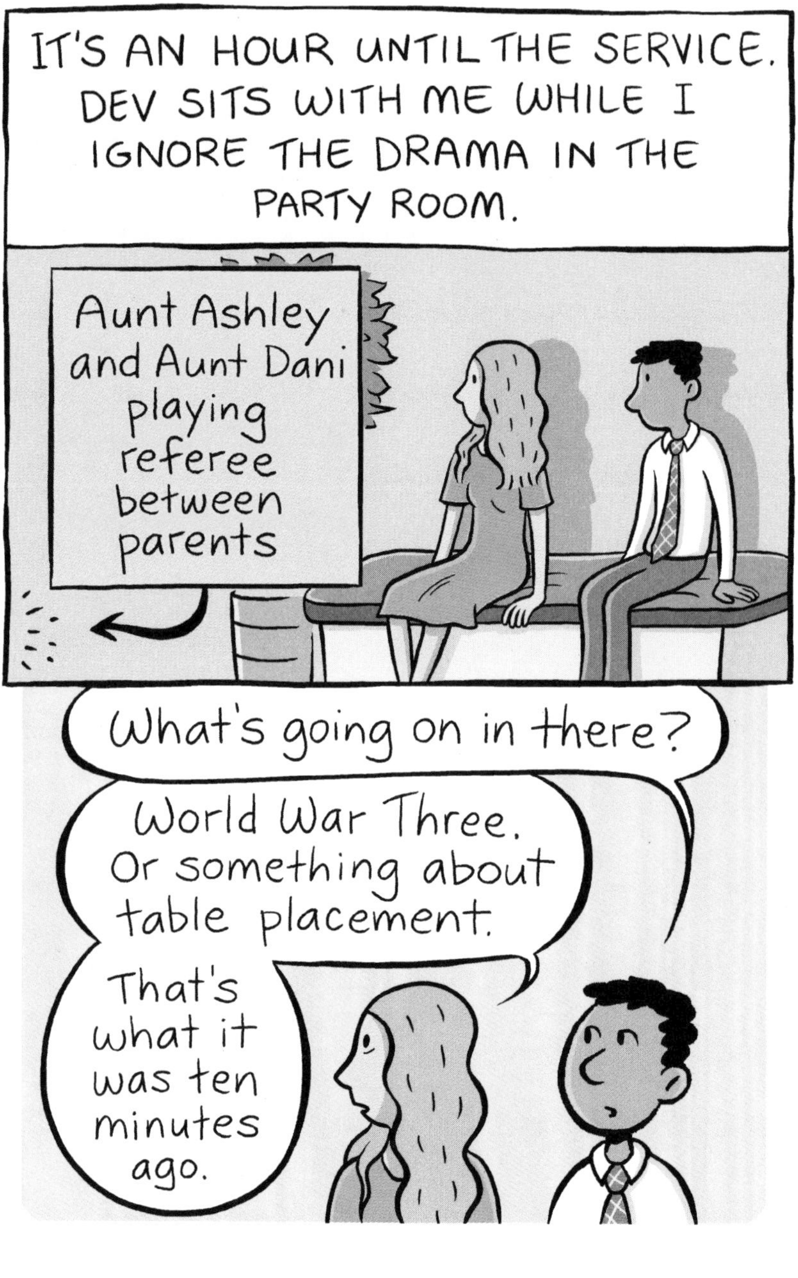
IT'S AN HOUR UNTIL THE SERVICE. DEV SITS WITH ME WHILE I IGNORE THE DRAMA IN THE PARTY ROOM.
Aunt Ashley and Aunt Dani playing referee between parents
What's going on in there?
World War Three. Or something about table placement.
That's what it was ten minutes ago.

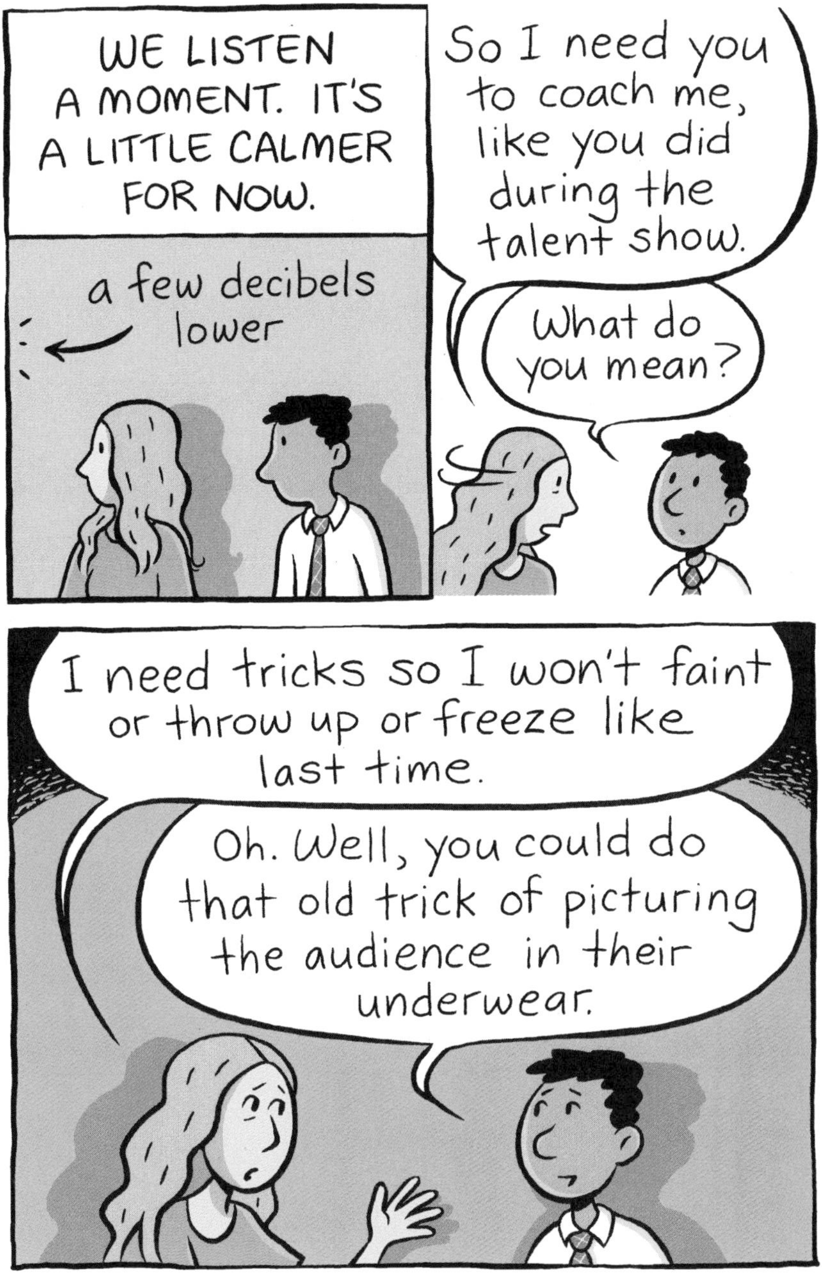
WE LISTEN A MOMENT. IT'S A LITTLE CALMER FOR NOW.
a few decibels lower
So I need you to coach me, like you did during the talent show.
What do you mean?
I need tricks so I won't faint or throw up or freeze like last time.
Oh. Well, you could do that old trick of picturing the audience in their underwear.

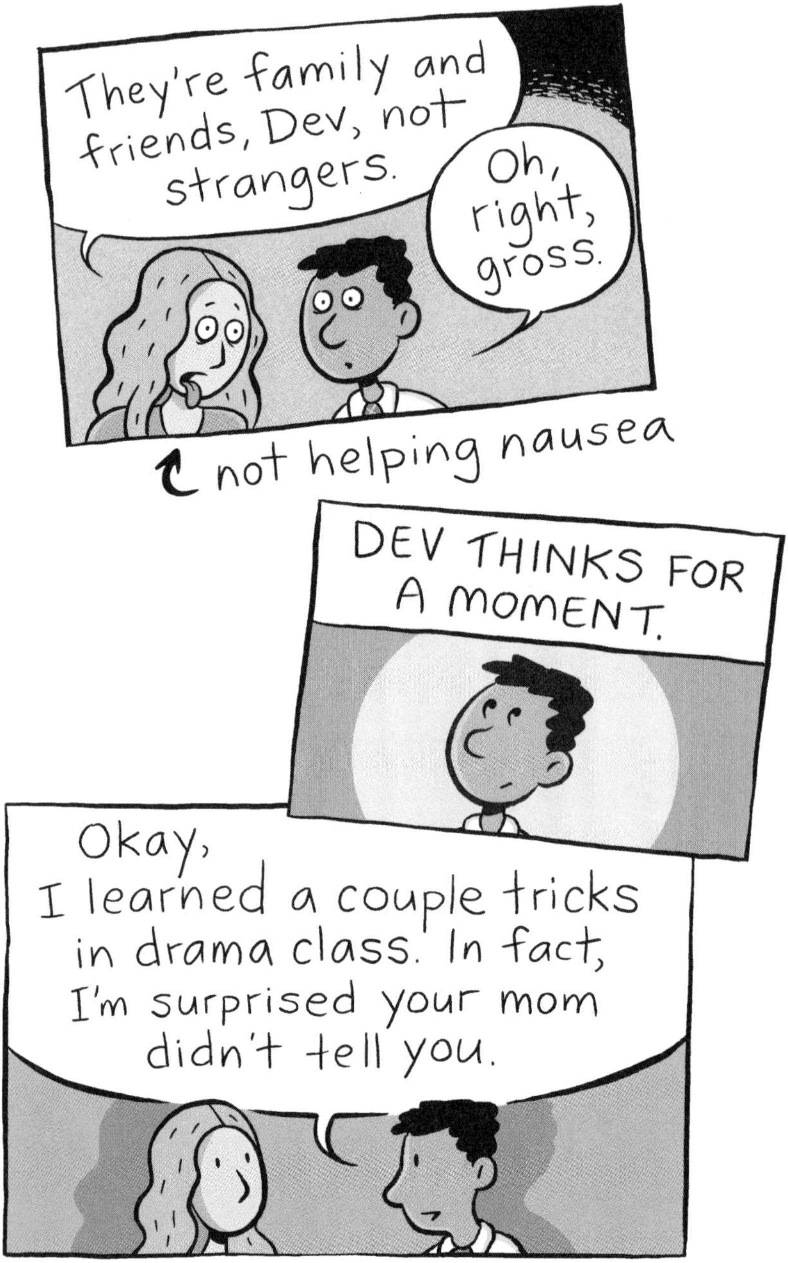
They're family and friends, Dev, not strangers.
Oh, right, gross.
not helping nausea
DEV THINKS FOR A MOMENT.
Okay, I learned a couple tricks in drama class. In fact, I'm surprised your mom didn't tell you.

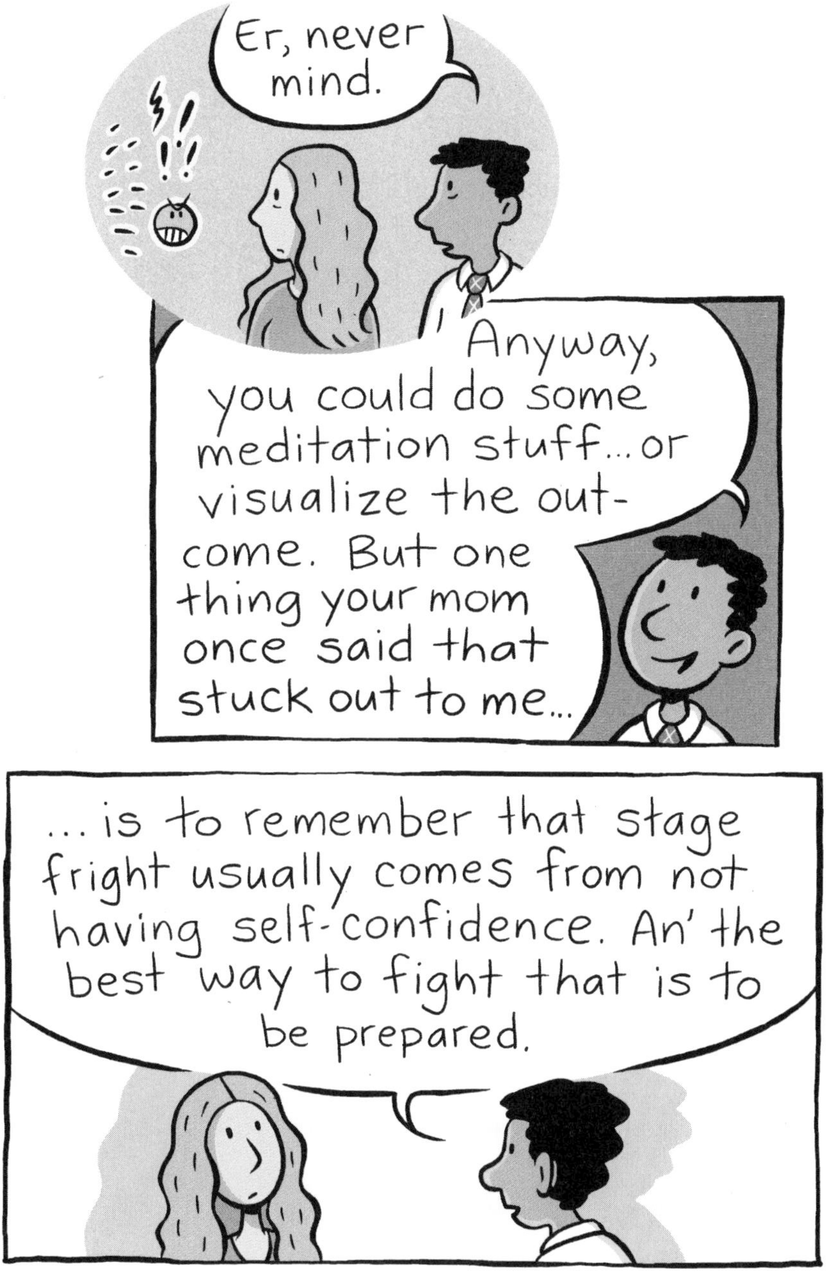
Er, never mind.
Anyway, you could do some meditation stuff... or visualize the outcome. But one thing your mom once said that stuck out to me...
... is to remember that stage fright usually comes from not having self-confidence. An' the best way to fight that is to be prepared.

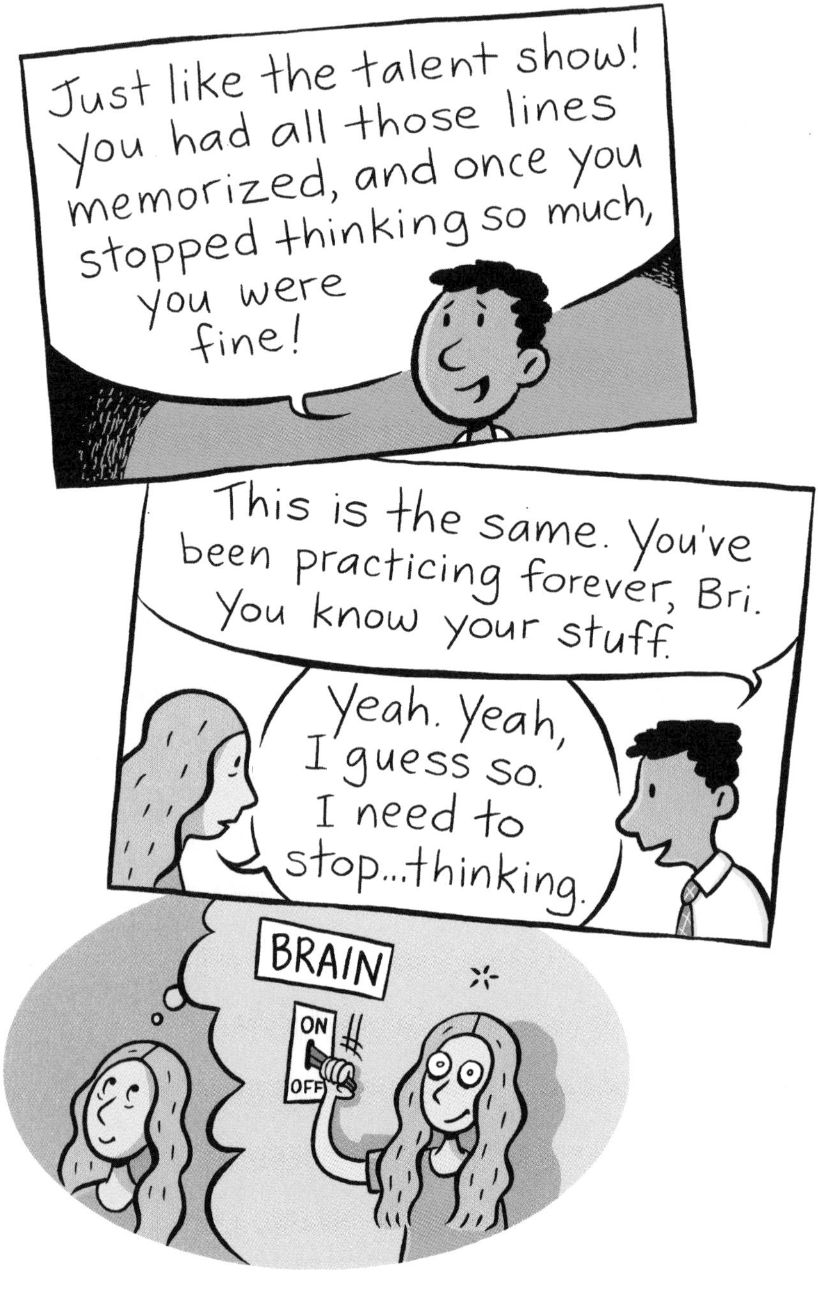
Just like the talent show! You had all those lines memorized, and once you stopped thinking so much, you were fine!
This is the same. You've been practicing forever, Bri. You know your stuff.
Yeah. Yeah, I guess so. I need to stop...thinking.
BRAIN
ON
OFF

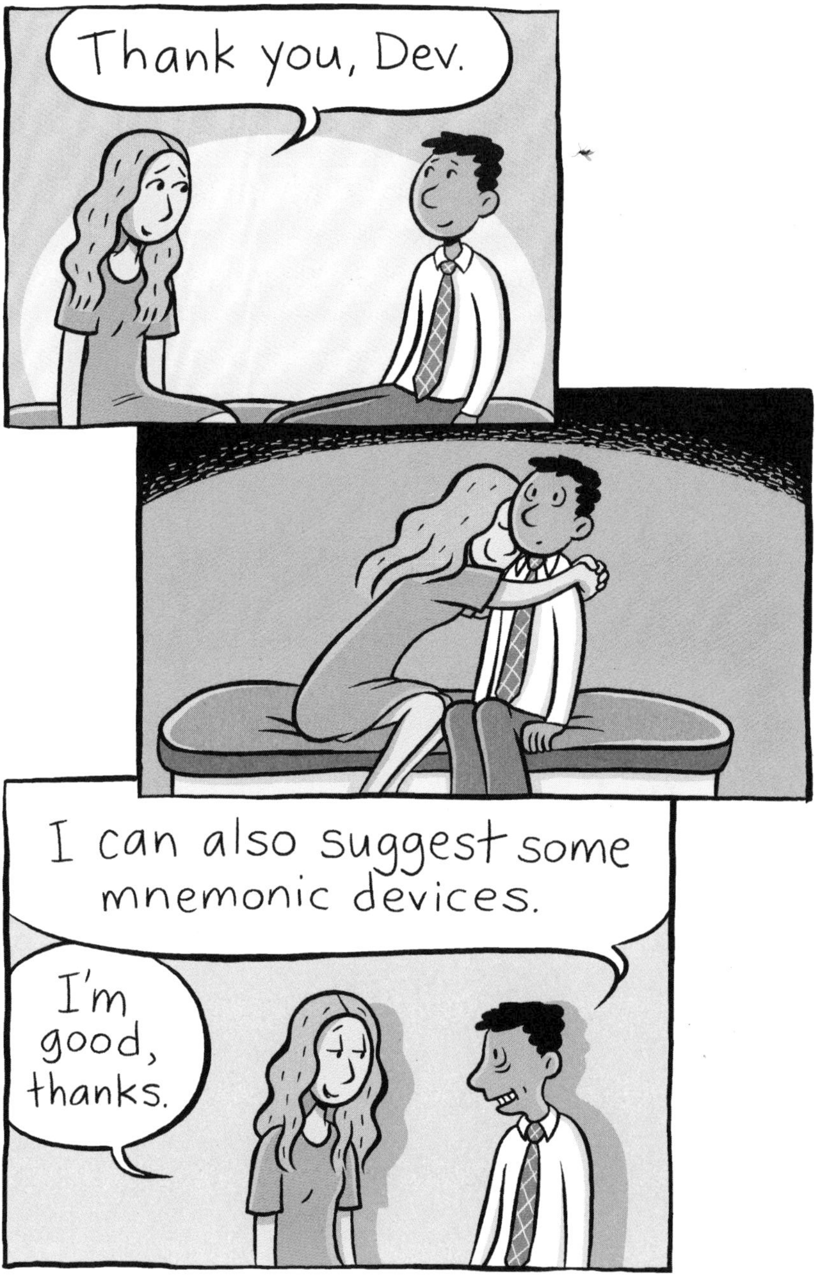
Thank you, Dev.
I can also suggest some mnemonic devices.
I'm good, thanks.

TWO AND A HALF MONTHS AGO

Just got ice cream with Dev at Taystee's.

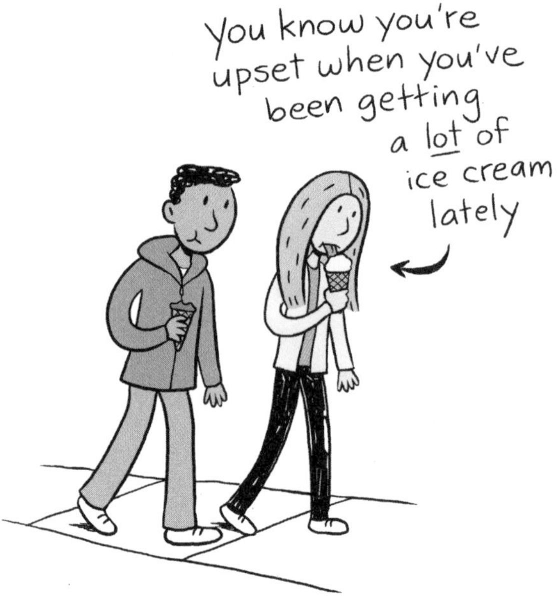
you know you're upset when you've been getting a lot of ice cream lately

Ever since the talent show, we've been hanging out more. Especially now that Em and I aren't speaking to each other.

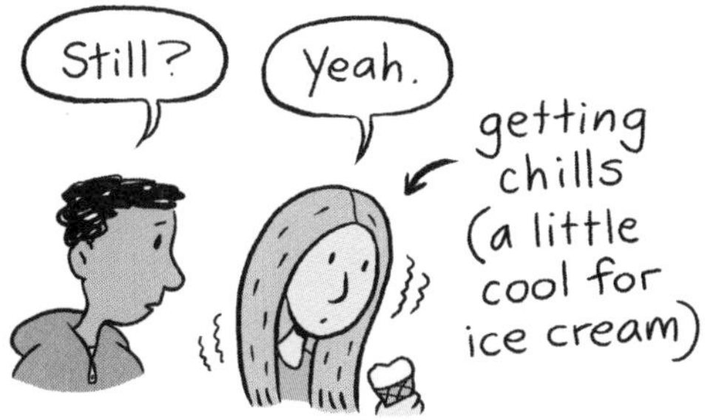
Still?
Yeah.
getting chills (a little cool for ice cream)

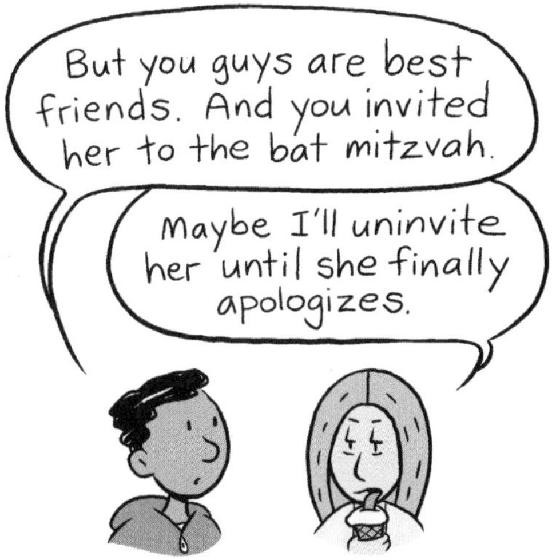
But you guys are best friends. And you invited her to the bat mitzvah.
Maybe I'll uninvite her until she finally apologizes.

It's been two weeks. Em tried telling me her side of things again, but I'm still mad and I know how to hold a grudge. Besides, she did **not** apologize.

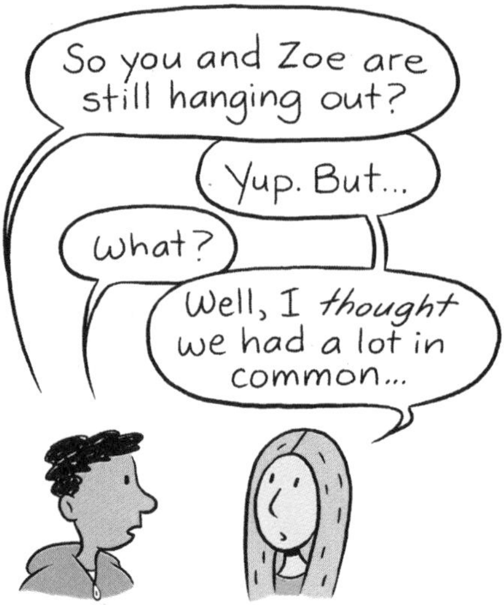
So you and Zoe are still hanging out?
Yup. But...
What?
Well, I *thought* we had a lot in common...

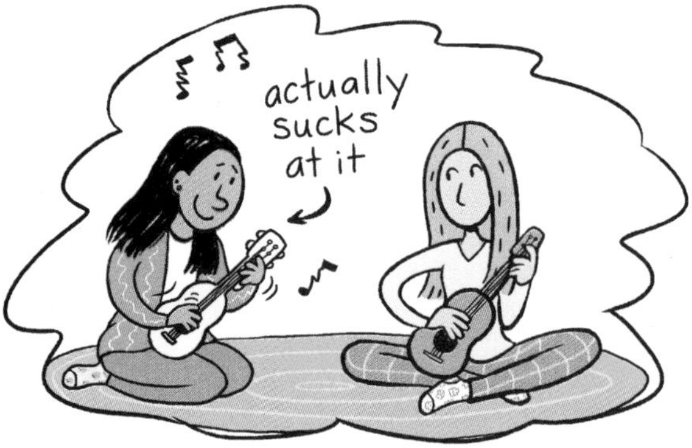
actually sucks at it

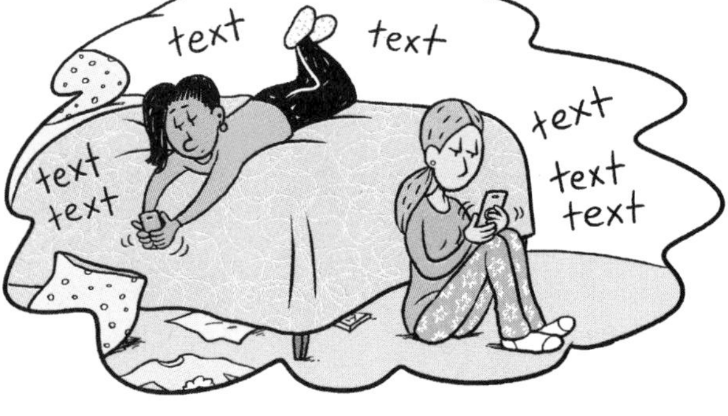
text
text
text text
text
text text

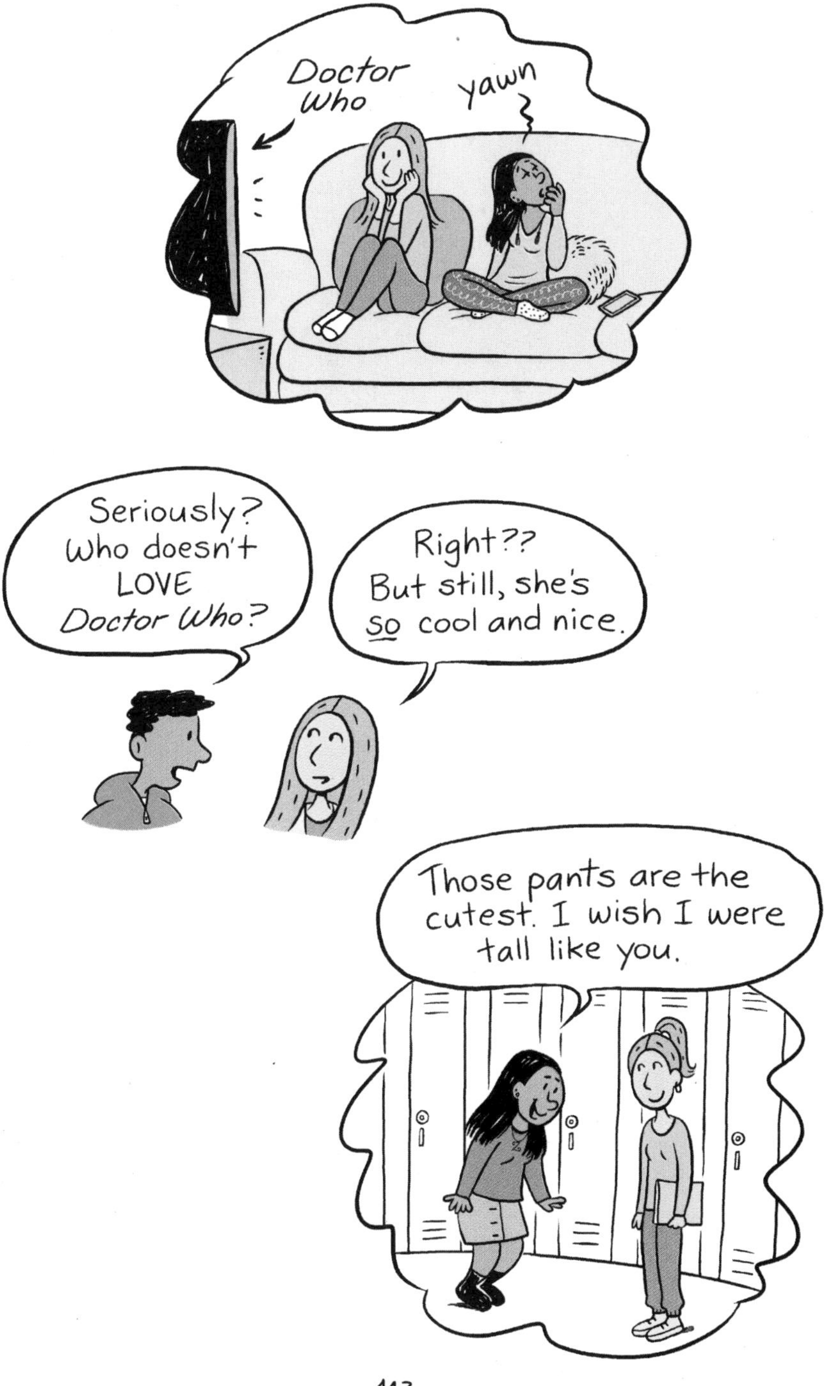
Doctor Who
yawn
Seriously? Who doesn't LOVE Doctor Who?
Right?? But still, she's so cool and nice.
Those pants are the cutest. I wish I were tall like you.

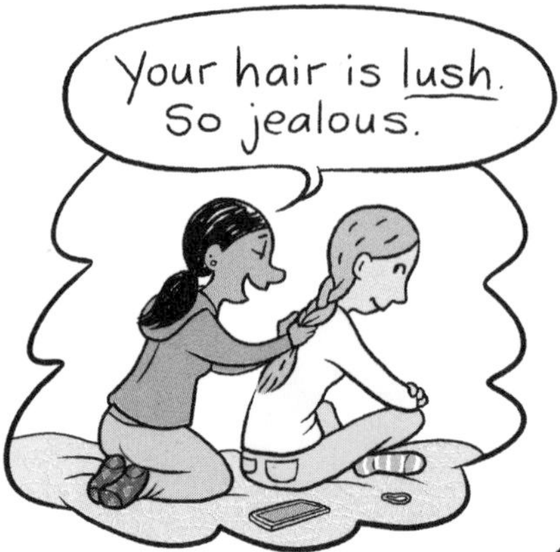
Your hair is lush. So jealous.

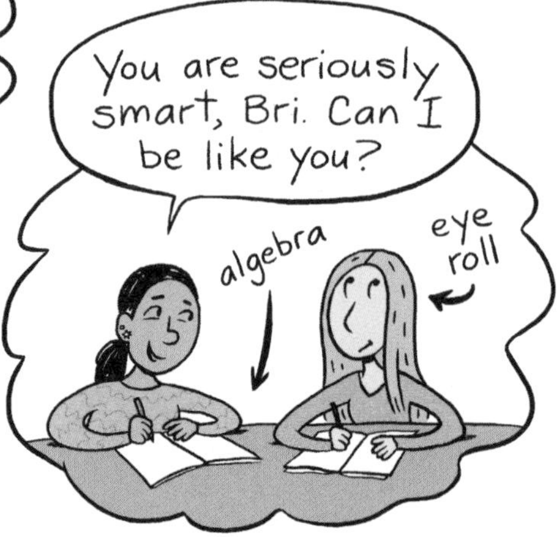
You are seriously smart, Bri. Can I be like you?
algebra
eye roll

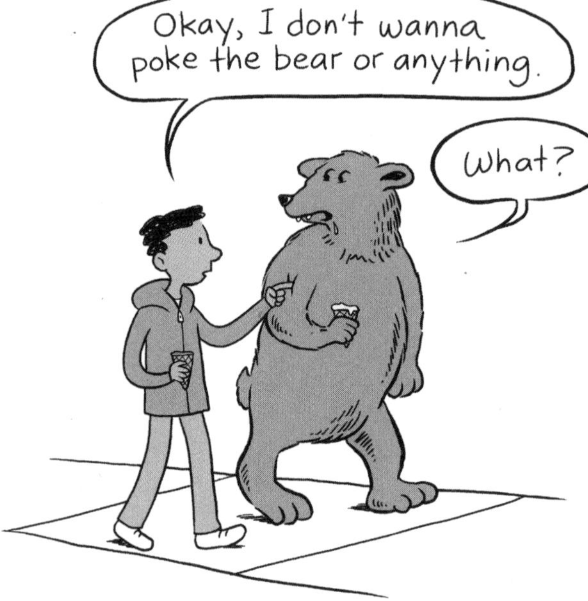
Okay, I don't wanna poke the bear or anything.
What?

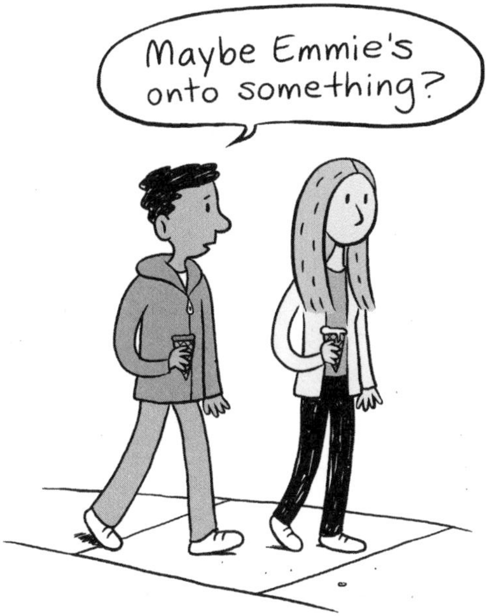
Maybe Emmie's onto something?

I stop.

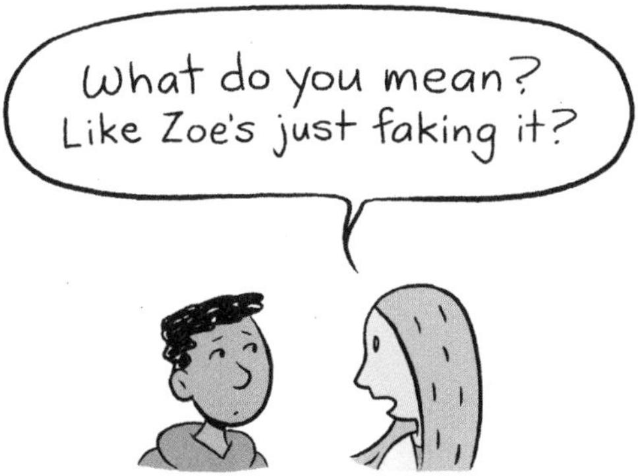
What do you mean? Like Zoe's just faking it?

Dev stops a little behind me, like he's scared to catch up.

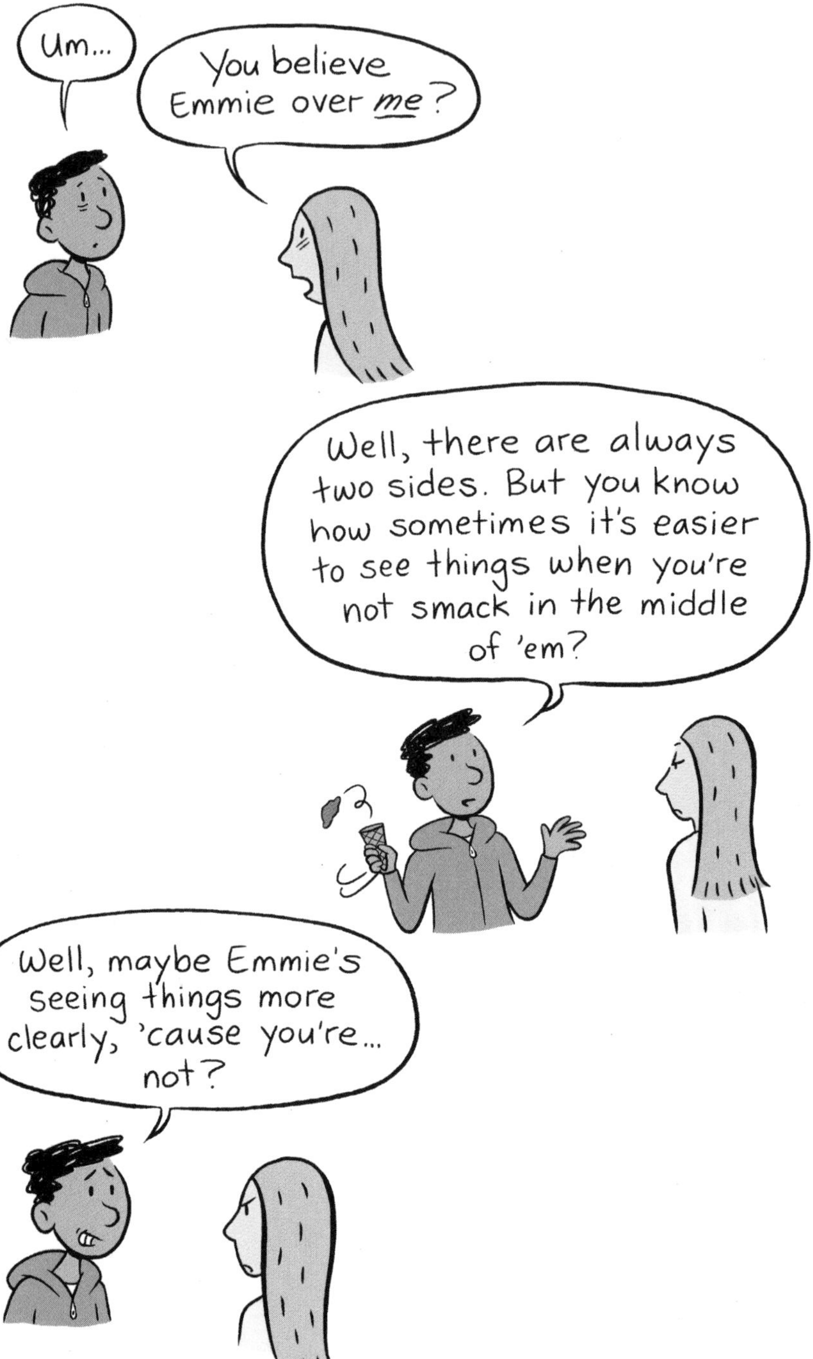
Um...
You believe Emmie over *me*?
Well, there are always two sides. But you know how sometimes it's easier to see things when you're not smack in the middle of 'em?
Well, maybe Emmie's seeing things more clearly, 'cause you're... not?

I start marching in long angry strides. Dev sprints to catch up.

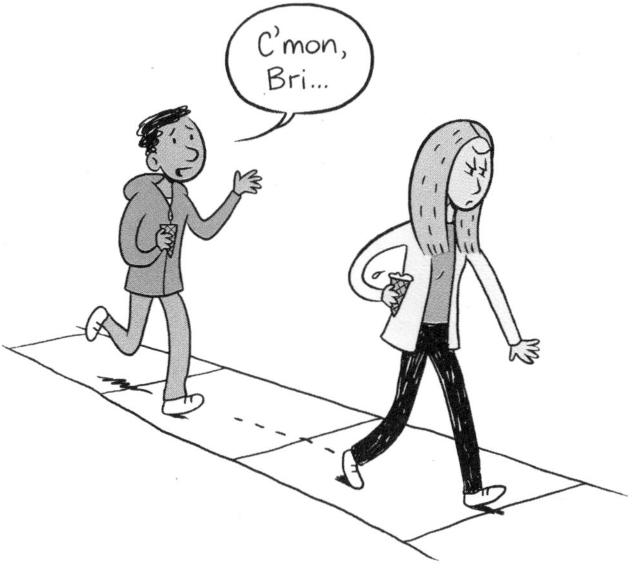
C'mon, Bri...

I slow down, but I don't stop brooding.

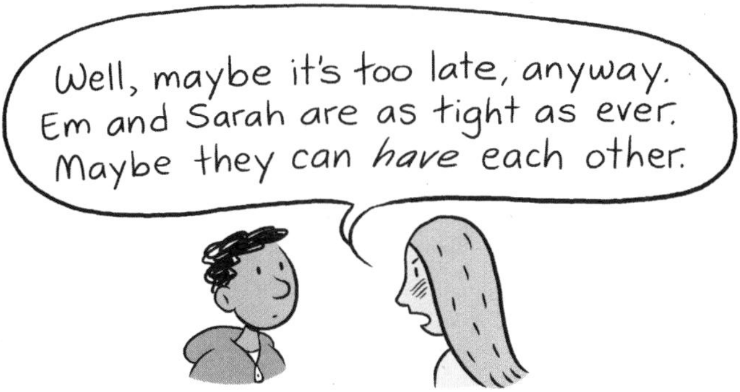
Well, maybe it's too late, anyway. Em and Sarah are as tight as ever. Maybe they can *have* each other.

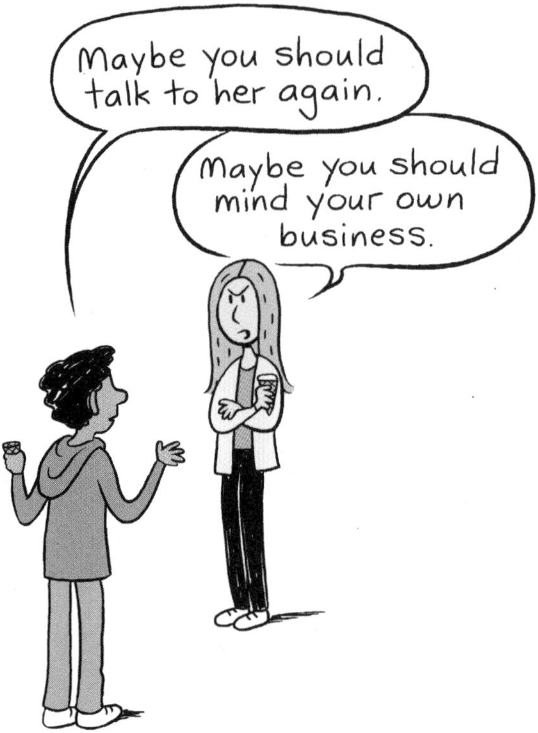
Maybe you should talk to her again.
Maybe you should mind your own business.

I keep marching in long strides, with Dev doing little leaps to keep up. We're the same height, but my legs are probably five inches longer.

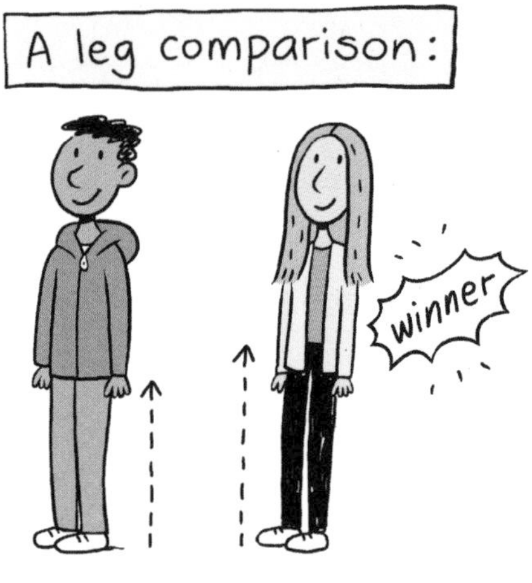
A leg comparison:
winner

I smile at his efforts. I can't help it. Dev can be annoying, but it's hard to stay mad at him.

But what's harder . . .

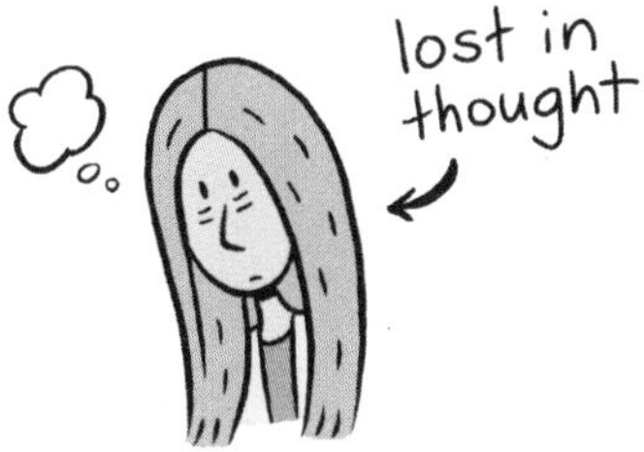
lost in thought

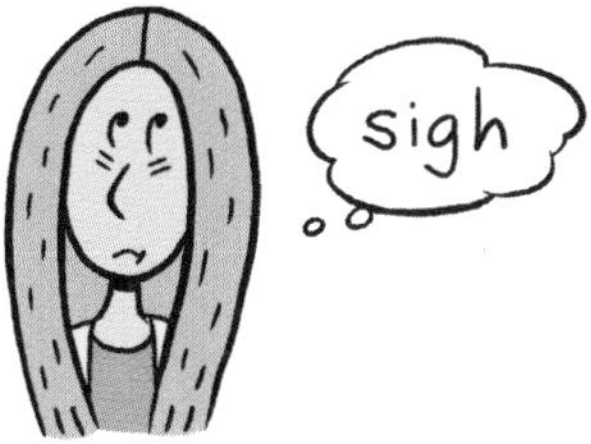
sigh

. . . is wondering if he might make sense.

NOW

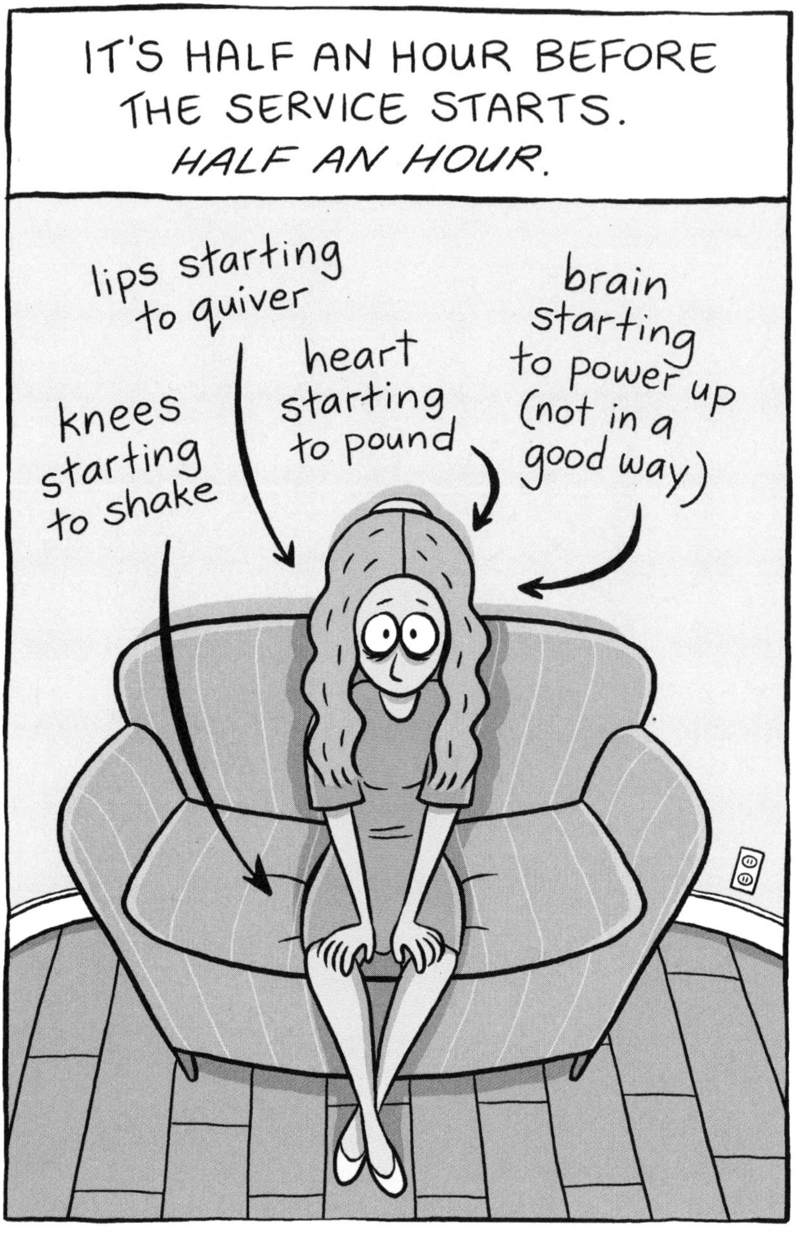
IT'S HALF AN HOUR BEFORE THE SERVICE STARTS.
HALF AN HOUR.
lips starting to quiver
knees starting to shake
heart starting to pound
brain starting to power up (not in a good way)

I'M IN THE RABBI'S OFFICE, WHICH HAS A SECRET DOOR AND HALL THAT LEAD RIGHT TO THE SANCTUARY STAGE. HE SHOWED IT TO ME LAST TIME.

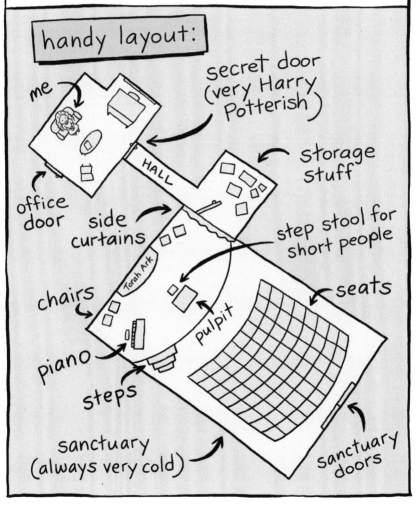

handy layout:

me

secret door
(very Harry Potterish)

HALL

storage stuff

office door

side curtains

step stool for short people

Torah Ark

chairs

seats

piano

pulpit

steps

sanctuary
(always very cold)

sanctuary doors

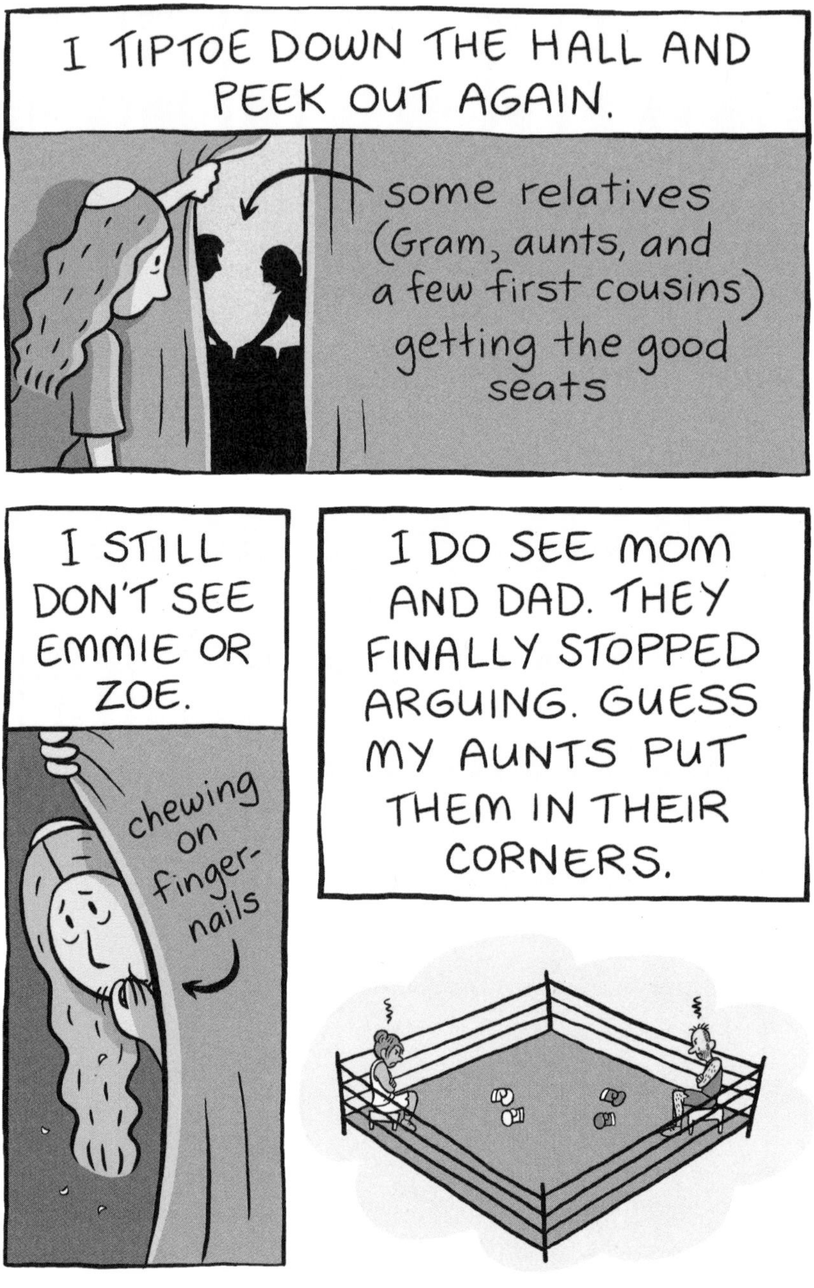
I TIPTOE DOWN THE HALL AND PEEK OUT AGAIN.
some relatives (Gram, aunts, and a few first cousins) getting the good seats
I STILL DON'T SEE EMMIE OR ZOE.
chewing on finger-nails
I DO SEE MOM AND DAD. THEY FINALLY STOPPED ARGUING. GUESS MY AUNTS PUT THEM IN THEIR CORNERS.

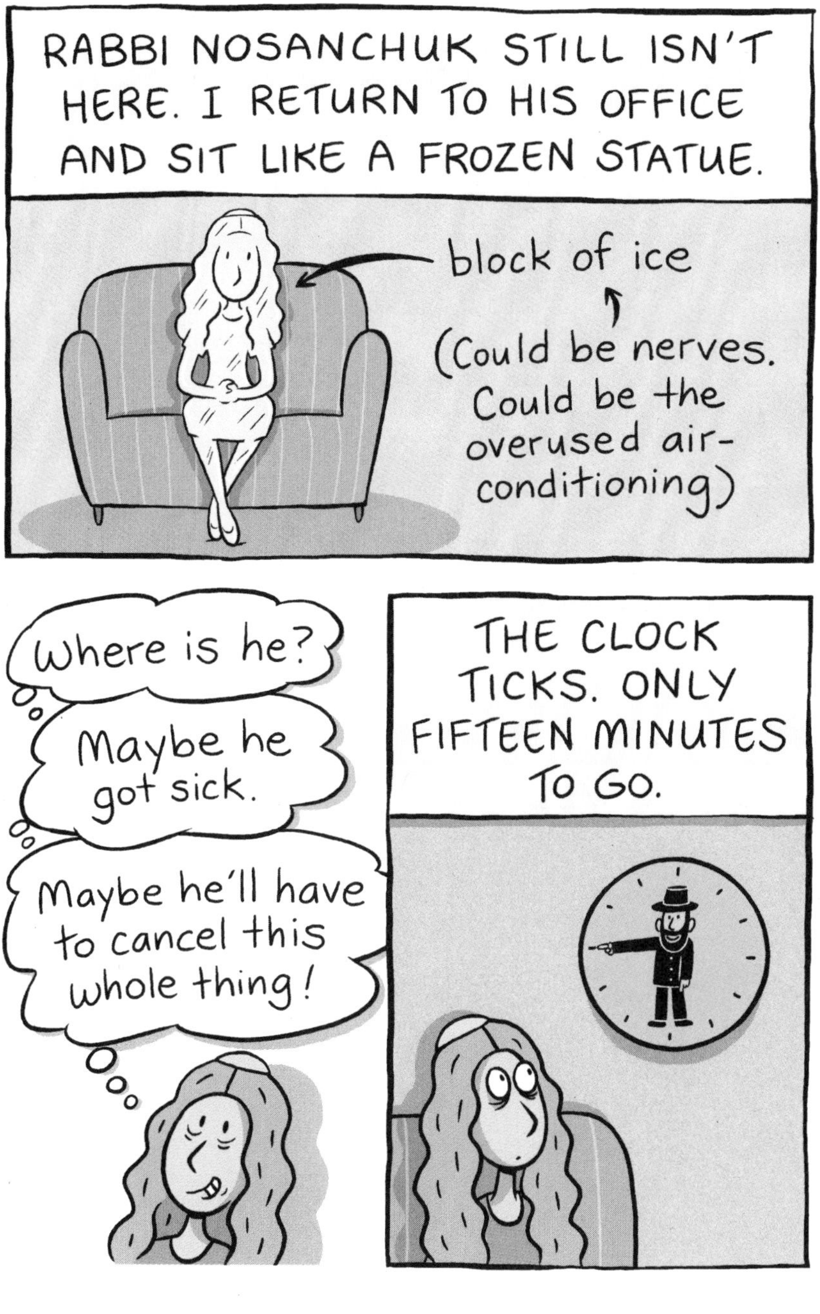
RABBI NOSANCHUK STILL ISN'T HERE. I RETURN TO HIS OFFICE AND SIT LIKE A FROZEN STATUE.
block of ice
(Could be nerves. Could be the overused air-conditioning)
Where is he?
Maybe he got sick.
Maybe he'll have to cancel this whole thing!
THE CLOCK TICKS. ONLY FIFTEEN MINUTES TO GO.

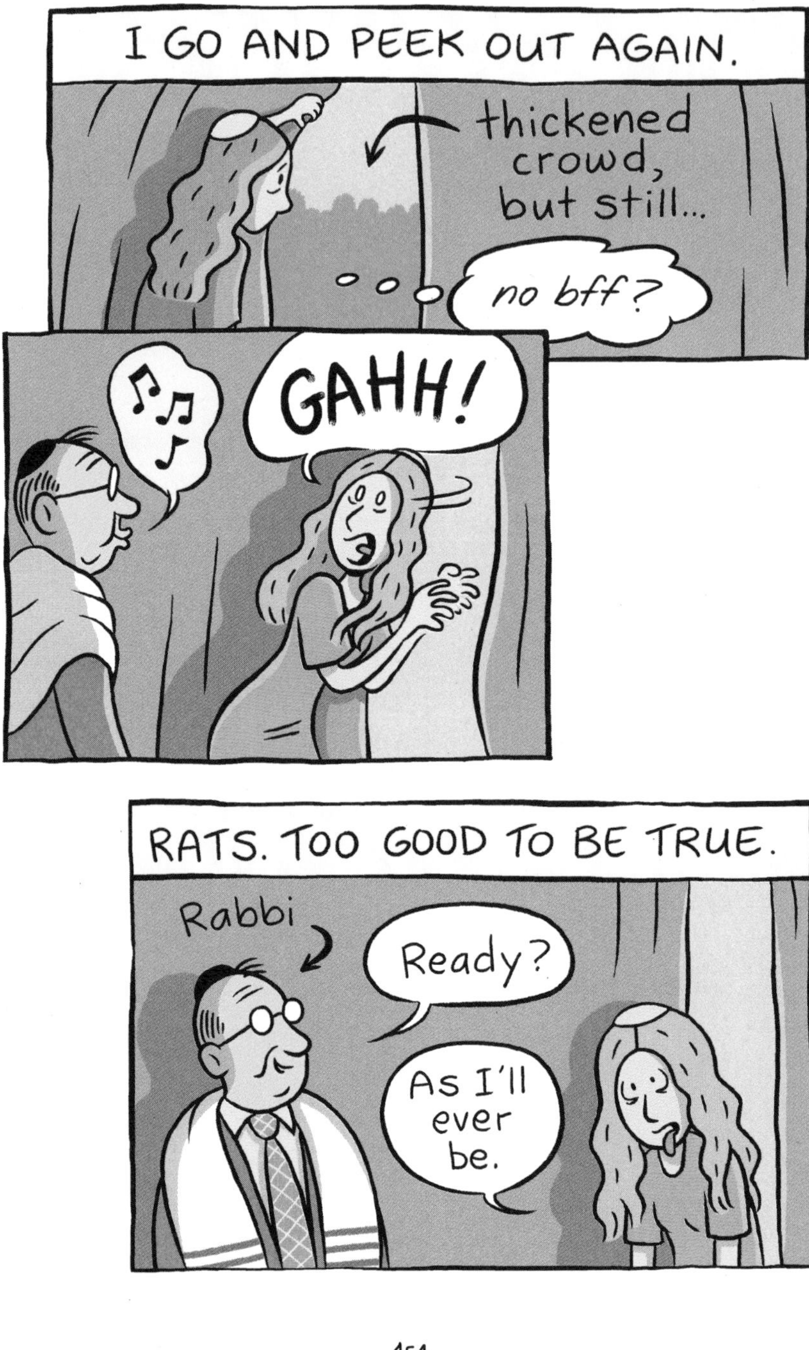
I GO AND PEEK OUT AGAIN.
thickened crowd, but still...
no bff?
GAHH!
RATS. TOO GOOD TO BE TRUE.
Rabbi
Ready?
As I'll ever be.

TWO MONTHS AGO

I'm sitting at the kitchen table at my dad's, trying to tackle my bat mitzvah speech. I'm purposely doing it here 'cause I need to get away from my mom, who continues to drive me batty.

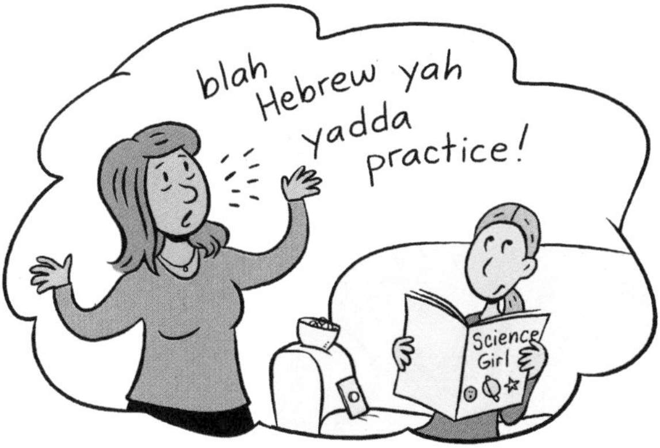

blah
Hebrew yah
yadda
practice!
Science Girl

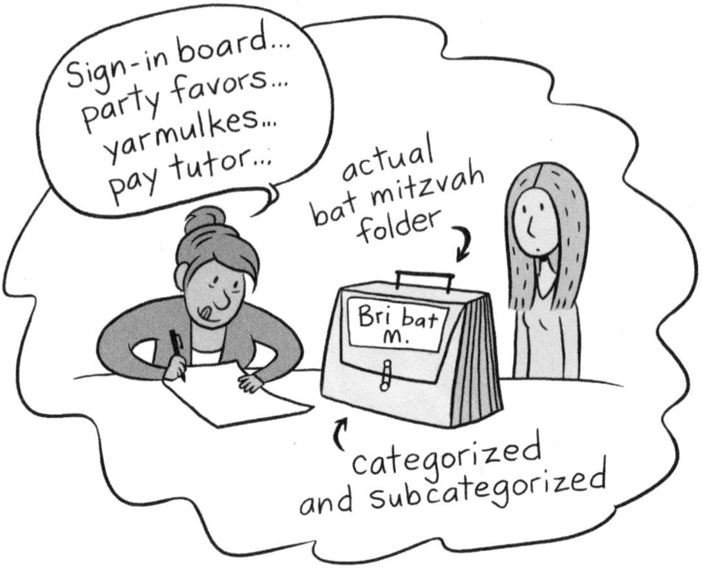

Sign-in board...
party favors...
yarmulkes...
pay tutor...
actual
bat mitzvah
folder
Bri bat
M.
categorized
and subcategorized

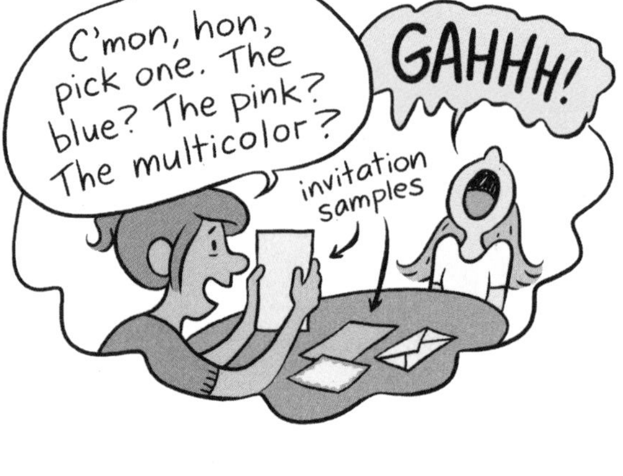

C'mon, hon, pick one. The blue? The pink? The multicolor?
GAHHH!
invitation
samples

It's been a rough month. Em and I still aren't talking. She's always hanging with Sarah. (By the way, doesn't **she** have any other friends?) Every time I think about making up with Emmie, I either see them together or think about them doing the same stuff we used to.

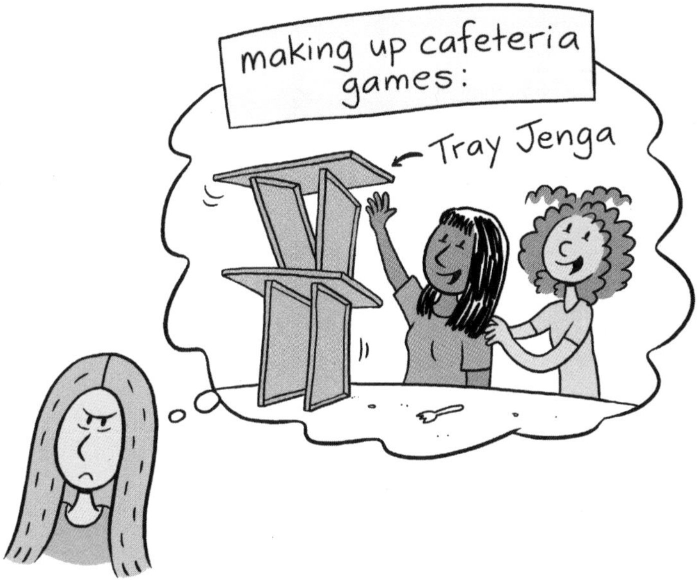
making up cafeteria games:
Tray Jenga

The one bright spot: ever since I got friendly with Zoe and Olivia, a lot of other kids in school have noticed. They're acting nicer and friendlier to me, too. Between all the friendliness and the bat mitzvah party hype, I'm suddenly . . . almost . . .

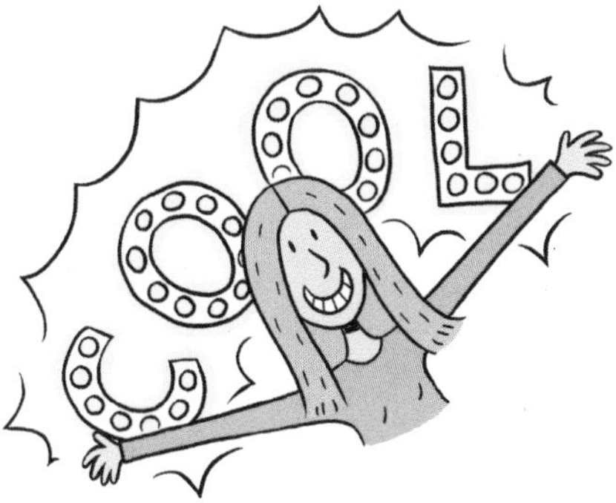
COOL

It's a strange feeling. And kinda exhilarating.

"Winn Word of the Week"

(Mrs. Winn, English teacher)

Anyway, I decided to put my fears about Zoe to rest. So we don't have a lot in common—that's natural in the beginning of a friendship, right? Anyway, Zoe texts me all the time. If this is her way of using me . . .

snicker

...then it's a strange way of showing it.

funny meme

The not-so-bright spot: I don't have time to enjoy any of this. I've got so much going on. Like homework. And my hyperfocused mom. And all the Hebrew. And this speech, which I've made no real progress with.

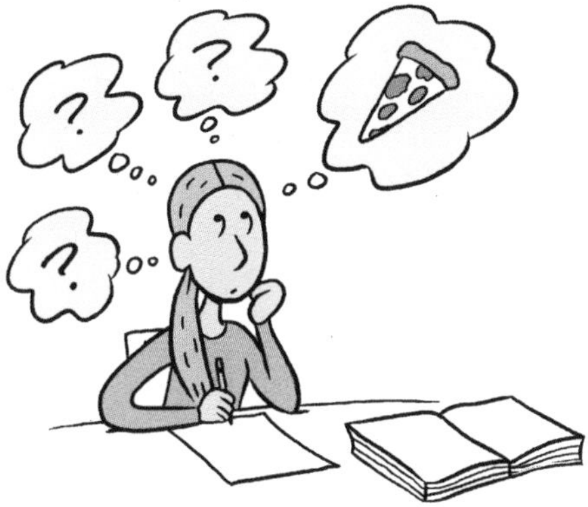

I've tried. Well, once. I met with the rabbi, and we started working on it together. He gave me the whole overview of the Torah portion. The big takeaway is the line from the ancient Jews to God: "We will do and we will hear." Which basically amounts to: "I will blindly follow you."

Part of me thinks:

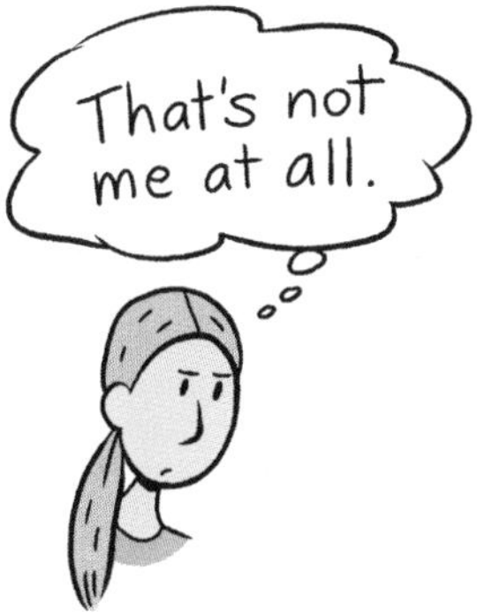
That's not me at all.

The other part of me thinks:

Then why am I blindly following my mom?

I groan and ball up my umpteenth sheet of paper, which my dad won't be happy about. He wants me to type this on his laptop, but I always work better writing on plain, old-school computer paper (aka "forest murdering").

AH HA HA HA HA HA

AHHH!

Okay, one more time. I read to myself from the prayer book. It contains many, many, **many** paragraphs about thunder, lightning, dense clouds, smoke, blasts of horns, and mountains trembling . . .

. . . all because people are getting their town laws and tax codes.

Not only that, they decide to just accept it all. Blindly. Without questioning anything.

Okay, so there's more to it. They also receive the Ten Commandments—which I guess deserves all that dramatic fanfare. Those are the biggies. The huge moral codes: Do not kill, blah, blah, blah. But even some of those I've already broken, so how can I get on board with them?

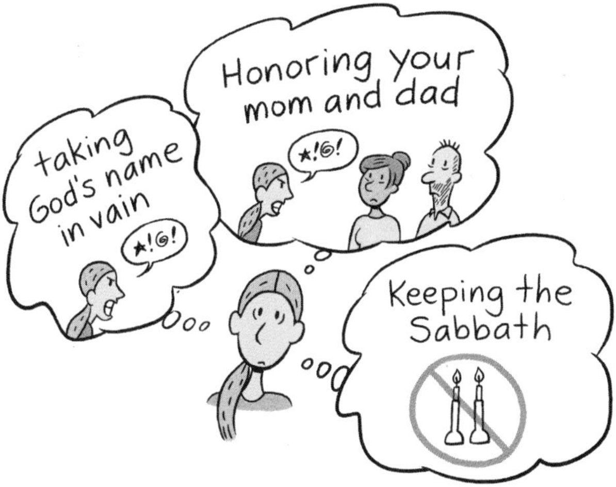
taking God's name in vain
*!@!
Honoring your mom and dad
*!@!
Keeping the Sabbath

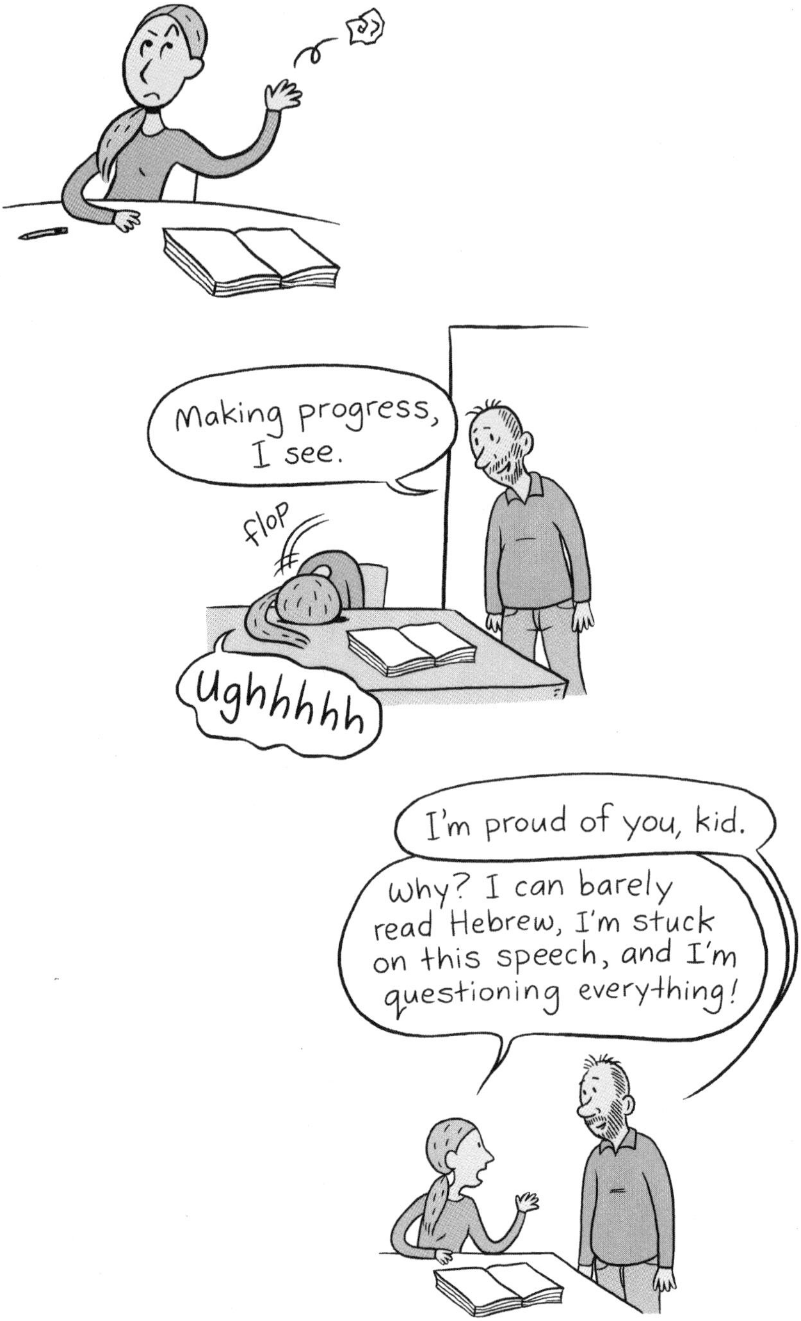
Making progress, I see.
flop
Ughhhhh
I'm proud of you, kid.
Why? I can barely read Hebrew, I'm stuck on this speech, and I'm questioning everything!

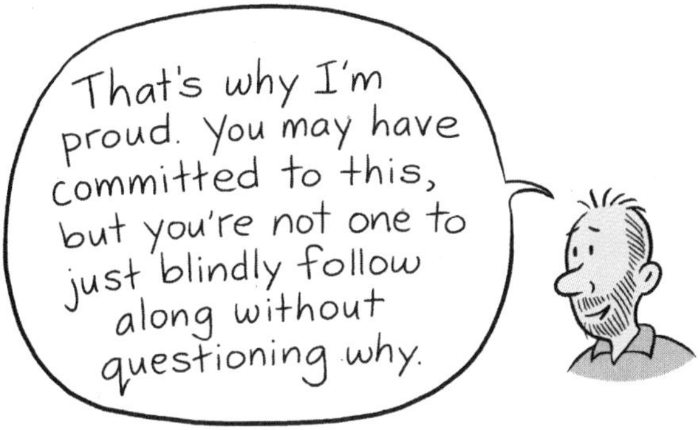
That's why I'm proud. You may have committed to this, but you're not one to just blindly follow along without questioning why.

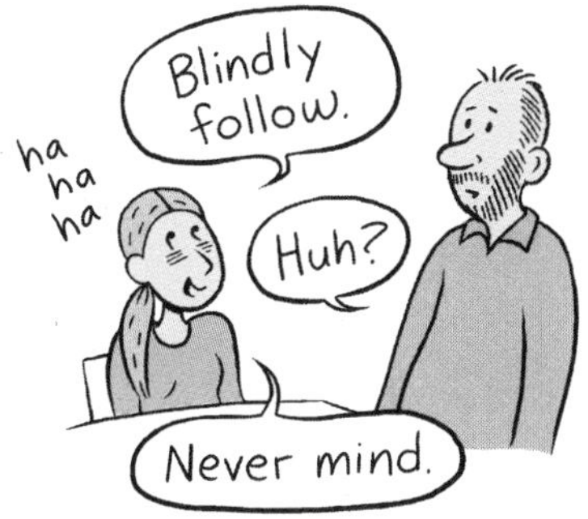
ha
ha
ha
Blindly follow.
Huh?
Never mind.

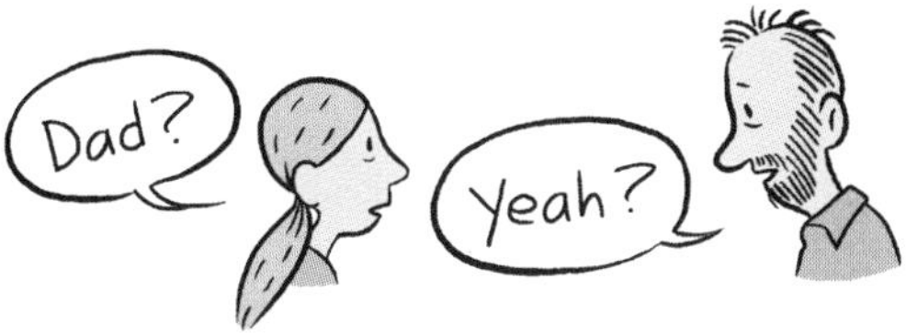
Dad?
Yeah?

I start to ask if he thinks this whole thing is a good idea. But I change my mind. I don't know if I wanna know the answer. It's too late, anyway. I'm committed.

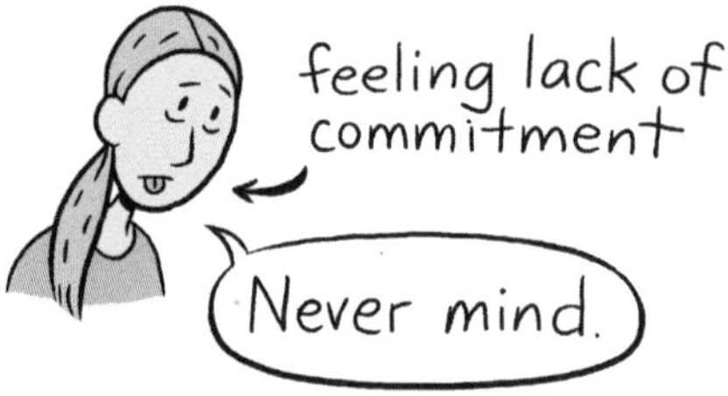
feeling lack of commitment
Never mind.

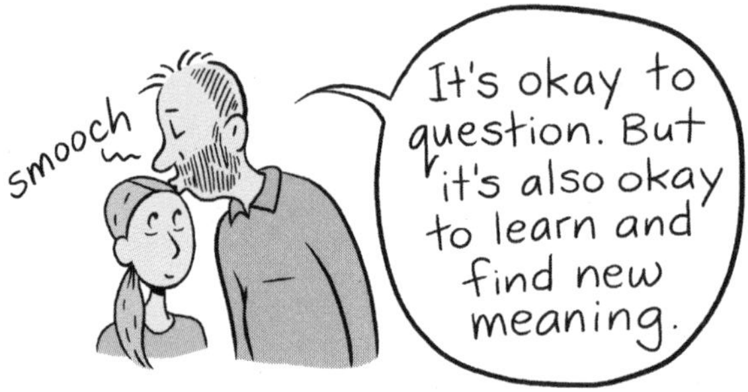
smooch
It's okay to question. But it's also okay to learn and find new meaning.

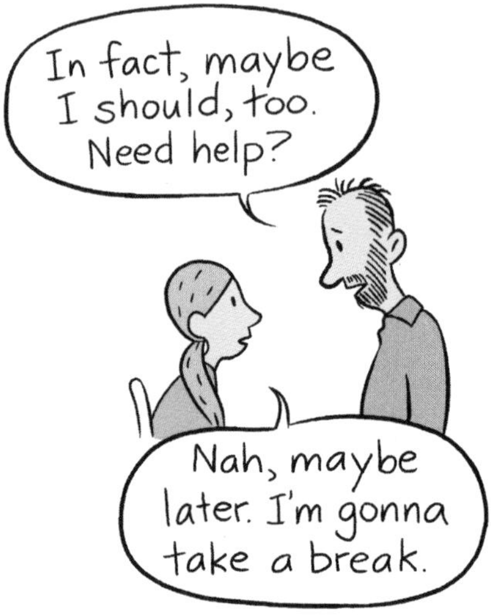
In fact, maybe I should, too. Need help?
Nah, maybe later. I'm gonna take a break.

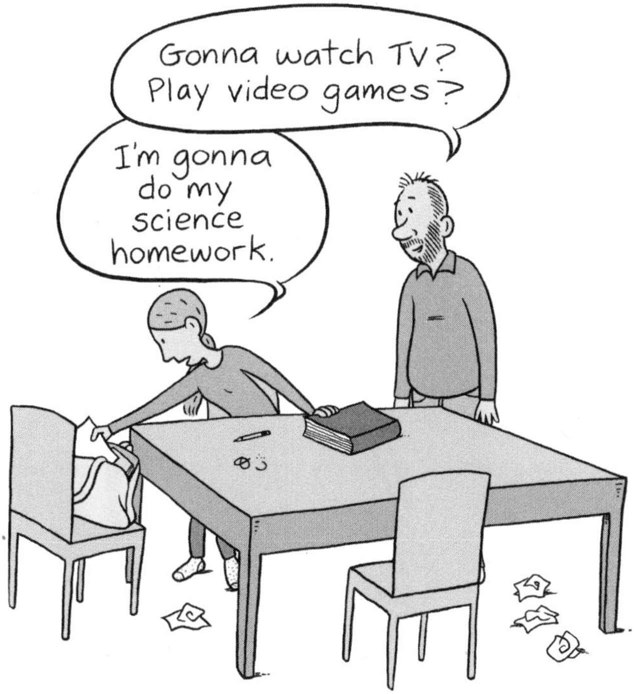
Gonna watch TV? Play video games?
I'm gonna do my science homework.

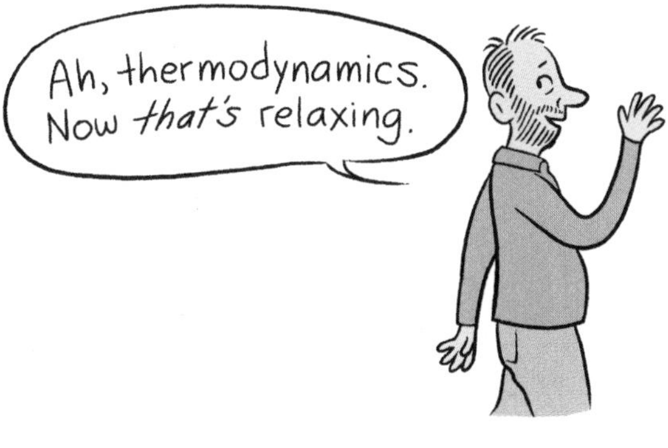
Ah, thermodynamics. Now *that's* relaxing.

NOW

RABBI NOSANCHUK'S WHISTLING SOUNDS FAMILIAR. I RECOGNIZE IT AS A CARDI B SONG. I LAUGH.

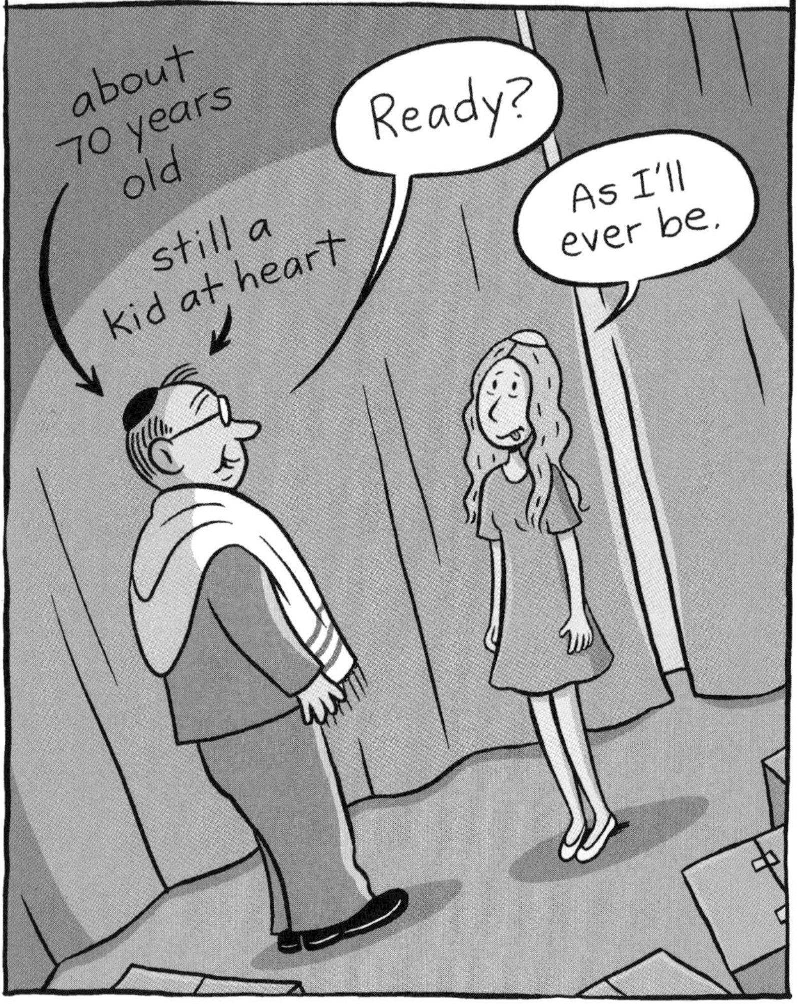
about 70 years old
still a kid at heart
Ready?
As I'll ever be.

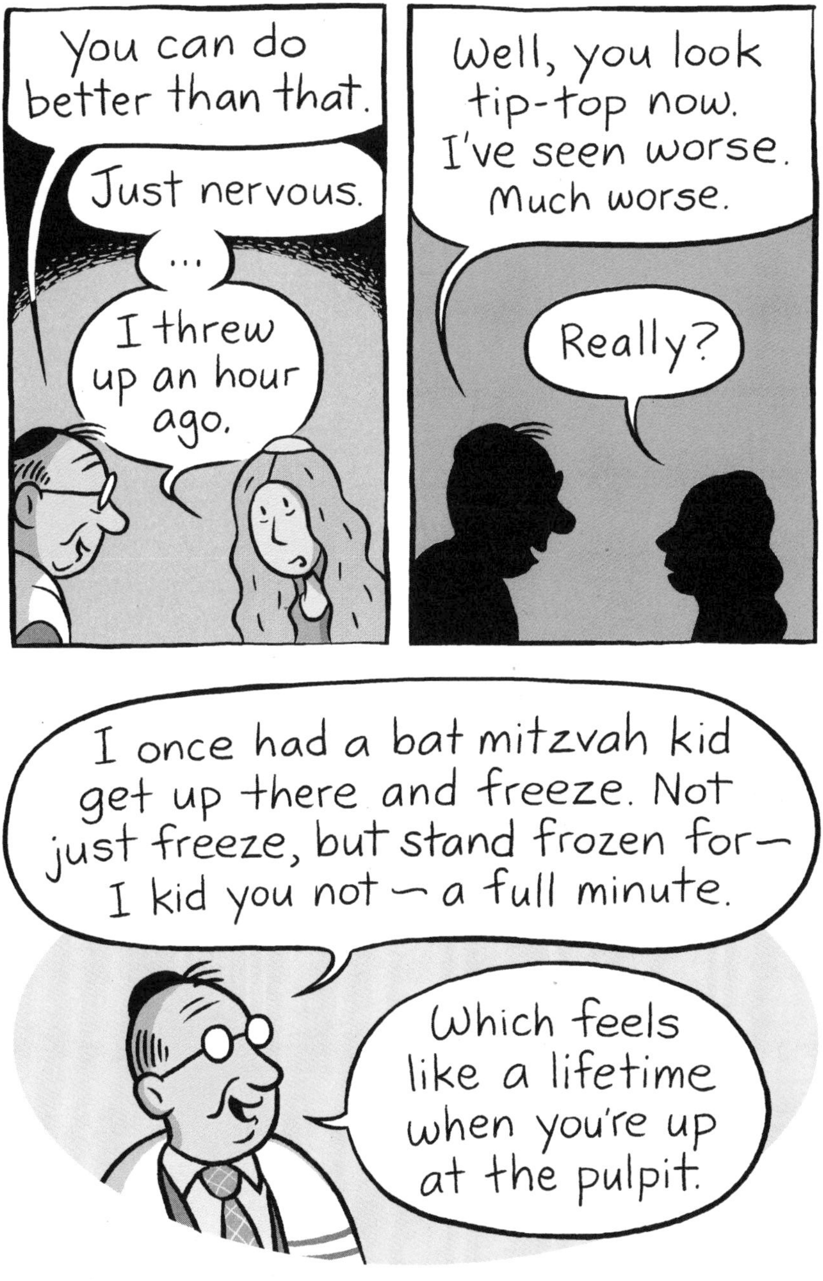
You can do better than that.
Just nervous.
...
I threw up an hour ago.
Well, you look tip-top now. I've seen worse. Much worse.
Really?
I once had a bat mitzvah kid get up there and freeze. Not just freeze, but stand frozen for— I kid you not — a full minute.
Which feels like a lifetime when you're up at the pulpit.

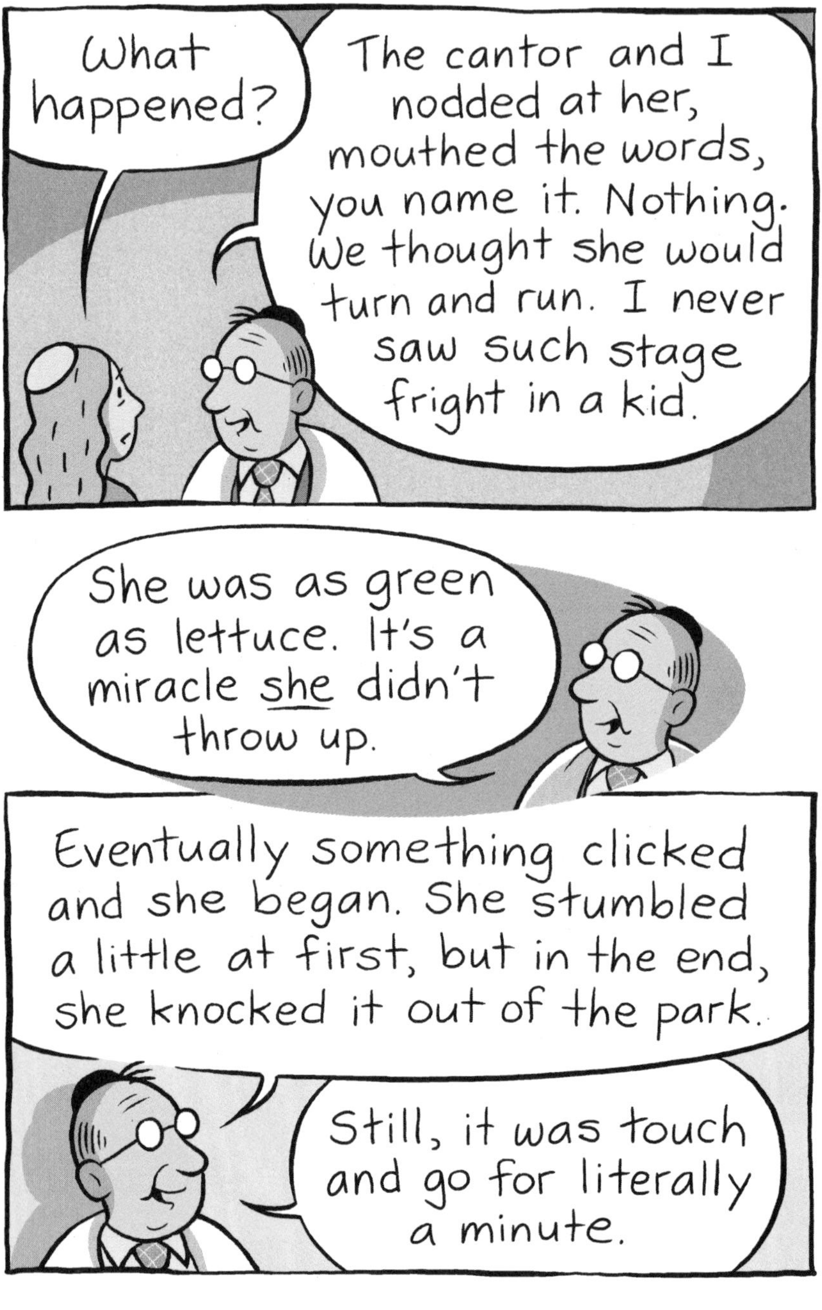
What happened?
The cantor and I nodded at her, mouthed the words, you name it. Nothing. We thought she would turn and run. I never saw such stage fright in a kid.
She was as green as lettuce. It's a miracle she didn't throw up.
Eventually something clicked and she began. She stumbled a little at first, but in the end, she knocked it out of the park.
Still, it was touch and go for literally a minute.

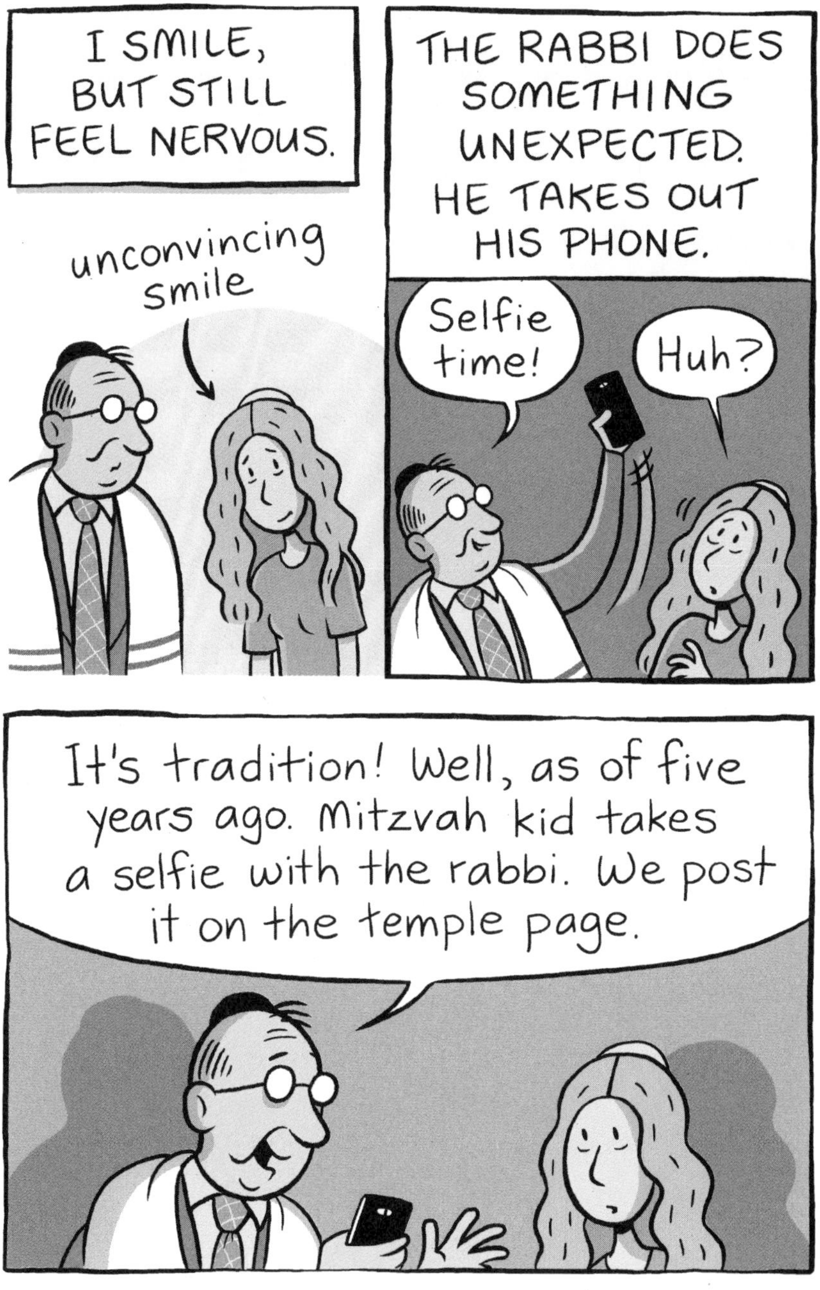
I SMILE, BUT STILL FEEL NERVOUS.
unconvincing smile
THE RABBI DOES SOMETHING UNEXPECTED. HE TAKES OUT HIS PHONE.
Selfie time!
Huh?
It's tradition! Well, as of five years ago. Mitzvah kid takes a selfie with the rabbi. We post it on the temple page.

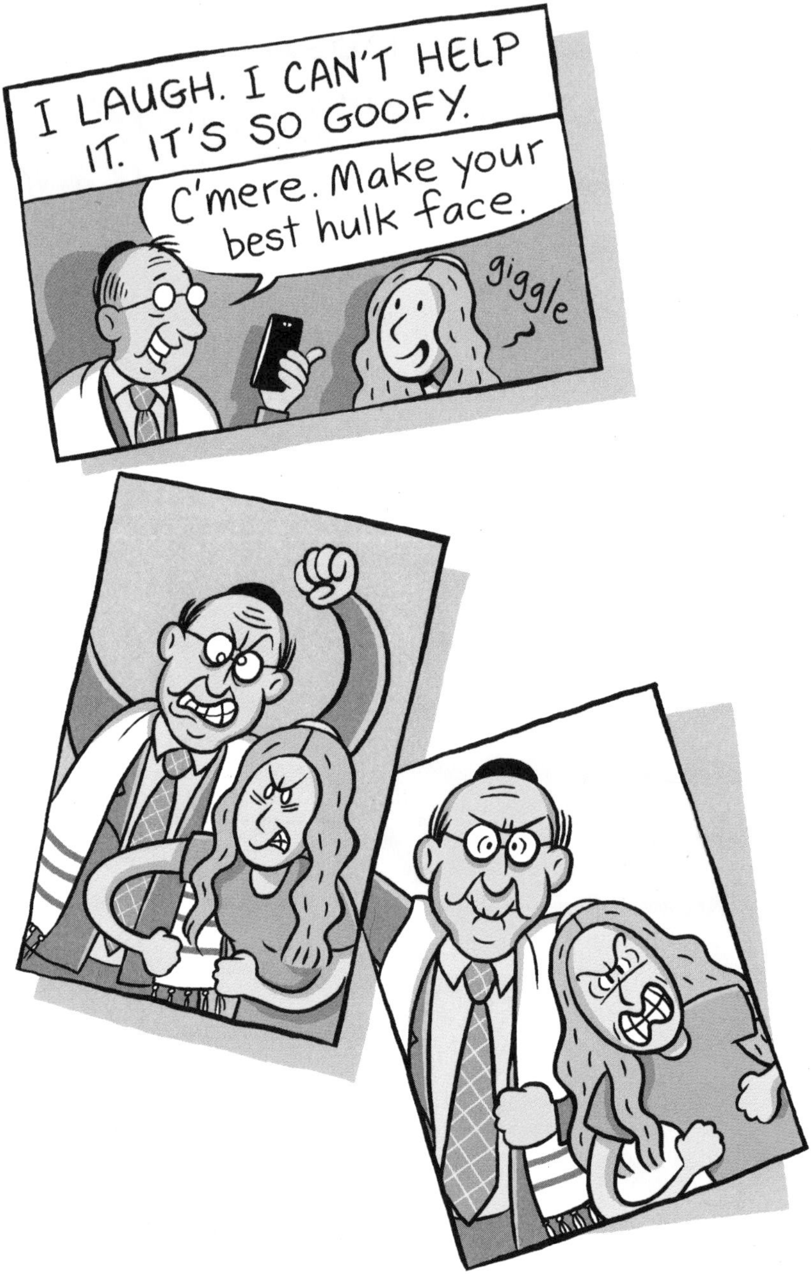
I LAUGH. I CAN'T HELP IT. IT'S SO GOOFY.
C'mere. Make your best hulk face.
giggle

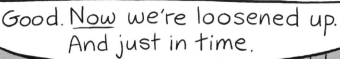
Good. Now we're loosened up. And just in time.

HE LEADS ME BACK TO THE CURTAIN. I CAN HEAR THE CROWD MURMURING.

Showtime, Bina.

THAT'S MY HEBREW NAME. IT MEANS "UNDER-STANDING AND WISDOM"...

...A COUPLE THINGS I COULD USE RIGHT NOW.

ONE MONTH AGO

I'm on my way to lunch. Meeting Dev. I've been sitting with him and a few other kids from Science Club.

It's finally May. And unusually hot. **And** there's no air-conditioning.

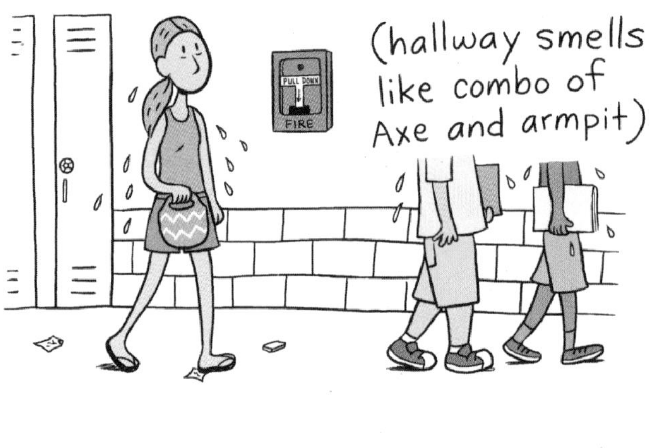
(hallway smells like combo of Axe and armpit)
PULL DOWN
FIRE

I see Zoe and Olivia walking from the opposite end of the hall, and I wave. For a split second, it looks like they saw me and pretended they didn't, but then they wave and smile, all friendly.

I think they're going to stop and talk, but they keep going. Guess they're in a hurry. Seems like that's been happening a lot lately.

At the same time, Zoe's still sending me plenty of SnapGab messages.

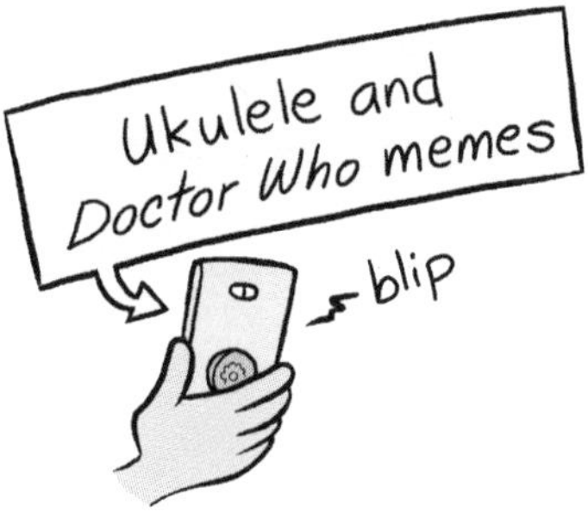
Ukulele and Doctor Who memes
blip

It's so confusing.

I invited her and Olivia to the bat mitzvah. When Zoe got the invite, she texted me this.

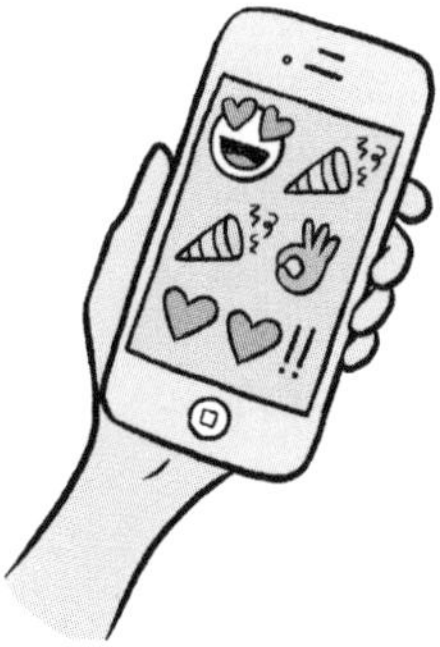
!!

At first, it made me happy that she was so excited. She kept asking me questions.

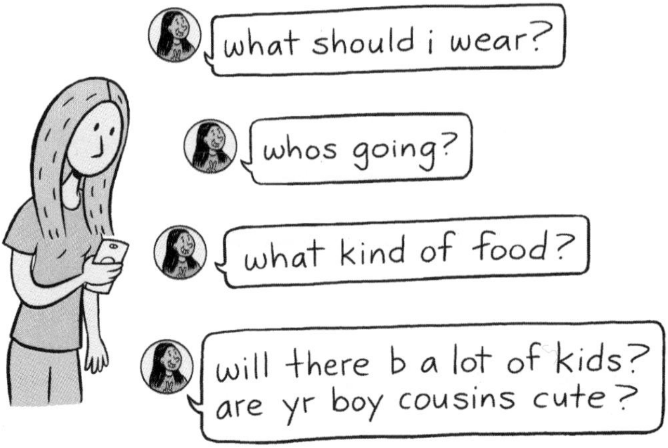
what should i wear?
whos going?
what kind of food?
will there b a lot of kids?
are yr boy cousins cute?

She only asked me about the party and the people, not about the ceremony, which was a little weird. But then, that's Zoe. She likes excitement.

I couldn't tell her much 'cause my mom is still keeping everything a secret.

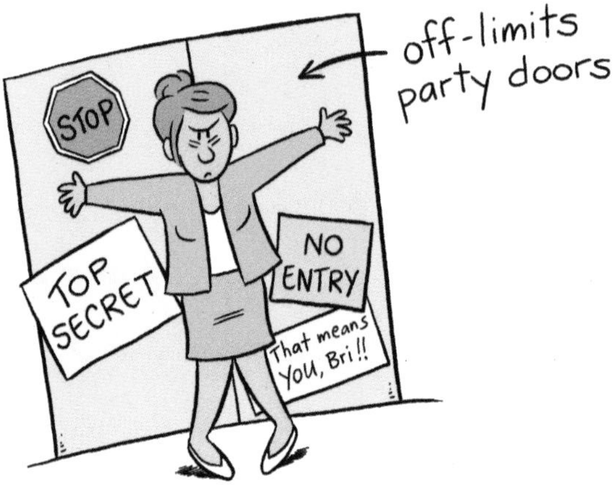
off-limits
party doors
STOP
TOP SECRET
NO ENTRY
That means YOU, Bri!!

Emmie was right about one thing, though. There are still rumors flying around about my "blowout event." I think the last one I heard from Dev was that Shawn Mendes is going to make a surprise appearance by zip-lining into the party room.

As soon as I walk into the cafeteria, I see Emmie and Sarah sitting in our (old) usual spot.

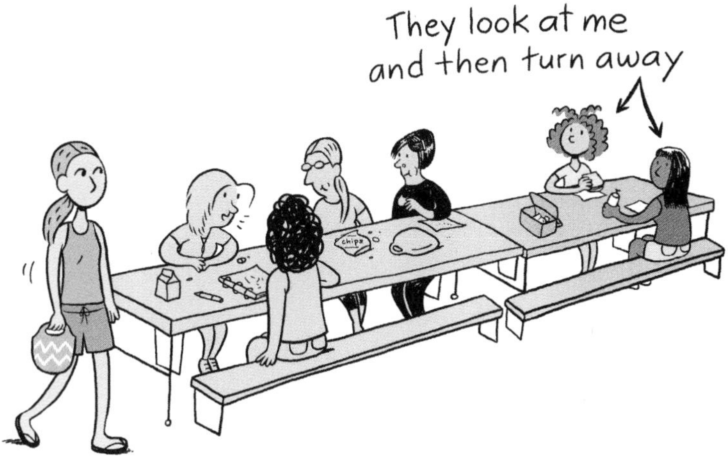
They look at me
and then turn away
chips

It's now been a month. Sarah tried to get us to talk once, but by then Emmie and I were both so mad at each other, it felt too late.

It hits me. Finally. Is it **really** over?

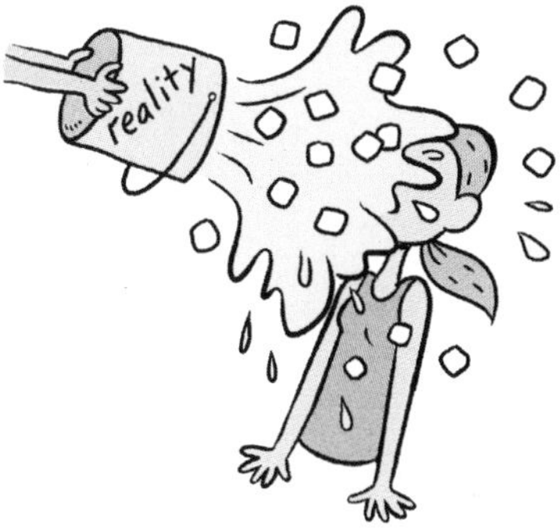
reality

Honestly, I don't even know if I'm mad anymore. I don't know **anything**.

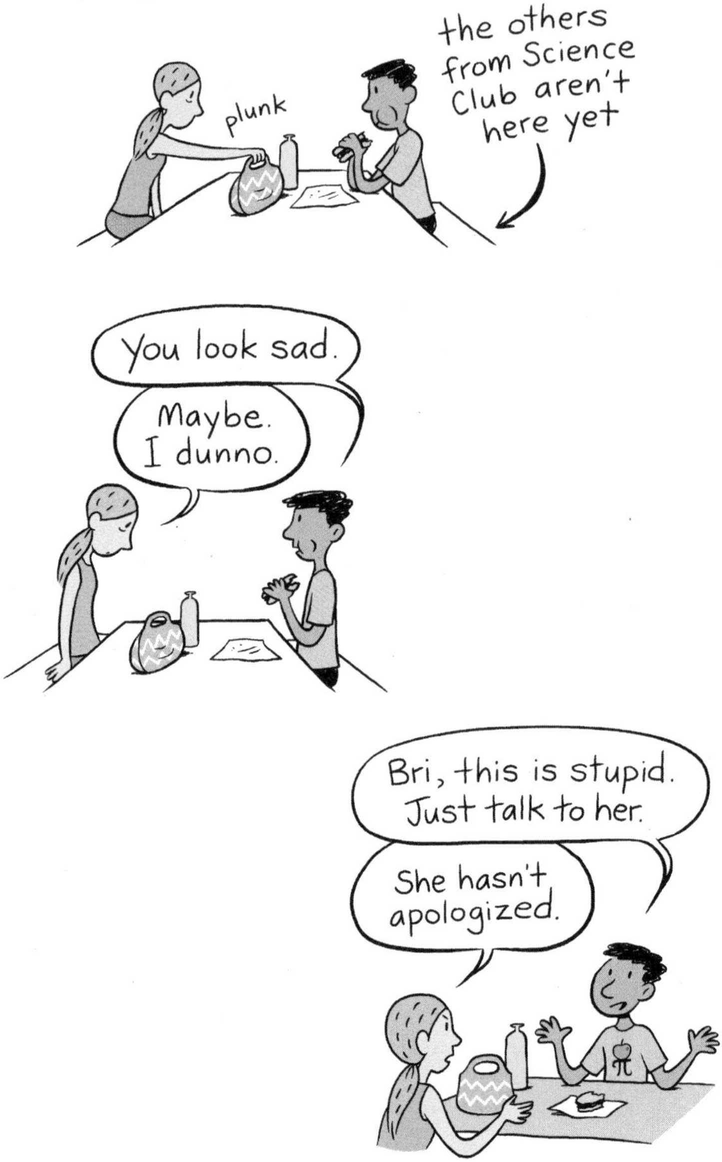
plunk
the others from Science Club aren't here yet
You look sad.
Maybe. I dunno.
Bri, this is stupid. Just talk to her.
She hasn't apologized.

Soon, we see Zoe and Olivia sit at their usual table. To my surprise, Zoe waves me over. Usually, they like to eat quickly and then head to the yearbook room. They're both on the committee. They also hate the cafeteria.

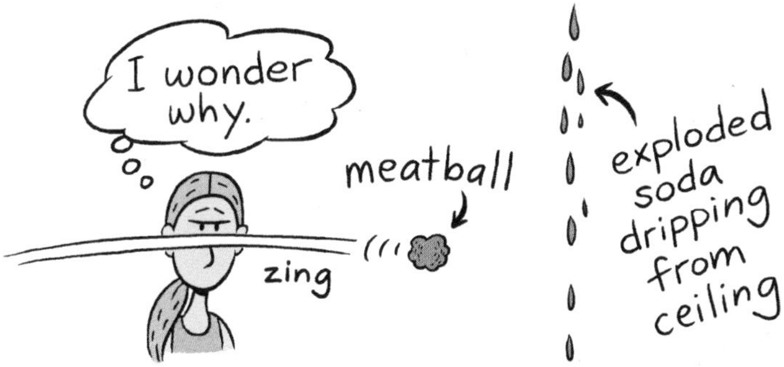

I wonder why.
meatball
zing
exploded soda dripping from ceiling

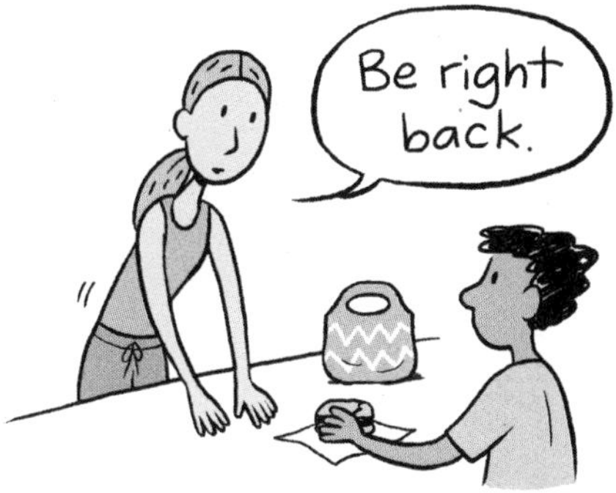

Be right back.

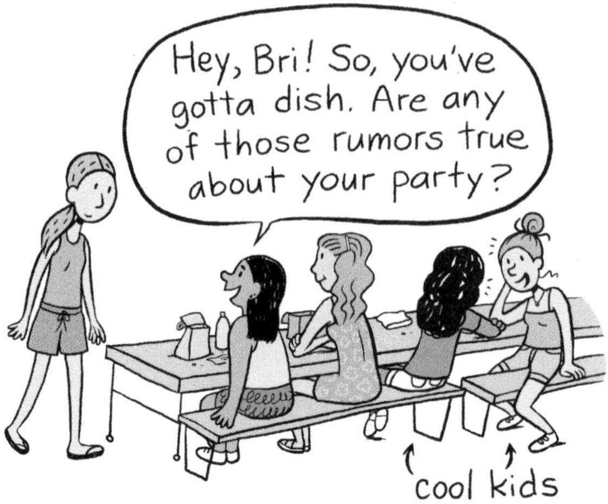
Hey, Bri! So, you've gotta dish. Are any of those rumors true about your party?
cool kids

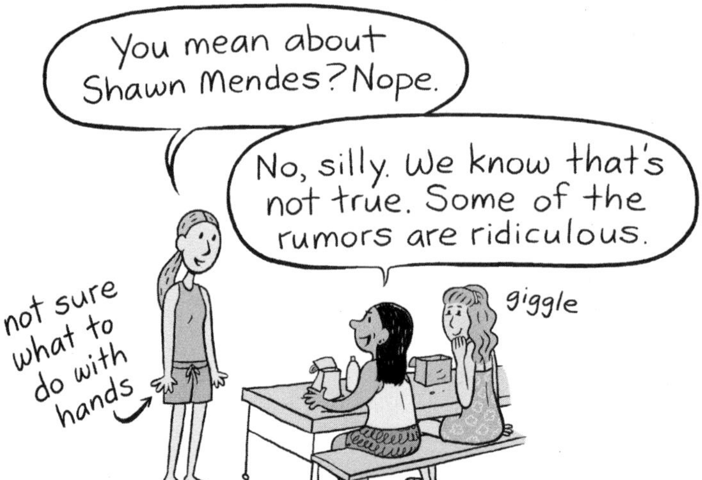
You mean about Shawn Mendes? Nope.
No, silly. We know that's not true. Some of the rumors are ridiculous.
giggle
not sure what to do with hands

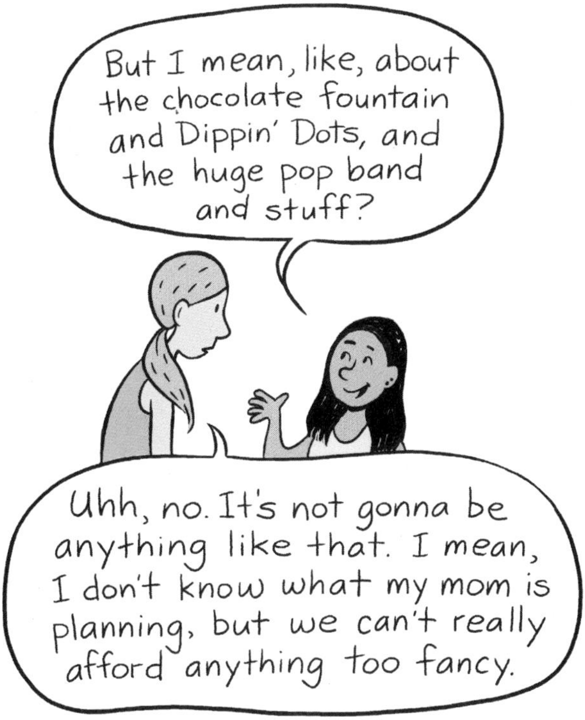
But I mean, like, about the chocolate fountain and Dippin' Dots, and the huge pop band and stuff?
Uhh, no. It's not gonna be anything like that. I mean, I don't know what my mom is planning, but we can't really afford anything too fancy.

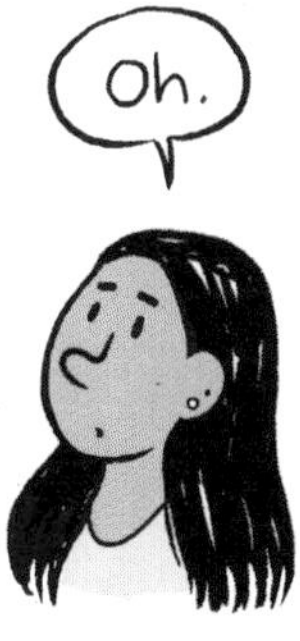
Oh.

There is literally dead silence.

Olivia finally clears her throat, and Zoe snaps back to life from her zombie state.

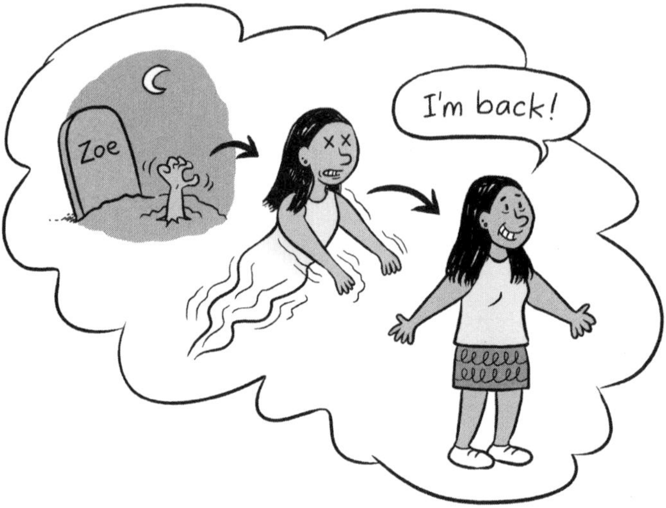
Zoe
I'm back!

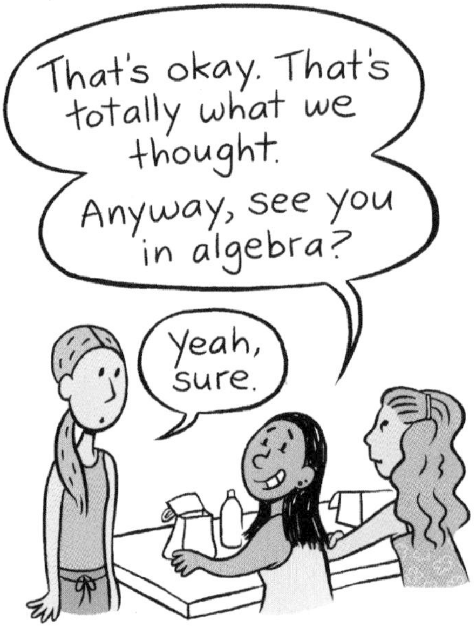
That's okay. That's totally what we thought.
Anyway, see you in algebra?
Yeah, sure.

Guess I've been dismissed. I sit back down across from Dev.

For a minute, I thought you were ditching me.

Nope. It kinda feels like I've been ditched, though.

What do you mean?

I dunno. They're nice to me, and we still do stuff. But our friendship seems kinda... off.

It's like they wanna be friends but also... don't.

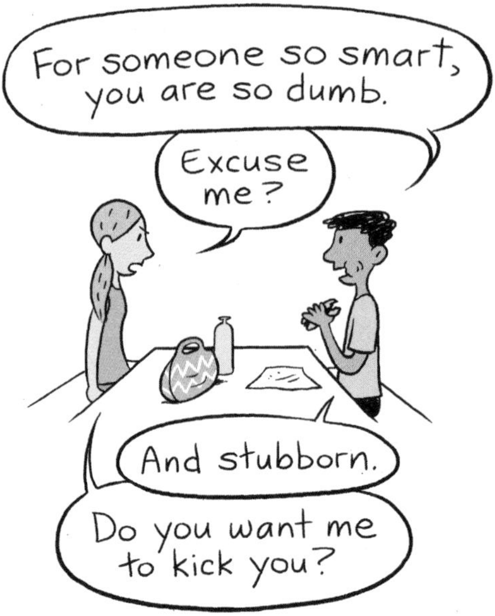
For someone so smart, you are so dumb.
Excuse me?
And stubborn.
Do you want me to kick you?

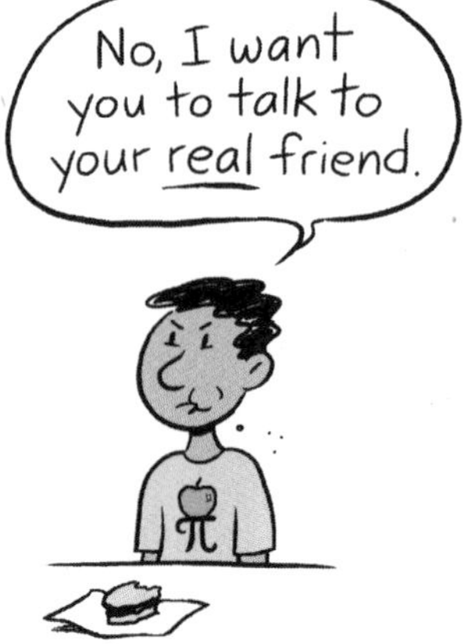
No, I want you to talk to your real friend.

I've never seen Dev look like this. Angry and serious at once. The same look he had when we were performing a drama scene in the talent show.

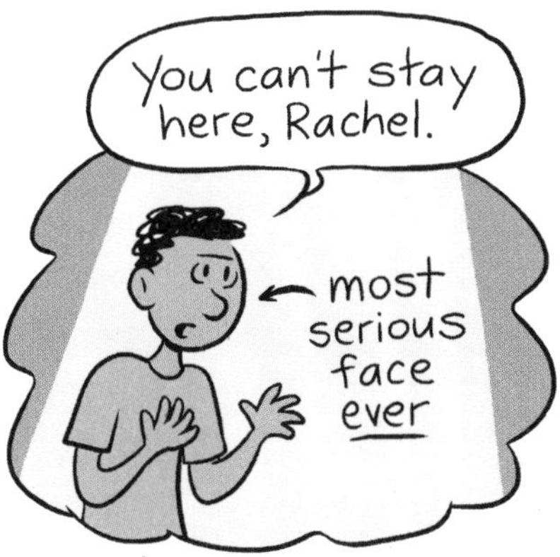
You can't stay here, Rachel.
most serious face ever

He means business.

I watch Zoe and Olivia get up. I catch their eye and wave bye. They wave back, but this time not so enthusiastically.

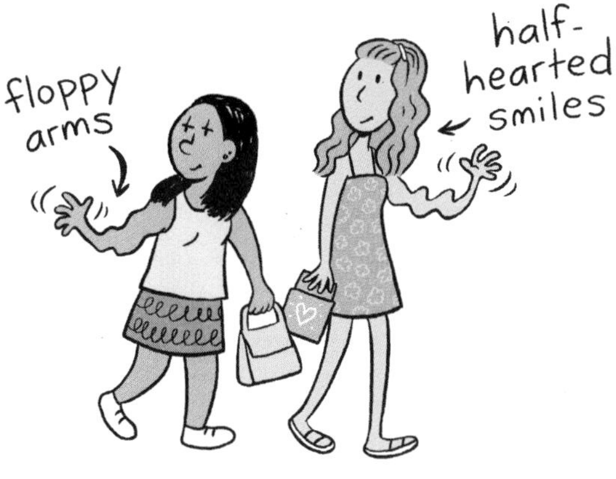
floppy arms
half-hearted smiles

My sponge brain finally kicks in, and it's like a spotlight shines on my memories.

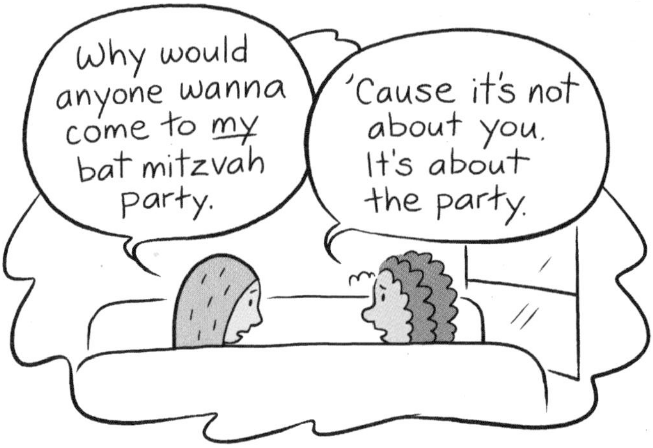
Why would anyone wanna come to my bat mitzvah party.
'Cause it's not about you. It's about the party.

And:

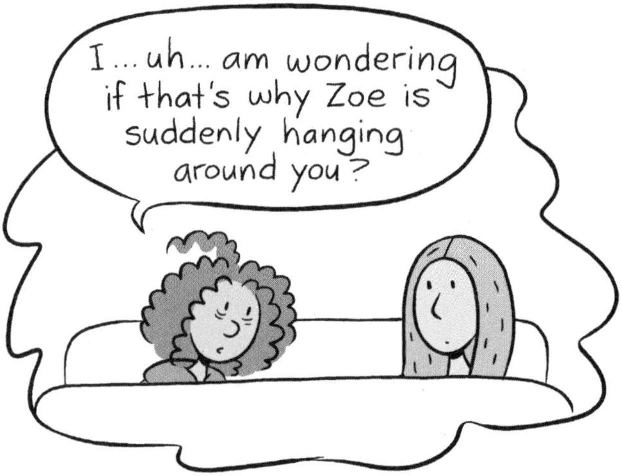
I... uh... am wondering if that's why Zoe is suddenly hanging around you?

And:

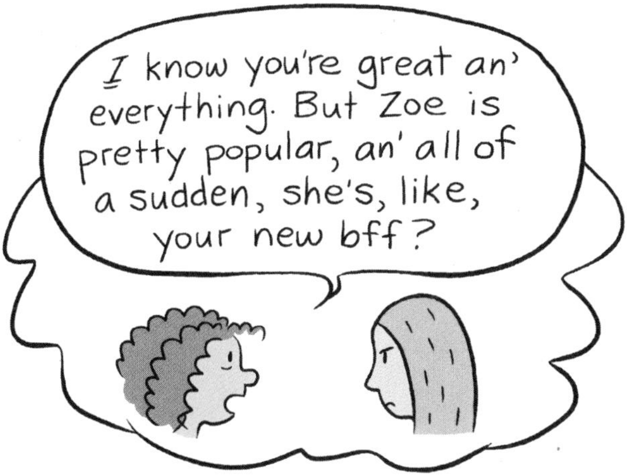
I know you're great an' everything. But Zoe is pretty popular, an' all of a sudden, she's, like, your new bff?

Over the last couple months, kids I barely know have come up to me and asked how they could get an invitation to my bat mitzvah. They must've bought into all those crazy rumors. Their intentions were so obvious, and at the time I couldn't believe their (here's where Gram's Yiddish comes in) chutzpah.

But the key word here is "obvious."

Now I think about Zoe looking bored during those **Doctor Who** marathons, texting her friends while we hung out, and seeming like she'd rather be in detention with Joe Lungo than doing stuff with me.

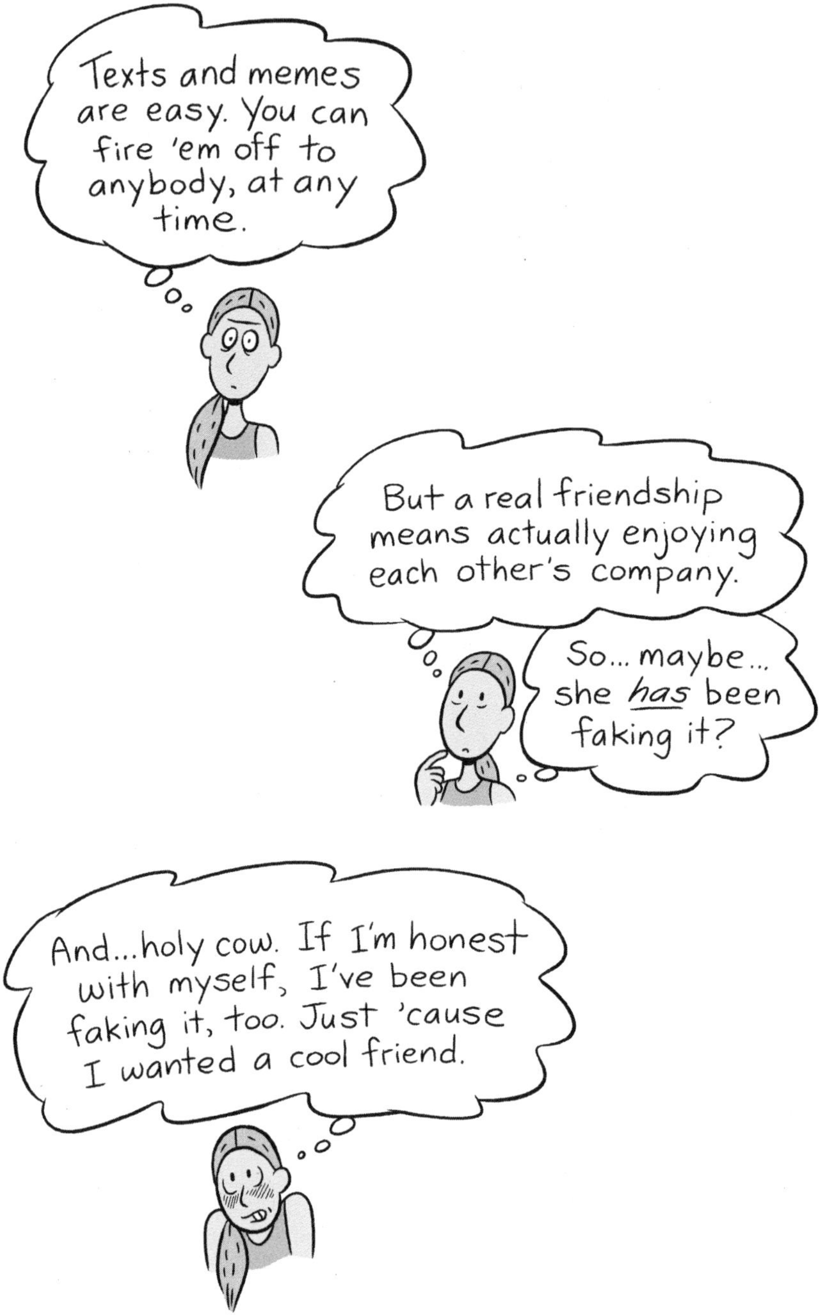
Texts and memes are easy. You can fire 'em off to anybody, at any time.
But a real friendship means actually enjoying each other's company.
So... maybe... she *has* been faking it?
And...holy cow. If I'm honest with myself, I've been faking it, too. Just 'cause I wanted a cool friend.

I'm silent as this all sinks in.

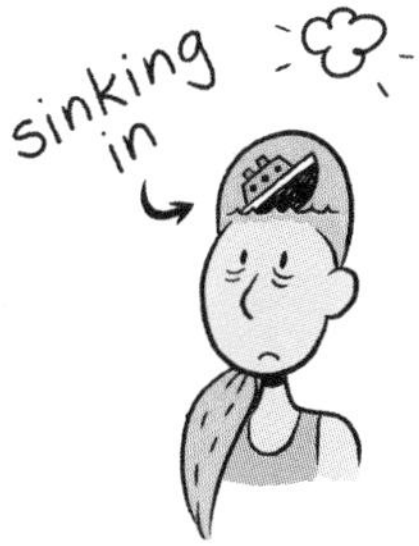
sinking in

Weirdly, I don't feel so sad. I just feel dumb, like Dev said. And also ashamed. I should have seen it sooner.

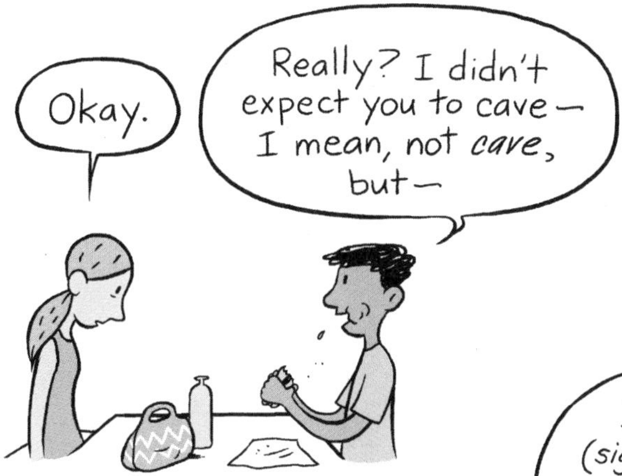
Okay.
Really? I didn't expect you to cave— I mean, not *cave*, but—

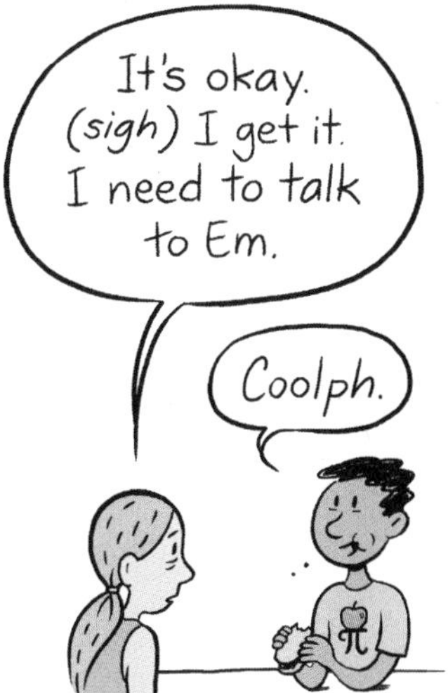
It's okay. (*sigh*) I get it. I need to talk to Em.
Coolph.

I see Emmie and Sarah finish their lunches and leave.

I ignore my packed lunch of—you guessed it—cold pizza and wave bye to Dev. I hurry out just as the science kids come in. Probably for the best—I'm in no mood to talk about rock formations today.

I hurry and catch up to Emmie before I change my mind.

And stop. And hesitate. This could be harder than I thought.

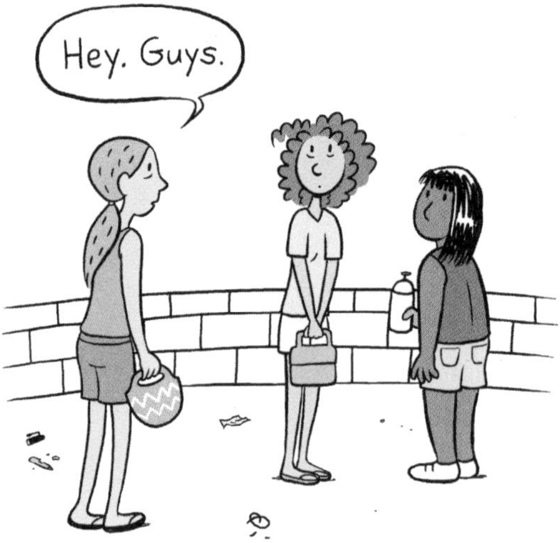
Hey. Guys.

I look at Emmie, a little shyly.

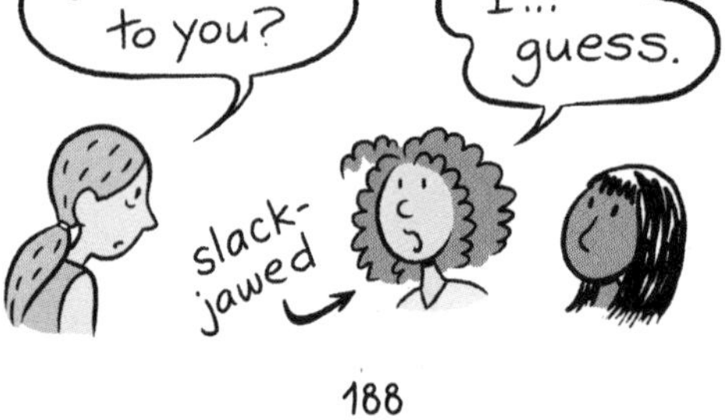
Can I talk to you?
I... guess.
slack-jawed

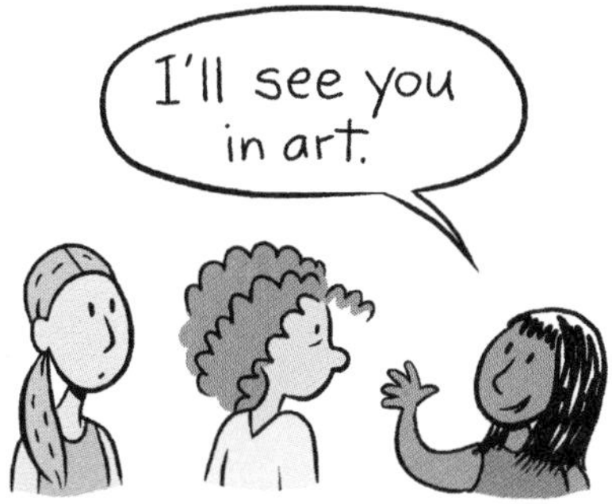
I'll see you in art.

I notice we're right near our once-usual little hideaway meeting place.

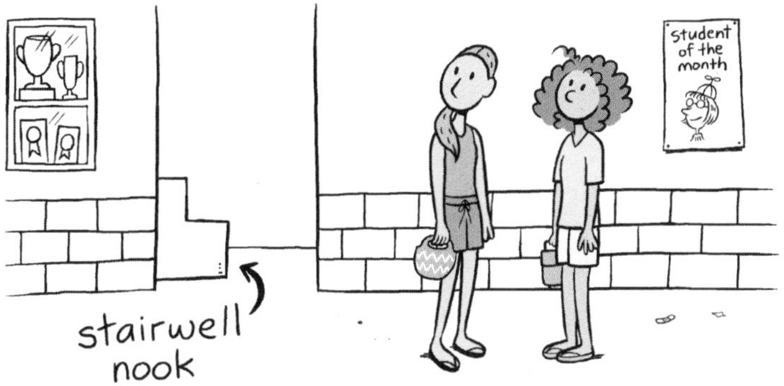
student of the month
stairwell nook

Like a reflex, we both sit on the steps at once. We watch everyone hurrying back and forth to the cafeteria.

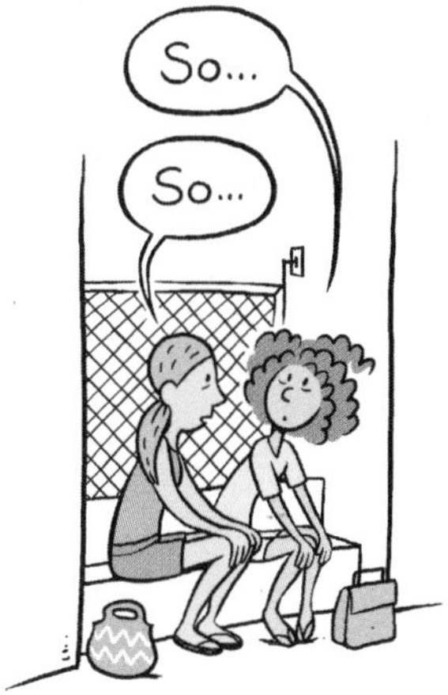
So...
So...

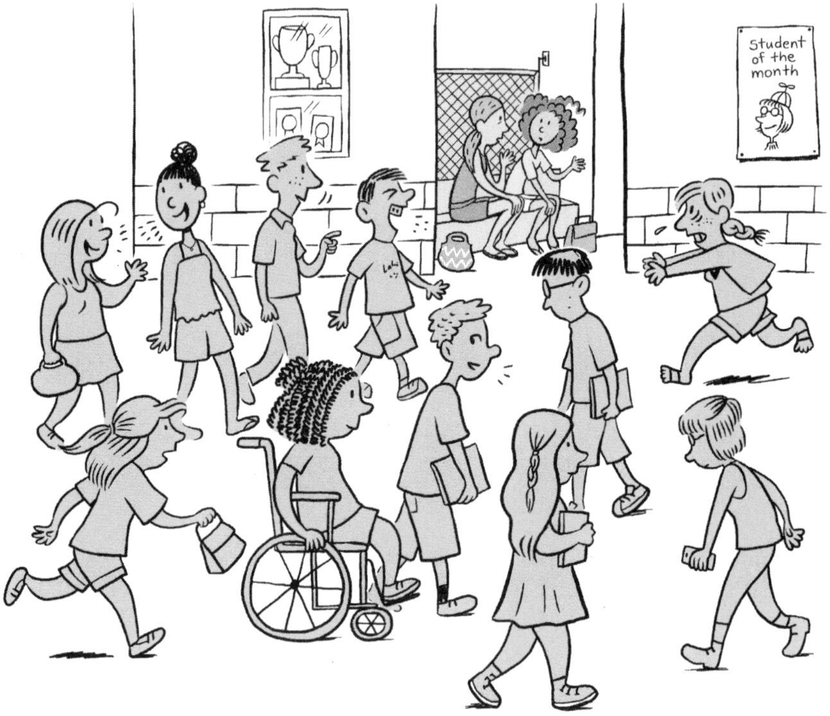
Student of the month

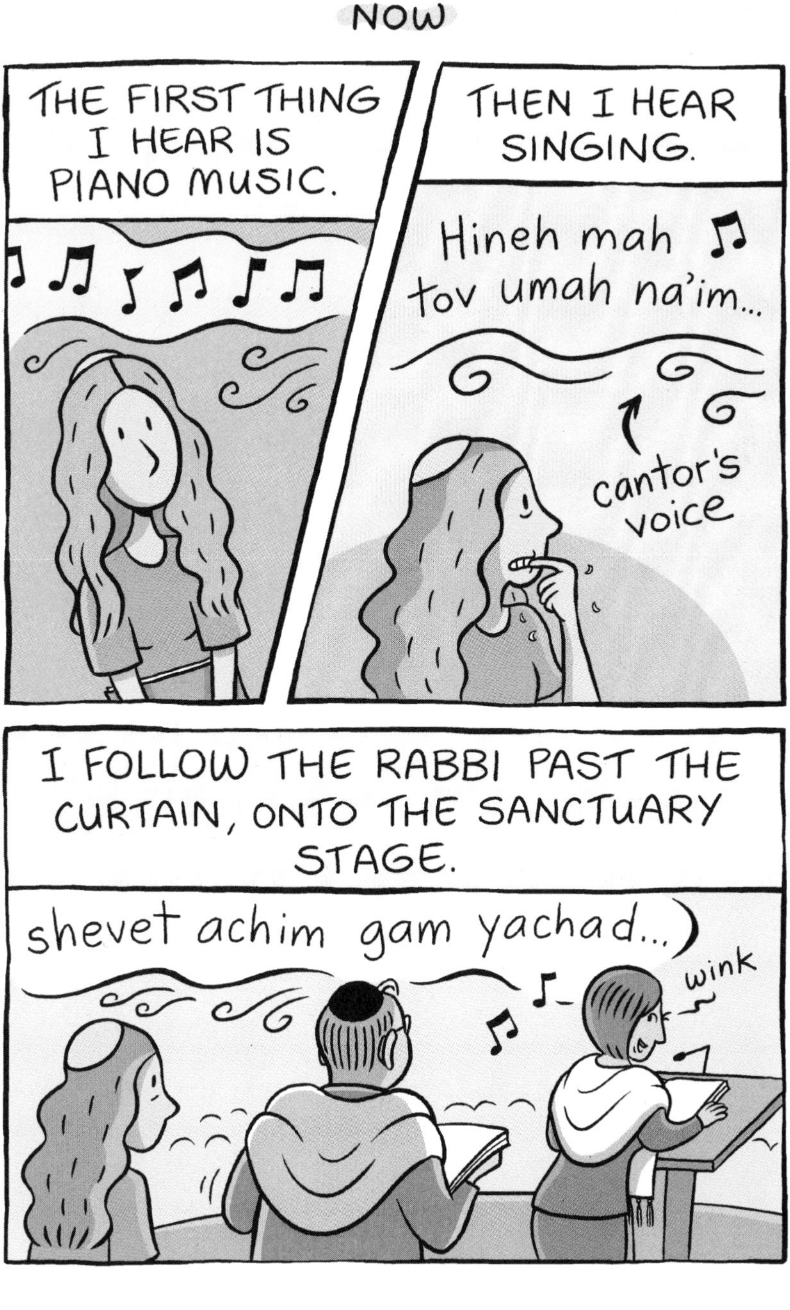
NOW
THE FIRST THING I HEAR IS PIANO MUSIC.
THEN I HEAR SINGING.
Hineh mah tov umah na'im...
cantor's voice
I FOLLOW THE RABBI PAST THE CURTAIN, ONTO THE SANCTUARY STAGE.
shevet achim gam yachad...
wink

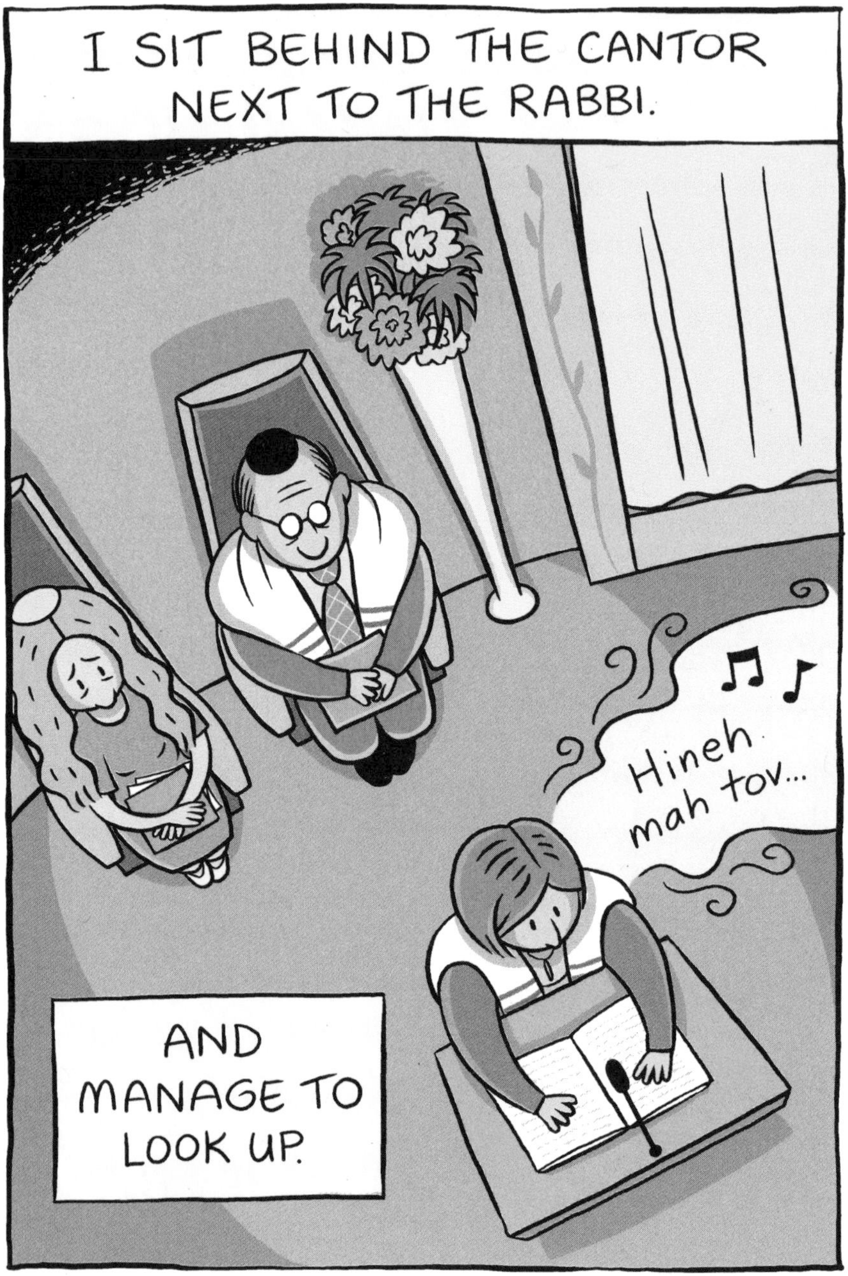
I SIT BEHIND THE CANTOR NEXT TO THE RABBI.
Hineh mah tov...
AND MANAGE TO LOOK UP.

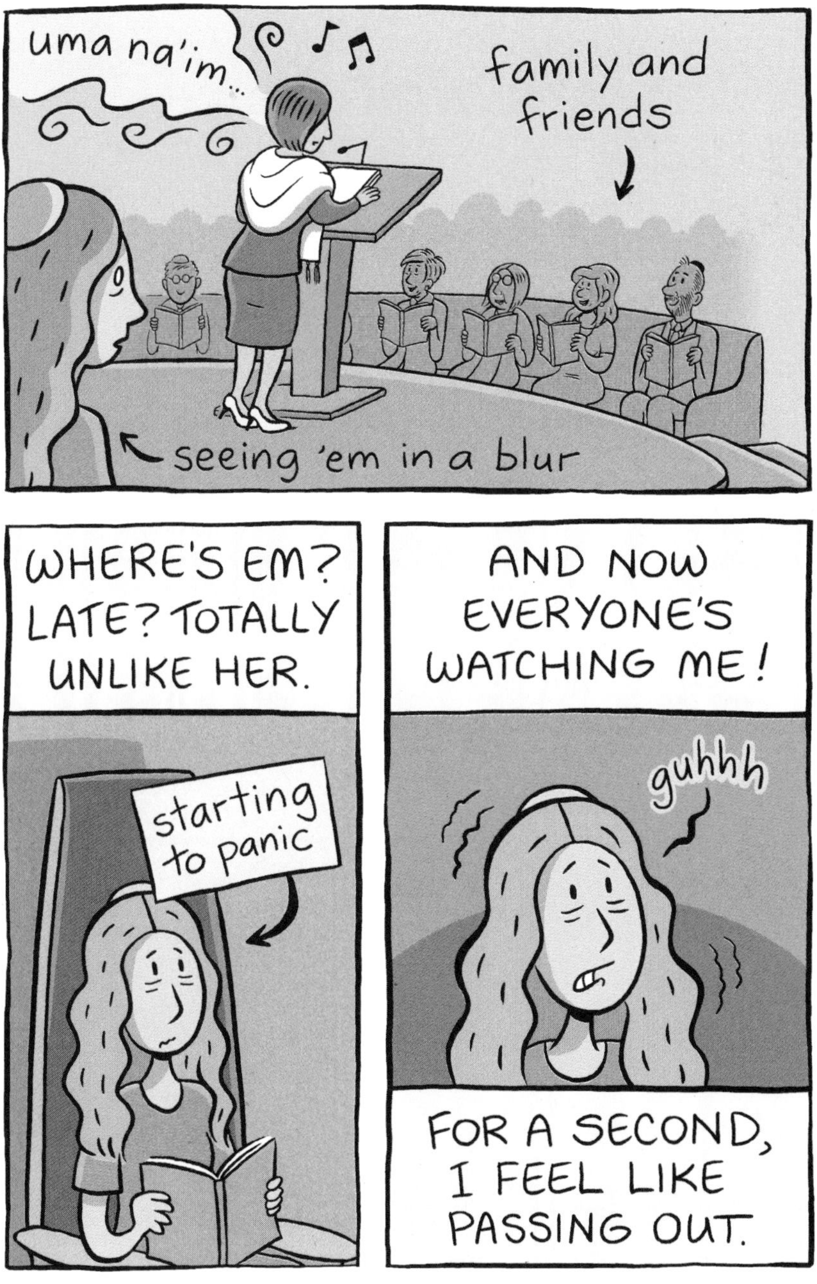
uma na'im...
family and friends
seeing 'em in a blur
WHERE'S EM? LATE? TOTALLY UNLIKE HER.
starting to panic
AND NOW EVERYONE'S WATCHING ME!
guhhh
FOR A SECOND, I FEEL LIKE PASSING OUT.

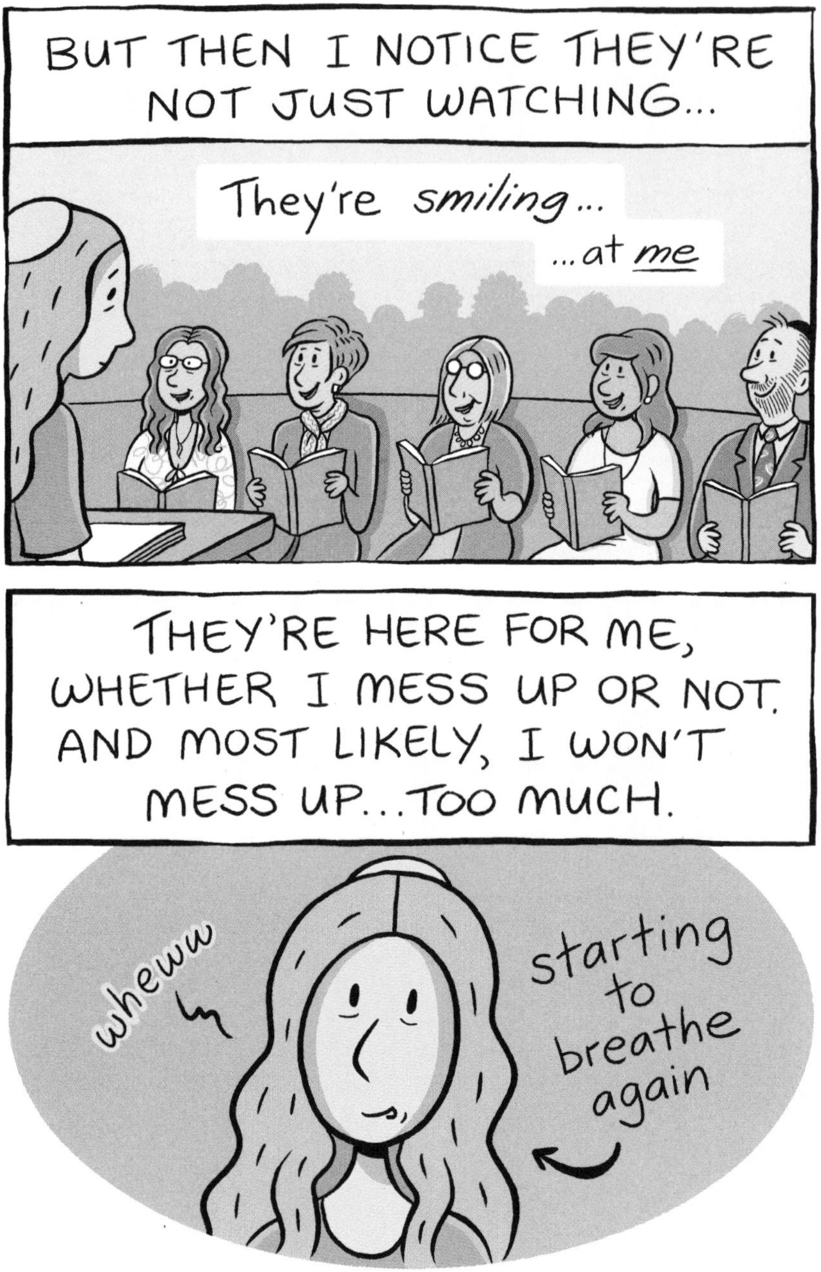
BUT THEN I NOTICE THEY'RE NOT JUST WATCHING...
They're *smiling*...
...at <u>me</u>
THEY'RE HERE FOR ME, WHETHER I MESS UP OR NOT. AND MOST LIKELY, I WON'T MESS UP...TOO MUCH.
wheww
starting to breathe again

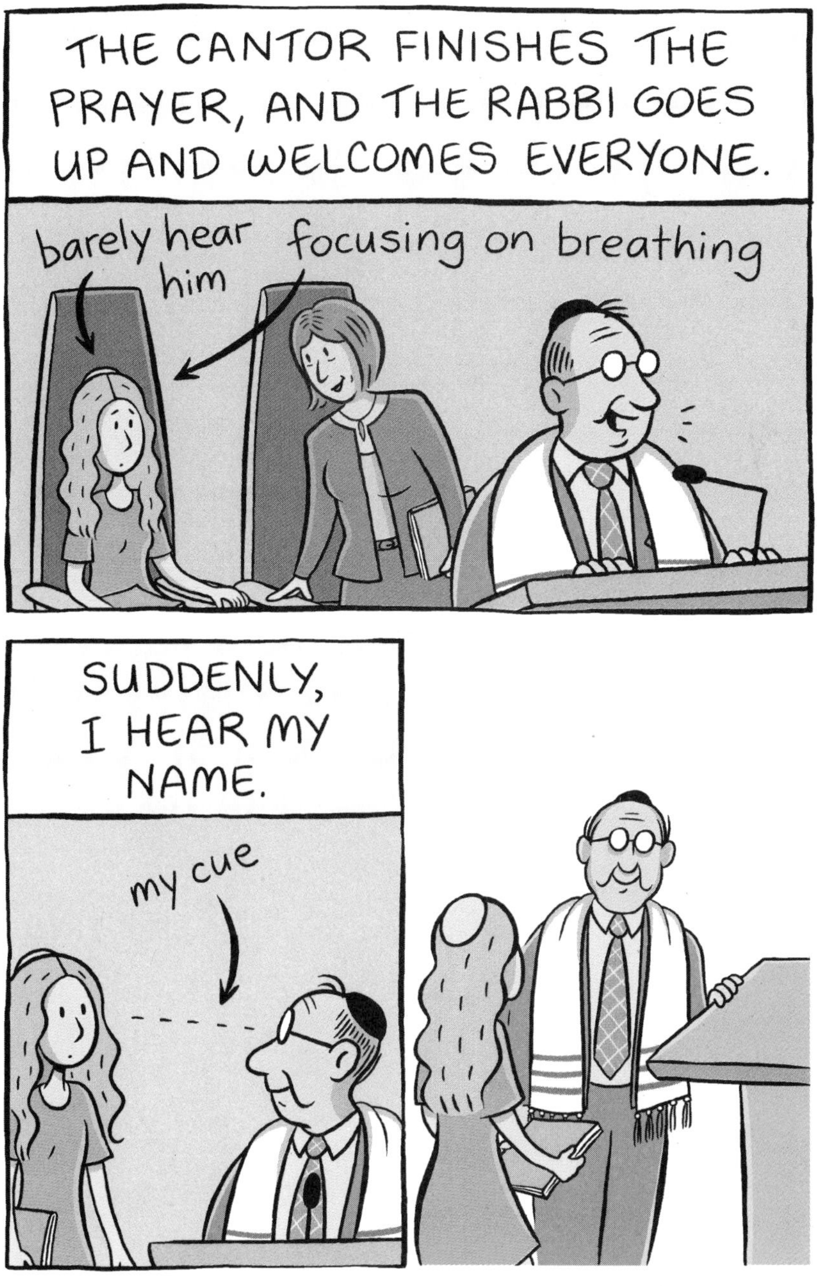
THE CANTOR FINISHES THE PRAYER, AND THE RABBI GOES UP AND WELCOMES EVERYONE.
barely hear him
focusing on breathing
SUDDENLY, I HEAR MY NAME.
my cue

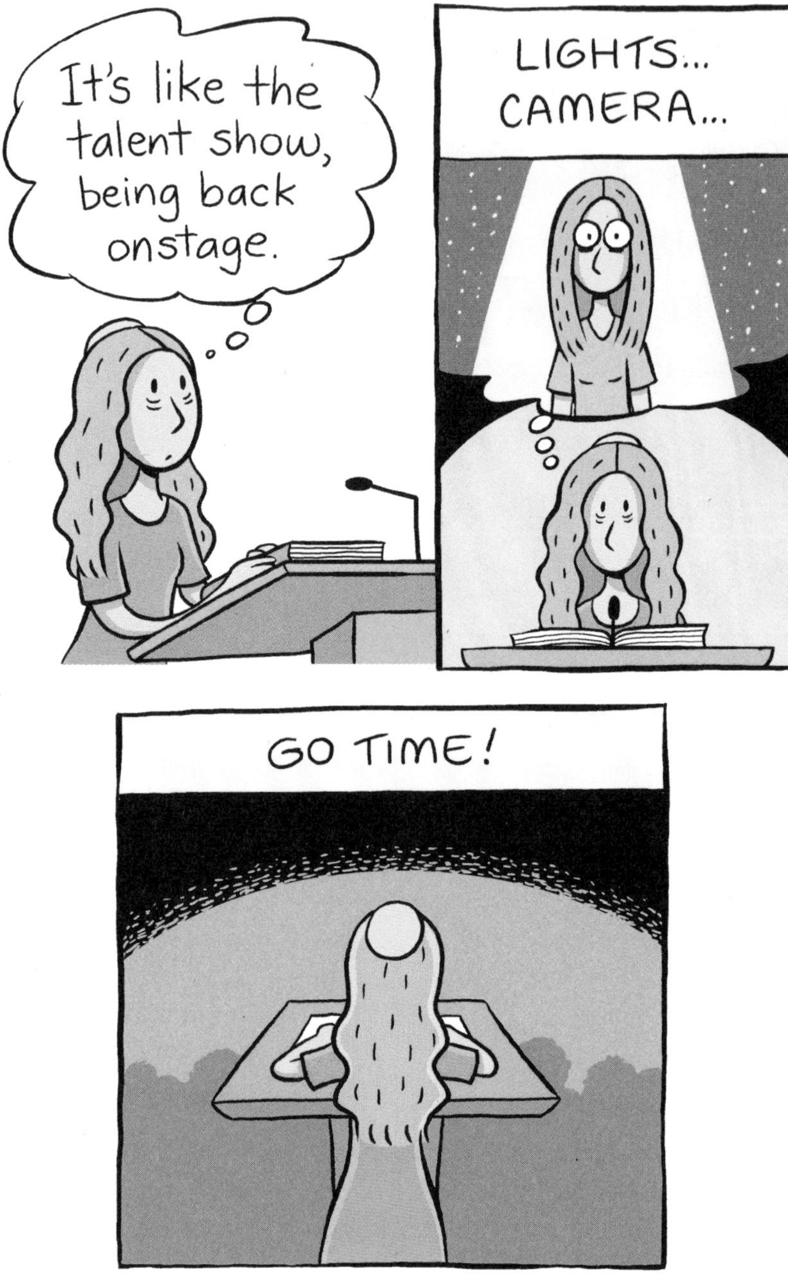
It's like the talent show, being back onstage.
LIGHTS... CAMERA...
GO TIME!

THREE WEEKS AGO

At Mom's this week. She's running errands. I'm taking advantage of the quiet evening and doing my Spanish homework.

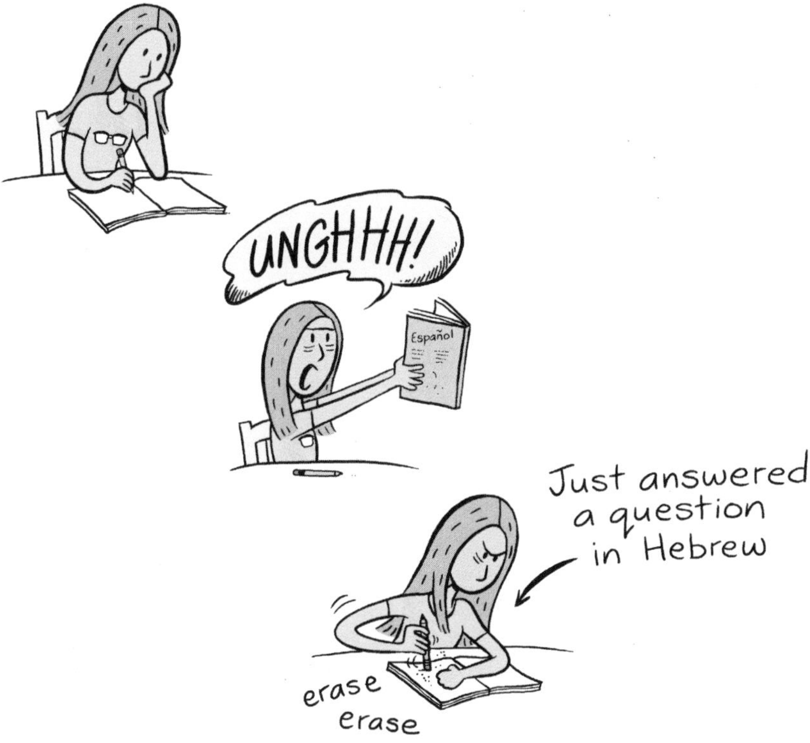
UNGHHH!
Español
Just answered a question in Hebrew
erase
erase

Mom walks in, out of breath. She's holding a million bags.

Okay, I just picked up items for the out-of-towners' welcome bags. We can assemble these later.

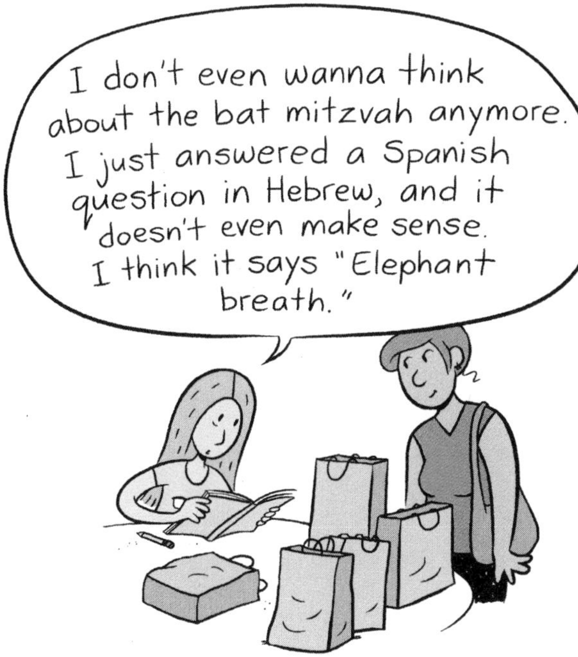
I don't even wanna think about the bat mitzvah anymore. I just answered a Spanish question in Hebrew, and it doesn't even make sense. I think it says "Elephant breath."

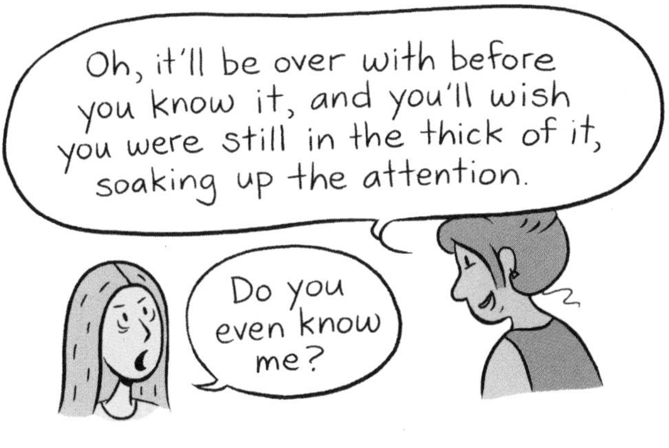
Oh, it'll be over with before you know it, and you'll wish you were still in the thick of it, soaking up the attention.
Do you even know me?

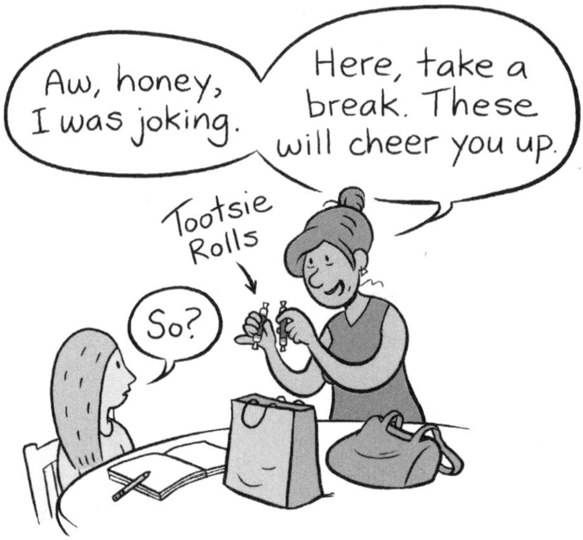
Aw, honey, I was joking.
Here, take a break. These will cheer you up.
Tootsie Rolls
So?

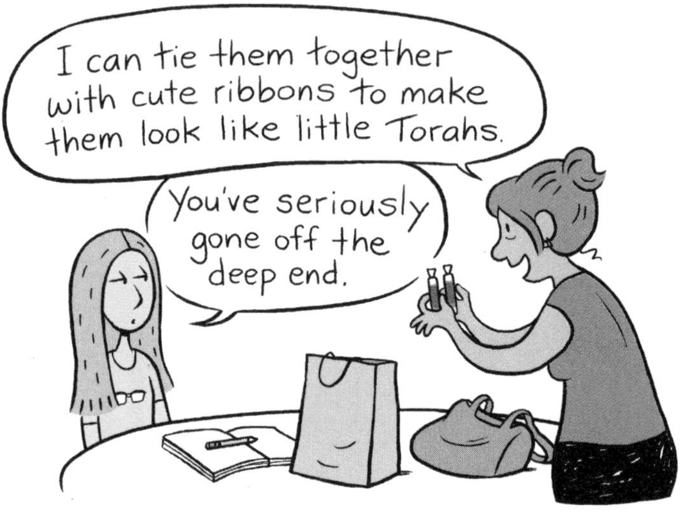
I can tie them together with cute ribbons to make them look like little Torahs.
You've seriously gone off the deep end.

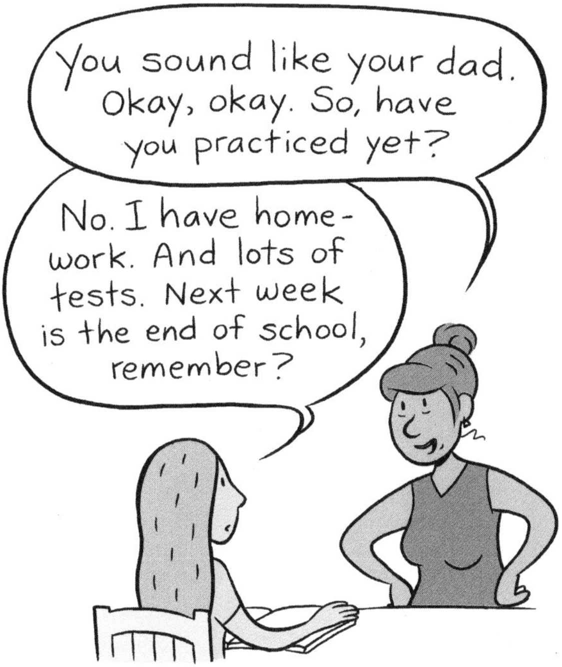
You sound like your dad. Okay, okay. So, have you practiced yet?
No. I have home-work. And lots of tests. Next week is the end of school, remember?

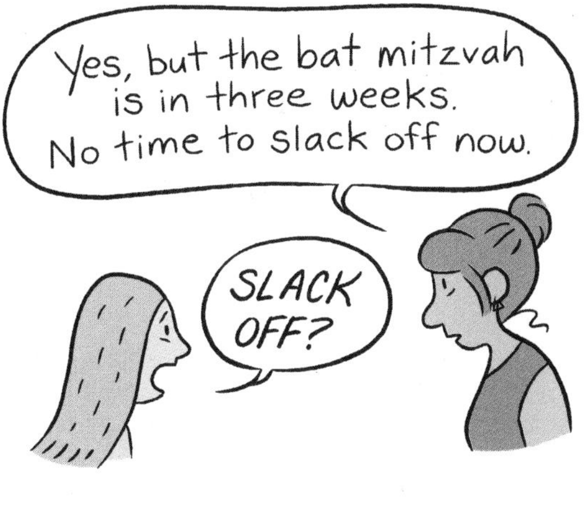
Yes, but the bat mitzvah is in three weeks. No time to slack off now.
SLACK OFF?

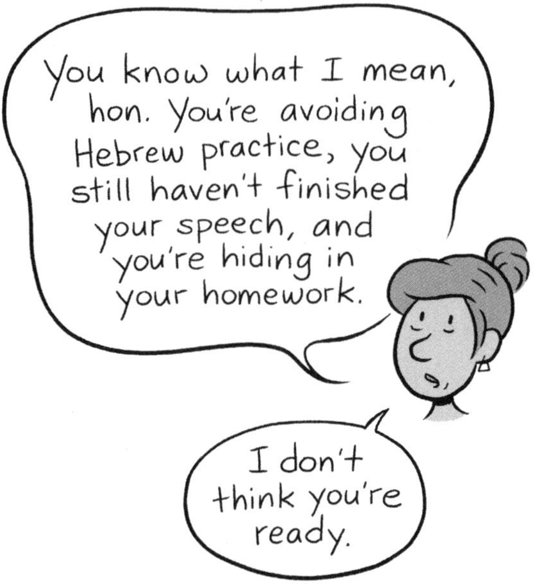
You know what I mean, hon. You're avoiding Hebrew practice, you still haven't finished your speech, and you're hiding in your homework.
I don't think you're ready.

I slam my Spanish book closed. And catch my fingers in it.

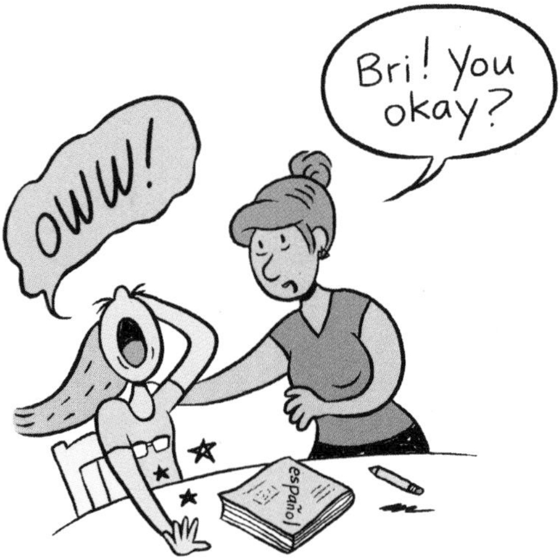
OWW!
Bri! You okay?
español

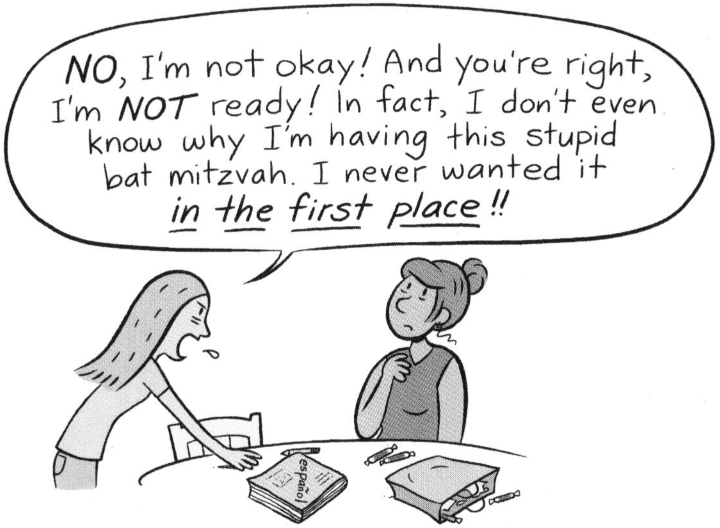
NO, I'm not okay! And you're right, I'm ***NOT*** ready! In fact, I don't even know why I'm having this stupid bat mitzvah. I never wanted it *in the first place*!!
español

I run to my room and slam the door. A couple photos flutter from my mirror frame, and my jewelry tree falls over. This condo isn't exactly the sturdiest structure.

I cry. Hard.

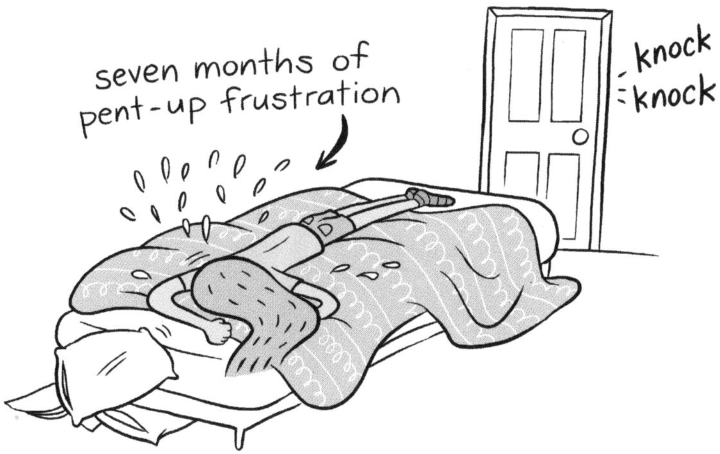
seven months of pent-up frustration
knock
knock

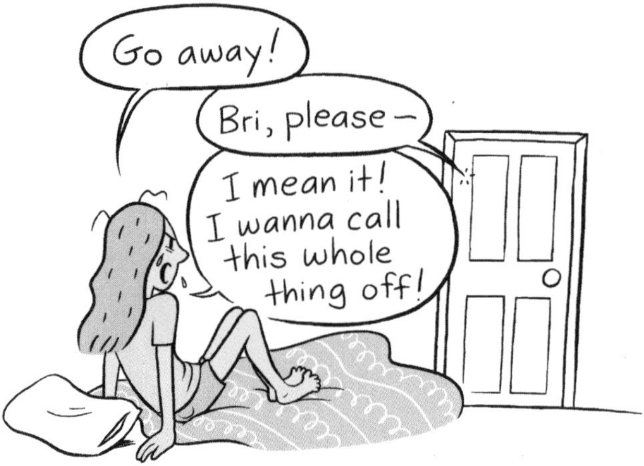
Go away!
Bri, please—
I mean it! I wanna call this whole thing off!

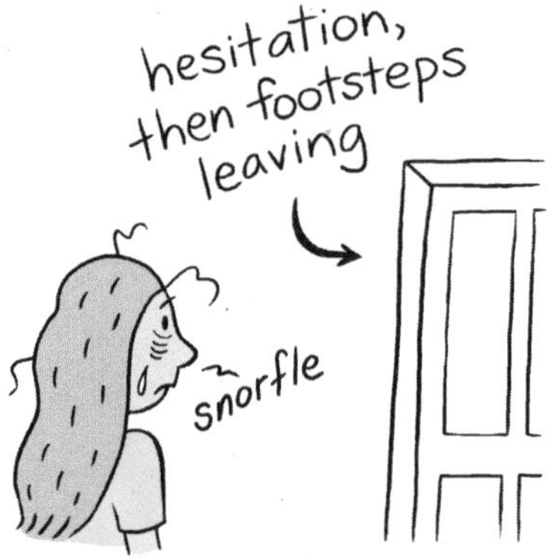
hesitation, then footsteps leaving
snorfle

I have a good cry over everything: my bickering parents (for Pete's sake, you're already divorced; stop fighting!), my nearly broken friendship with my bff, my so over friendship with a stupid user, seven months of learning prayers in an impossible language, and a yet-to-be-written speech—that has absolutely no meaning to me—which has to **knock the socks off everyone!**

I don't even have to wonder if it's worth it. It's not.

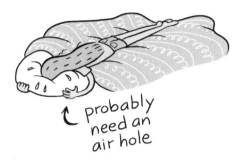

↰ probably
need an
air hole

I stay in my room for a long time before I hear knocking again.

What?

Bri, hon. Dad's here. Can we come in?

Great, she called in reinforcements. Don't know why she bothered. They'll probably end up arguing in front of me. What's frustrating is, they got along great before this whole bat mitzvah thing came about. Just another reason not to do it.

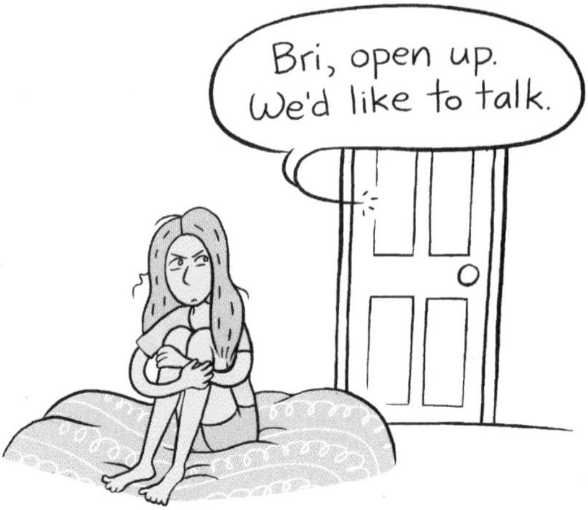
Bri, open up. We'd like to talk.

Fiiiine. I sniffle, get up, wipe the snot off my face, and open the door. My parents come in.

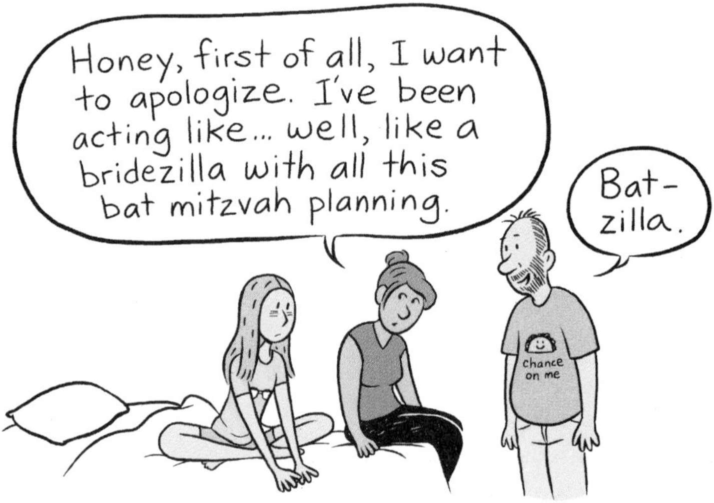
Honey, first of all, I want to apologize. I've been acting like... well, like a bridezilla with all this bat mitzvah planning.
Bat-zilla.
chance on me

They chuckle, and I try not to smile at his lame dad-joke.

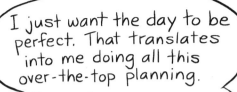

I just want the day to be perfect. That translates into me doing all this over-the-top planning.

I promise I'll try to keep it in check from now on.

And I admit, I probably haven't done enough to help. Your mom and I agreed to keep tabs on each other from now until your big day.

Can you stop calling it that?

They look at each other.

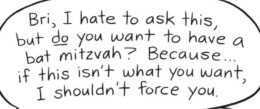

Bri, I hate to ask this, but <u>do</u> you want to have a bat mitzvah? Because... if this isn't what you want, I shouldn't force you.

I'm sorry, I realize it's so late in the game, but we can still cancel.

And don't say yes because this is some sort of big challenge you want to face, or a goal to check off.

We know you, honey.

I don't answer. I don't know what I want.

You don't have to decide right now. Sleep on it.

She smiles at me, and they head out, closing the door gently.

I flop on my back and stare at the ceiling. Even the cracks in the plaster look like Hebrew letters.

those look like "Bina"

I roll onto my stomach.

I guess I have some thinking to do.

IT'S TIME TO START
THE FIRST PRAYER.

eek!

I BEGIN, AND IMMEDI-
ATELY SCREW UP.

veyaftah...
I mean
v'ahav—
tah—...

OMG, THIS *IS* JUST LIKE
THE TALENT SHOW!

at least the
mike hasn't
emitted
screechy
feedback

210

I CAN'T HELP IT. I LOOK AT THE CONGREGATION.
Emmie, sneaking in from the back
empty seats
toddler pulling her mom's hair
not-so-empty seats
Cousin Bradley sneezing and scratching his armpit
Dev, giving me thumbs-up
Mom and Dad, smiling in terror
SHNOO!
Grandma and aunts, beaming
me

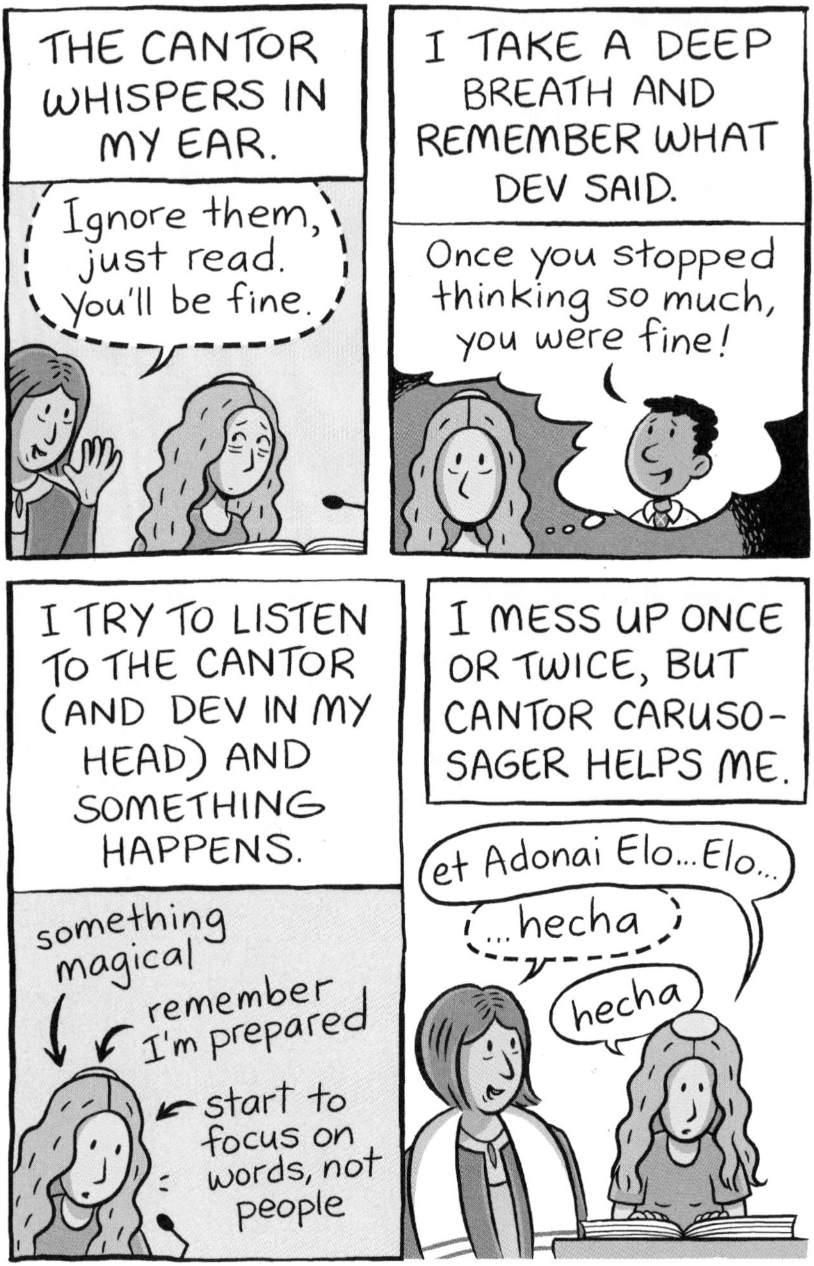

THE CANTOR WHISPERS IN MY EAR.
Ignore them, just read. You'll be fine.
I TAKE A DEEP BREATH AND REMEMBER WHAT DEV SAID.
Once you stopped thinking so much, you were fine!
I TRY TO LISTEN TO THE CANTOR (AND DEV IN MY HEAD) AND SOMETHING HAPPENS.
something magical
remember I'm prepared
start to focus on words, not people
I MESS UP ONCE OR TWICE, BUT CANTOR CARUSO-SAGER HELPS ME.
et Adonai Elo...Elo...
...hecha
hecha

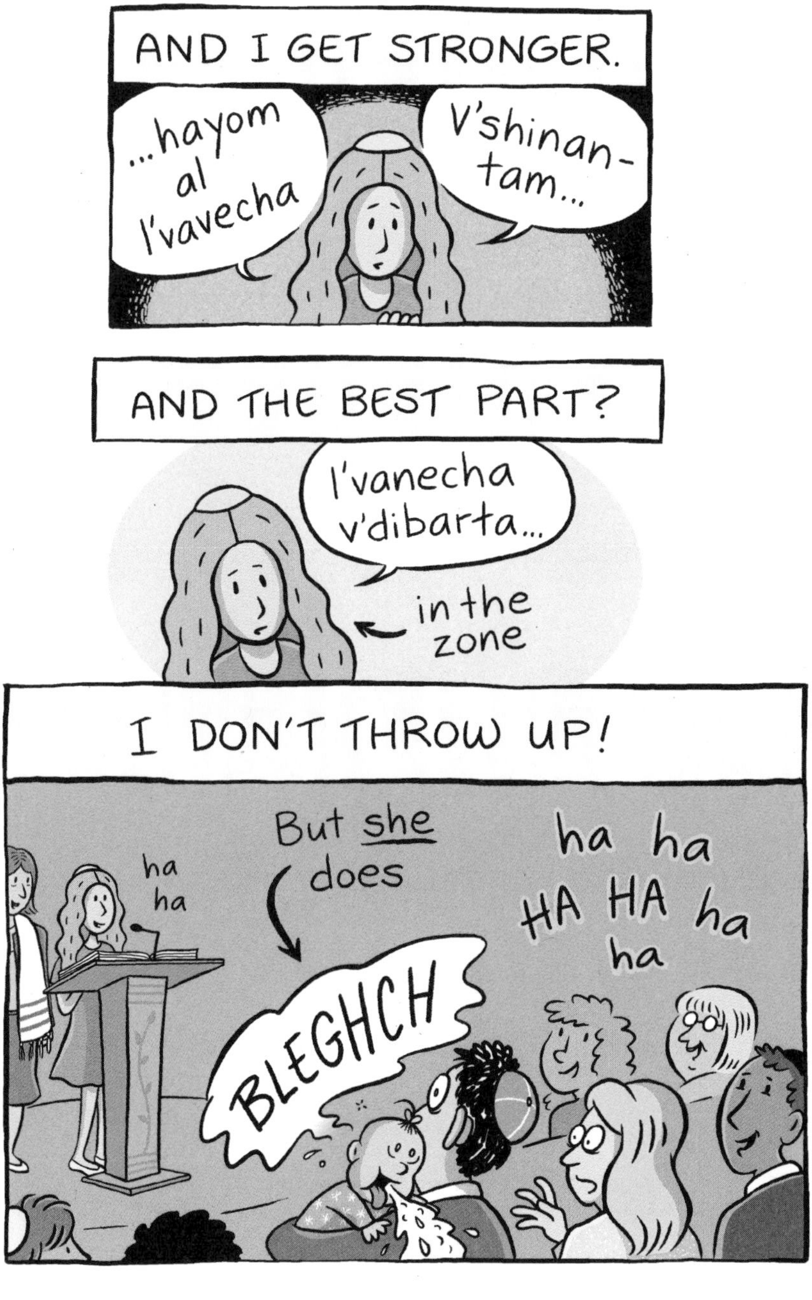
AND I GET STRONGER.
...hayom al l'vavecha
V'shinan-tam...
AND THE BEST PART?
l'vanecha v'dibarta...
in the zone
I DON'T THROW UP!
But she does
ha ha
ha ha HA HA ha ha
BLEGHCH

ONE WEEK AGO

School ended last week. It's been a ride.

Last day of school:

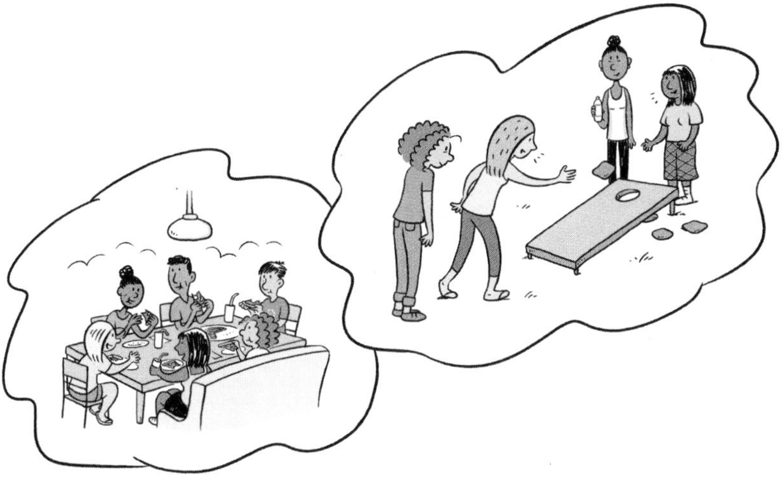

I've made some new friends and made up with an old one.

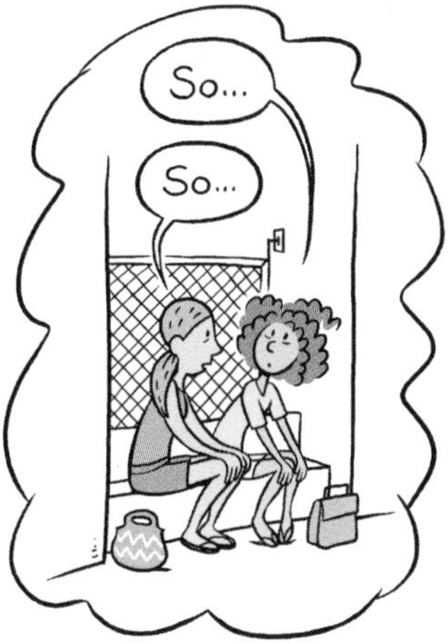

So...
So...

It hasn't been perfect or anything. Emmie forgave me, but I can tell she's still a little mad. She's just trying not to show it. She's hurt that I held a grudge for so long.

But it's Emmie. Which means she's really, really bad at being mad.

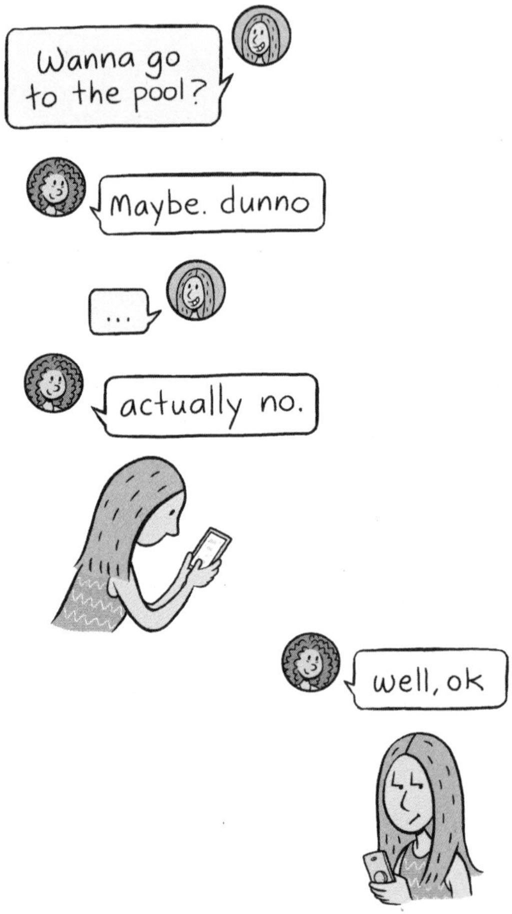
Wanna go to the pool?
Maybe. dunno
...
actually no.
well, ok

I deserve it. It's now super obvious that Zoe was just using me. She's still trying to be friendly, but I'm not having it anymore. I don't return her texts. I pretty much ignore her.

hey, u mad at me or something??
i don't understand what i did ☹
if i did something wrong, i'm sorry ☹

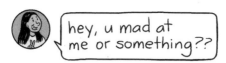

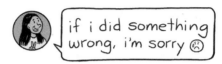

Yesterday I got tired of it and texted her back.

i'm just busy with bat mitzvah
k ☺

I probably should confront her, but I'm too tired and crazed. Honestly, I don't even want to deal with it.

One thing I wish I could do:

YOU ARE UN-INVITED to Brianna's Bat Mitzvah ♥

My only satisfaction is knowing she realizes this isn't gonna be the blowout event she once thought it would be.

Also . . .

one week ago:

You wanted to know who was invited?

invitation list

mostly kids from Science Club, Math Club, Robotics Camp, and Dev, Emmie, and Sarah

(can practically hear their faces falling)

Meanwhile, Emmie and Sarah are still tight, which scares me. It's not that I don't like Sarah. Actually, she's grown on me . . . a lot. But I still get scared that she's gonna replace me.

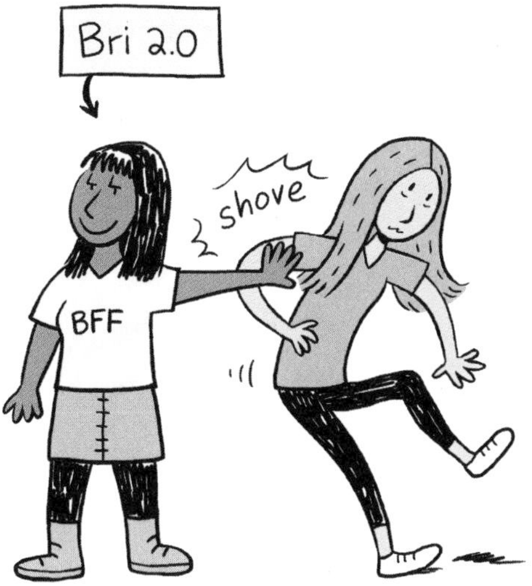

Bri 2.0
shove
BFF

Speaking of friends, I stopped talking about the bat mitzvah in front of them. I'm back to compartmentalizing, this time to the extreme. It's the only way to cope.

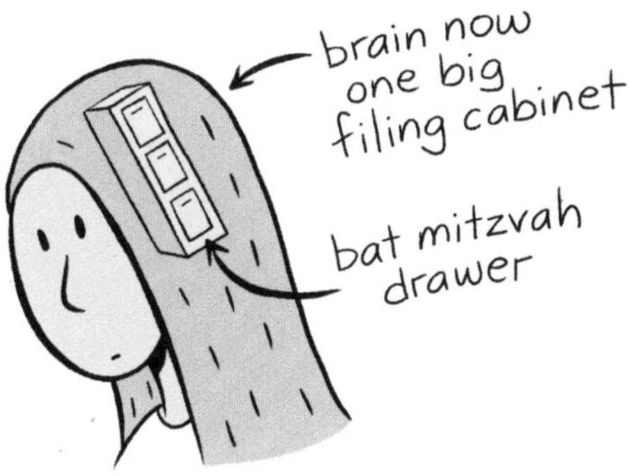

brain now one big filing cabinet
bat mitzvah drawer

But yes, I'm still going through with it. I admit, a big part of it is pride. The invites were sent, I made a commitment, and I need to see it through. I also learned a buttload of Hebrew this past year, and I'm not gonna let it go to waste!

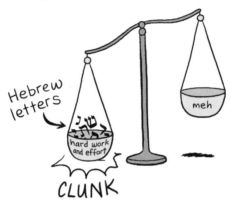

Hebrew letters

שמ
אבג
hard work and effort

meh

CLUNK

But I did think about it that night my parents talked to me. In fact, I barely slept. I realized I do want to have the bat mitzvah. Em and I video-chatted about it yesterday.

So, I realized I may not have gone to religious school all the time, I may not even <u>be</u> religious, but there's one big thing I like about my rabbi, cantor, and temple.

What's that?

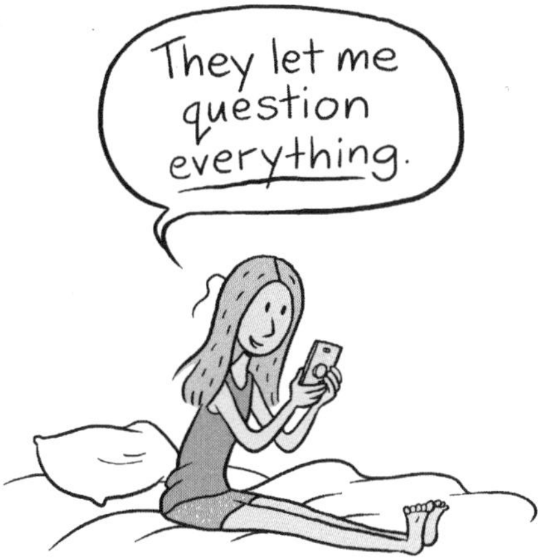
They let me question everything.

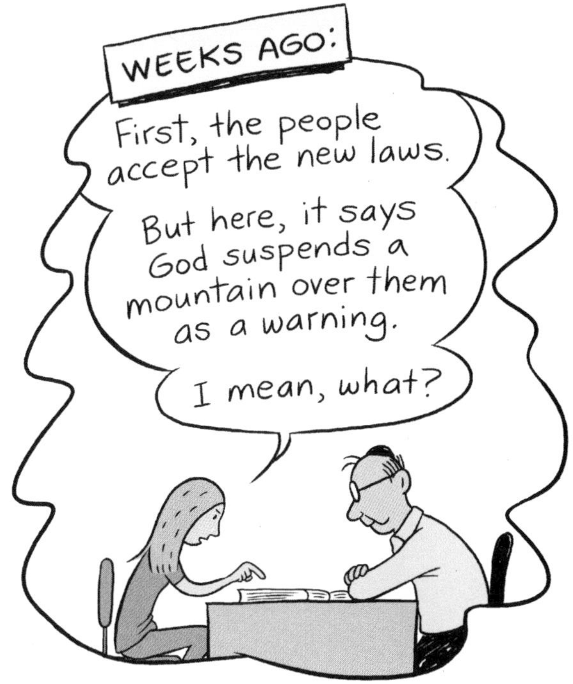
WEEKS AGO:
First, the people accept the new laws.
But here, it says God suspends a mountain over them as a warning.
I mean, what?

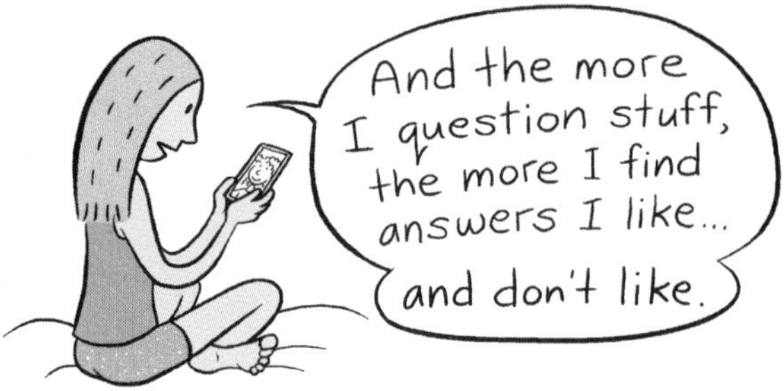
And the more I question stuff, the more I find answers I like...
and don't like.

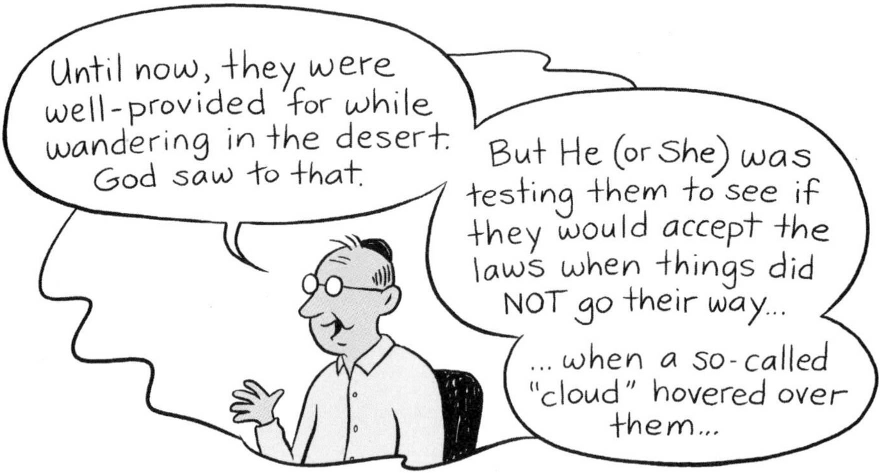
Until now, they were well-provided for while wandering in the desert. God saw to that.
But He (or She) was testing them to see if they would accept the laws when things did NOT go their way...
...when a so-called "cloud" hovered over them...

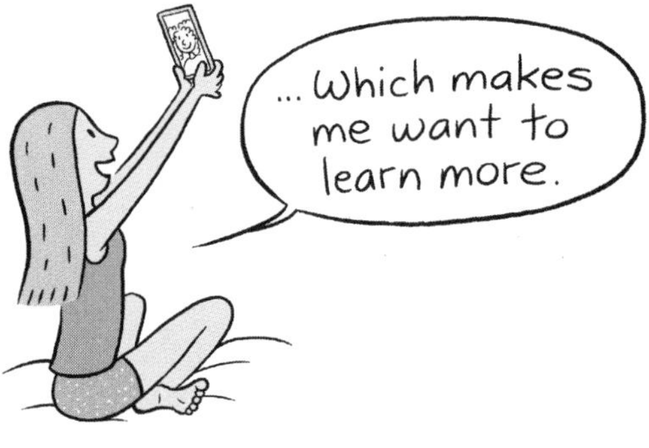
...Which makes me want to learn more.

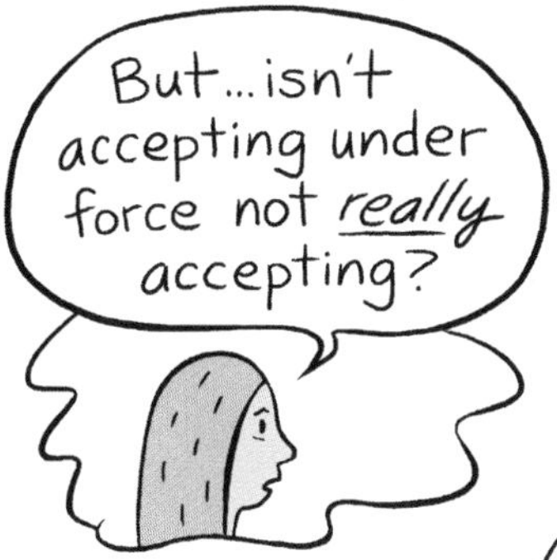

But... isn't accepting under force not *really* accepting?

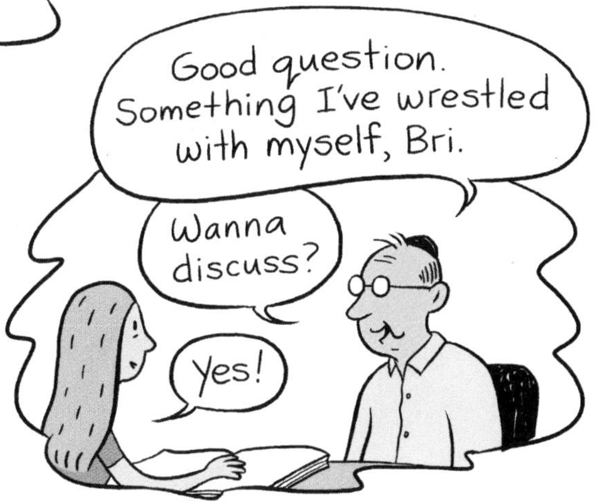

Good question. Something I've wrestled with myself, Bri.
Wanna discuss?
Yes!

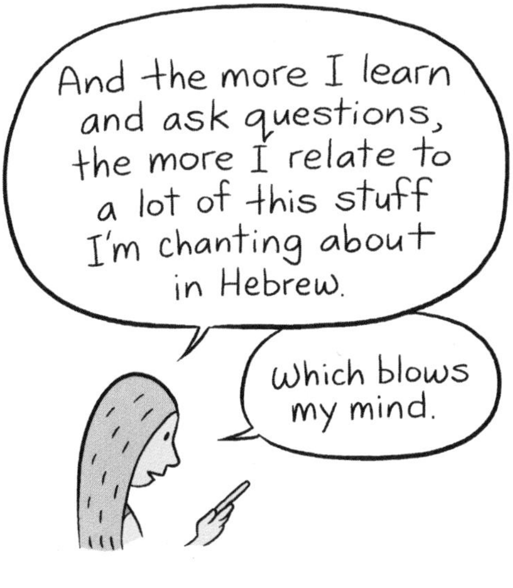

And the more I learn and ask questions, the more I relate to a lot of this stuff I'm chanting about in Hebrew.
Which blows my mind.

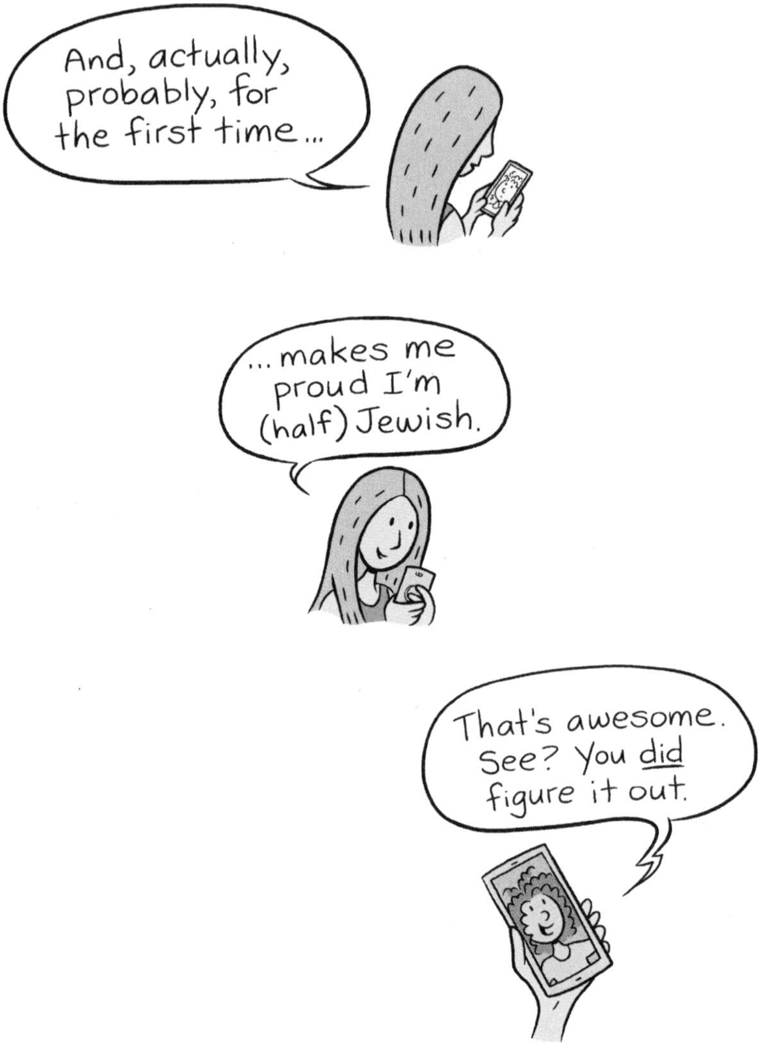
And, actually, probably, for the first time...
...makes me proud I'm (half) Jewish.
That's awesome. See? You did figure it out.

I guess I did. Maybe someday I'll be more spiritual and stuff, maybe not—but for now, this is huge.

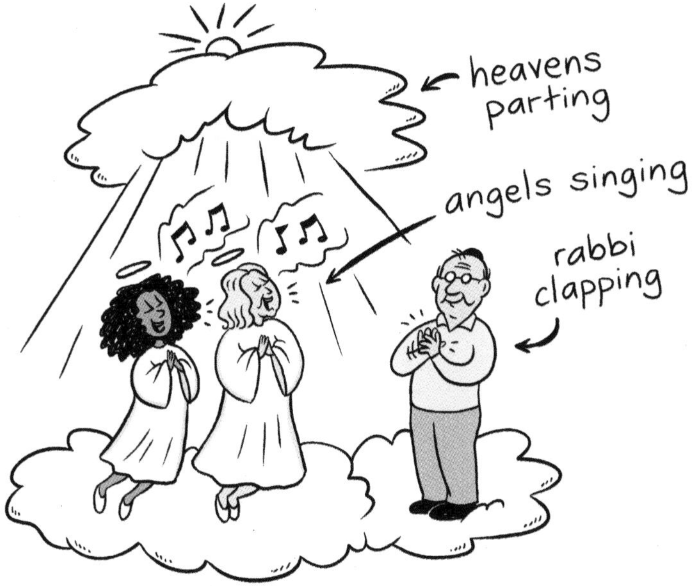
heavens parting
angels singing
rabbi clapping

I finished up the last of my Hebrew practice. The tutor just left. I think I'm set. I give myself a mental pat on the back.

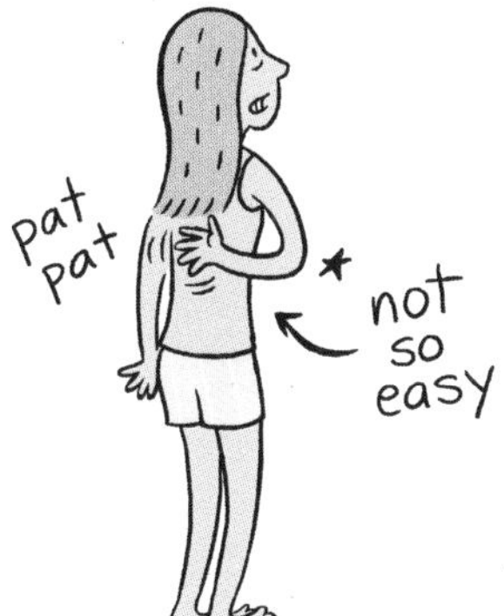
pat pat
not so easy

But . . . I still haven't written my speech. I know, I know, stupid. I just want to get it right. I lied to everyone and said it was all done. Besides, I will write it. Sometimes a last-minute deadline is the greatest motivator. That's what I tell myself, anyway.

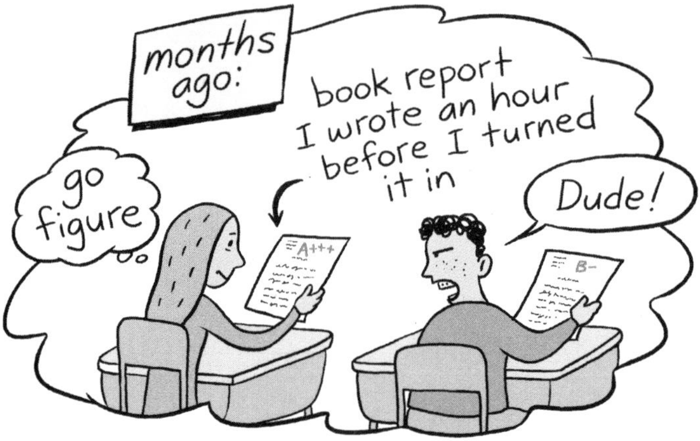
months ago:
book report I wrote an hour before I turned it in
go figure
Dude!
A+++
B-

Mom walks in the room. She's been true to her word, not bugging me about practicing or about the "big day" and stuff. She's really toned it down. That will probably change the day of, but for now, it's been helpful.

Still, I notice she smells like her favorite multipurpose cleaner. While the tutor was here, she must've been secretly deep-cleaning for the out-of-town guests.

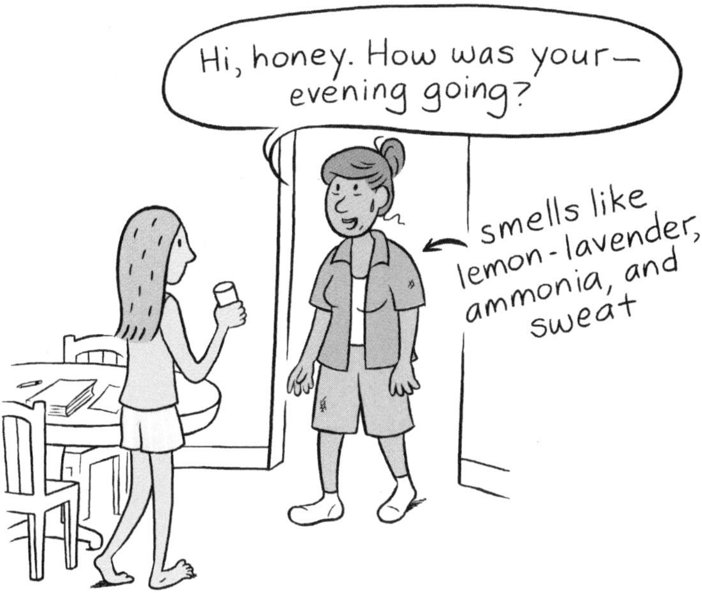
Hi, honey. How was your— evening going?
smells like lemon-lavender, ammonia, and sweat

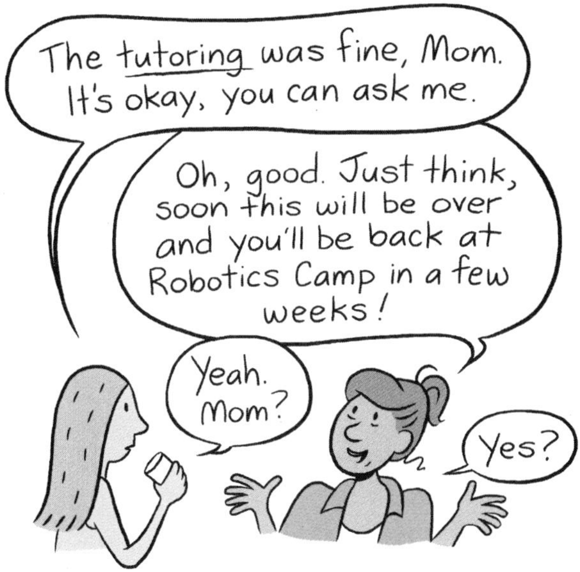
The tutoring was fine, Mom. It's okay, you can ask me.
Oh, good. Just think, soon this will be over and you'll be back at Robotics Camp in a few weeks!
Yeah. Mom?
Yes?

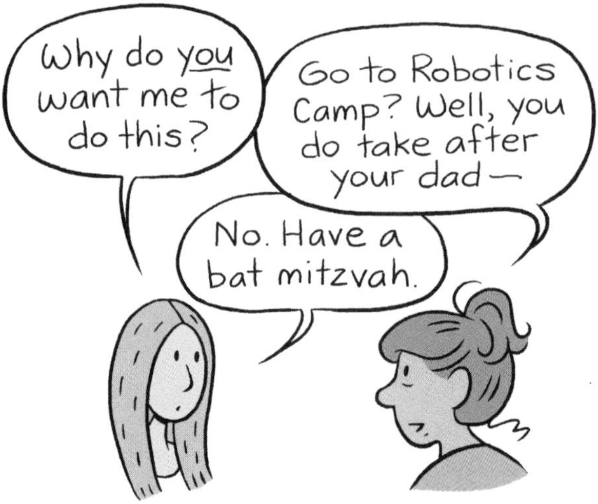
Why do you want me to do this?
Go to Robotics Camp? Well, you do take after your dad—
No. Have a bat mitzvah.

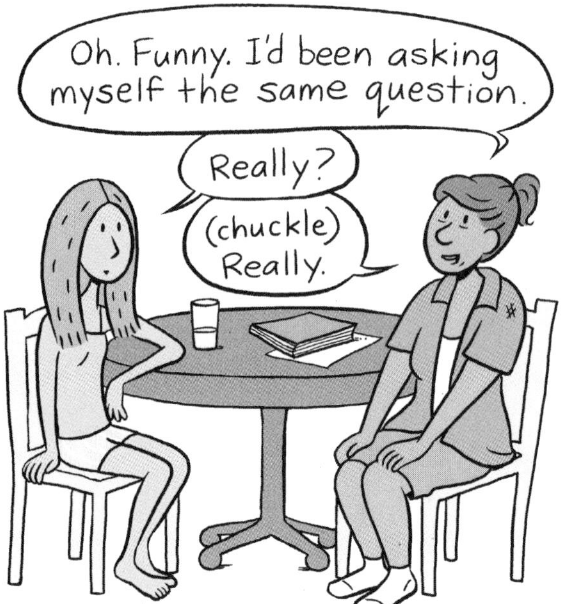
Oh. Funny. I'd been asking myself the same question.
Really?
(chuckle) Really.

She hesitates.

Well, at first I told myself it was about tradition and rite of passage and all that. But then I dove a little deeper.

What do you mean?

(sigh) I hate to admit this, but I think it became a vanity project. I wanted you to do it because _I_ did it. I wanted you to shine because _I_ wanted to shine.

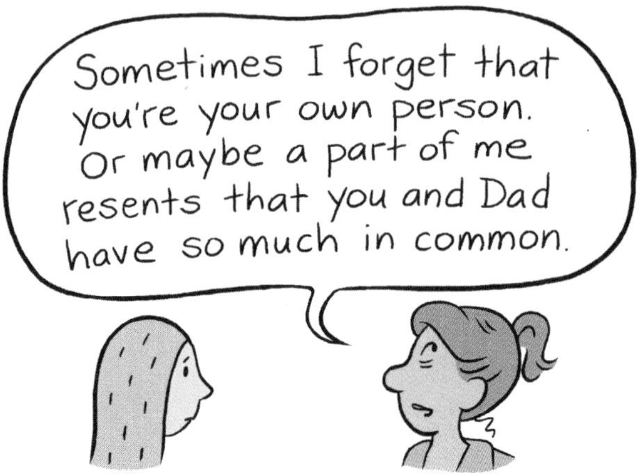
Sometimes I forget that you're your own person. Or maybe a part of me resents that you and Dad have so much in common.

She suddenly smiles.

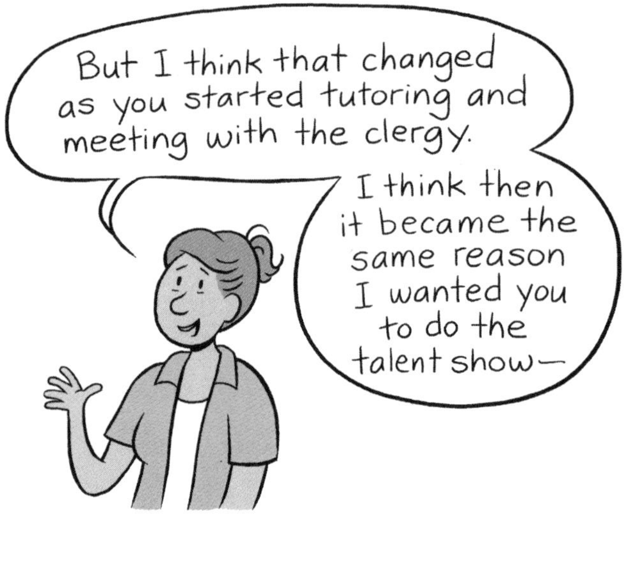
But I think that changed as you started tutoring and meeting with the clergy.
I think then it became the same reason I wanted you to do the talent show—

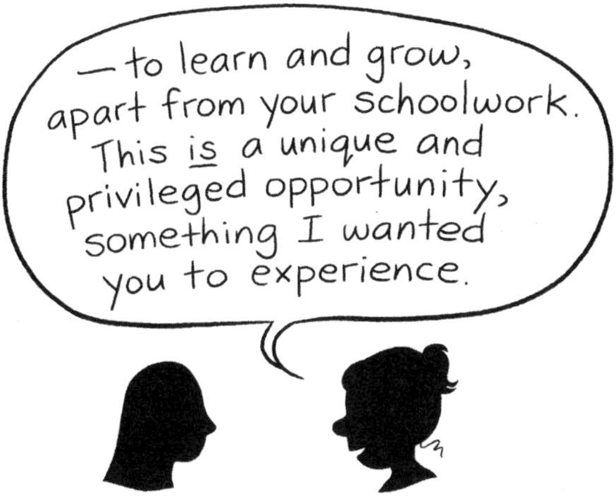
—to learn and grow, apart from your schoolwork. This is a unique and privileged opportunity, something I wanted you to experience.

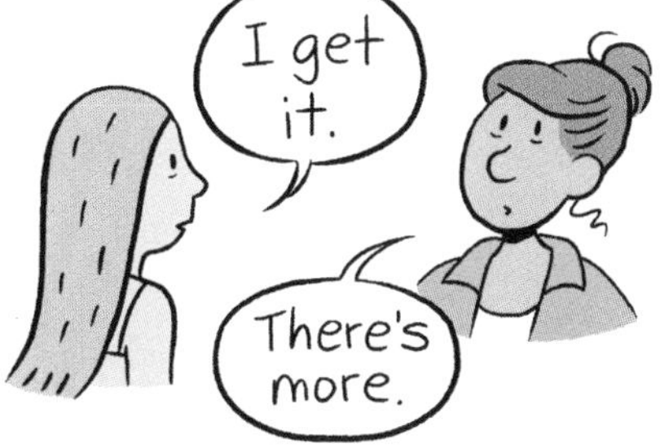
I get it.
There's more.

Her face becomes harder to read.

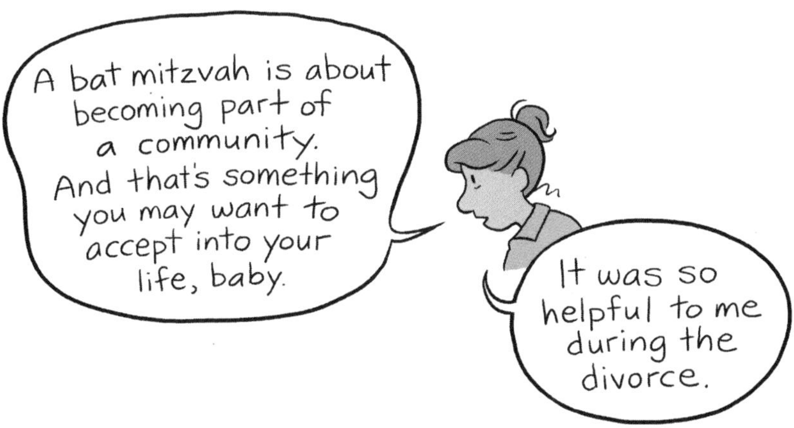
A bat mitzvah is about becoming part of a community. And that's something you may want to accept into your life, baby.
It was so helpful to me during the divorce.

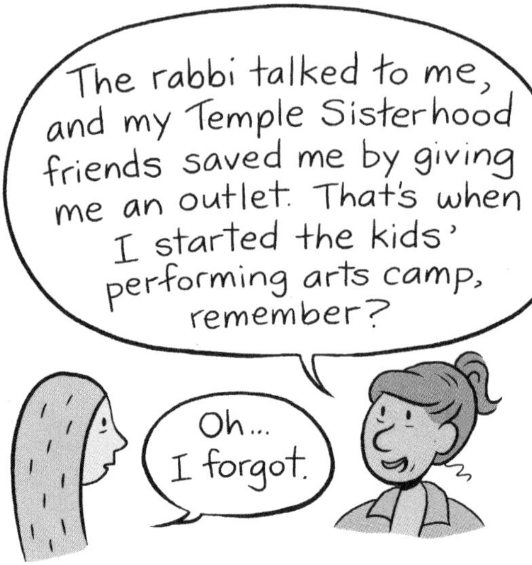
The rabbi talked to me, and my Temple Sisterhood friends saved me by giving me an outlet. That's when I started the kids' performing arts camp, remember?
Oh... I forgot.

I must have blocked it out. Or was just too busy feeling sorry for myself back then. The divorce was extra hard on my mom. She cried, like, forever. I remember hiding out at Emmie's house, holing up in our crazy little forts.

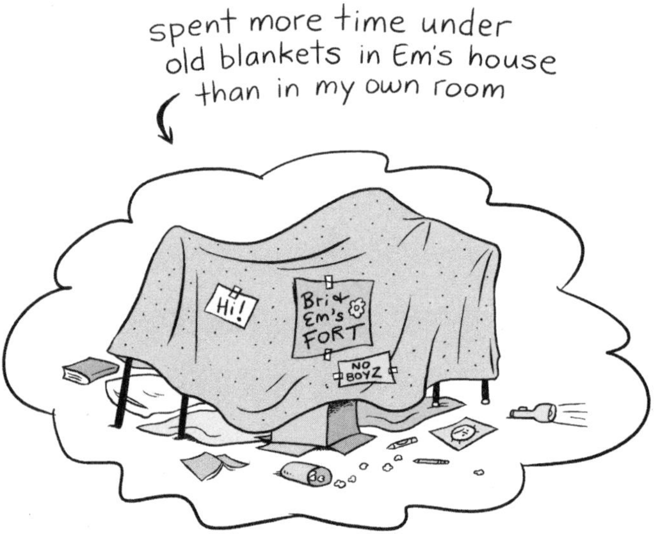
spent more time under old blankets in Em's house than in my own room
Hi!
Bri & Em's FORT
NO BOYZ

My mom runs a small performing arts camp every summer in the temple sanctuary. They put on a cute little ensemble show at the end of the four weeks. She **loves** it. I totally forgot she started that during her post-divorce mourning period. Makes sense now.

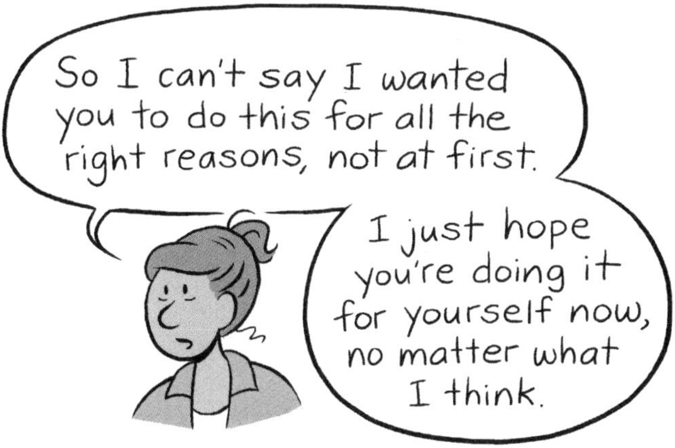
So I can't say I wanted you to do this for all the right reasons, not at first.
I just hope you're doing it for yourself now, no matter what I think.

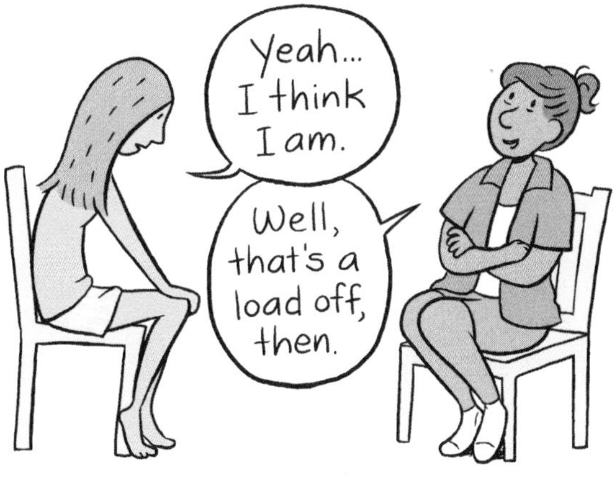
Yeah... I think I am.
Well, that's a load off, then.

I laugh.

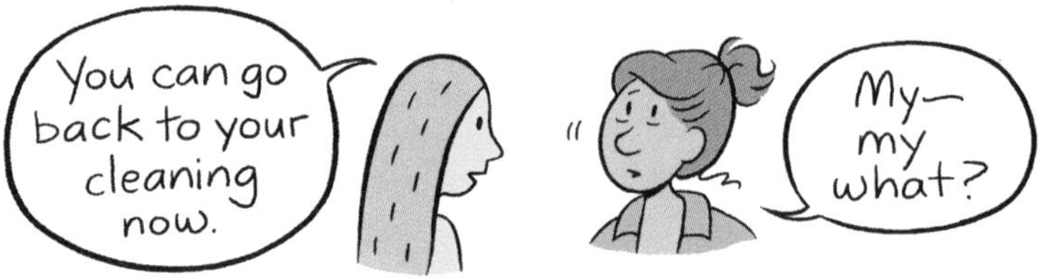
You can go back to your cleaning now.
My— my what?

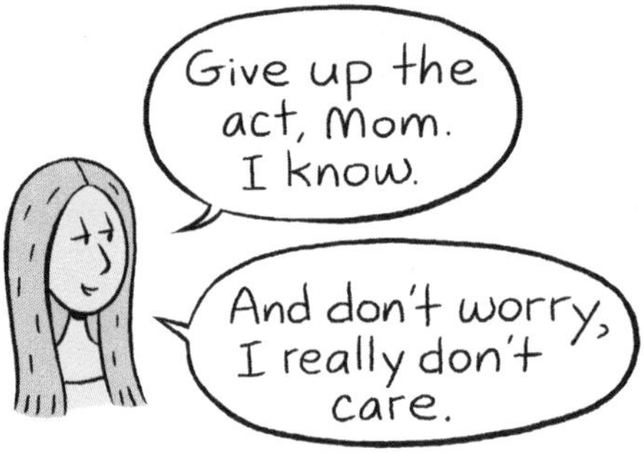
Give up the act, Mom. I know.
And don't worry, I really don't care.

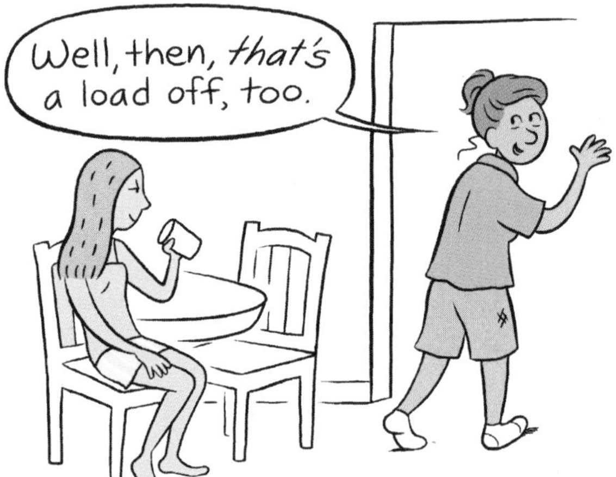
Well, then, *that's* a load off, too.

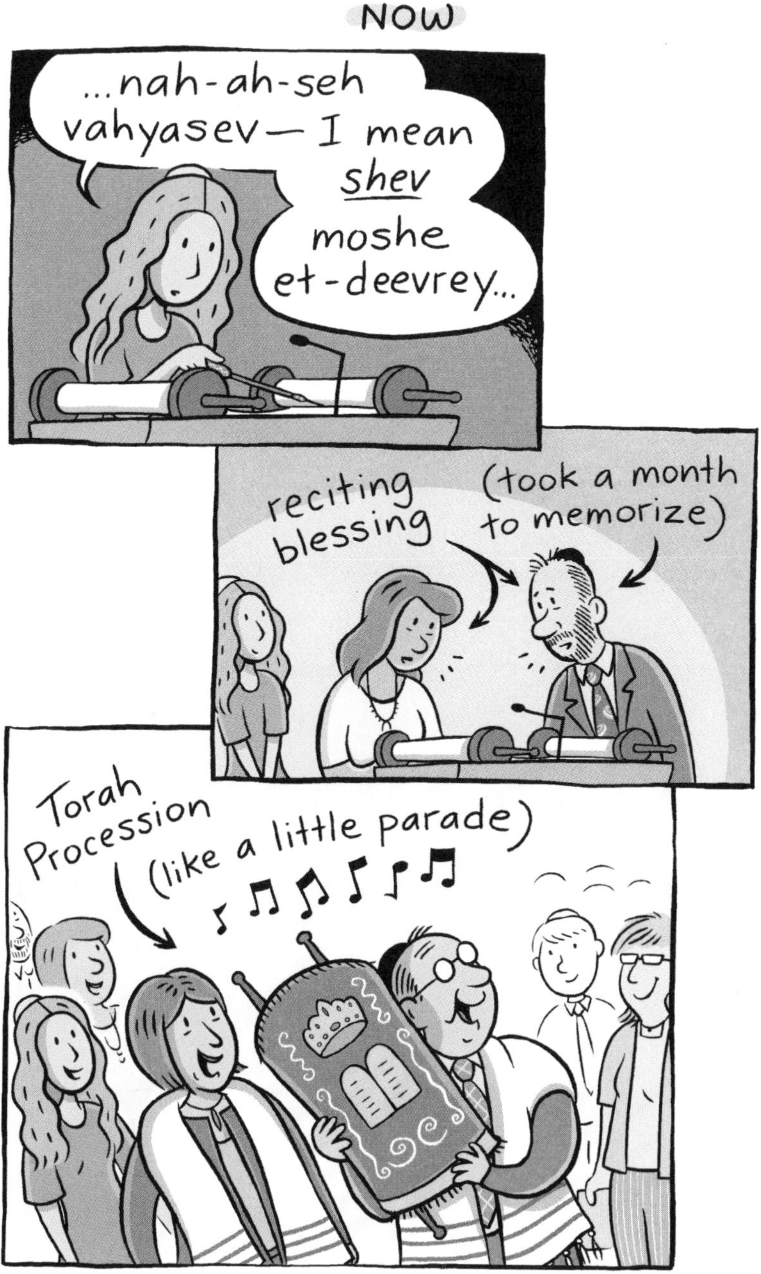
NOW
...nah-ah-seh vahyasev— I mean shev moshe et-deevrey...
reciting blessing
(took a month to memorize)
Torah Procession
(like a little parade)

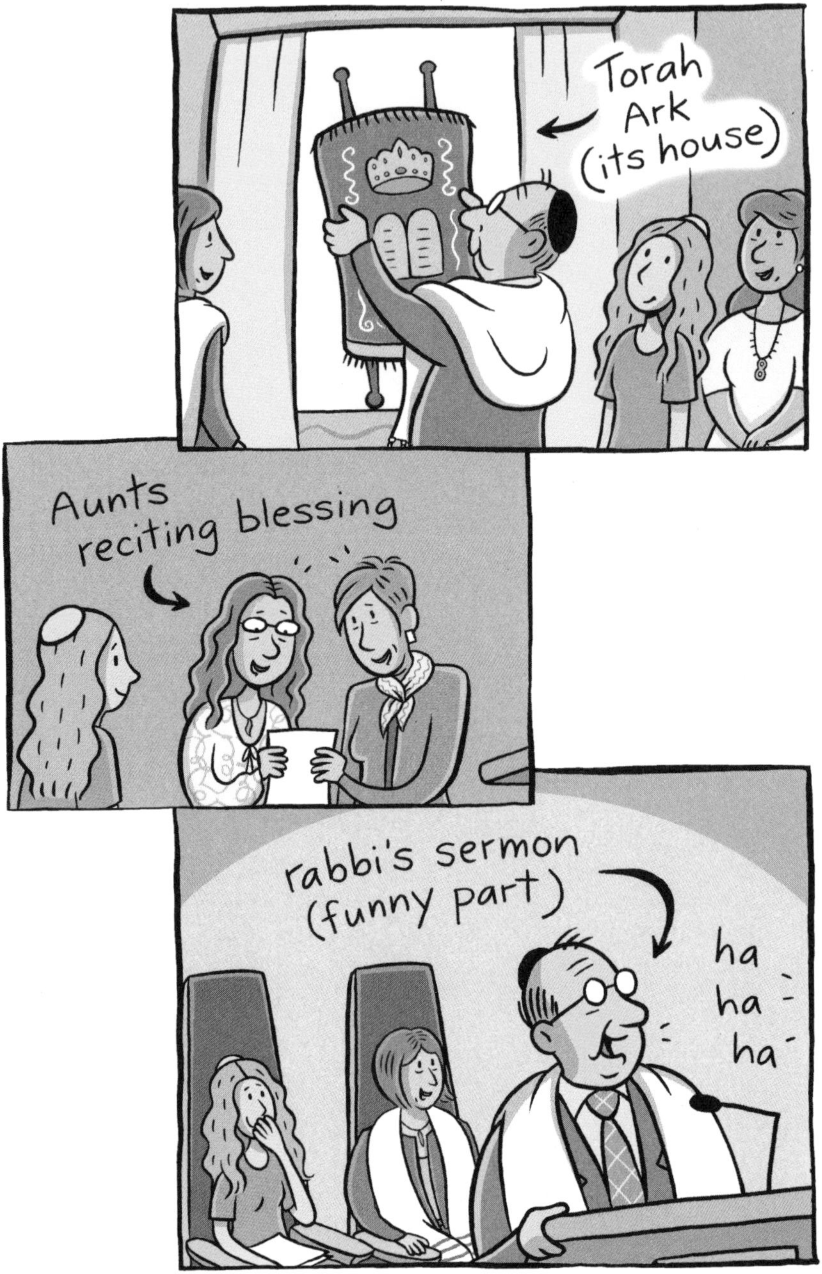
Torah Ark (its house)
Aunts reciting blessing
rabbi's sermon (funny part)
ha
ha
ha

FIVE DAYS AGO

It's morning. I'm sitting on the edge of my bed, feet resting on a pile of dirty clothes. I barely slept.

You see, I made a serious

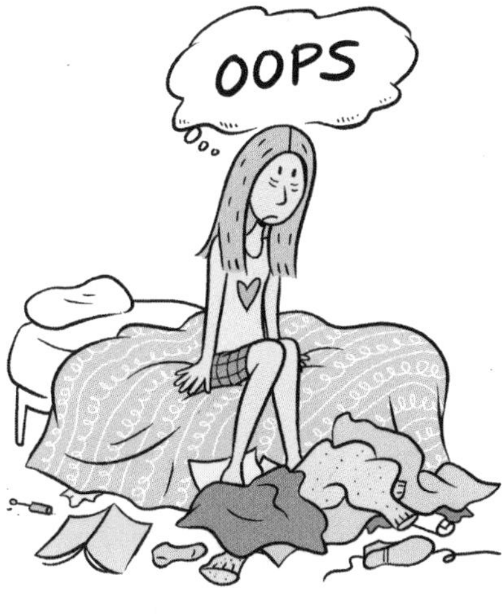
OOPS

I maybe, sort of, accidentally . . . invited four extra people to my bat mitzvah—without telling my mom.

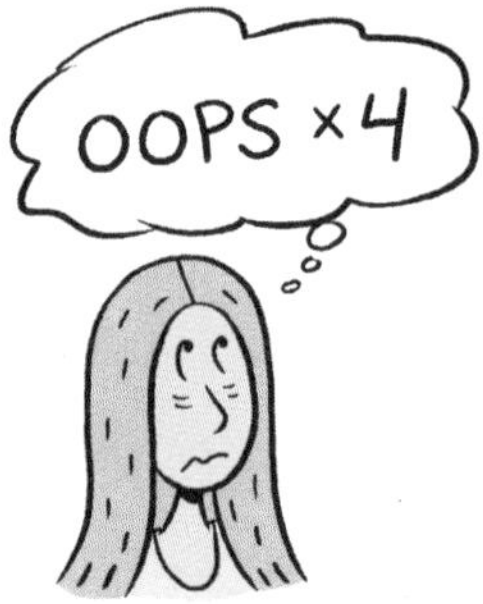
OOPS x 4

Yesterday, I was with Dev and Emmie at the pool, and we ran into Maya and Jaime. We all started hanging out, just like on the last day of school. Then Anthony and Tyler came, and we goofed around and decided to go to Taystee's afterward.

I was having so much fun (who knew?!), and in a moment of weakness . . .

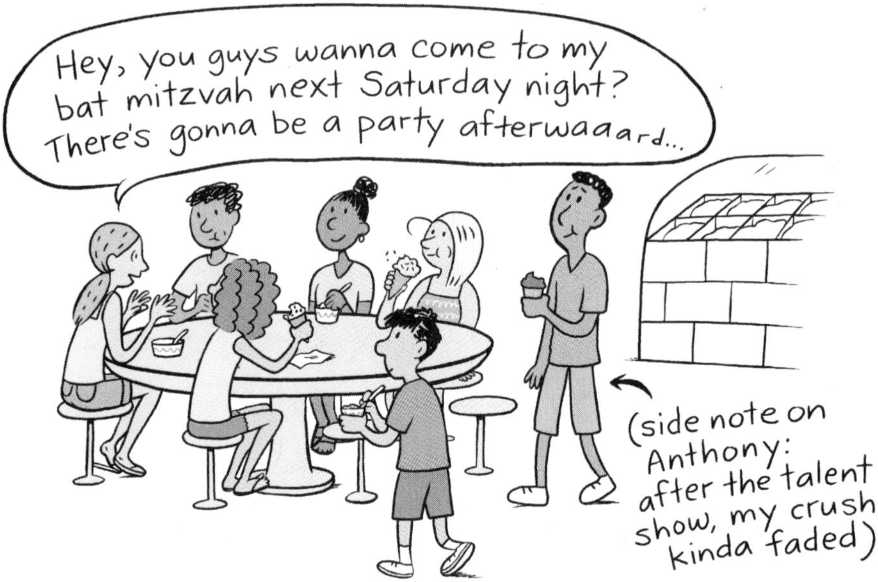
Hey, you guys wanna come to my bat mitzvah next Saturday night? There's gonna be a party afterwaaard...
(side note on Anthony: after the talent show, my crush kinda faded)

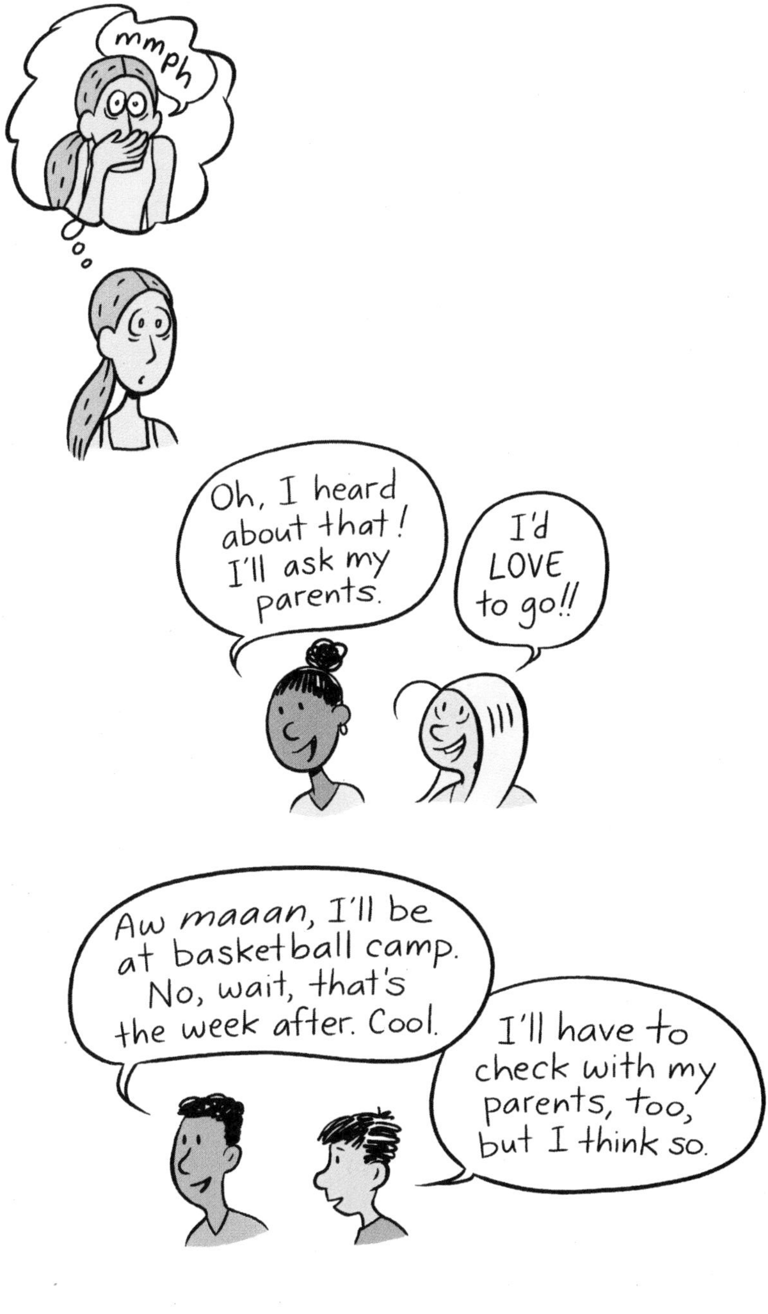
mmph
Oh, I heard about that! I'll ask my parents.
I'd LOVE to go!!
Aw *maaan*, I'll be at basketball camp. No, wait, that's the week after. Cool.
I'll have to check with my parents, too, but I think so.

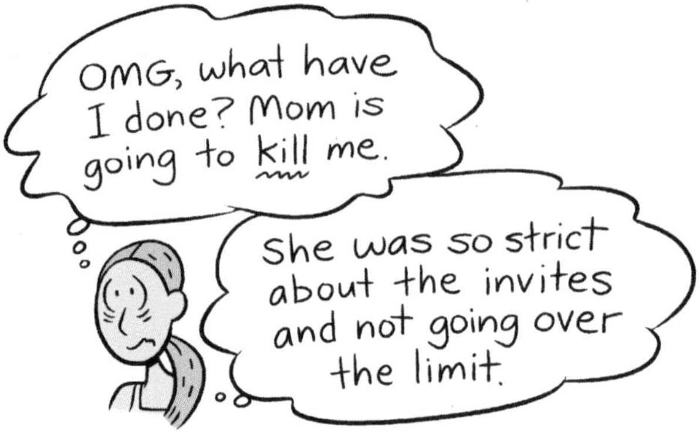
OMG, what have I done? Mom is going to kill me.
She was so strict about the invites and not going over the limit.

I get up and start pacing my room, practicing in my head what I'm going to tell her.

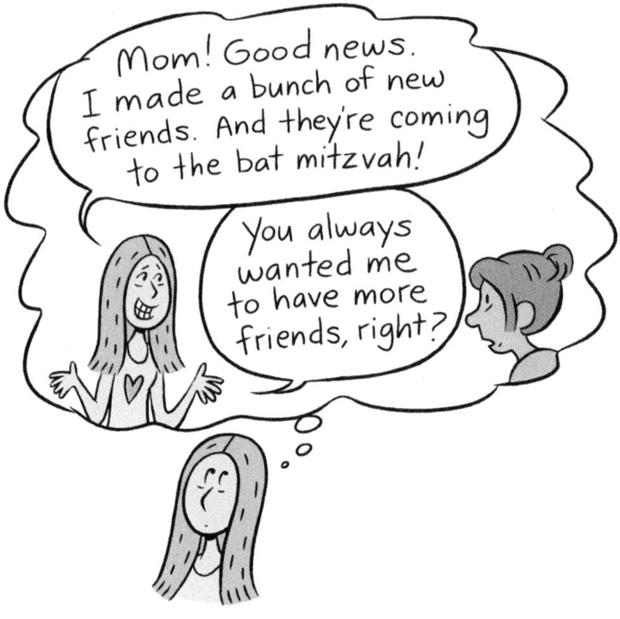
Mom! Good news. I made a bunch of new friends. And they're coming to the bat mitzvah!
You always wanted me to have more friends, right?

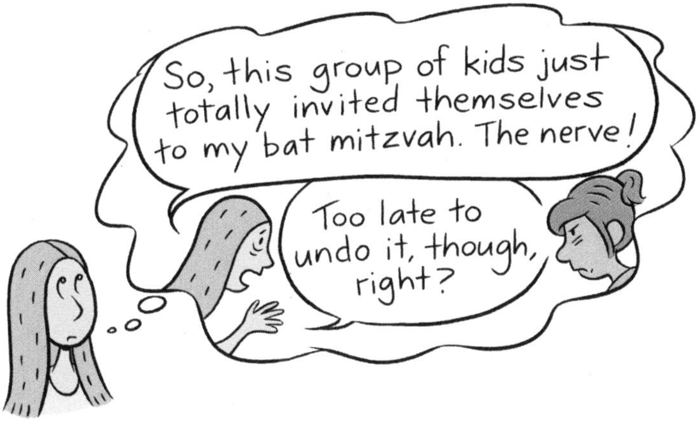
So, this group of kids just totally invited themselves to my bat mitzvah. The nerve!
Too late to undo it, though, right?

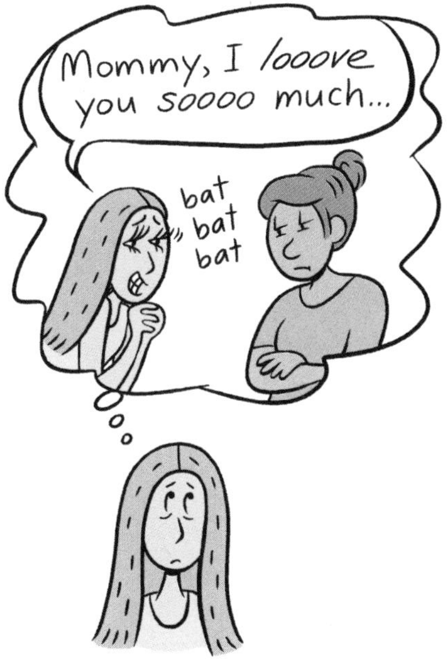
Mommy, I *looove* you *soooo* much...
bat bat bat

This is never going to work.

I wish I could just uninvite Zoe and Olivia. At least that would open up two slots.

I stop pacing and take a deep breath. Might as well rip the Band-Aid off. I head to the kitchen, where my mom is pouring cereal in a bowl and (loudly) sipping her coffee.

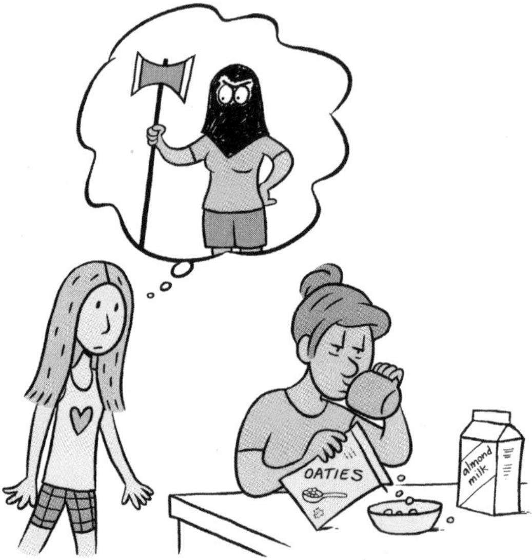
OATIES
almond milk

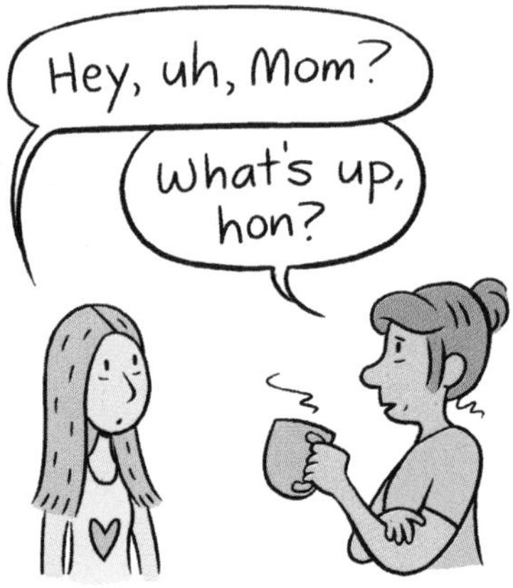
Hey, uh, Mom?
What's up, hon?

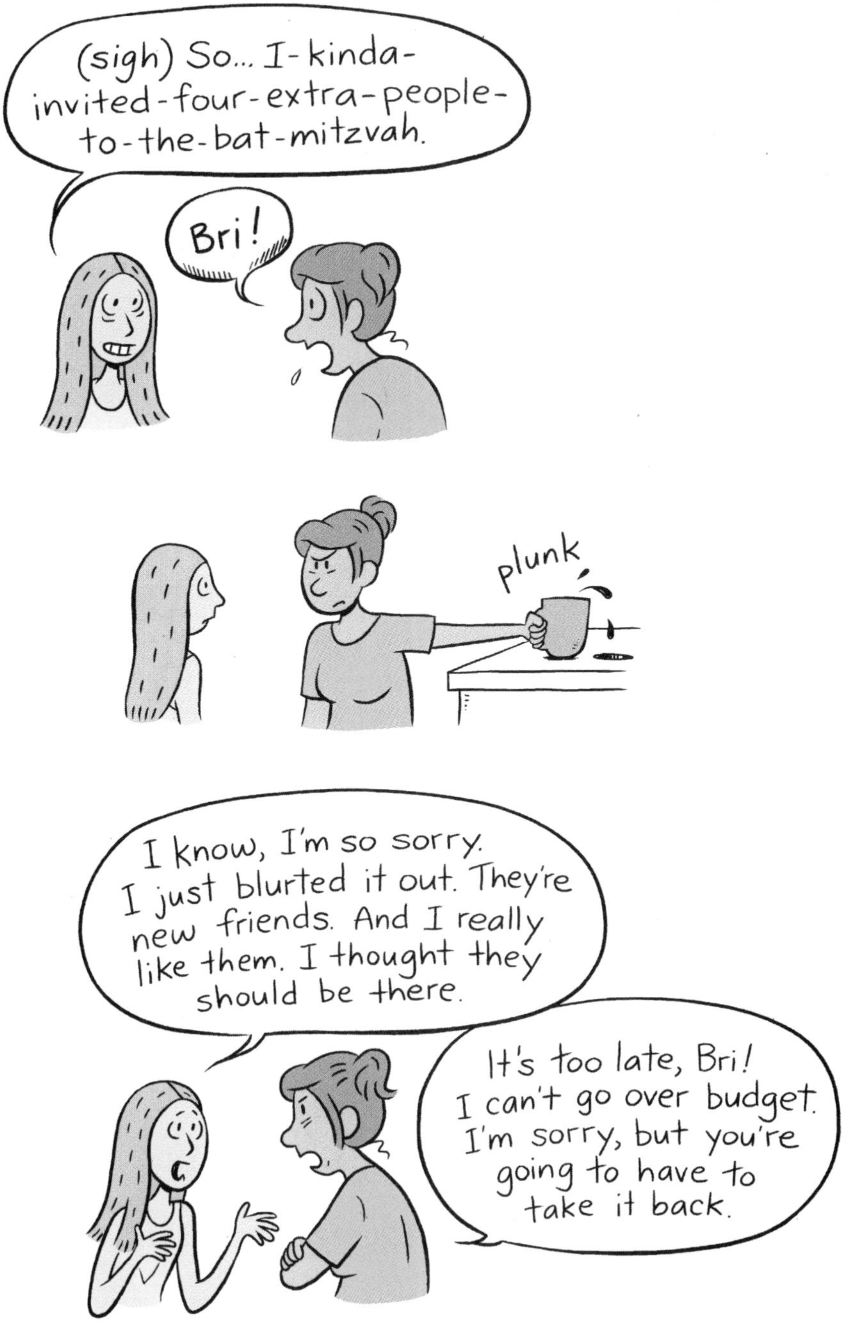
(sigh) So... I-kinda-invited-four-extra-people-to-the-bat-mitzvah.
Bri!
plunk
I know, I'm so sorry. I just blurted it out. They're new friends. And I really like them. I thought they should be there.
It's too late, Bri! I can't go over budget. I'm sorry, but you're going to have to take it back.

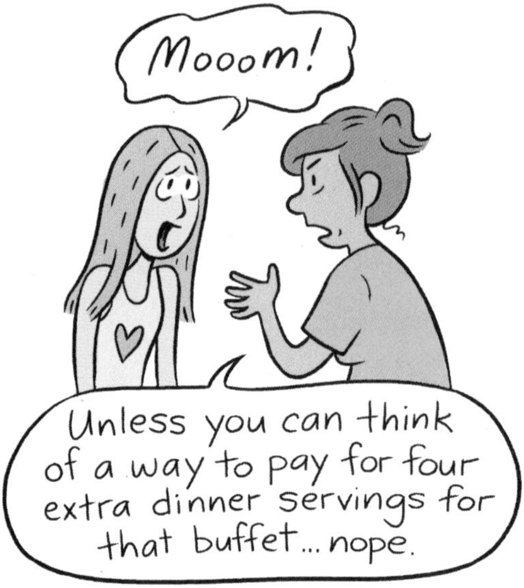
Mooom!
Unless you can think of a way to pay for four extra dinner servings for that buffet... nope.

I'm doomed. There's no way I can afford to pay for four extra people. I can barely afford to pay for a movie or treats with my pitiful allowance.

I head back to my room. I can hear my mom muttering under her breath.

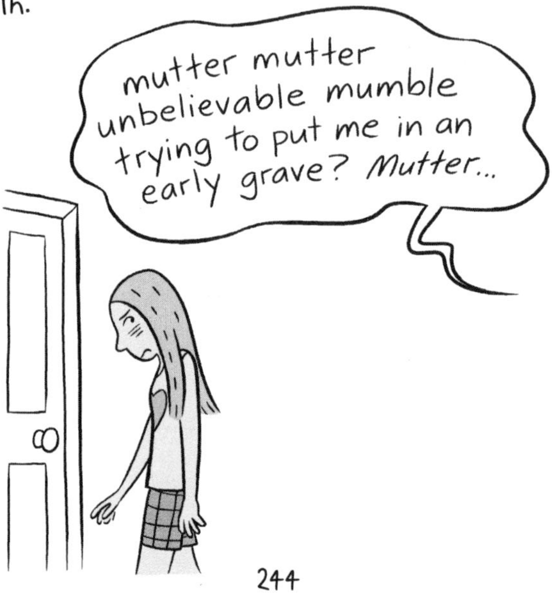
mutter mutter unbelievable mumble trying to put me in an early grave? *Mutter...*

I close my bedroom door and plop back on my bed. I try to clear all the brain cobwebs and **think.**

I'm either gonna have to take back my invitation—which would be totally **humiliating**, not to mention I'd feel so awful—or figure out a way to make some money fast.

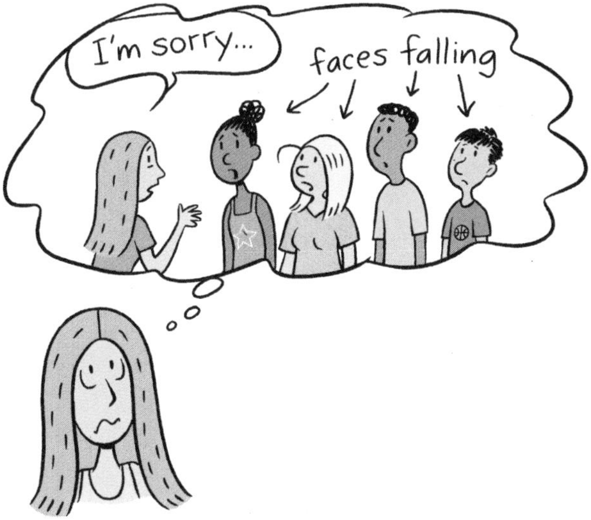
I'm sorry...
faces falling

There's no choice.

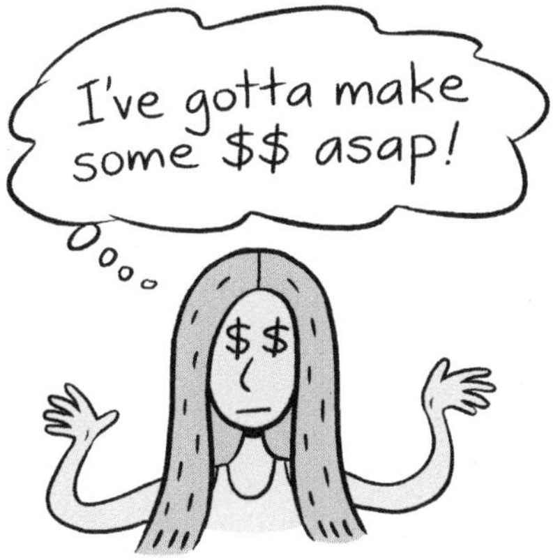
I've gotta make some $$ asap!

I need to brainstorm. I text Emmie and Sarah.

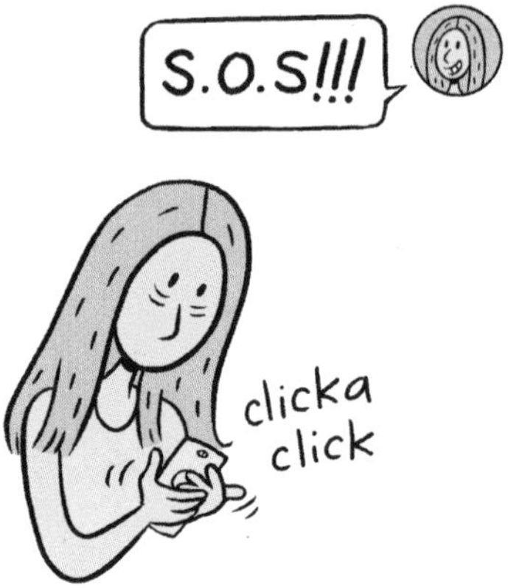
S.O.S!!!
clicka
click

After all, I may have a "gifted mind" . . .
but three heads are still better than one.

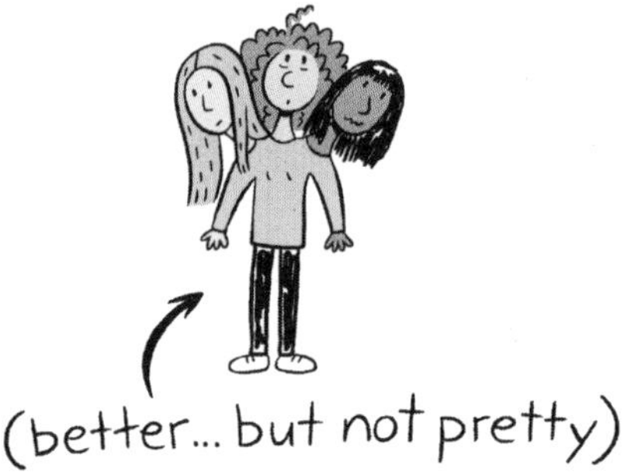
(better... but not pretty)

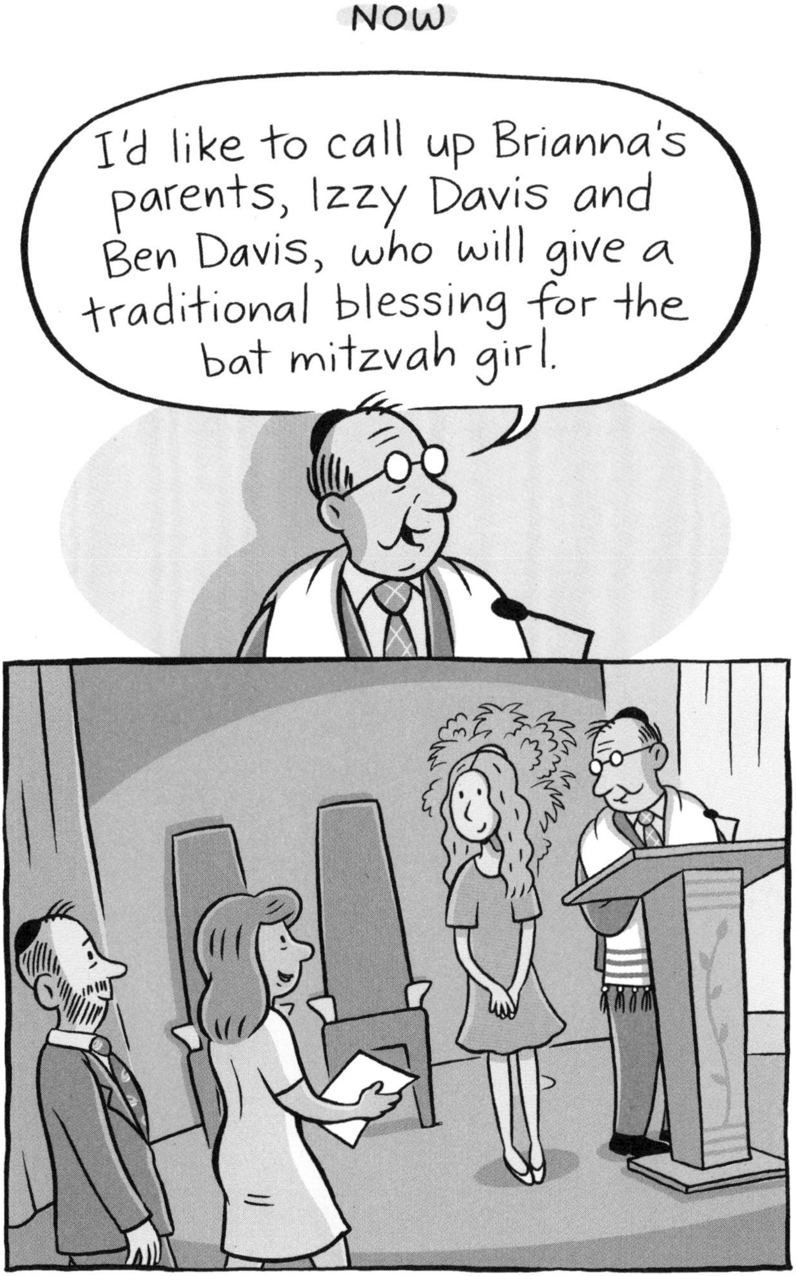
NOW
I'd like to call up Brianna's parents, Izzy Davis and Ben Davis, who will give a traditional blessing for the bat mitzvah girl.

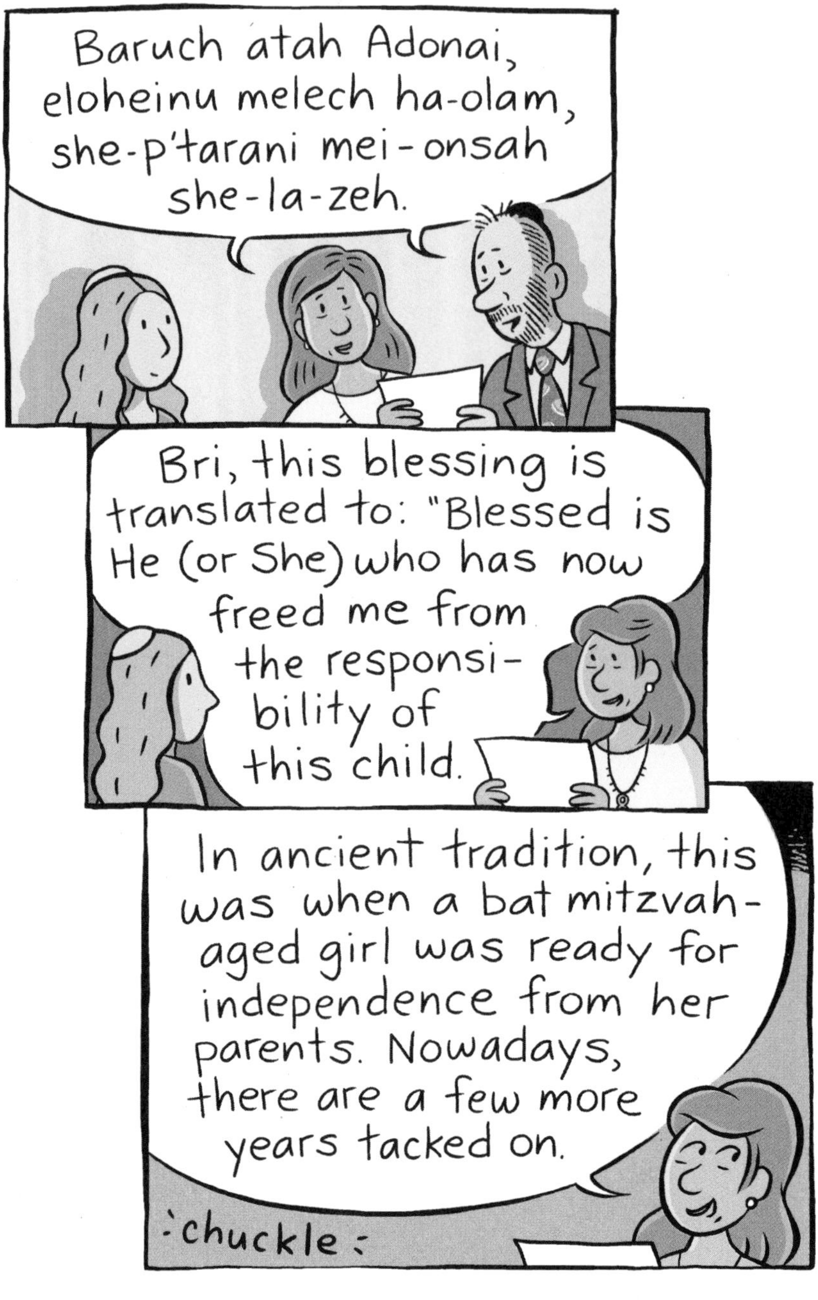
Baruch atah Adonai, eloheinu melech ha-olam, she-p'tarani mei-onsah she-la-zeh.
Bri, this blessing is translated to: "Blessed is He (or She) who has now freed me from the responsibility of this child.
In ancient tradition, this was when a bat mitzvah-aged girl was ready for independence from her parents. Nowadays, there are a few more years tacked on.
:chuckle:

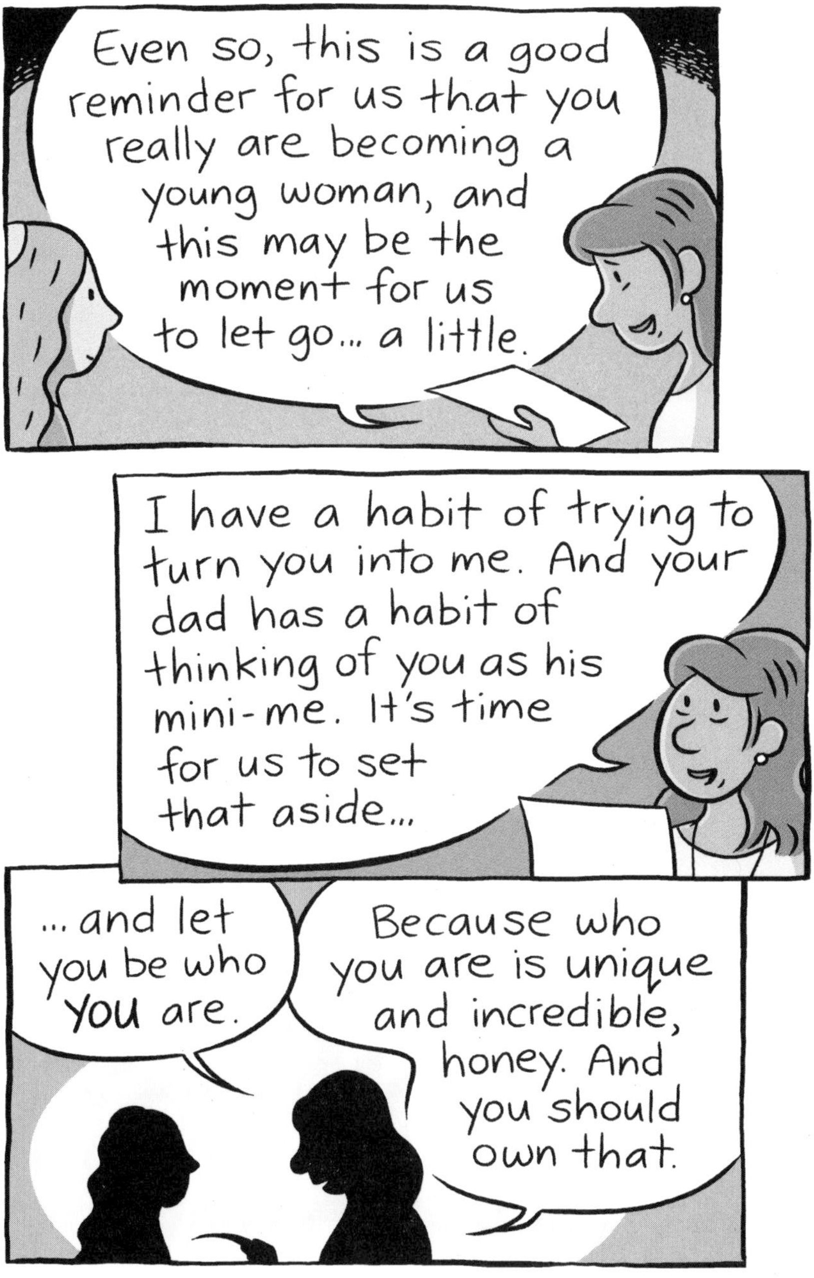
Even so, this is a good reminder for us that you really are becoming a young woman, and this may be the moment for us to let go... a little.
I have a habit of trying to turn you into me. And your dad has a habit of thinking of you as his mini-me. It's time for us to set that aside...
... and let you be who YOU are.
Because who you are is unique and incredible, honey. And you should own that.

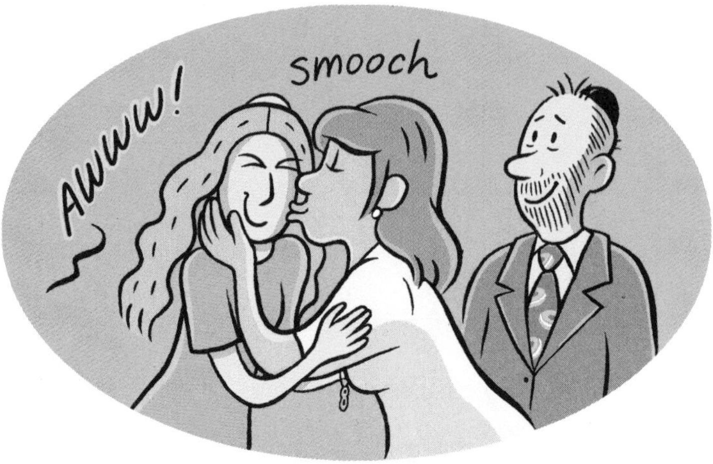
AWWW!
smooch

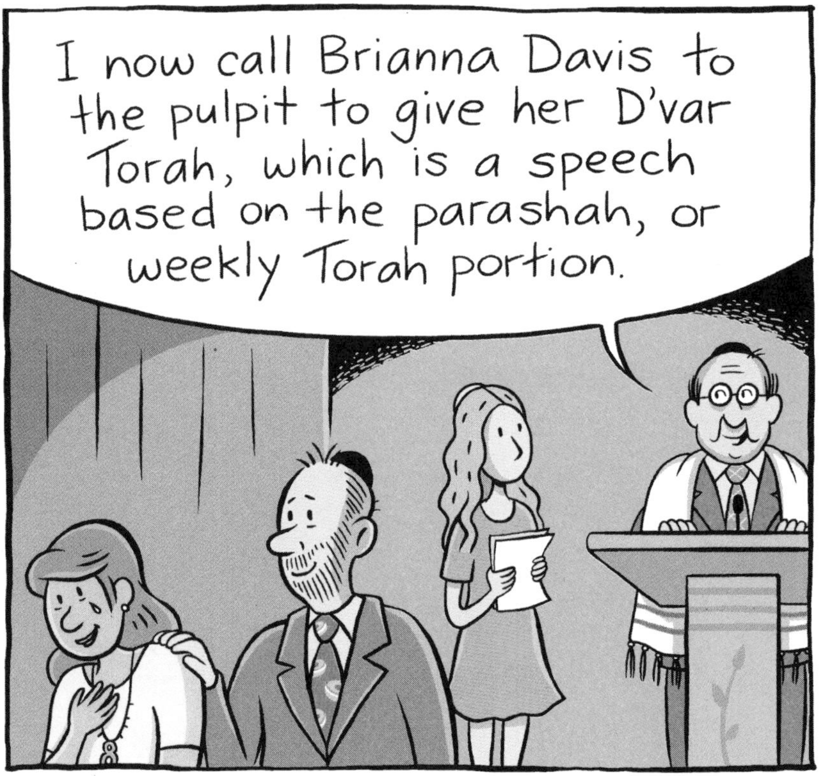
I now call Brianna Davis to the pulpit to give her D'var Torah, which is a speech based on the parashah, or weekly Torah portion.

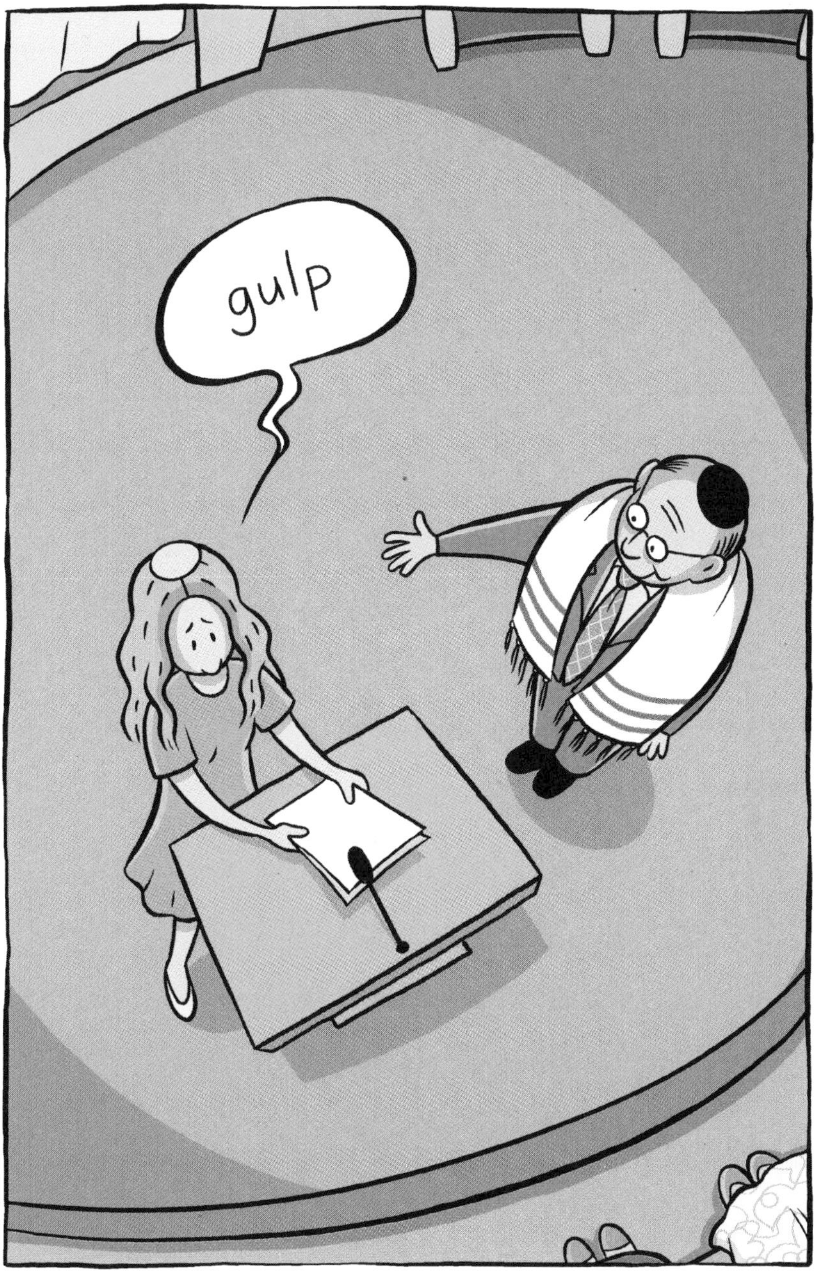
gulp

THREE DAYS AGO

I cannot believe I still haven't written my speech. What is wrong with me? Do I need some sort of speech-writing aversion therapy?

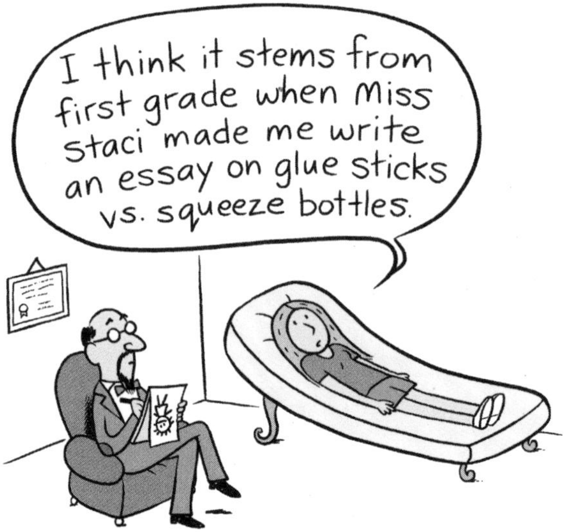
I think it stems from first grade when Miss Staci made me write an essay on glue sticks vs. squeeze bottles.

I'm at my dad's. Normally, I'd be at Mom's, but she gave up all pretense and is in the middle of deep-cleaning the entire condo.

We both decided it's best for our sanity that I stay at Dad's until Saturday.

probably cleaning our neighbors' places, too, at this point

wssh wssh

Glo

I've been sitting on my bed for, like, half an hour, trying to write this speech. I need to do it before Dad comes home. (He still thinks I wrote the darn thing.)

But my mind wanders . . . again.

I think back to a few days ago.

Unless you can think of a way to pay for four extra dinner servings for that buffet... nope.

Emmie, Sarah, and I had a group text. They offered to chip in for the four dinners, but I said no way.

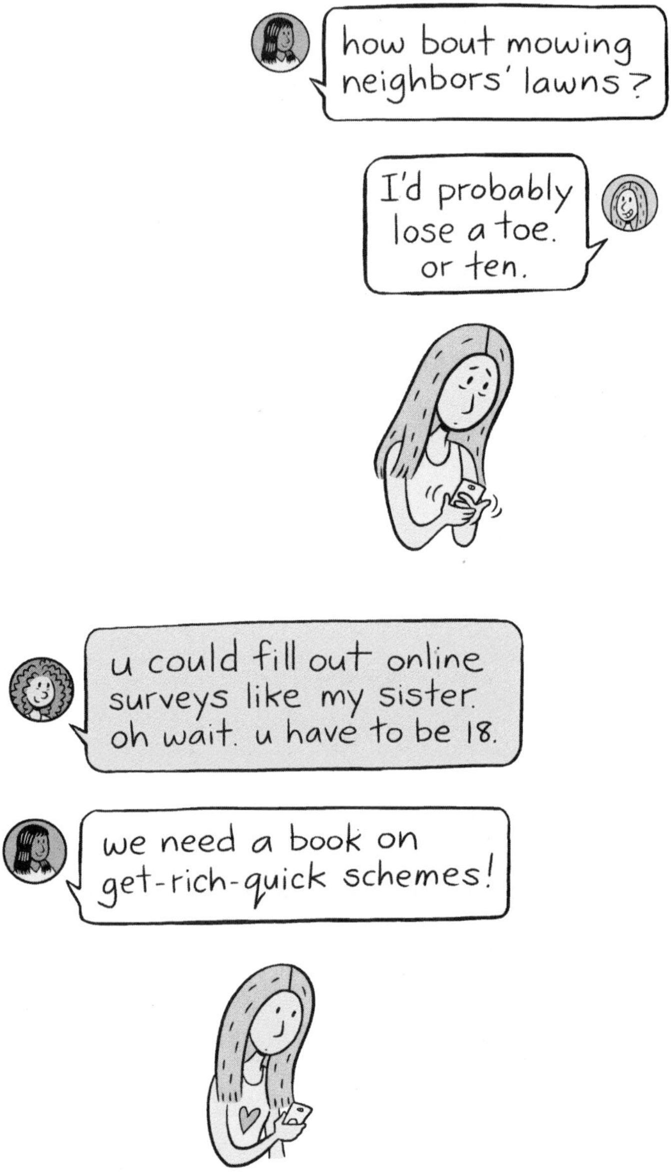
how bout mowing neighbors' lawns?
I'd probably lose a toe. or ten.
u could fill out online surveys like my sister. oh wait. u have to be 18.
we need a book on get-rich-quick schemes!

That's when an idea hit. Books!

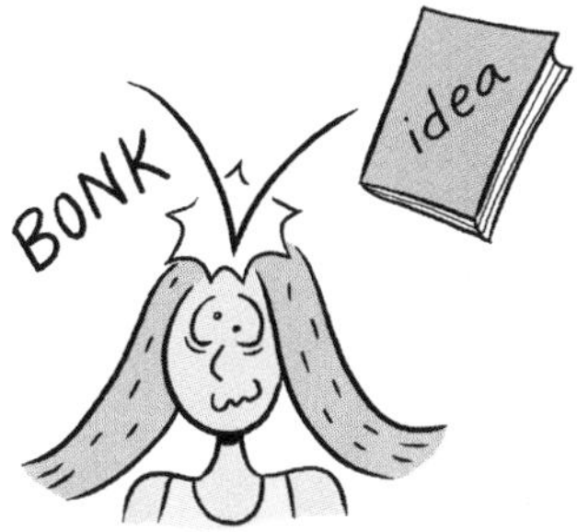
BONK
idea

During the next few hours, I ran back and forth between my mom's house, my dad's, Em's, and Sarah's. We all gathered as many books and clothes as we could and dumped them in the middle of my room.

There was a TON.

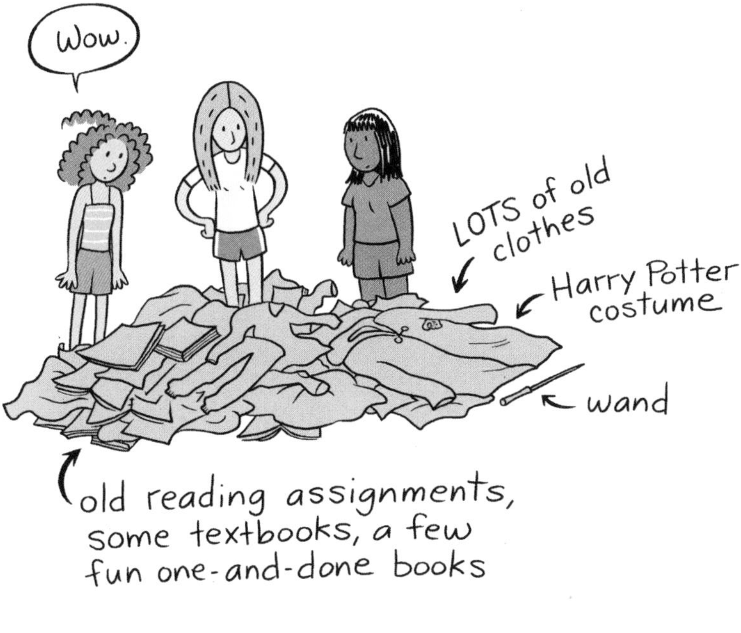
Wow.
LOTS of old clothes
Harry Potter costume
wand
old reading assignments, some textbooks, a few fun one-and-done books

I told Mom about the plan and asked if she would help. Luckily, she enthusiastically agreed.

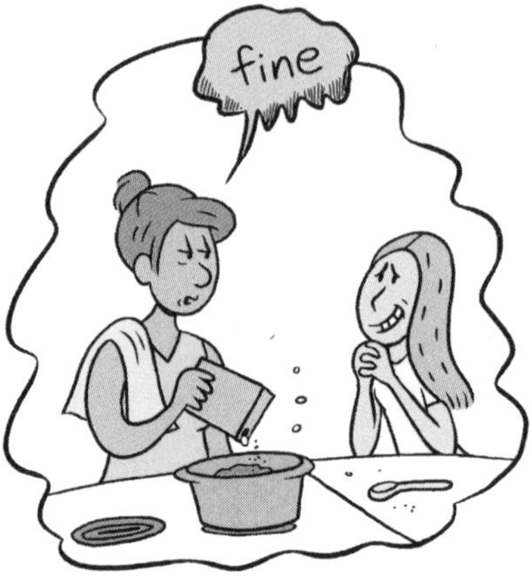
fine

So we drove to the used bookstore.

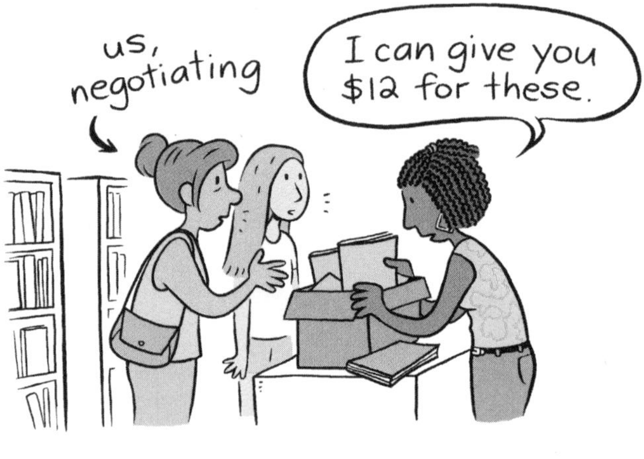
us, negotiating
I can give you $12 for these.

I groan. Not enough. But it helps.

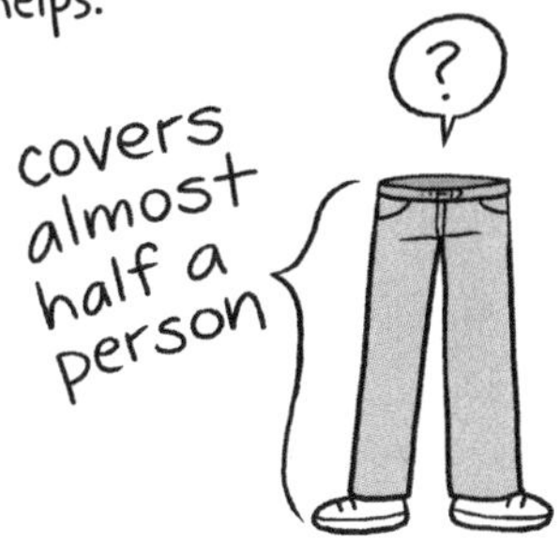
?
covers almost half a person

Then we drove to the consignment shop.

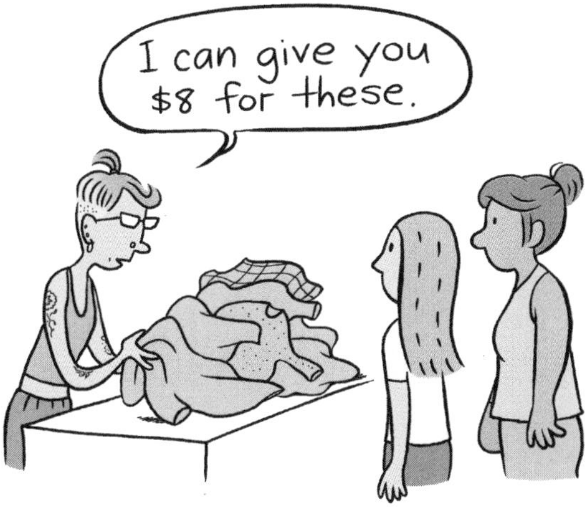
I can give you $8 for these.

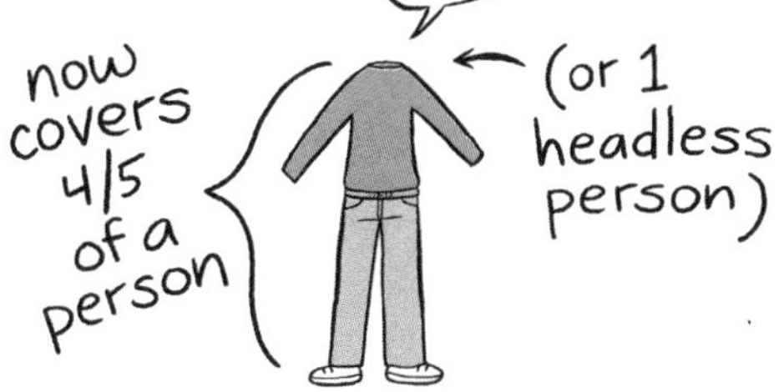
ahh!
now covers 4/5 of a person
(or 1 headless person)

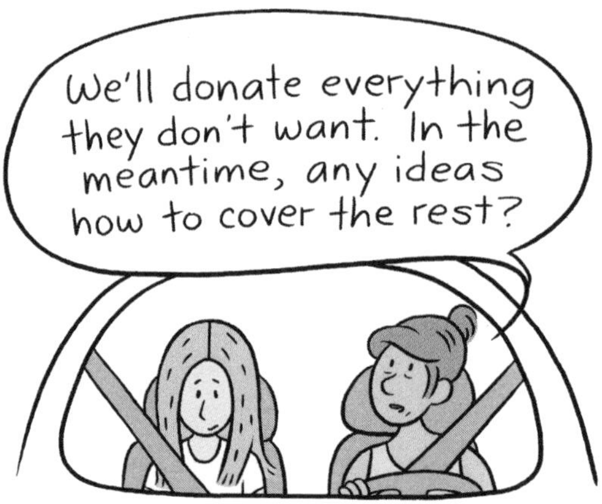
We'll donate everything they don't want. In the meantime, any ideas how to cover the rest?

Plan B. When I got home, I started rummaging through my bookshelf. In the fall, Emmie and I took a babysitting class at the YMCA, and we collected a bunch of phone numbers afterward from neighborhood parents. We were determined to make a pile of money during the school year. Em managed to snag a few jobs, but me . . .

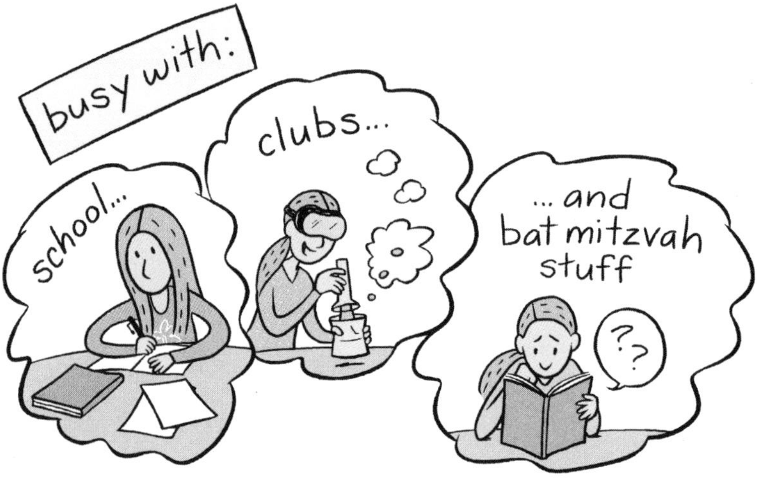
busy with:
school...
clubs...
...and bat mitzvah stuff
??

Found it!

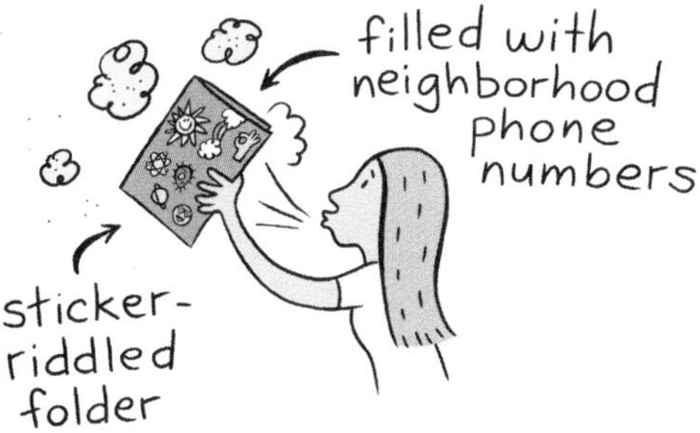
filled with neighborhood phone numbers
sticker-riddled folder

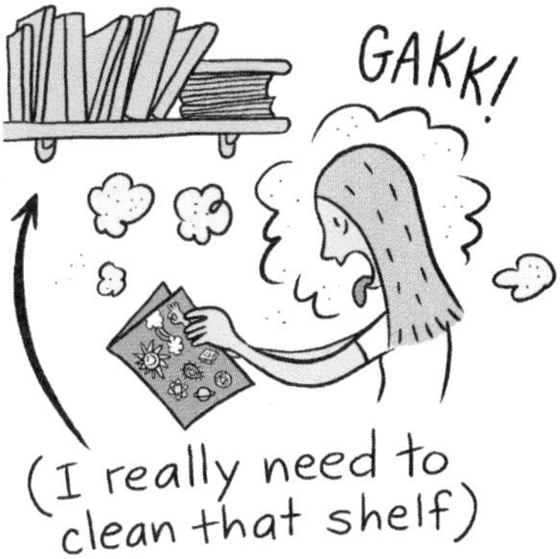
GAKK!
(I really need to clean that shelf)

I scanned all the numbers and chose a bunch that I thought would be a good fit. I texted the parents.

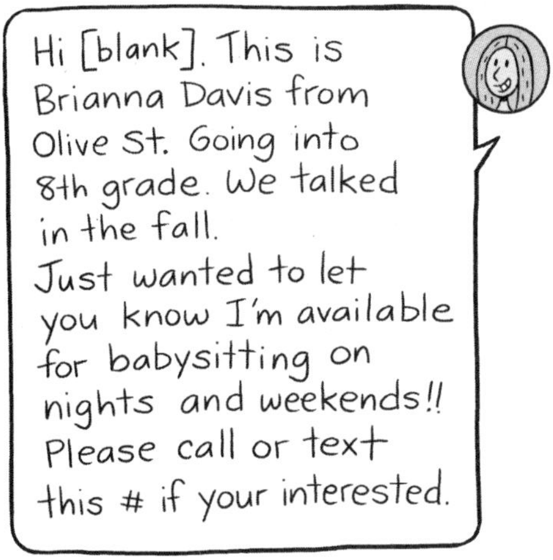
Hi [blank]. This is Brianna Davis from Olive St. Going into 8th grade. We talked in the fall.
Just wanted to let you know I'm available for babysitting on nights and weekends!! Please call or text this # if your interested.

Argh!!

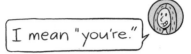

I mean "you're."

My English-teaching mom would have a fit.

Only one person responded. BUT—I have a babysitting job lined up after the bat mitzvah.

I can cover the rest with some of my bat mitzvah gift money, and then put it back in my savings as soon as I get enough babysitting cash.

Again, Mom enthusiastically agreed.

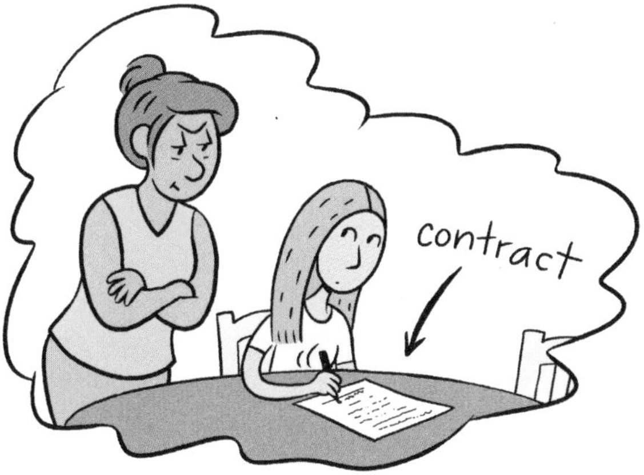
contract

It's not the ideal situation, but it works.

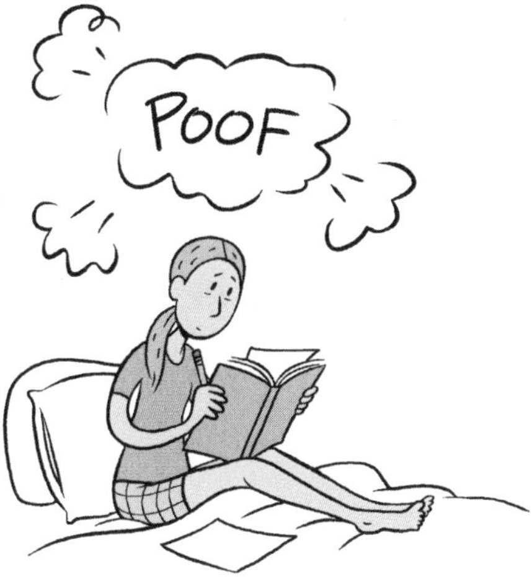
POOF

I snap out of my daydream and try to focus again. The speech!

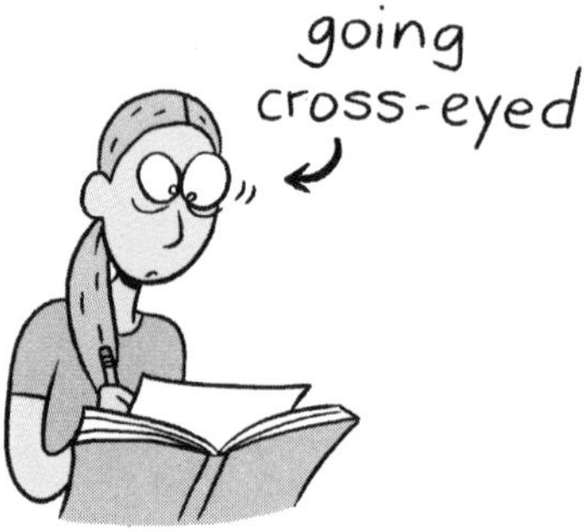
going cross-eyed

My dad knocks and peeks in before I can say anything.

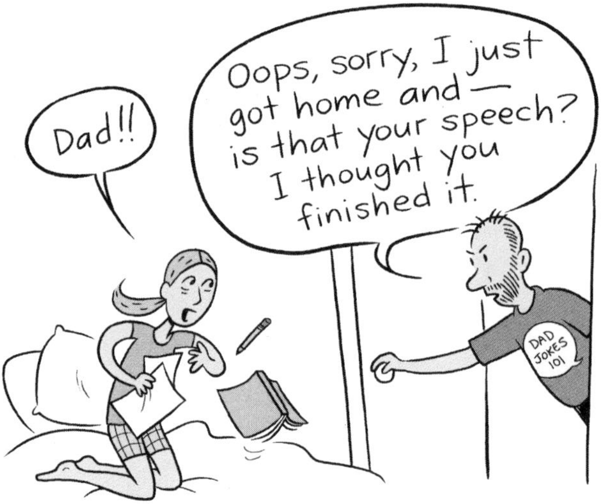
Dad!!
Oops, sorry, I just got home and— is that your speech? I thought you finished it.
DAD JOKES 101

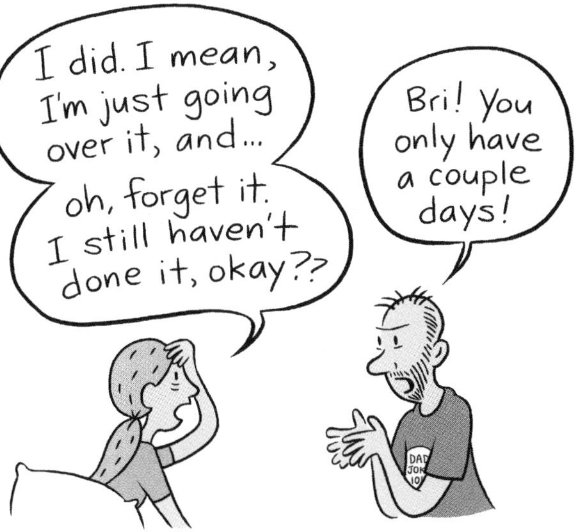
I did. I mean, I'm just going over it, and...
oh, forget it. I still haven't done it, okay??
Bri! You only have a couple days!
DAD JOK 10

He catches himself. Dad doesn't like to be one of those parents who flies off the handle.

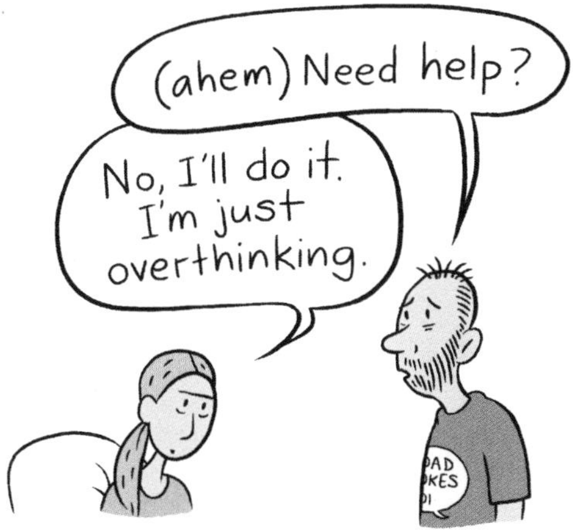
(ahem) Need help?
No, I'll do it. I'm just overthinking.
DAD KES 1

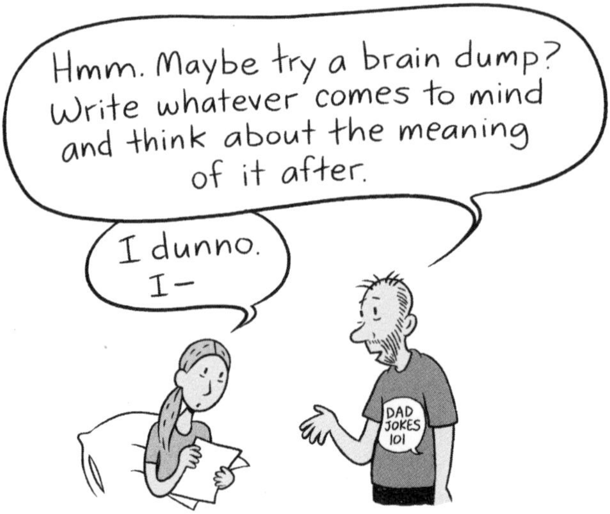
Hmm. Maybe try a brain dump? Write whatever comes to mind and think about the meaning of it after.
I dunno. I–
DAD JOKES 101

I sit up.

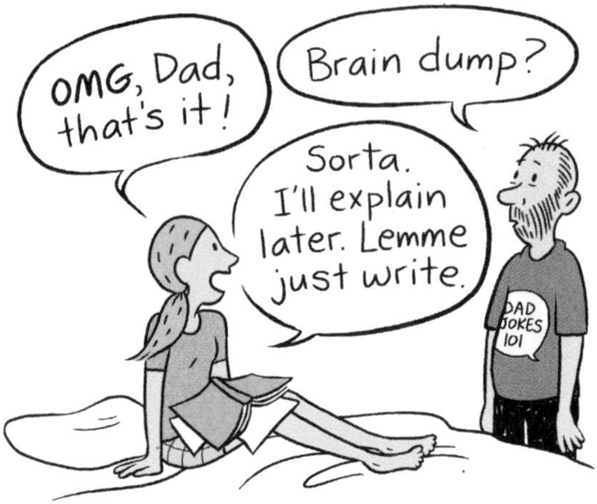
OMG, Dad, that's it!
Brain dump?
Sorta. I'll explain later. Lemme just write.
DAD JOKES 101

I start penning furiously. It's about time.

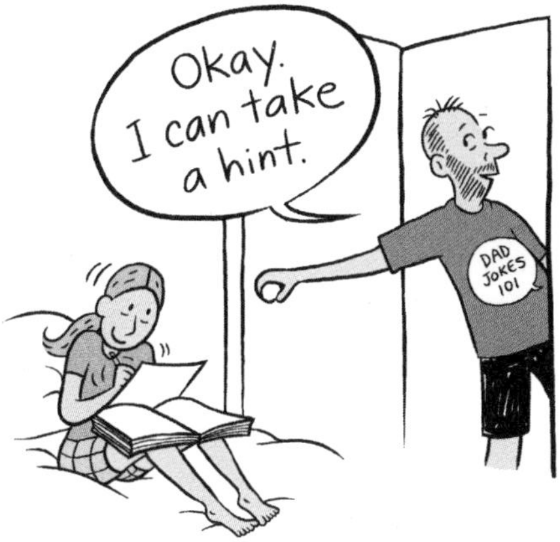
Okay. I can take a hint.
DAD JOKES 101

He closes the door.

I'm finally dumping! An avalanche! Well, maybe a couple big pieces of rock, but it's a start.

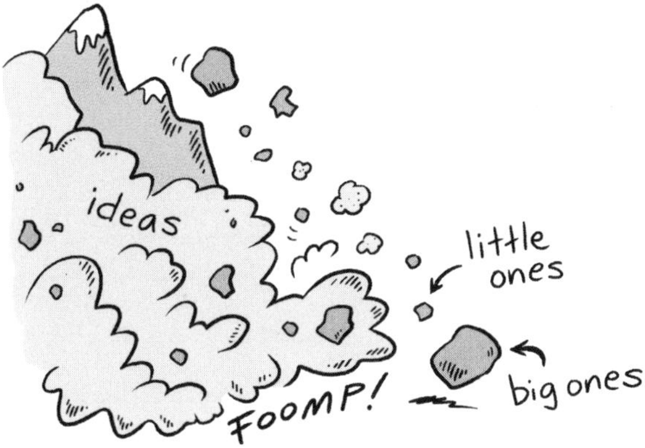
ideas
little ones
big ones
FOOMP!

I write and write until Dad calls me for dinner.

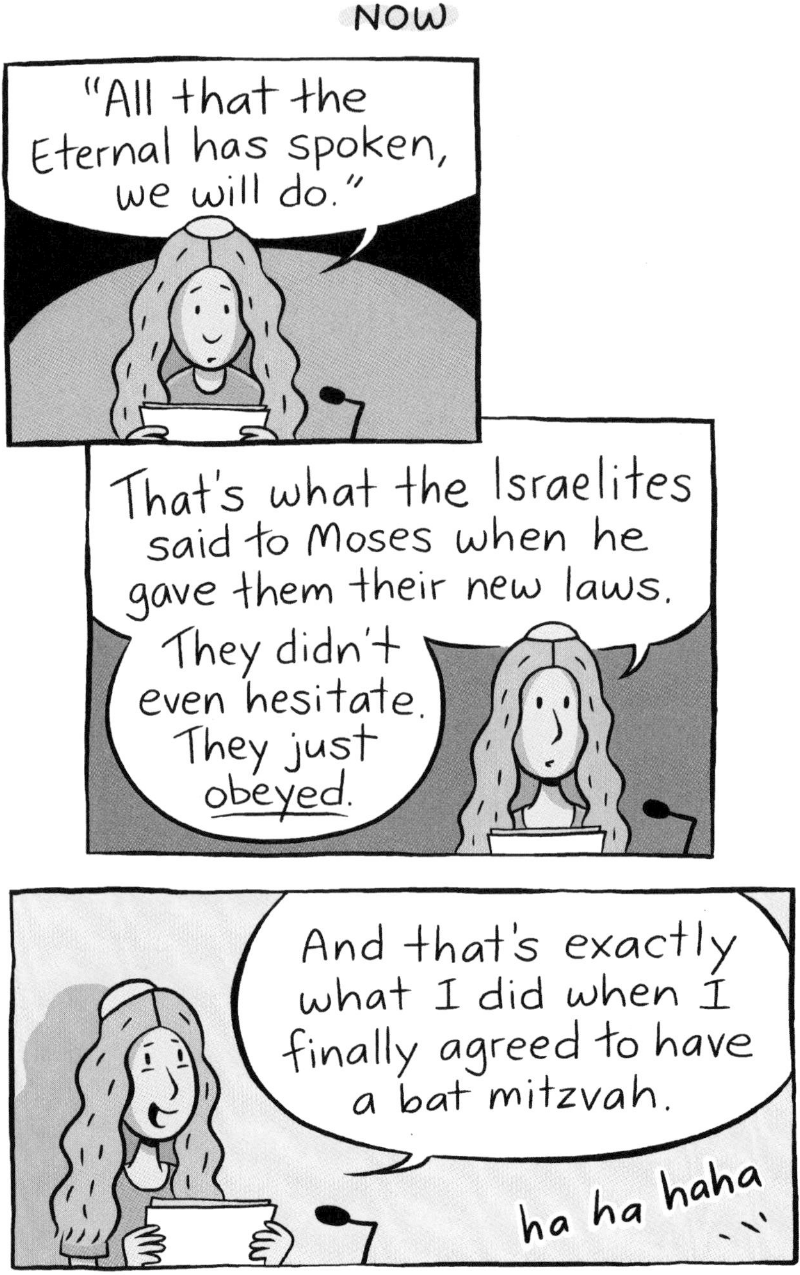
NOW
"All that the Eternal has spoken, we will do."
That's what the Israelites said to Moses when he gave them their new laws.
They didn't even hesitate. They just obeyed.
And that's exactly what I did when I finally agreed to have a bat mitzvah.
ha ha haha

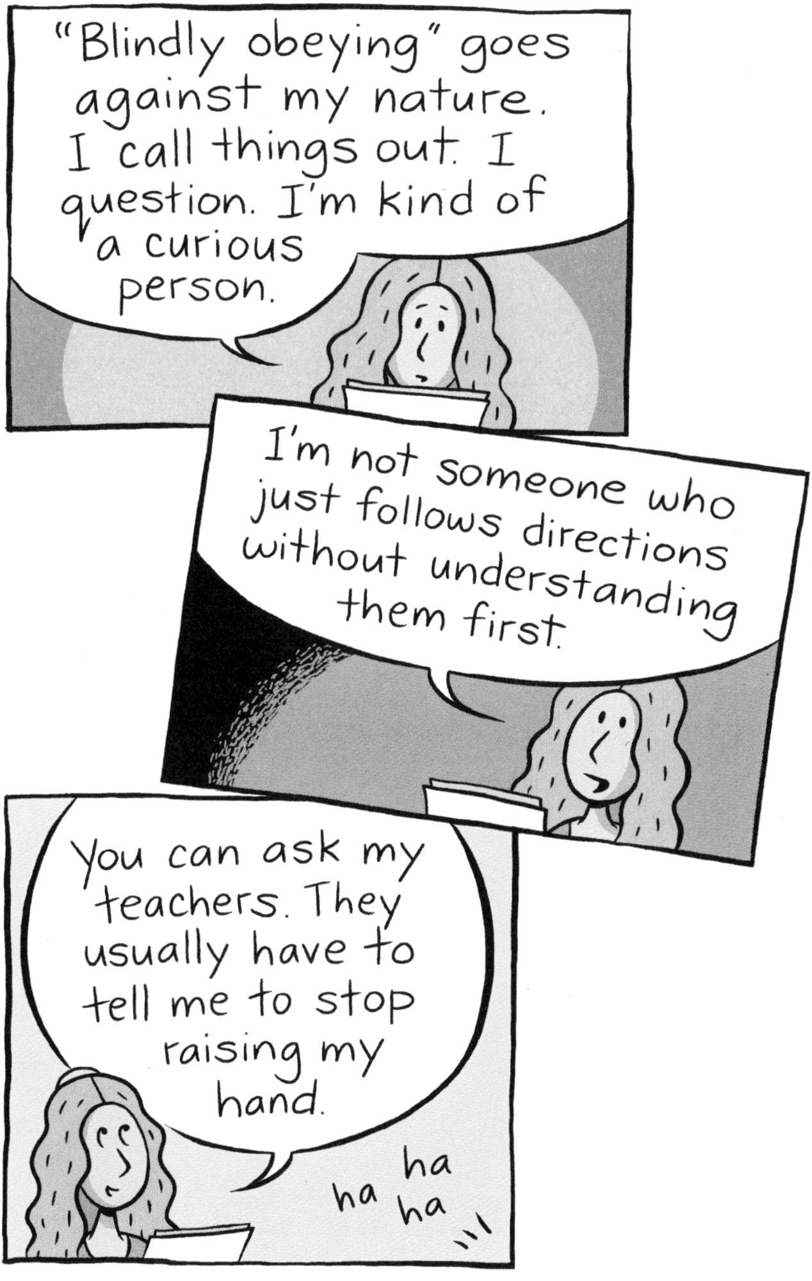
"Blindly obeying" goes against my nature. I call things out. I question. I'm kind of a curious person.
I'm not someone who just follows directions without understanding them first.
You can ask my teachers. They usually have to tell me to stop raising my hand.
ha ha ha

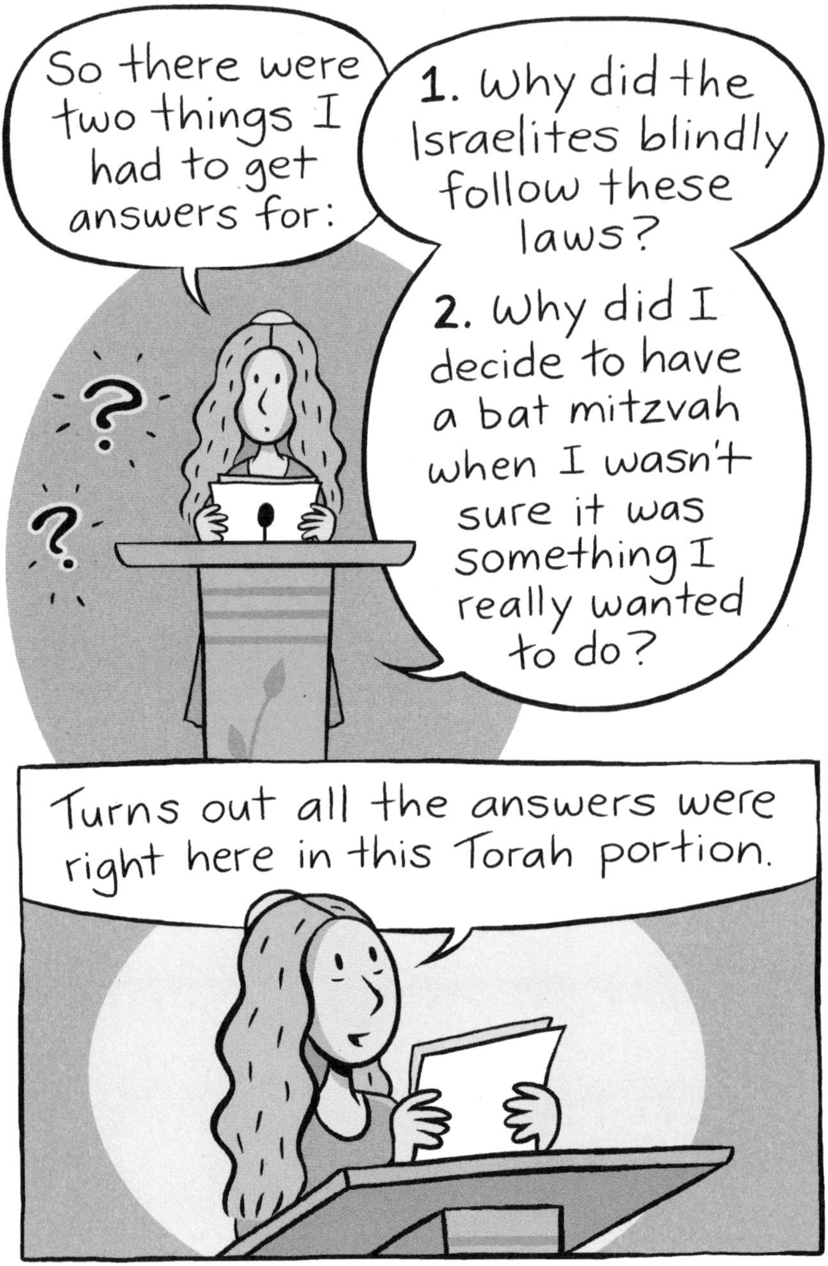
So there were two things I had to get answers for:
1. Why did the Israelites blindly follow these laws?
2. Why did I decide to have a bat mitzvah when I wasn't sure it was something I really wanted to do?
Turns out all the answers were right here in this Torah portion.

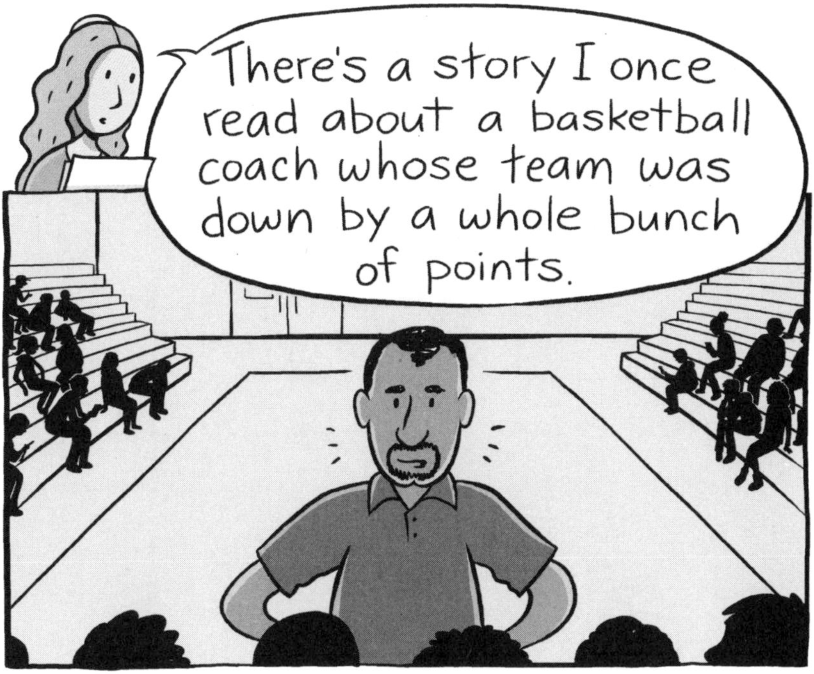
There's a story I once read about a basketball coach whose team was down by a whole bunch of points.

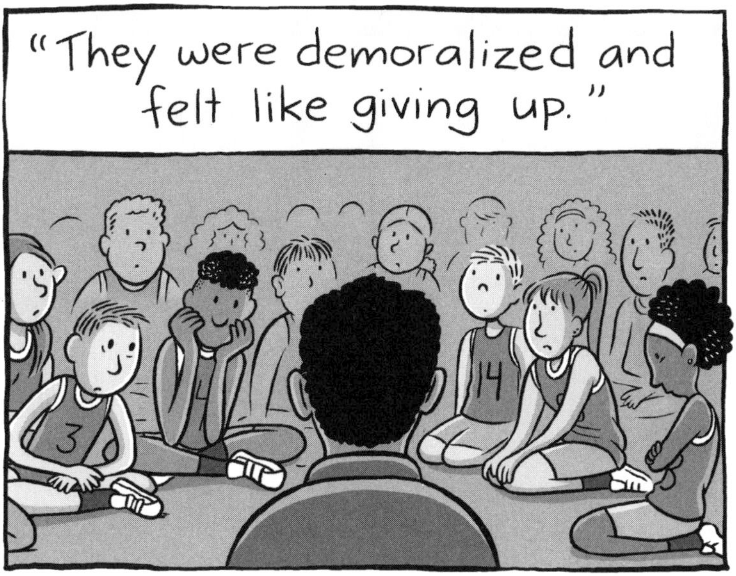
"They were demoralized and felt like giving up."
14
3

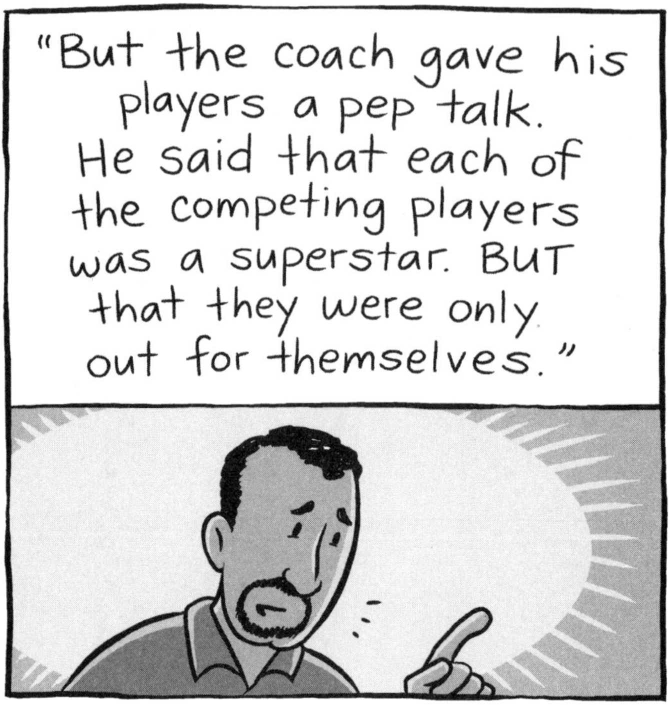
"But the coach gave his players a pep talk. He said that each of the competing players was a superstar. BUT that they were only out for themselves."

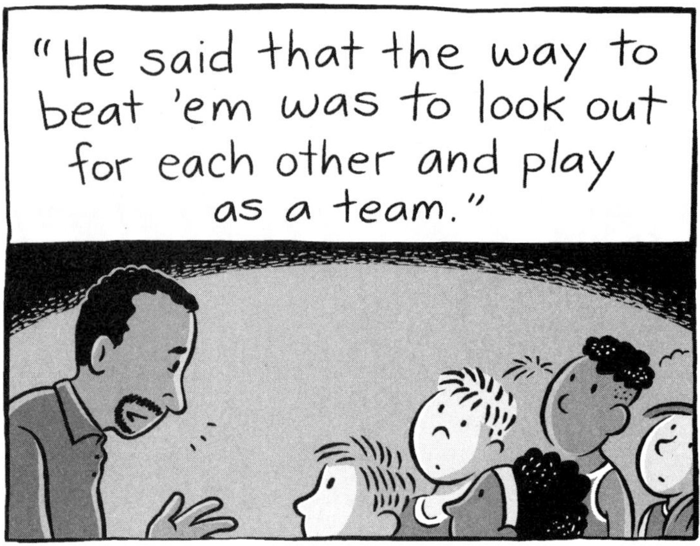
"He said that the way to beat 'em was to look out for each other and play as a team."

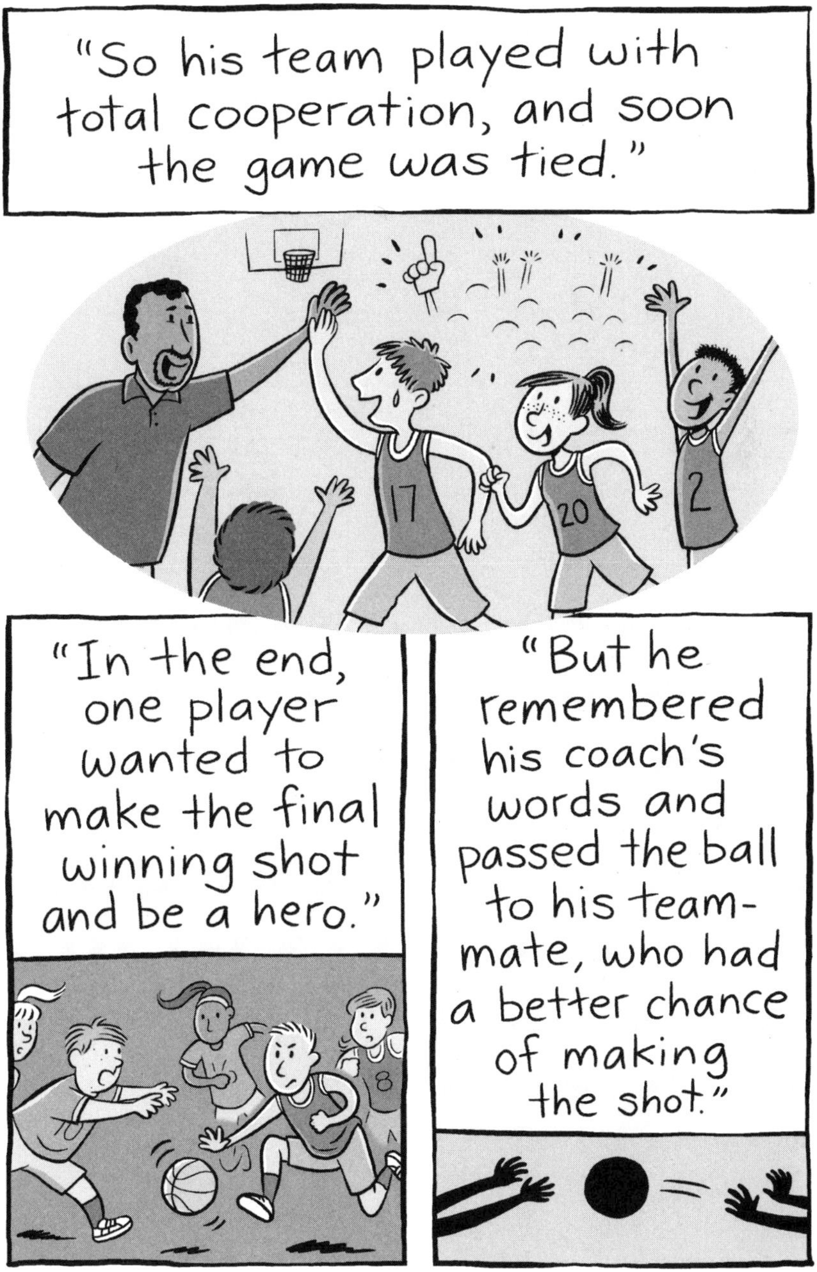
"So his team played with total cooperation, and soon the game was tied."
"In the end, one player wanted to make the final winning shot and be a hero."
"But he remembered his coach's words and passed the ball to his teammate, who had a better chance of making the shot."

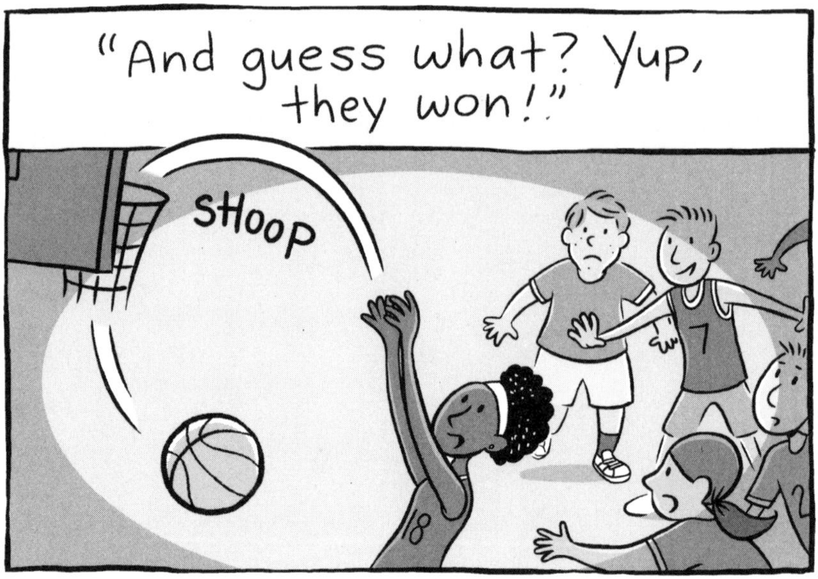
"And guess what? Yup, they won!"
SHOOP
18
7

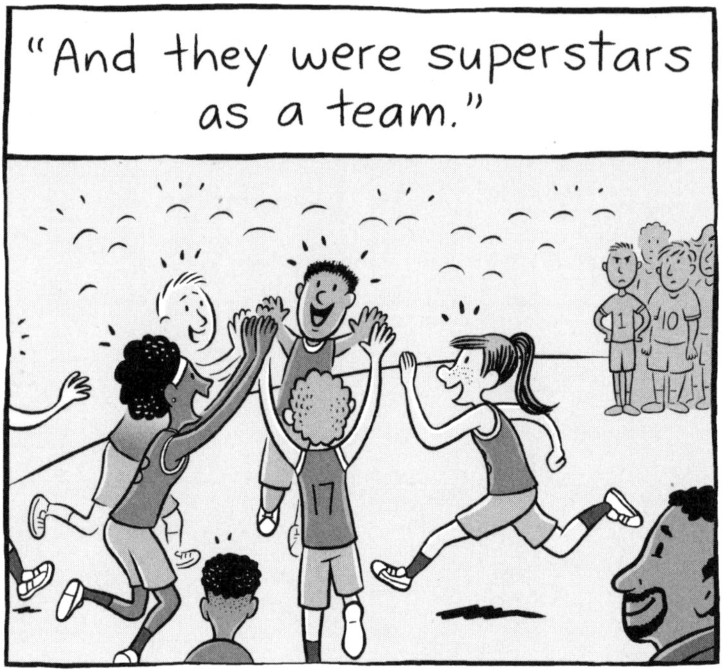
"And they were superstars as a team."
17
1
10

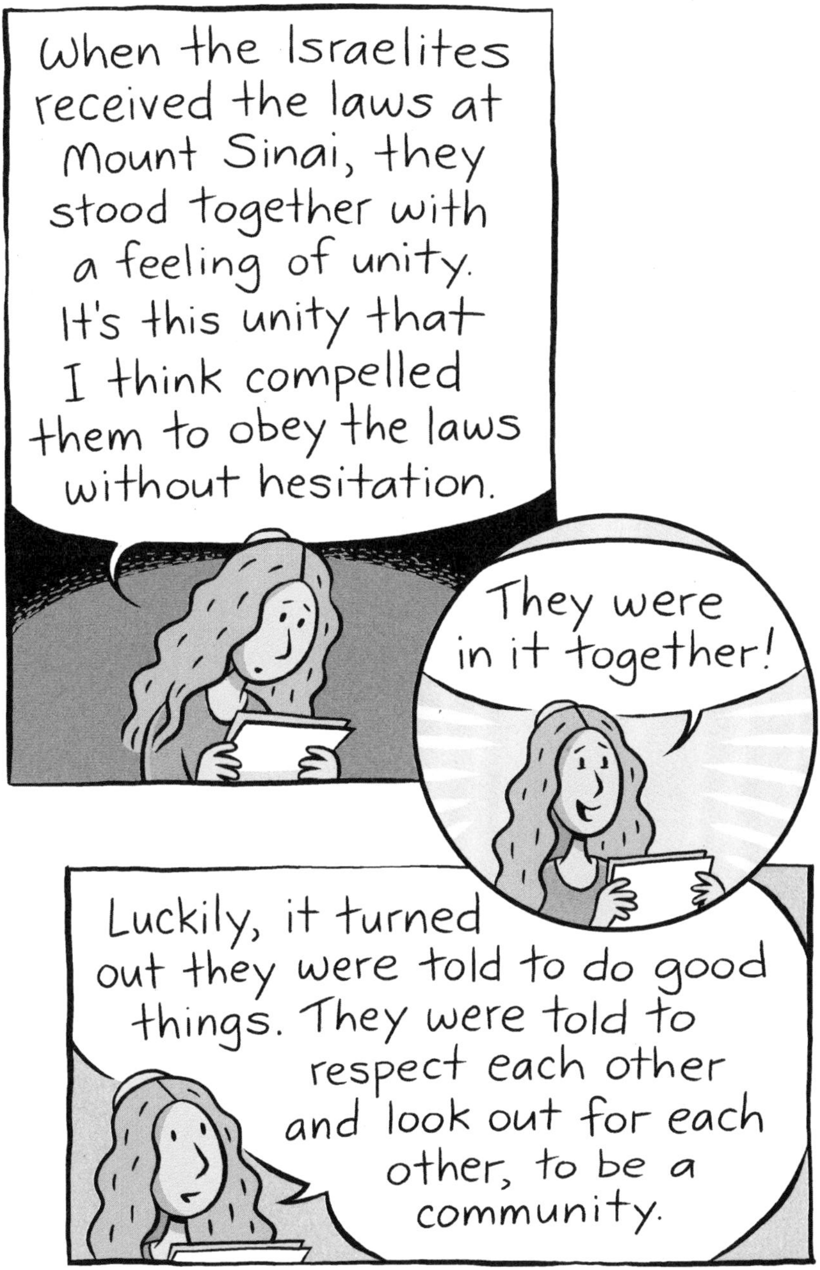
When the Israelites received the laws at Mount Sinai, they stood together with a feeling of unity. It's this unity that I think compelled them to obey the laws without hesitation.
They were in it together!
Luckily, it turned out they were told to do good things. They were told to respect each other and look out for each other, to be a community.

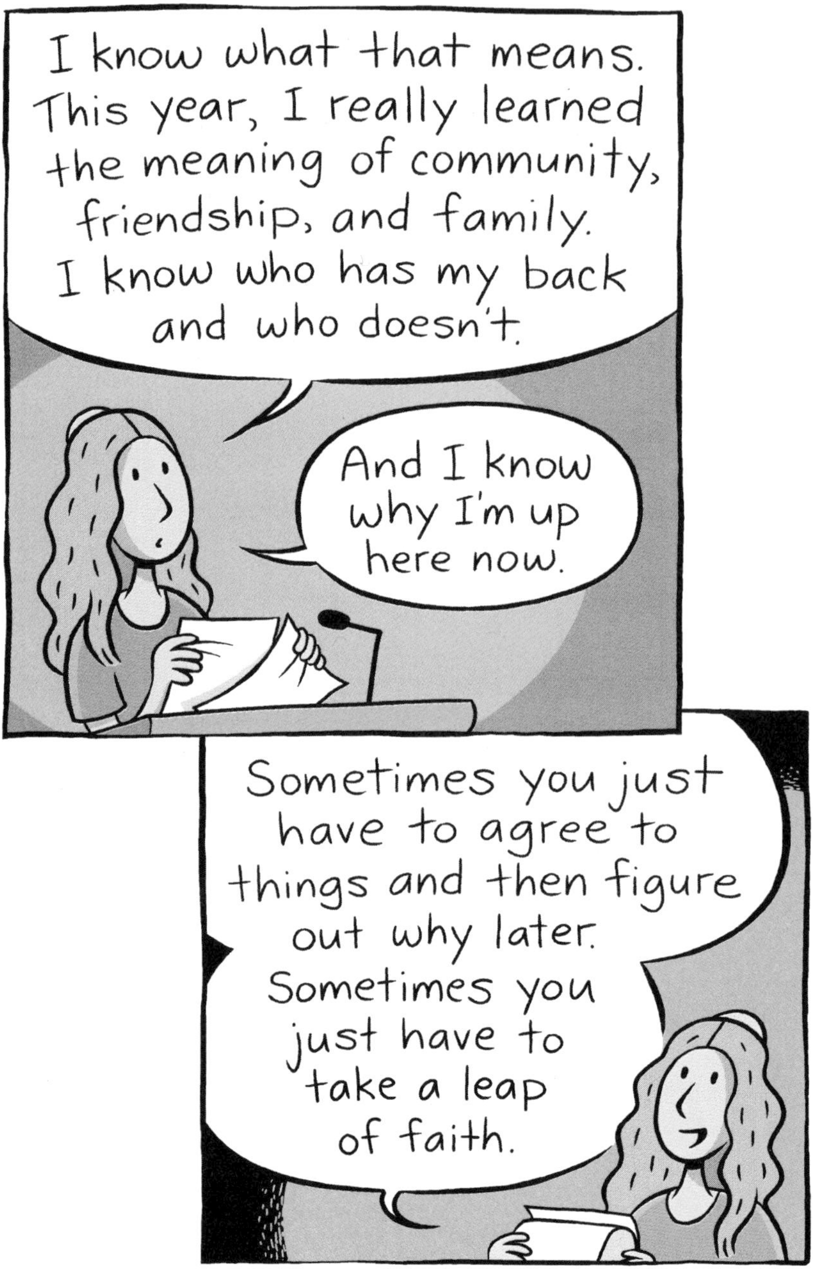
I know what that means. This year, I really learned the meaning of community, friendship, and family. I know who has my back and who doesn't.
And I know why I'm up here now.
Sometimes you just have to agree to things and then figure out why later. Sometimes you just have to take a leap of faith.

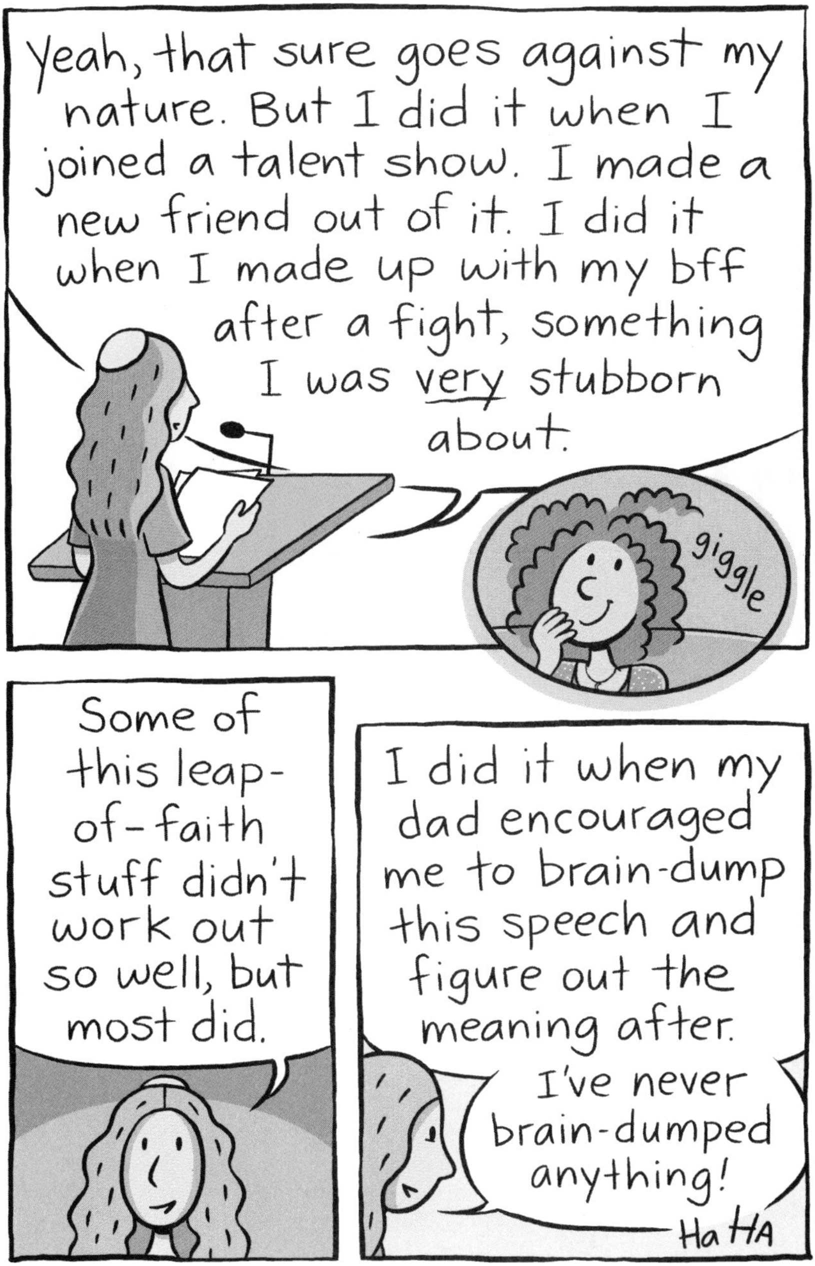

Yeah, that sure goes against my nature. But I did it when I joined a talent show. I made a new friend out of it. I did it when I made up with my bff after a fight, something I was very stubborn about.
giggle
Some of this leap-of-faith stuff didn't work out so well, but most did.
I did it when my dad encouraged me to brain-dump this speech and figure out the meaning after.
I've never brain-dumped anything!
Ha HA

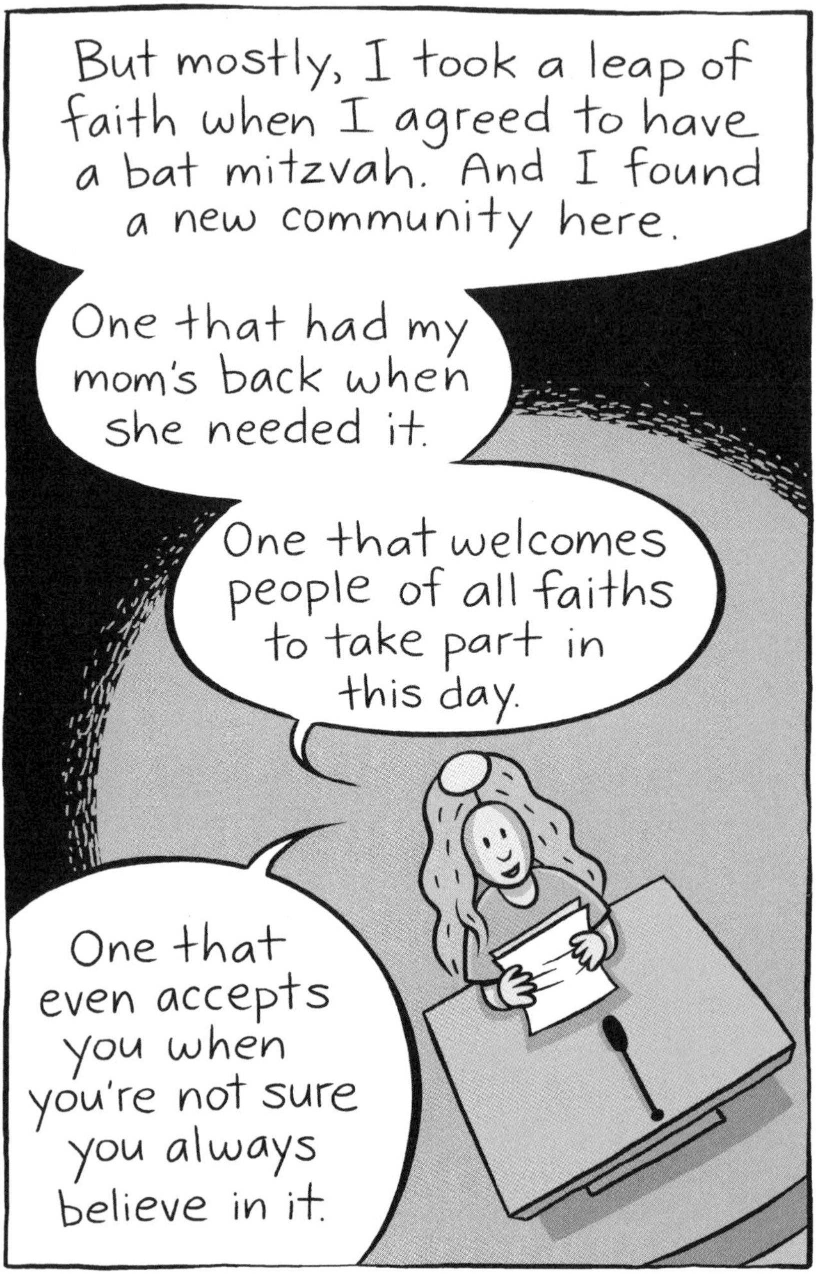
But mostly, I took a leap of faith when I agreed to have a bat mitzvah. And I found a new community here.
One that had my mom's back when she needed it.
One that welcomes people of all faiths to take part in this day.
One that even accepts you when you're not sure you always believe in it.

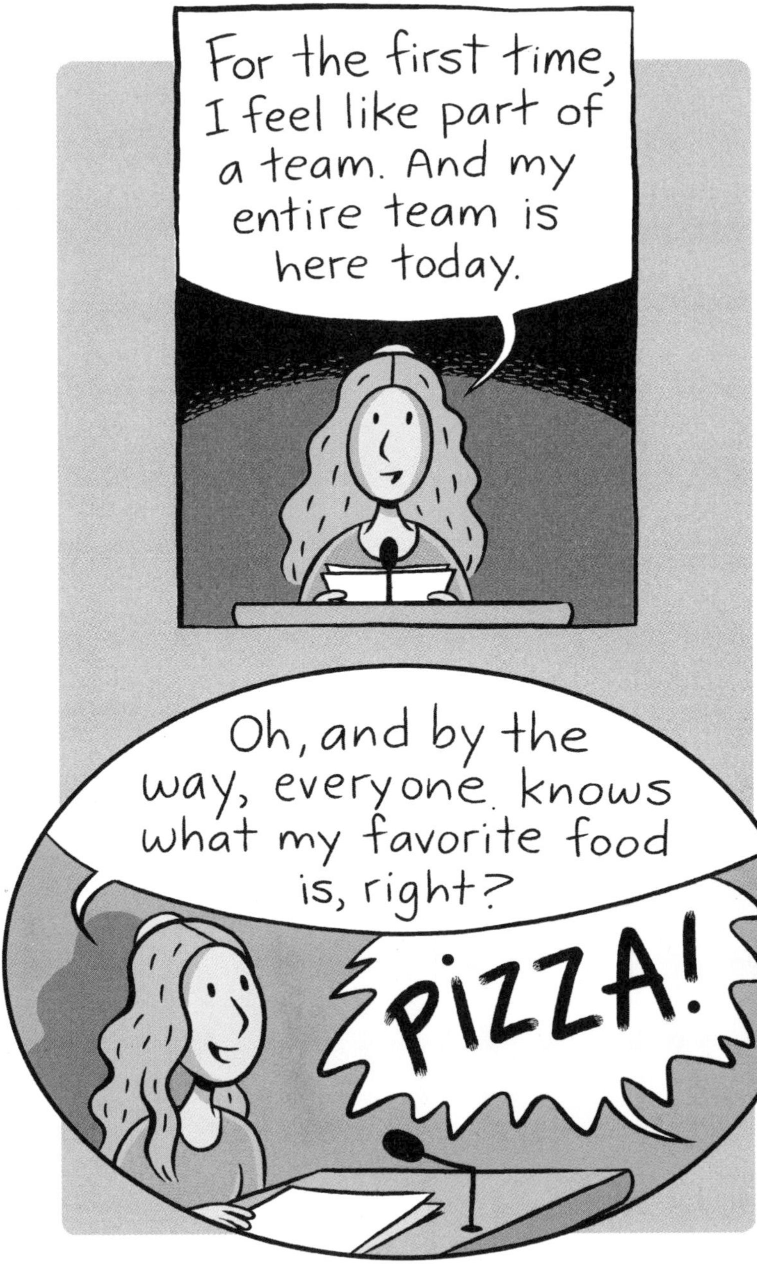
For the first time, I feel like part of a team. And my entire team is here today.
Oh, and by the way, everyone knows what my favorite food is, right?
PIZZA!

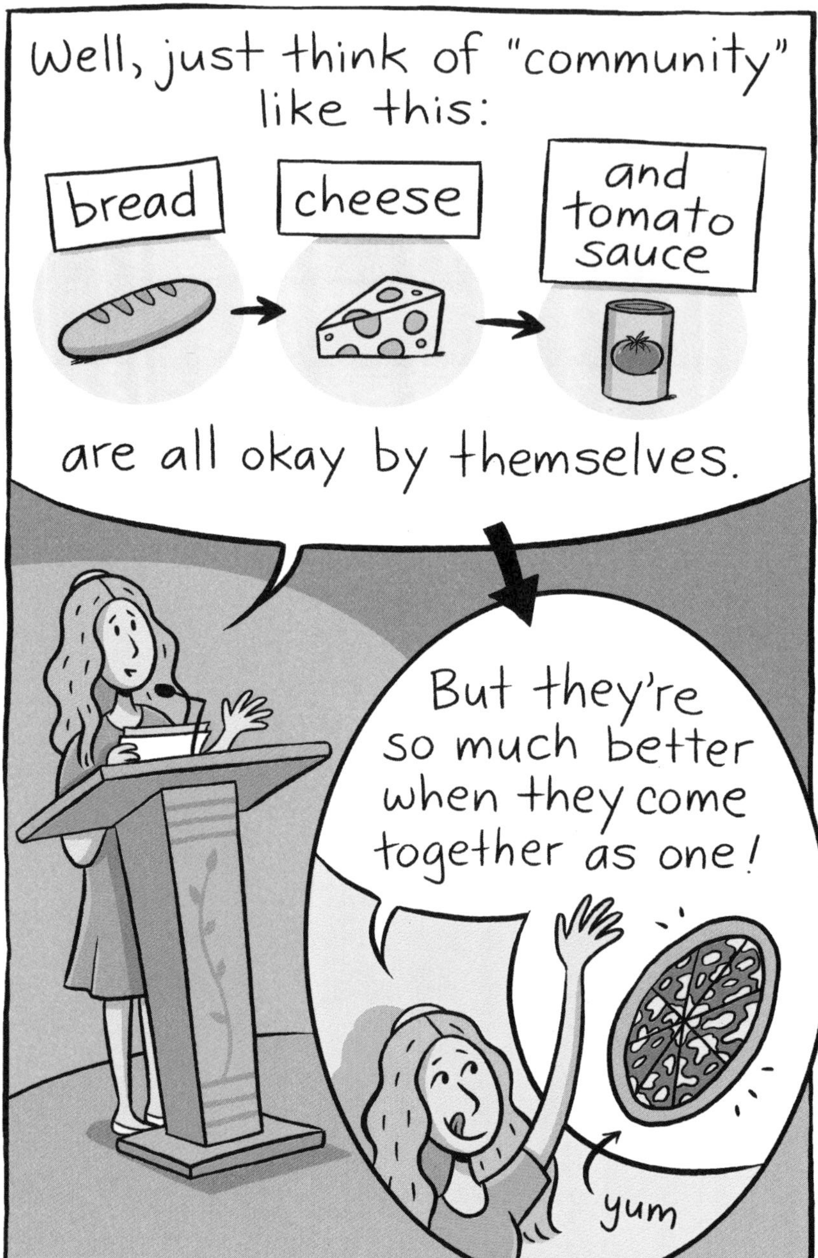
Well, just think of "community" like this:
bread
cheese
and tomato sauce
are all okay by themselves.
But they're so much better when they come together as one!
yum

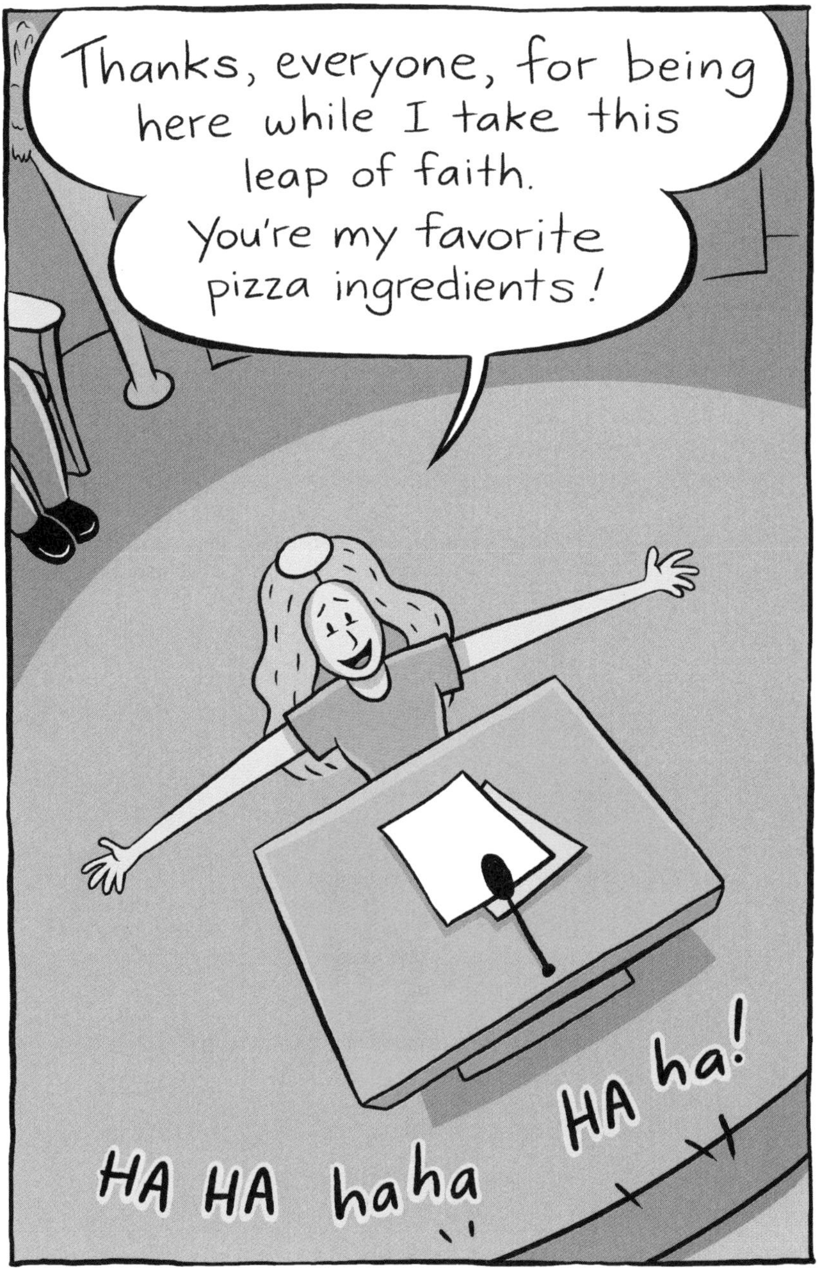
Thanks, everyone, for being here while I take this leap of faith. You're my favorite pizza ingredients!
HA HA haha
HA ha!

NOW

We're all back in the atrium, snacking on little appetizers. The cantor just led a totally beautiful havdalah ceremony, marking the end of Shabbat (Sabbath), which is sundown Friday to sundown Saturday.

Shavua Tov, Shavua Tov...

havdalah candle

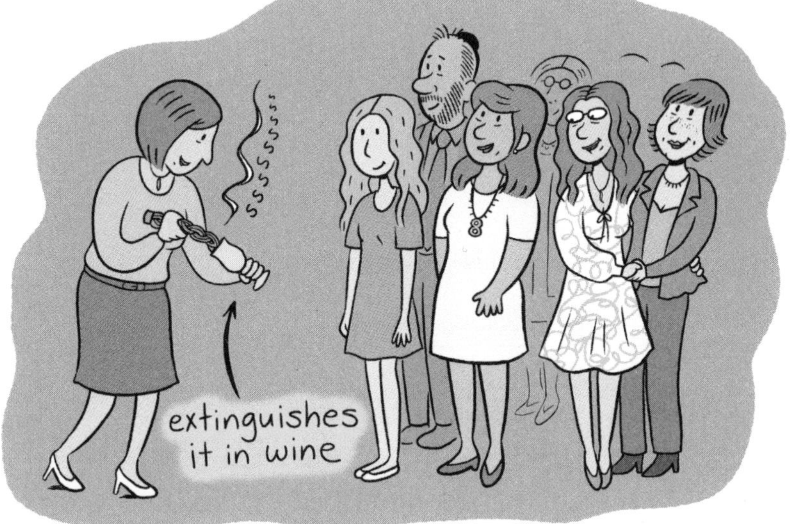
sssssssss
extinguishes
it in wine

Now I'm in full-fledged relief mode.

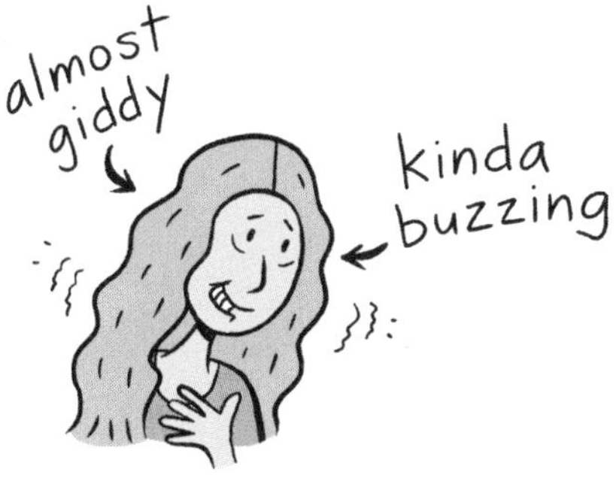
almost
giddy
kinda
buzzing

But I still have to be "on" 'cause people are congratulating me left and right.

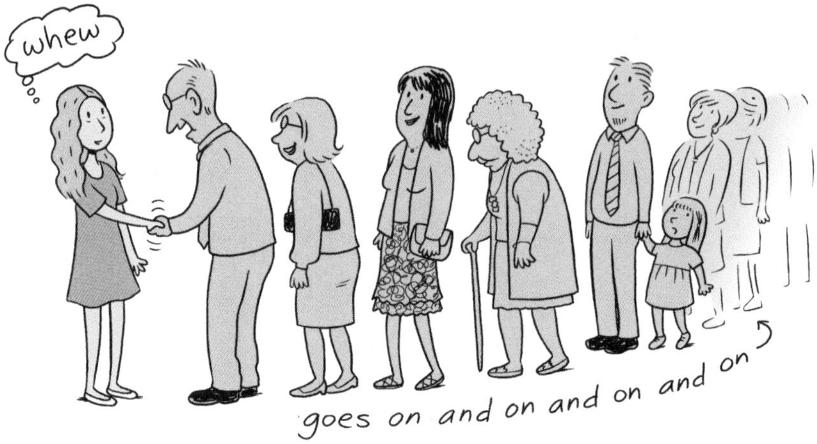
whew
goes on and on and on and on

Also, I'm so hungry, I just asked (okay, ordered) Dev to grab some snacks for me.

The doors suddenly open—loudly—and I see Zoe and Olivia walk in, dressed to the nines.

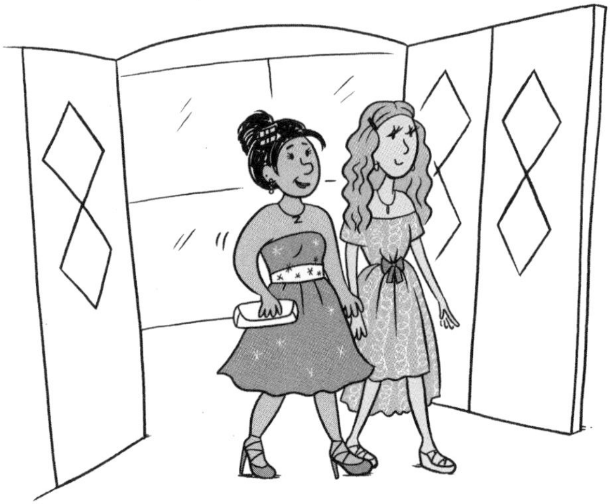

I can't believe it. They didn't even come to the service; they just came for the party!

I shake my head. I'm momentarily angry, but I **won't** let this ruin anything.

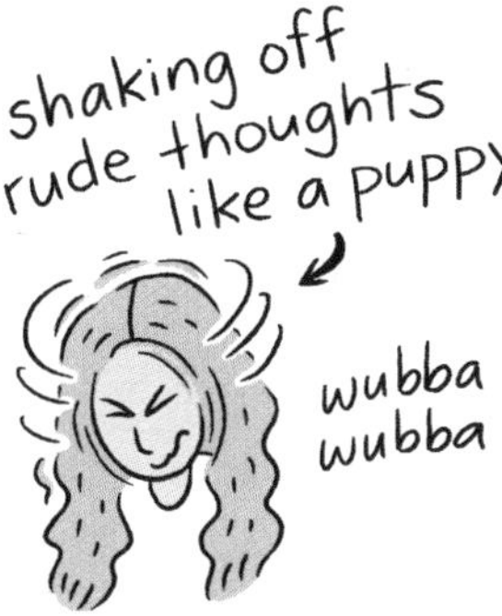
shaking off rude thoughts like a puppy
wubba wubba

The rabbi walks over, a stuffed grape leaf shoved in his mouth. Guess I'm not the only hungry one.

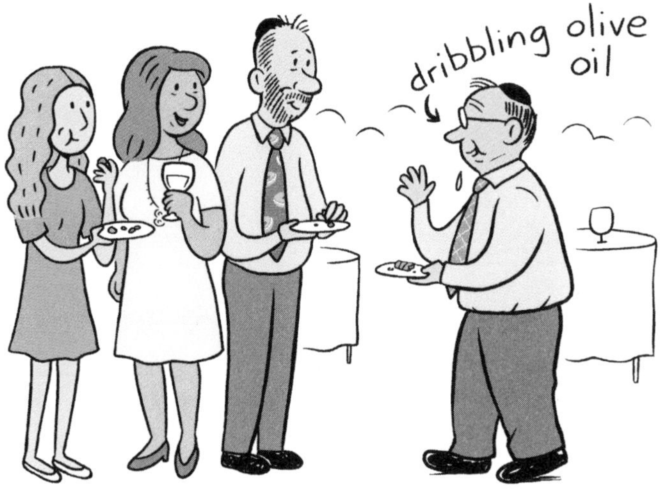
dribbling olive oil

Thankfully, he swallows the appetizer before he speaks.

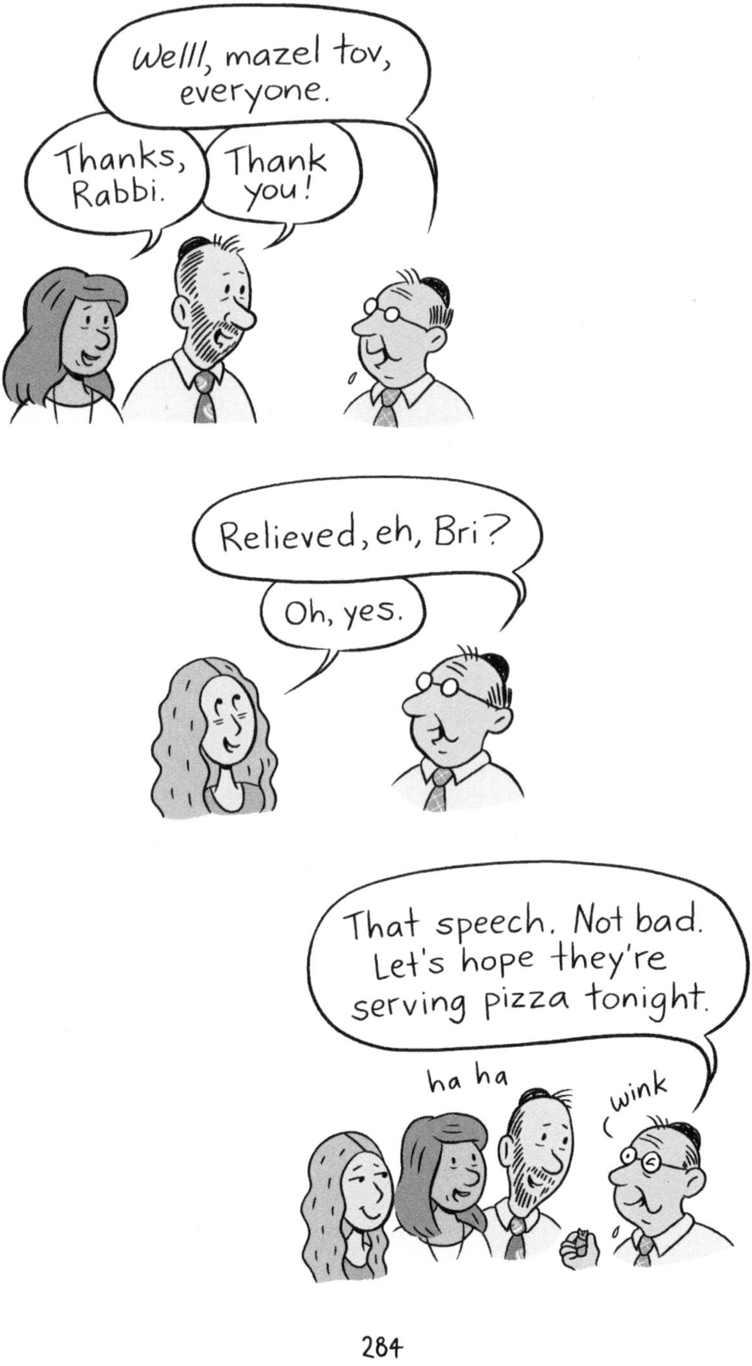
Welll, mazel tov, everyone.
Thanks, Rabbi.
Thank you!
Relieved, eh, Bri?
Oh, yes.
That speech. Not bad. Let's hope they're serving pizza tonight.
ha ha
wink

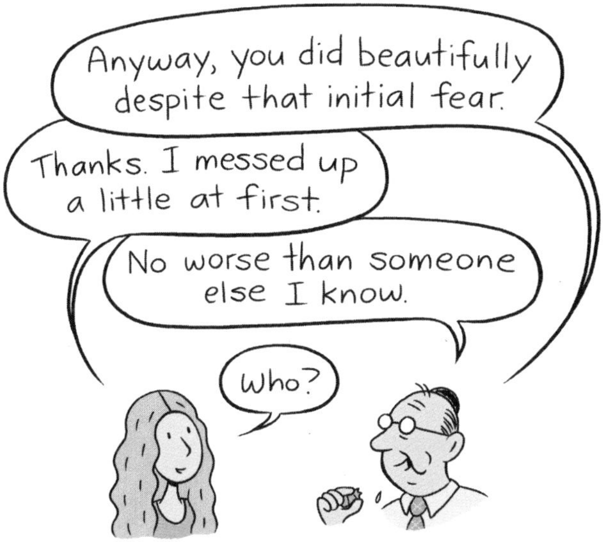
Anyway, you did beautifully despite that initial fear.
Thanks. I messed up a little at first.
No worse than someone else I know.
Who?

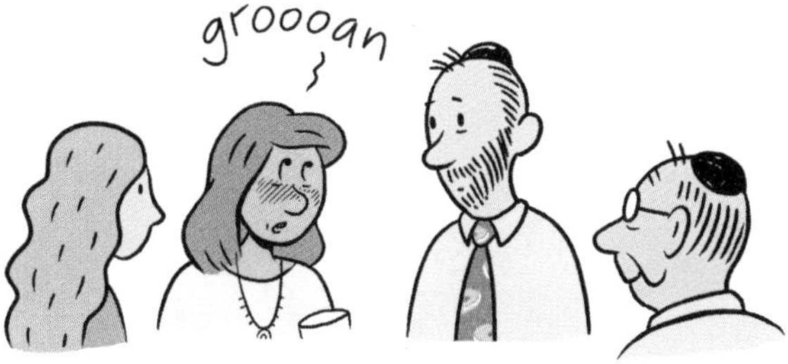
grooooan

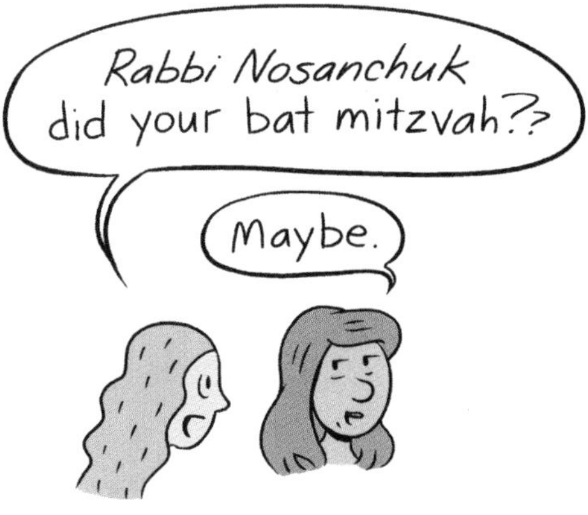
Rabbi Nosanchuk did your bat mitzvah?>
Maybe.

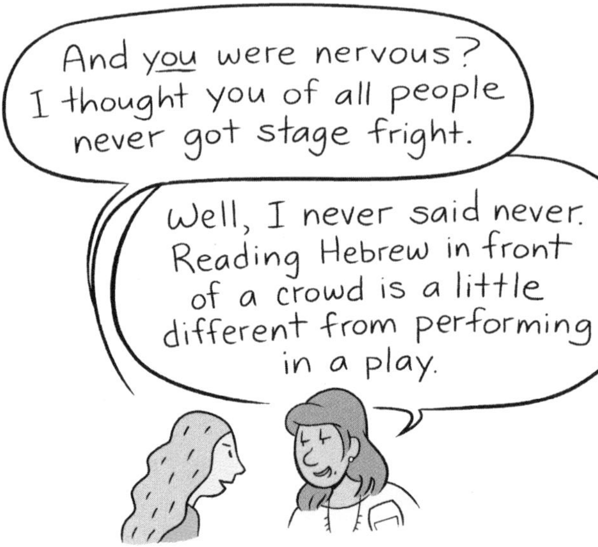
And you were nervous? I thought you of all people never got stage fright.
Well, I never said never. Reading Hebrew in front of a crowd is a little different from performing in a play.

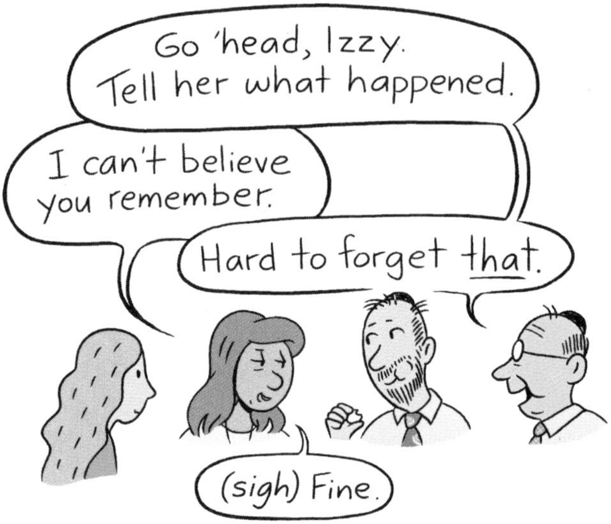
Go 'head, Izzy. Tell her what happened.
I can't believe you remember.
Hard to forget that.
(sigh) Fine.

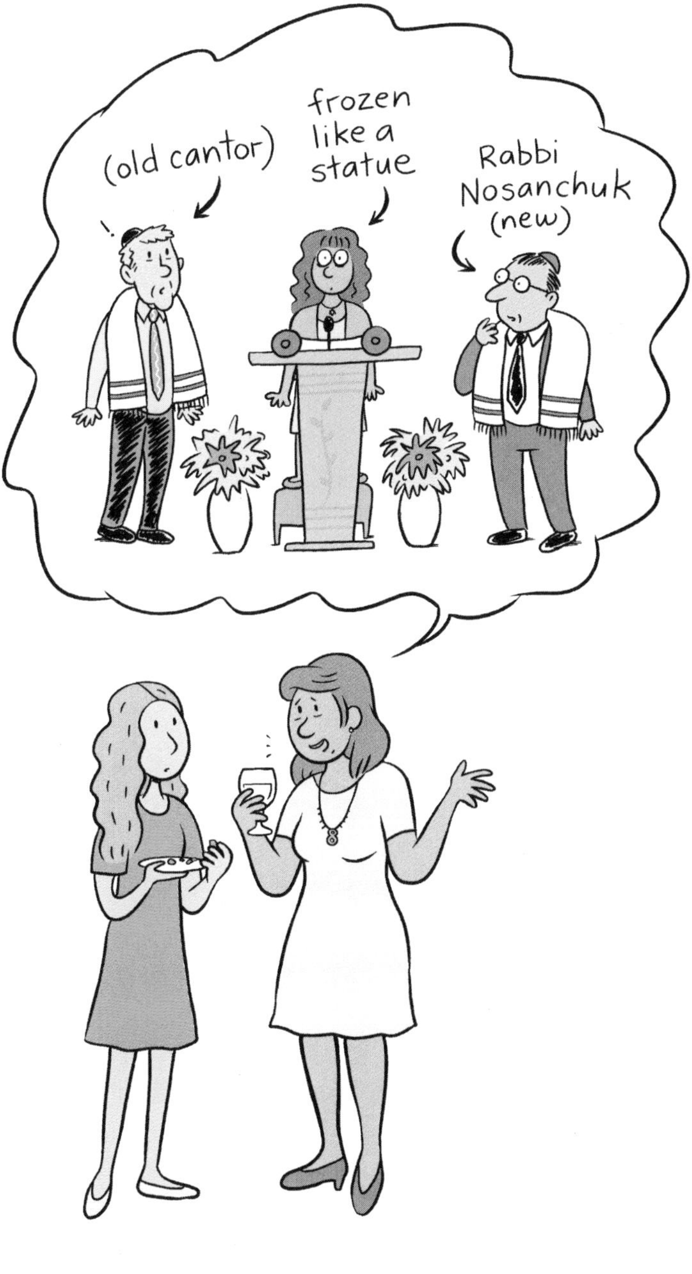
frozen like a statue
(old cantor)
Rabbi Nosanchuk (new)

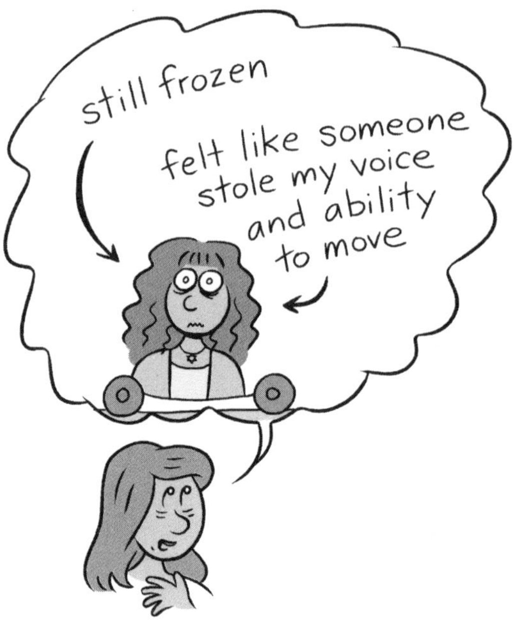
still frozen
felt like someone stole my voice and ability to move

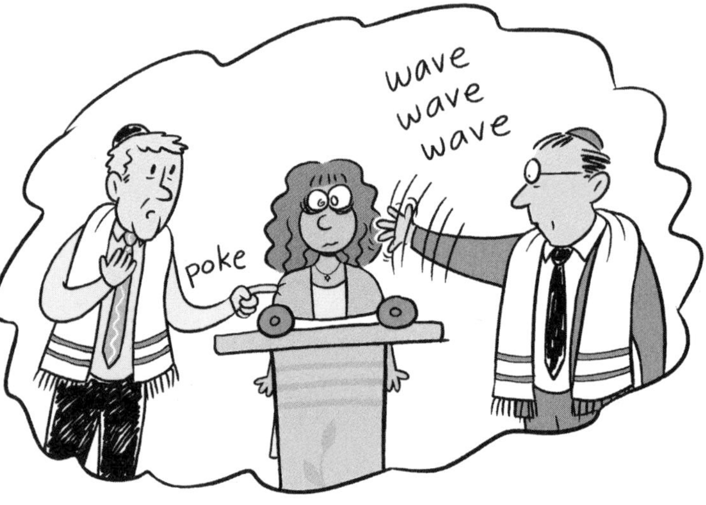
wave
wave
wave
poke

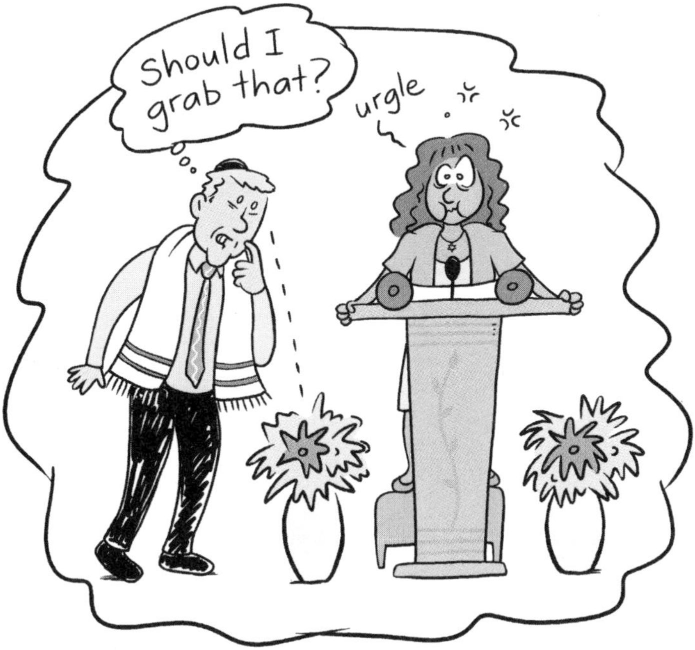
Should I grab that?
urgle

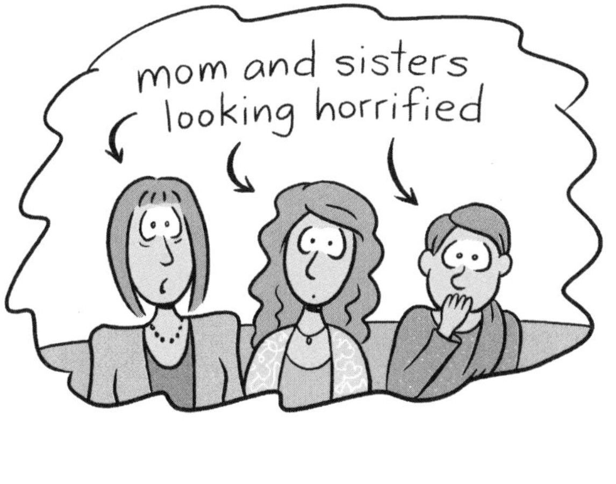
mom and sisters looking horrified

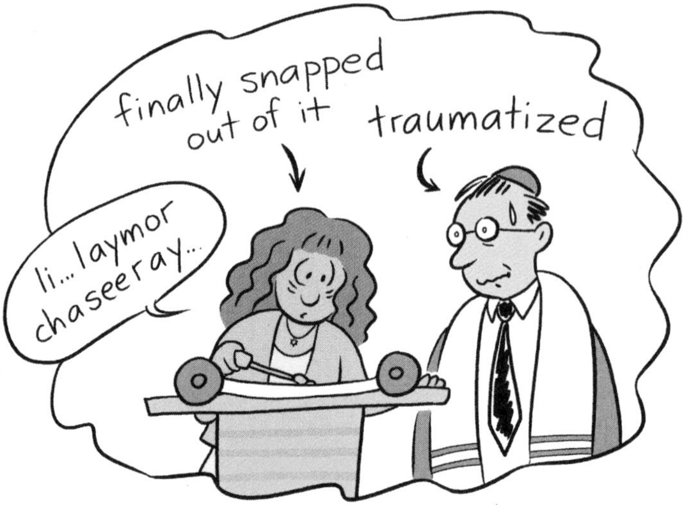
finally snapped out of it
traumatized
li... laymor chaseeray...

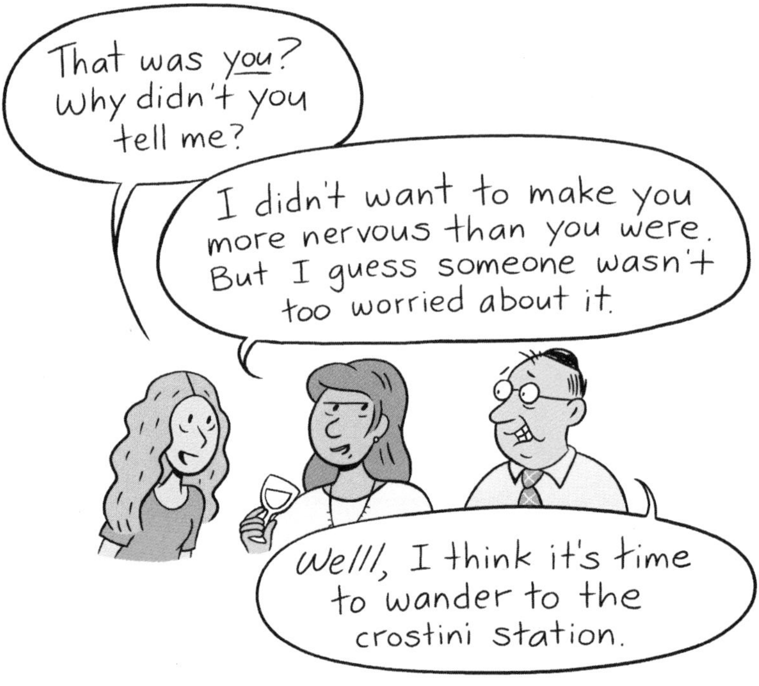
That was you? Why didn't you tell me?
I didn't want to make you more nervous than you were. But I guess someone wasn't too worried about it.
Welll, I think it's time to wander to the crostini station.

I'm still chuckling at my mom, who rolls her eyes.
Guess we aren't so different after all.

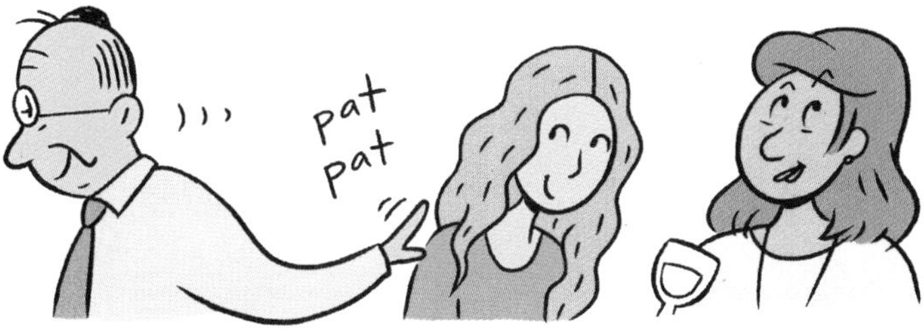
pat
pat

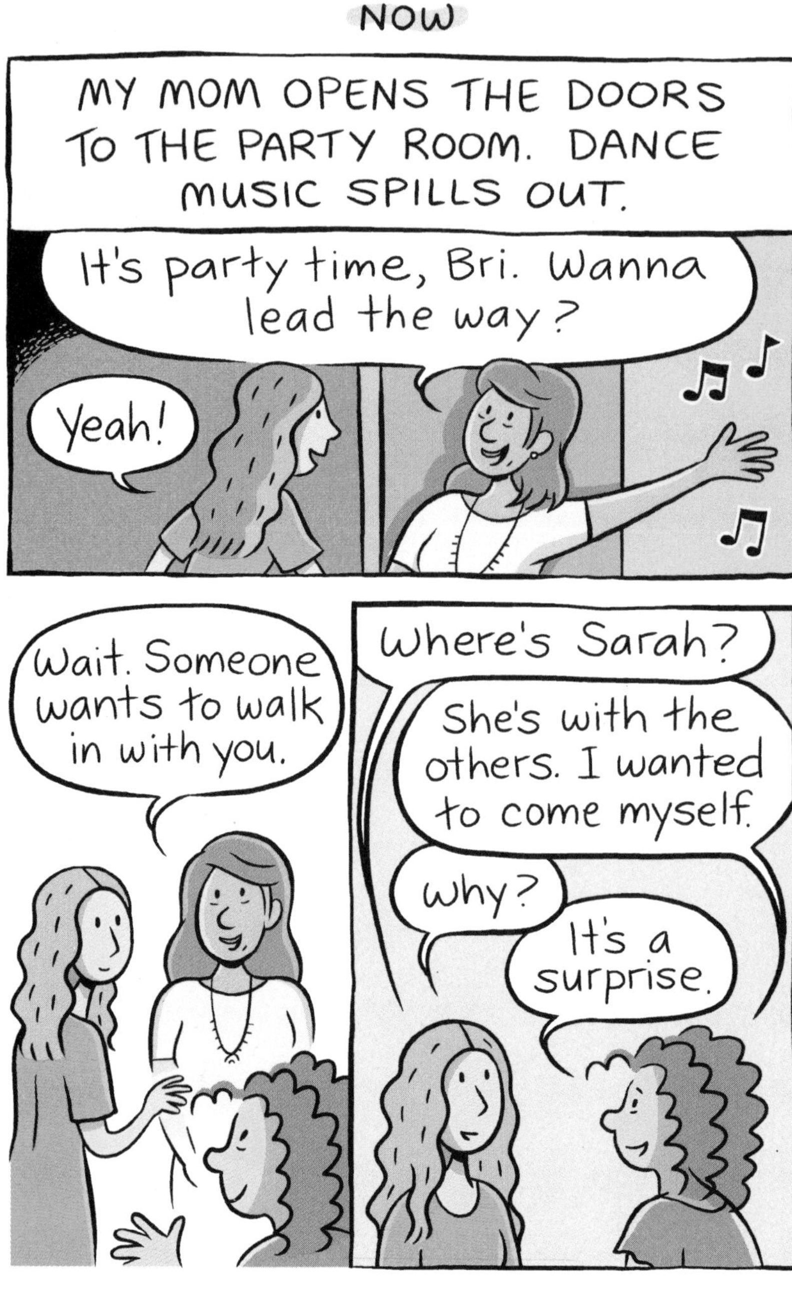
NOW
MY MOM OPENS THE DOORS TO THE PARTY ROOM. DANCE MUSIC SPILLS OUT.
It's party time, Bri. Wanna lead the way?
Yeah!
Wait. Someone wants to walk in with you.
Where's Sarah?
She's with the others. I wanted to come myself.
Why?
It's a surprise.

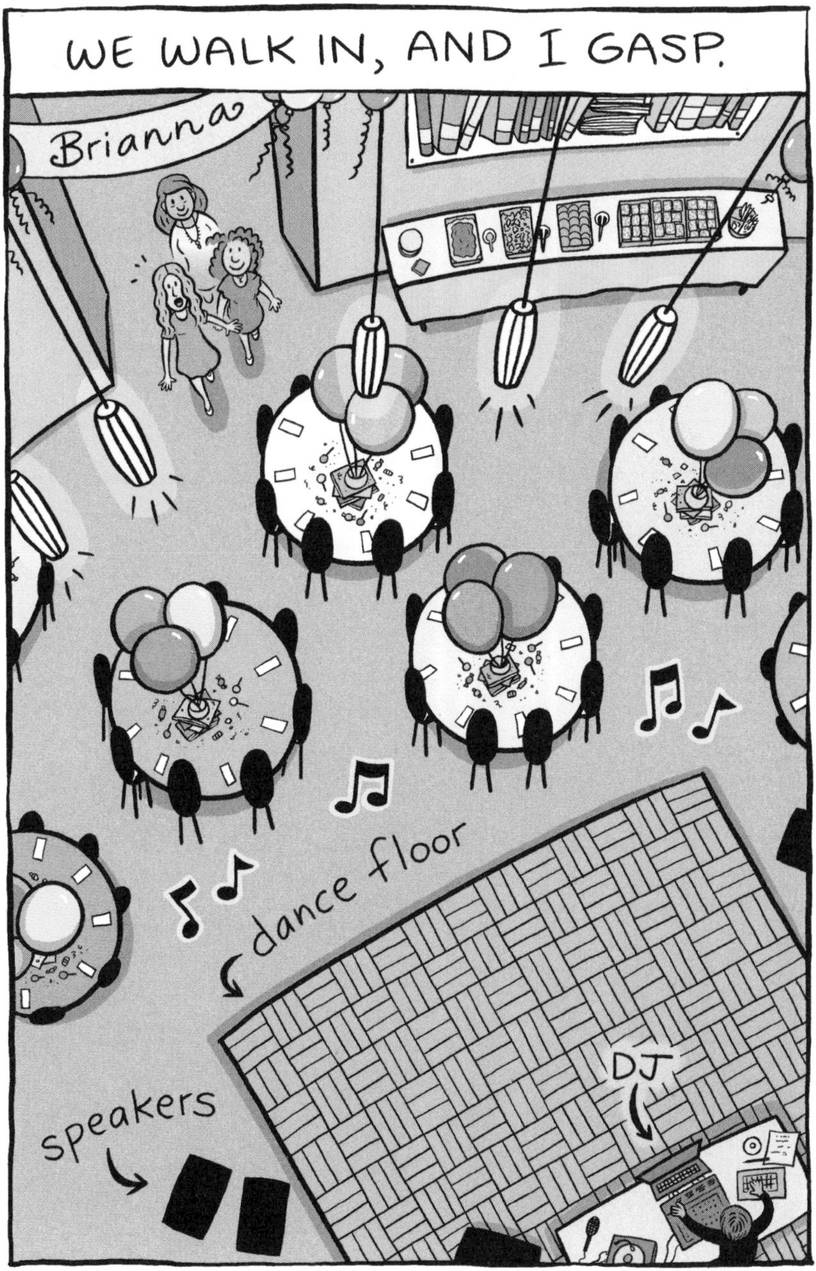
WE WALK IN, AND I GASP.
Brianna
dance floor
DJ
speakers

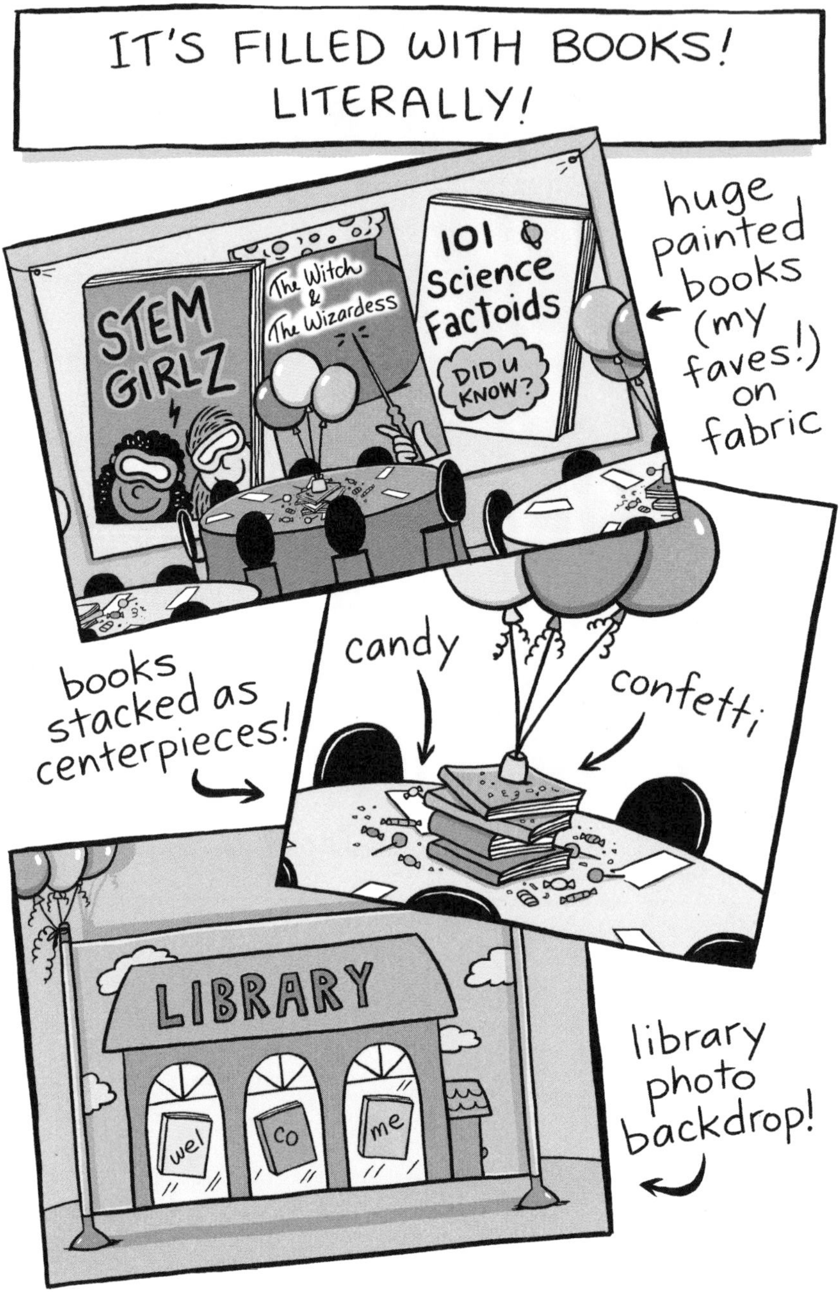
IT'S FILLED WITH BOOKS! LITERALLY!
STEM GIRLZ
The Witch & The Wizardess
101 Science Factoids
DID U KNOW?
huge painted books (my faves!) on fabric
candy
confetti
books stacked as centerpieces!
LIBRARY
wel
co
me
library photo backdrop!

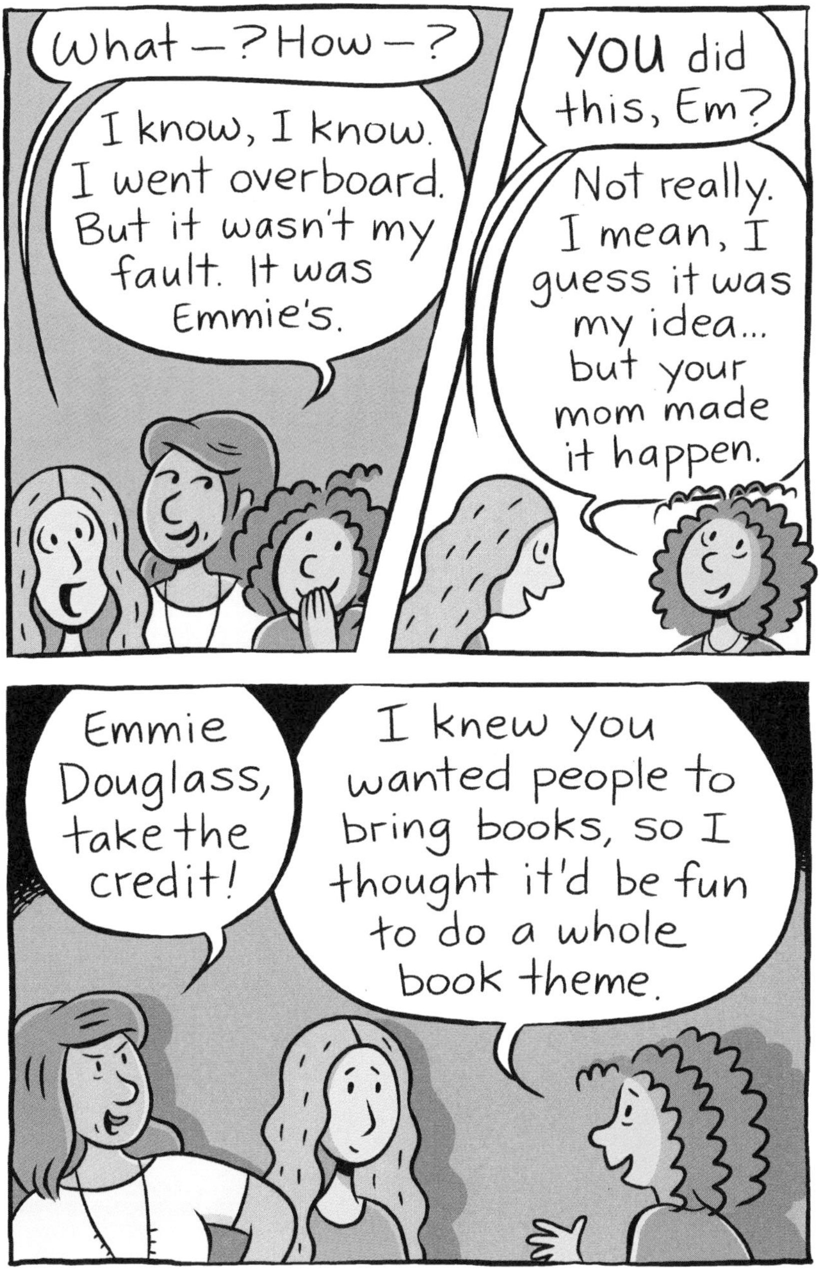
What—? How—?
I know, I know. I went overboard. But it wasn't my fault. It was Emmie's.
YOU did this, Em?
Not really. I mean, I guess it was my idea... but your mom made it happen.
Emmie Douglass, take the credit!
I knew you wanted people to bring books, so I thought it'd be fun to do a whole book theme.

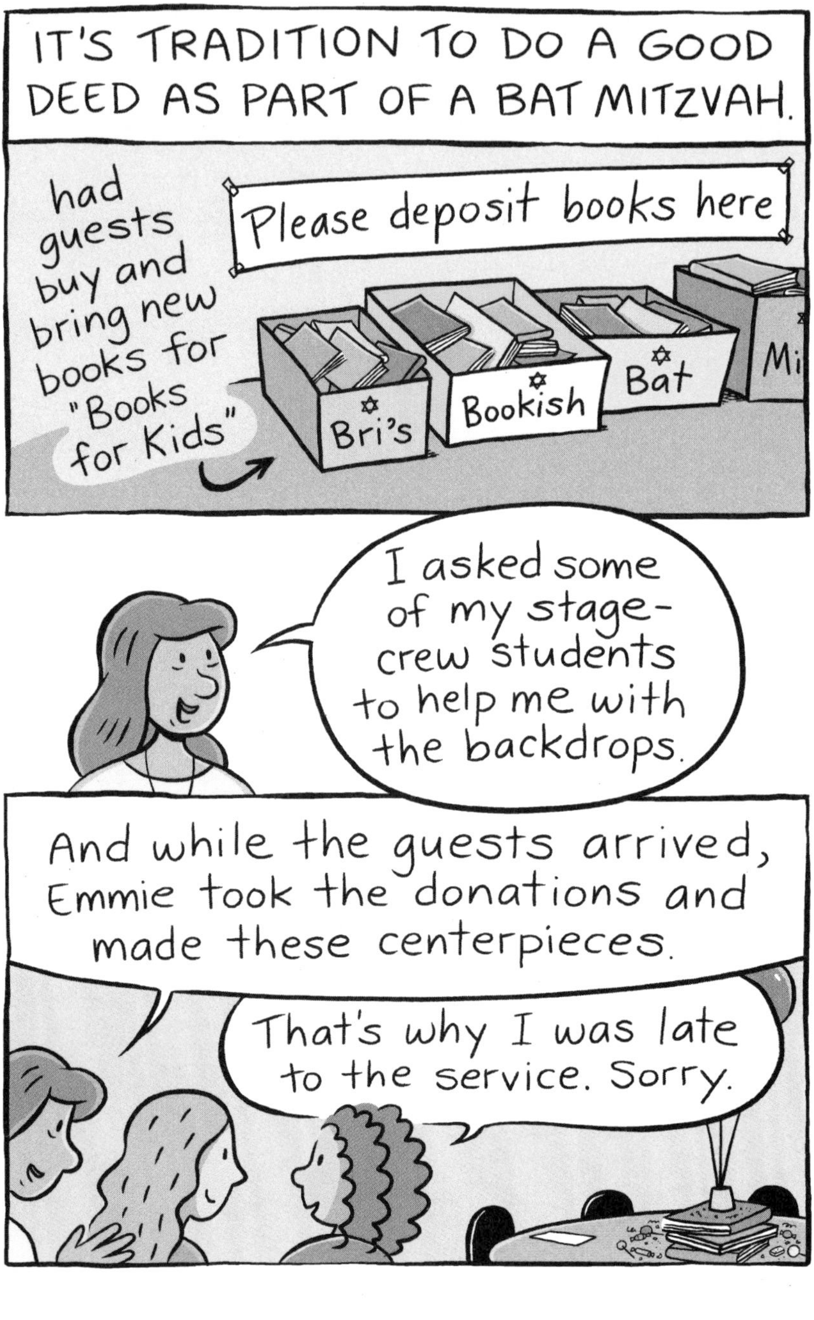
IT'S TRADITION TO DO A GOOD DEED AS PART OF A BAT MITZVAH.
had guests buy and bring new books for "Books for Kids"
Please deposit books here
Bri's
Bookish
Bat
Mi
I asked some of my stage-crew students to help me with the backdrops.
And while the guests arrived, Emmie took the donations and made these centerpieces.
That's why I was late to the service. Sorry.

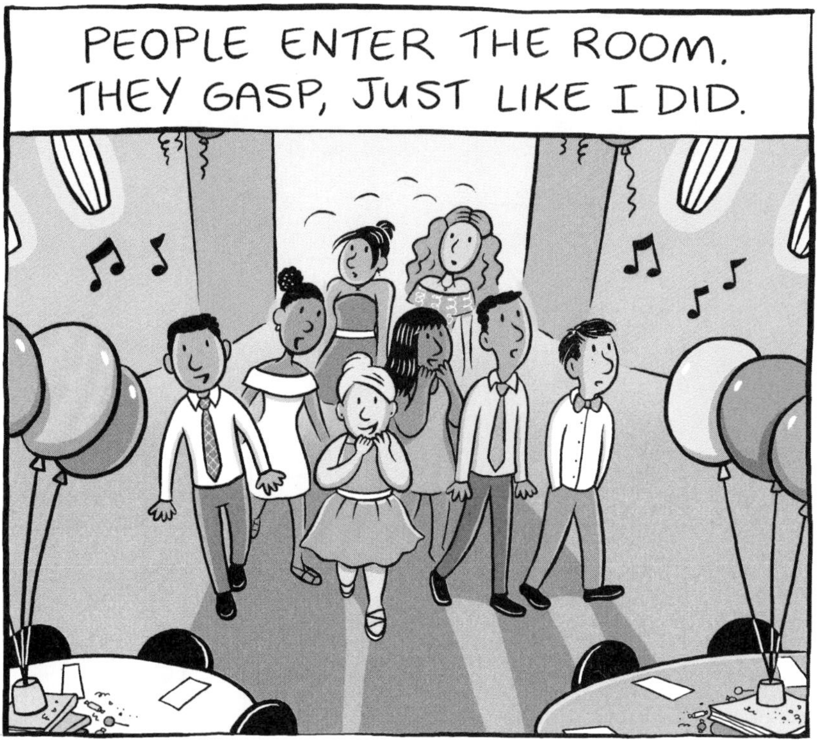
PEOPLE ENTER THE ROOM. THEY GASP, JUST LIKE I DID.

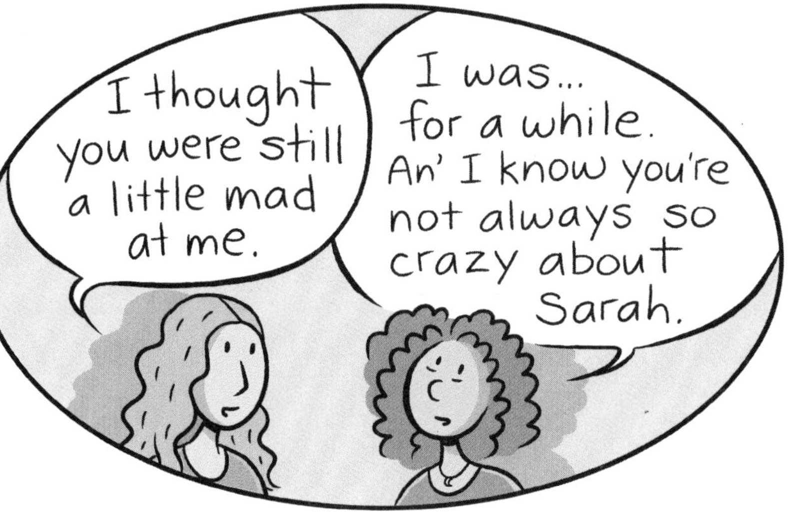
I thought you were still a little mad at me.
I was... for a while. An' I know you're not always so crazy about Sarah.

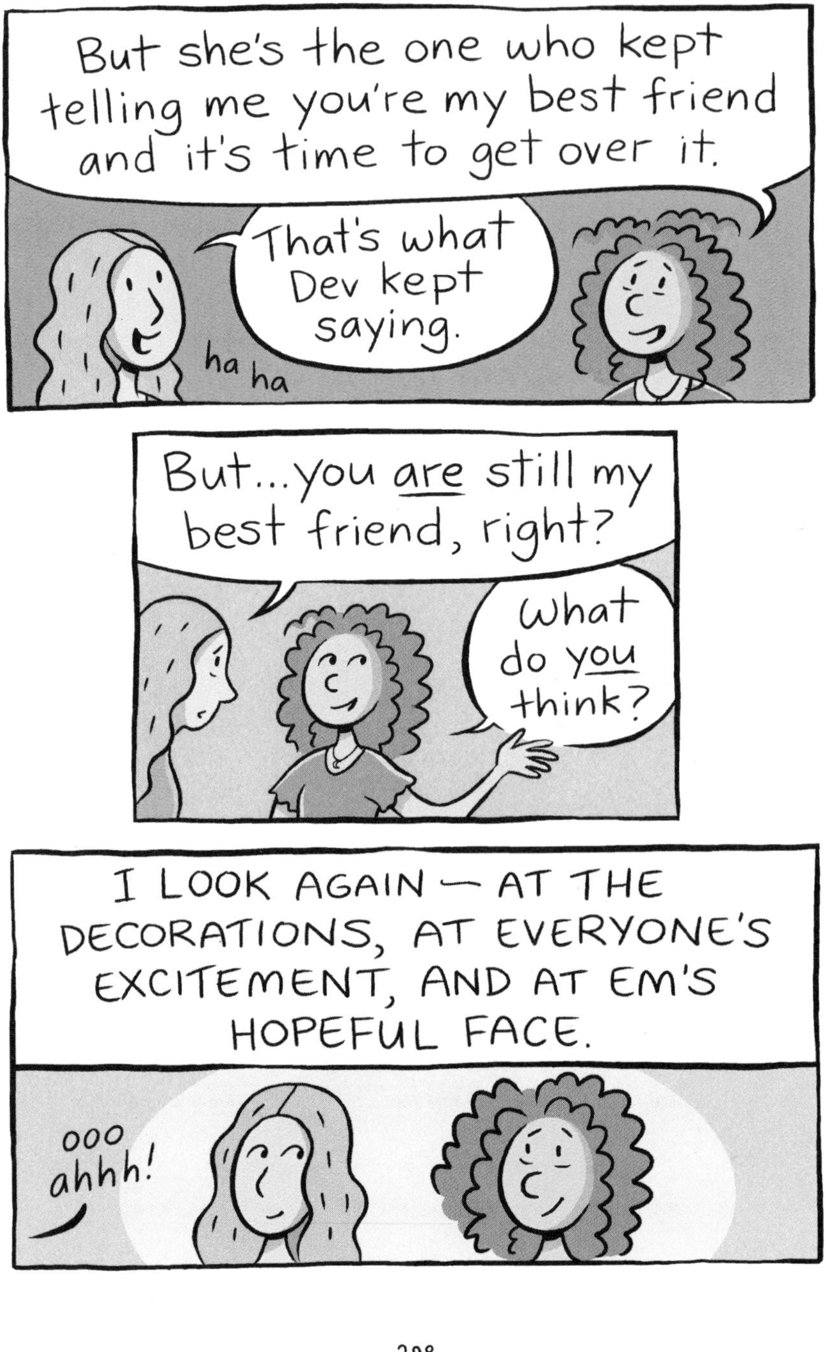

But she's the one who kept telling me you're my best friend and it's time to get over it.
That's what Dev kept saying.
ha ha
But...you are still my best friend, right?
What do you think?
I LOOK AGAIN — AT THE DECORATIONS, AT EVERYONE'S EXCITEMENT, AND AT EM'S HOPEFUL FACE.
ooo ahhh!

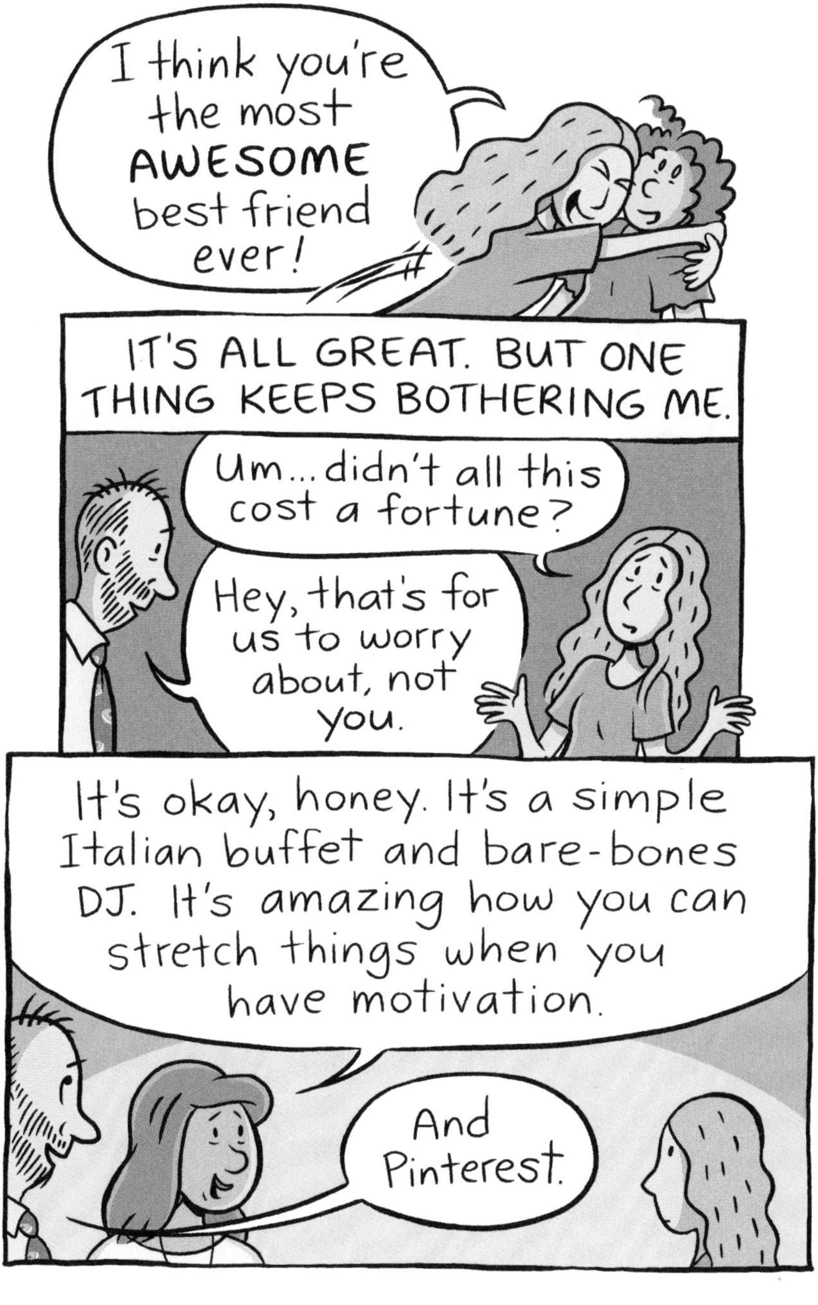
I think you're the most AWESOME best friend ever!
IT'S ALL GREAT. BUT ONE THING KEEPS BOTHERING ME.
Um... didn't all this cost a fortune?
Hey, that's for us to worry about, not you.
It's okay, honey. It's a simple Italian buffet and bare-bones DJ. It's amazing how you can stretch things when you have motivation.
And Pinterest.

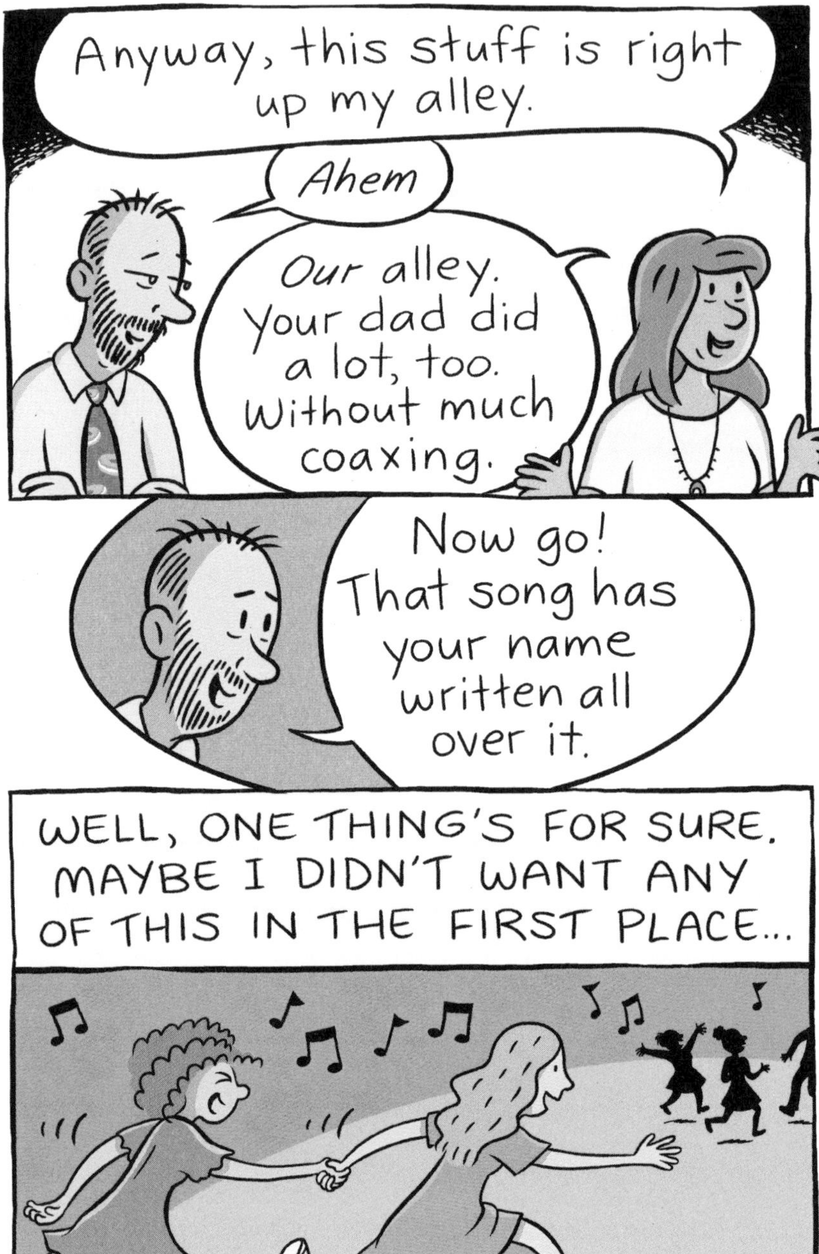
Anyway, this stuff is right up my alley.
Ahem
Our alley. Your dad did a lot, too. Without much coaxing.
Now go! That song has your name written all over it.
WELL, ONE THING'S FOR SURE. MAYBE I DIDN'T WANT ANY OF THIS IN THE FIRST PLACE...

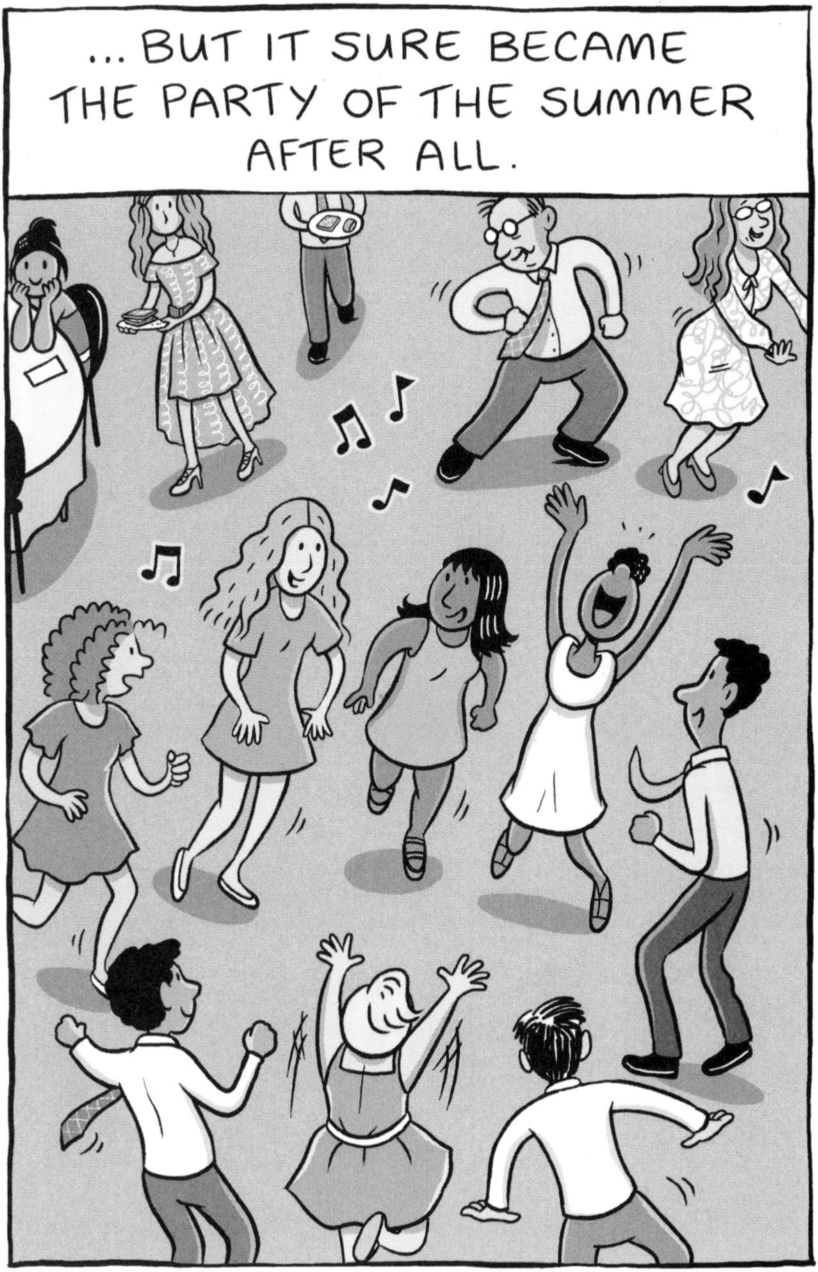
... BUT IT SURE BECAME THE PARTY OF THE SUMMER AFTER ALL.

EPILOGUE

I'm having a fun time, for sure. My friends and I have already danced our buns off.

We took a little break to eat (pizza and pasta!), ogle the sundae bar, and rest our feet (buh-bye, shoes!), but now we're back on the dance floor. If there's one thing thirteen-year-olds can do, it's dance all night.

The DJ's a little corny, but I think he got the hint and has finally laid off the bad jokes. Anyway, he plays good music, and that's the important part.

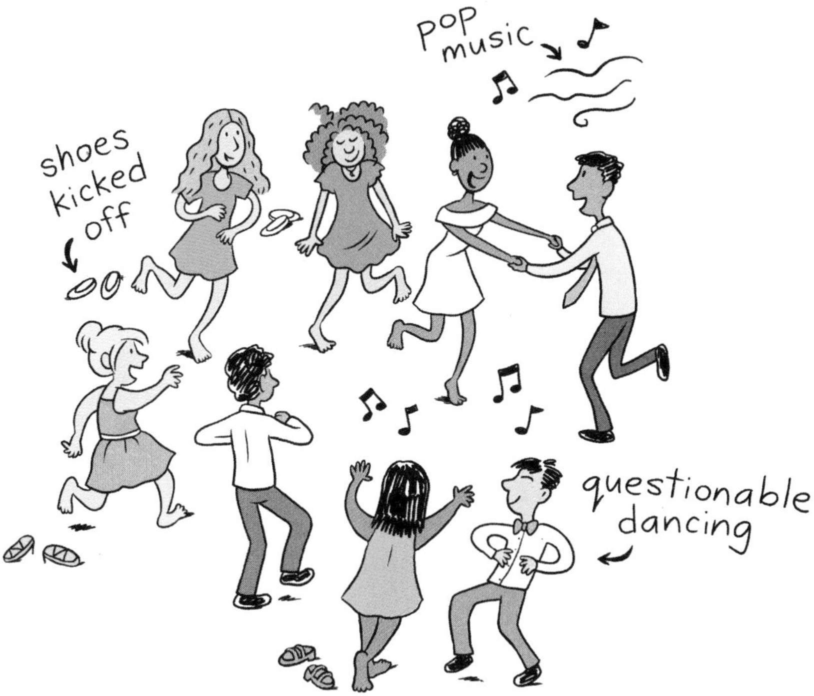
pop music
shoes kicked off
questionable dancing

The best thing is watching all the grown-ups get down. This is probably the only time I'm not embarrassed by horrible dancing.

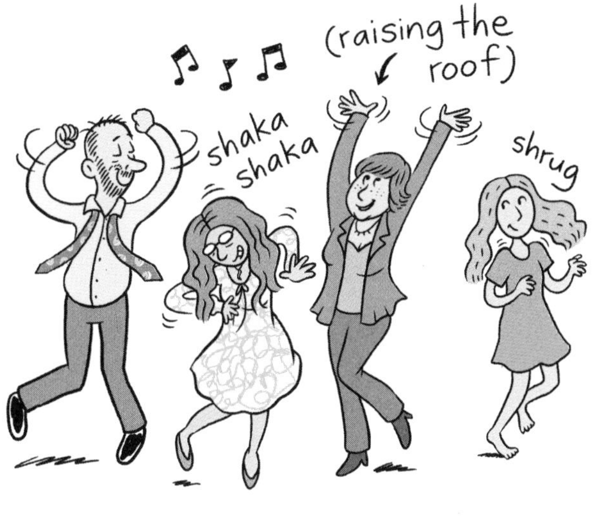
(raising the roof)
shaka shaka
shrug

Not including the cantor. Who knew she had moves!

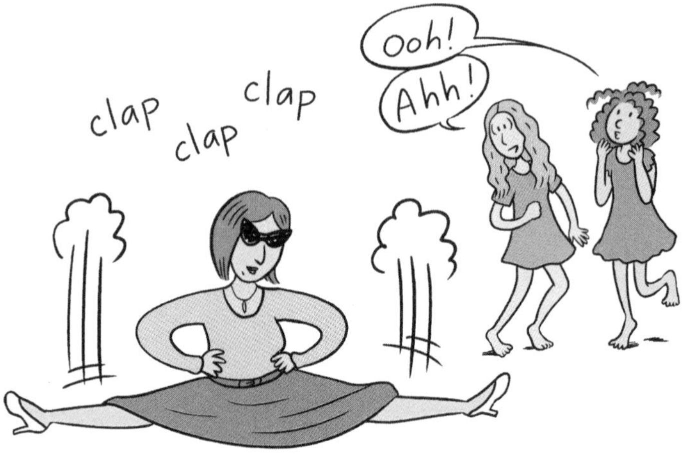
clap
clap
clap
Ooh!
Ahh!

I notice Zoe and Olivia are keeping to themselves. They came up to me earlier and said congrats, but that was about it. They're not besties with Jaime, Maya, Anthony, and Tyler, but they run in the same sort of crowd. Still . . . it almost looks like they're avoiding everyone.

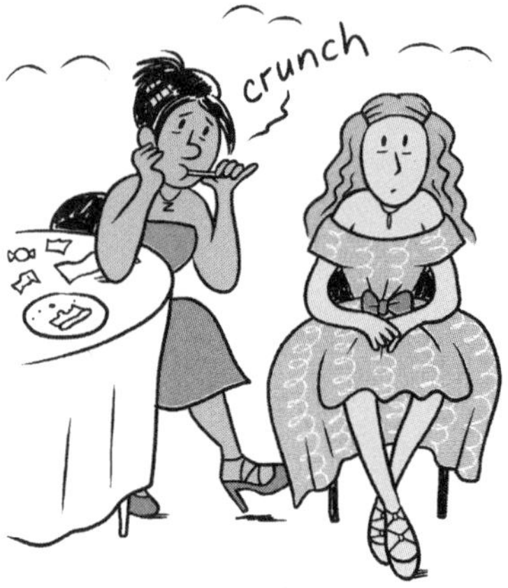
crunch

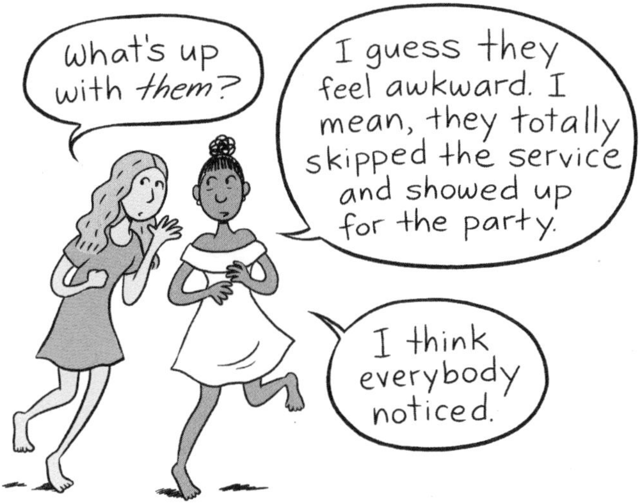
What's up with them?
I guess they feel awkward. I mean, they totally skipped the service and showed up for the party.
I think everybody noticed.

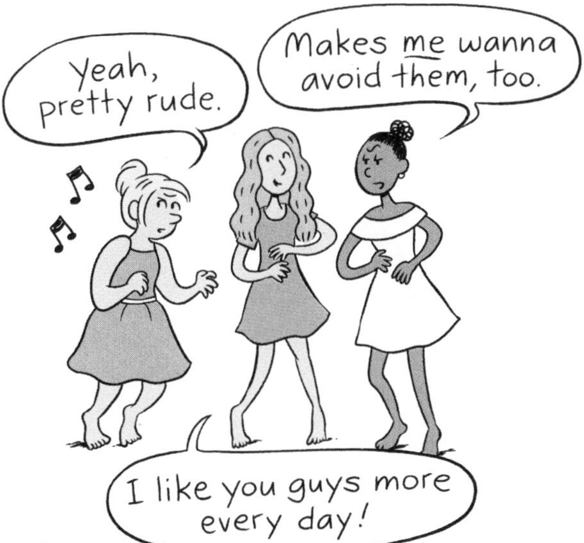
Yeah, pretty rude.
Makes me wanna avoid them, too.
I like you guys more every day!

We laugh. I had told them how those crafty girls used me to score an invite.

But I stop laughing when I look back over at Zoe and Olivia. They watch us awkwardly while sitting and nibbling on some candy that my mom had scattered on the tables.

If I didn't know their motives, I'd feel sorry for them. This is the first time I've seen them look totally out of place.

I guess "cool" depends on context. And if their regular context is "school," then they are way out of their environment.

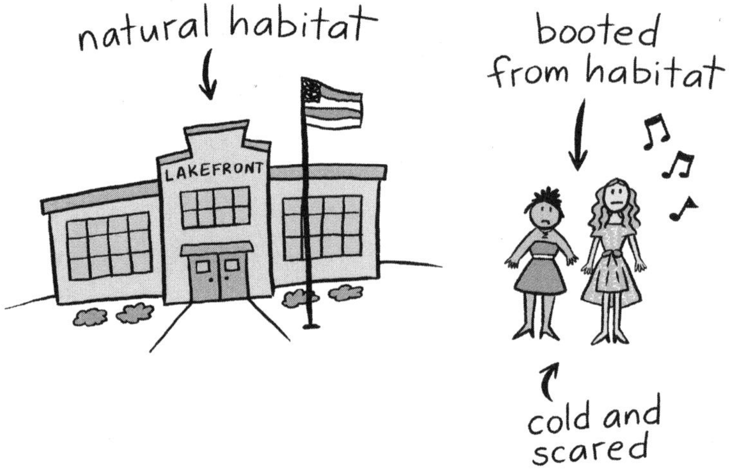
natural habitat
LAKEFRONT
booted from habitat
cold and scared

My thoughts are interrupted as Dev does a bizarre imitation of a moonwalk over to me.

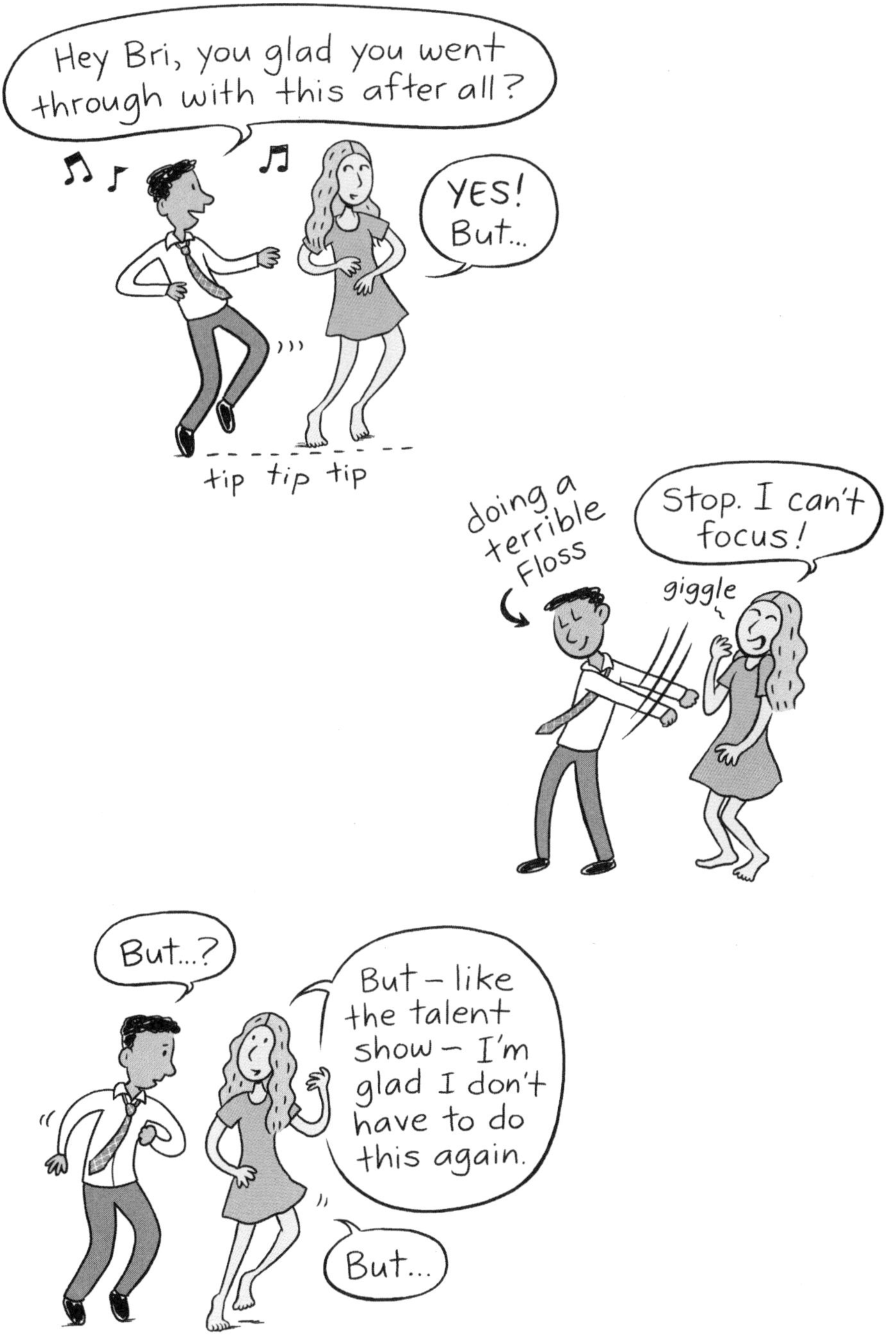
Hey Bri, you glad you went through with this after all?
YES! But...
tip tip tip
doing a terrible Floss
Stop. I can't focus!
giggle
But...?
But – like the talent show – I'm glad I don't have to do this again.
But...

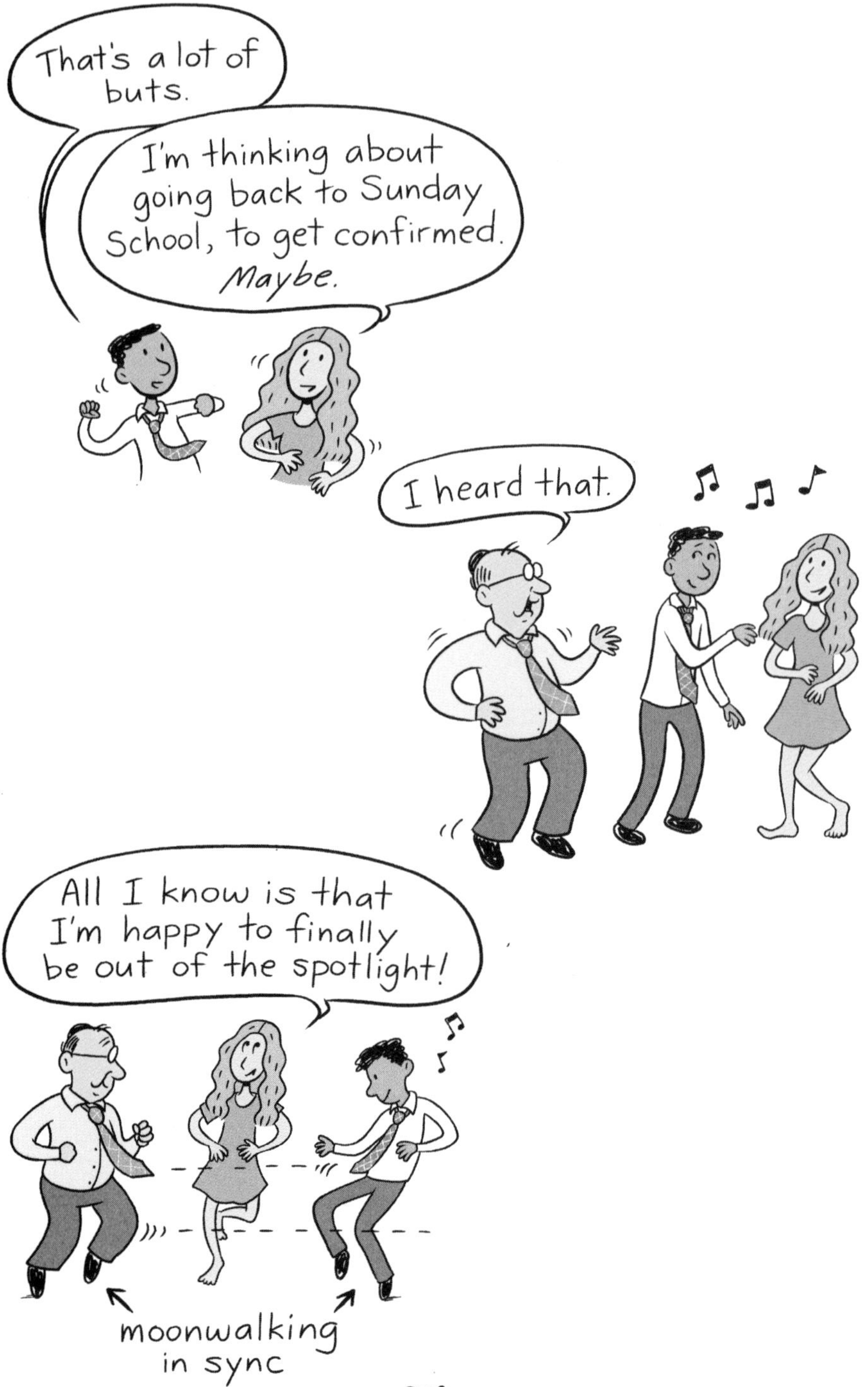
That's a lot of buts.
I'm thinking about going back to Sunday School, to get confirmed. *Maybe.*
I heard that.
All I know is that I'm happy to finally be out of the spotlight!
moonwalking in sync

The song ends. Something is nagging at my gut. I glance over at Zoe and Olivia again, who look miserable or bored or both.

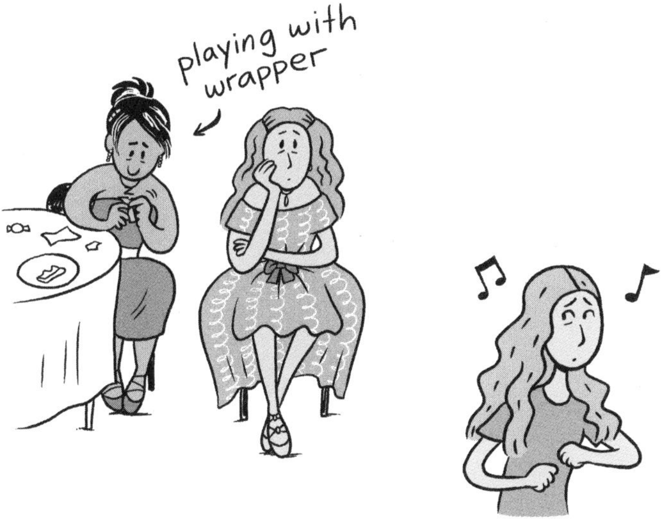
playing with wrapper

Before I can talk myself out of it, I walk over to them.

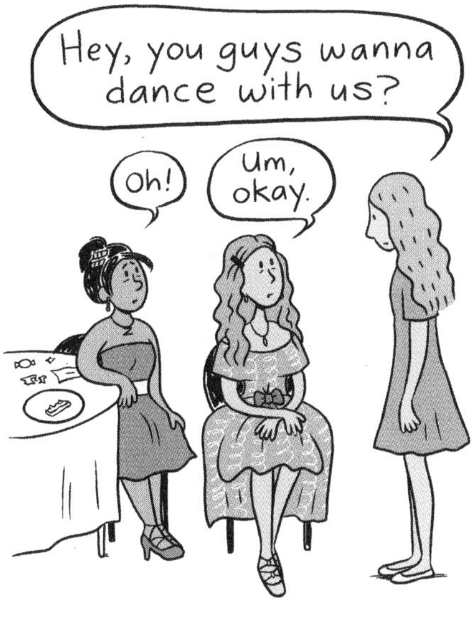
Hey, you guys wanna dance with us?
Oh!
Um, okay.

They look surprised but also grateful. They get up to follow me, then Zoe stops and taps me on the arm.

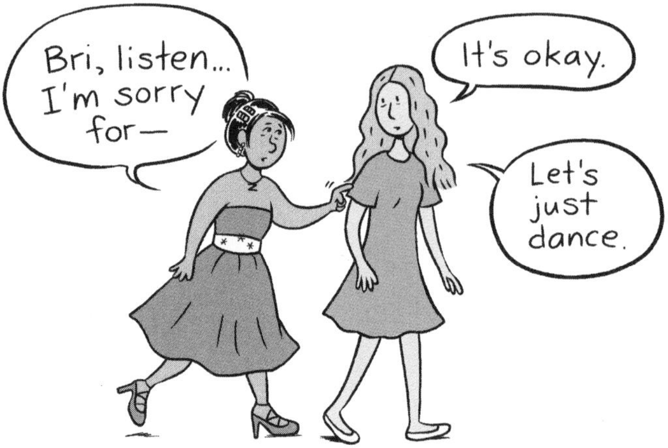
Bri, listen...
I'm sorry
for—
It's okay.
Let's
just
dance.

I lead them to my circle of friends. It's weird seeing Zoe and Olivia so awkward. And my friends are kinda frosty. But I smile and start to dance. Everyone follows my lead, and my friends start to smile and dance, too. I guess they figure if a grudge holder like me can forgive those two, so can they.

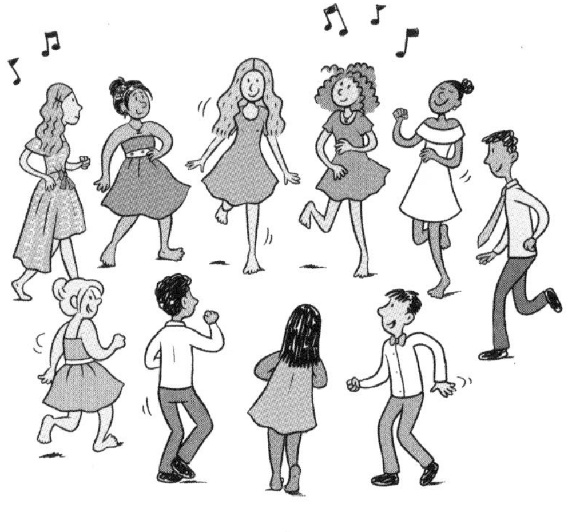

Soon I'm having so much fun, I almost don't notice when the song ends and the DJ picks up the mike.

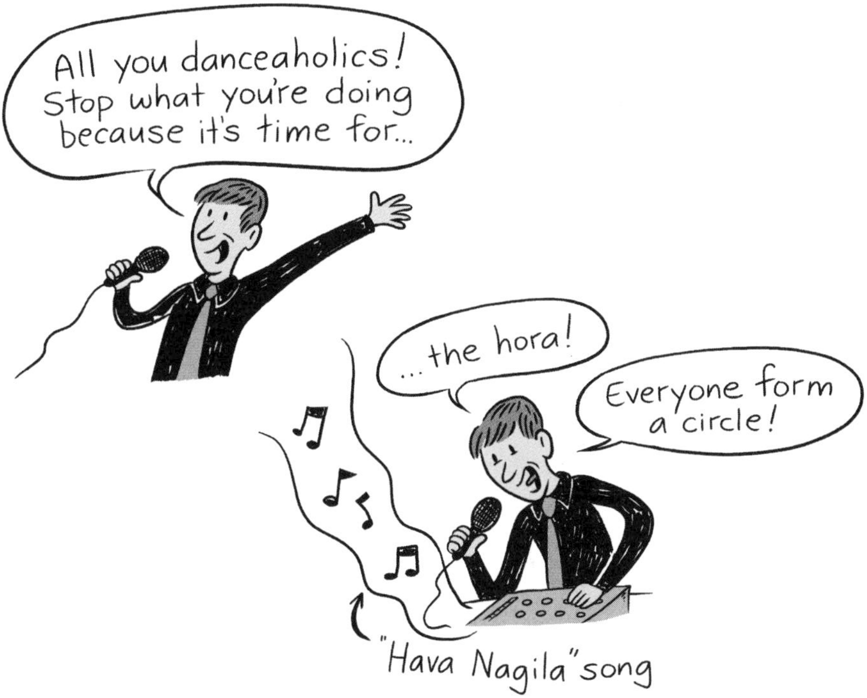
All you danceaholics! Stop what you're doing because it's time for...
...the hora!
Everyone form a circle!
"Hava Nagila" song

Before I can think, someone grabs a chair from one of the tables, and my aunt Dani coaxes me into it. Suddenly I'm lifted up, up, up—almost to the ceiling! I scream, half from excitement, half from pure terror. My dad, uncle Ryan, cousin Bradley, and one of my dad's teacher friends have each grabbed a chair leg and lifted me over the crowd!

The music plays loudly, and the crowd dances and cheers in a circle around me while I bob up and down. Even the ones who don't know the hora have caught on fast (it's not complicated).

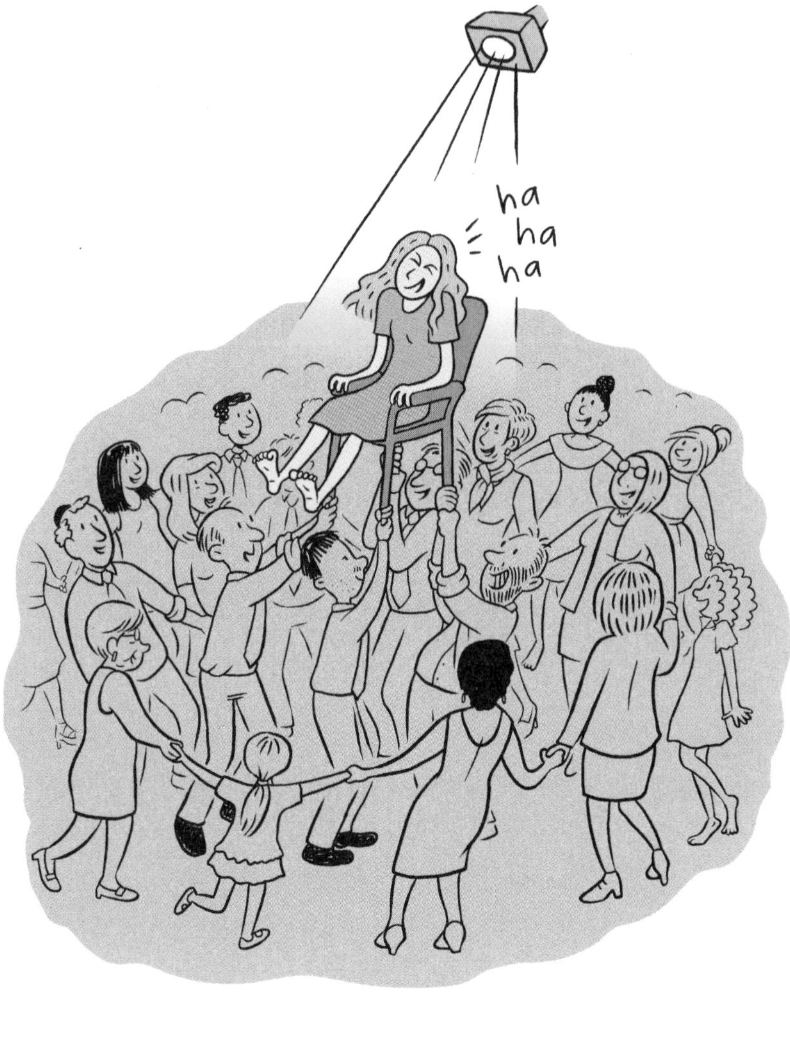
ha
ha
ha

What was it that I said to Dev?

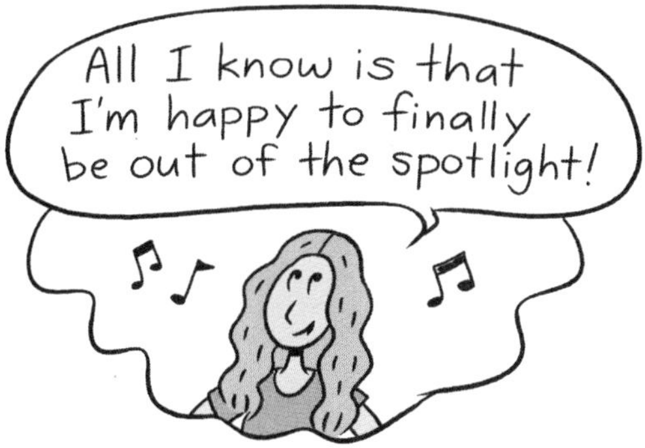
All I know is that I'm happy to finally be out of the spotlight!

Me and my big mouth!

A "BAT MITZVAH" GLOSSARY

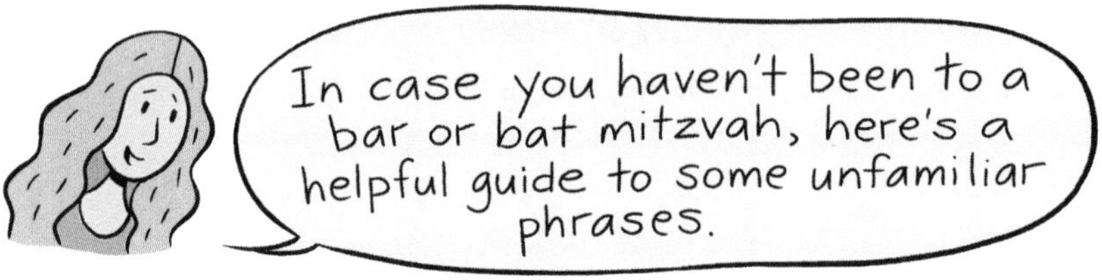
In case you haven't been to a bar or bat mitzvah, here's a helpful guide to some unfamiliar phrases.

Bar or Bat Mitzvah: This means son or daughter of the commandments. It signifies the coming of age in the Jewish community and becoming responsible for the performance of **mitzvot** . . . (plural of mitzvah), or duties of Jewish life.

You can have a bar or bat mitzvah at any time in your life [author's note: my in-laws had theirs when they were in their sixties!] although it's most common to have one around age thirteen. These days, non-binary kids sometimes call their ceremony a b'nai mitzvah (b'nai is plural and can refer to a mixed-gender group of people).

Bimah: A raised platform, pulpit, or podium where Jewish services are conducted.

Cantor: A Jewish religious official who leads the musical part of a service.

D'var Torah: A talk based on topics relating to a parashah, or Torah portion.

Havdalah Ceremony: Marks the conclusion of the Sabbath (Friday sundown to Saturday sundown). This consists of blessings over wine, bread, and the light of a candle.

Hebrew language (biblical): ancient native language of Israel.

Hora: A Jewish circle dance, usually done at celebrations like weddings and bar or bat mitzvahs. The music for the dance is "Hava Nagila," an Israeli folk song that means "Let us rejoice." It's customary to raise the honorees on chairs during the hora.

Parashah: A portion of the Torah that is recited every week until the entire Torah is read in a year's time.

Rabbi: A Jewish leader, scholar, or teacher. Usually the chief religious official of a synagogue.

Synagogue: A place of Jewish worship. Many also call it a temple or a shul.

Torah: A sacred handwritten parchment scroll that contains all the prayers and laws of the Jewish people. It is written in Hebrew.

Yarmulke: Also called a kippah; a head covering (looks like a beanie) worn by Jewish men and sometimes women. It is a sign of reverence. It's often worn when reading from the Torah.

ACKNOWLEDGMENTS:

Brianna was a joy to create, and it couldn't have been done without my invaluable support team:

Donna Bray, my wise and intuitive editor, who can coax the best ideas out of me, even when they're buried in the back of my mind.

Dan Lazar, my fearless, kind, and supportive agent, who always has my back.

Laura Mock and Dana Fritts at HarperCollins, who are skilled at fitting together these puzzle pieces that are the art and text of my books. You rock!

Everyone at HarperCollins who has had a hand in the Emmie and Friends series. You're the best!

Rabbi Josh Caruso, who helped me in the early stages of this book and inspired much of its meaningful content.

My family—Mike, Mollie, and Nikki—who surround me with love, support, and bags of potato chips when I lose it.

My mom and siblings—Meral, Brad, and Tina—who are my creative cheerleaders and always spread the word about my books (whether I like it or not).

Aaron, who is no longer with us but I'm sure is rooting for Brianna from above.

Mina, my sister from another mister, who I always ~~ask~~ force to read my manuscripts, and whose opinion I trust.

And, as always, my readers, who make this the ultimate dream job!